Ace Books by William C. Dietz

WHERE THE SHIPS DIE

WITHDRAWN

WILLIAM C. DIETZ

ACE BOOKS, NEW YORK

This book is an Ace original edition,
and has never been previously published.

WHERE THE SHIPS DIE

An Ace Book / published by arrangement with
the author

PRINTING HISTORY
Ace edition / August 1996

All rights reserved.
Copyright © 1996 by William C. Dietz.
Cover art by Bruce Jensen.
This book may not be reproduced in whole or in part,
by mimeograph or any other means, without permission.
For information address: The Berkley Publishing Group,
200 Madison Avenue, New York, New York 10016.

The Putnam Berkley World Wide Web site address is
http://www.berkley.com

ISBN: 0-441-00354-0

ACE®
Ace Books are published by The Berkley Publishing Group,
200 Madison Avenue, New York, New York 10016.
ACE and the "A" design are trademarks
belonging to Charter Communications, Inc.

PRINTED IN THE UNITED STATES OF AMERICA

10 9 8 7 6 5 4

For those who work with primitive tools—
for whom survival is nearly always in doubt—
and still care about others.
Our hope lies in them.

My eternal thanks to Marjorie, Allison, and Jessica.
You make everything possible.

WHERE THE SHIPS DIE

1

It is said the warrior's is the twofold way of pen and sword, and he should have a taste for both ways. . . .

Miyamoto Musashi
A Book of Five Rings
Standard year 1643

The Planet New Hope

The Milford Academy for Young Men was more notable for its location on the fashionable side of First Hill than for the quality of its architecture. Still, the cream-colored columns and reddish-black bricks *were* reminiscent of the universities the students hoped to attend, and made the institution seem more dignified.

A series of long, hill-hugging terraces had been carved out of the slope below the academy. Dorn Voss followed a flight of stairs down past the field where a soccer game swirled, past the pavilion where first-formers thrashed around the swimming pool and into the overgrown jungle that he regarded as his own private domain. The garden had been an orderly place once, rich with green foliage, colorful flowers, exotic scents, and the sound of steadily dripping water. The microhabitats, some twenty-five in all, had been designed by Mr. Halworthy and maintained by his students.

Dorn knew he'd never forget the fringe of gray-white hair,

the black X where Halworthy's suspenders crossed the vast
expanse of white shirt, and the old man's barely heard voice
as he delivered the lecture to the plants rather than his students.

Many of the boys had disliked Halworthy, and found his
subject dry and boring, but Dorn was the exception. He liked
anything connected with space travel, and the scientist had
been a member of a survey team in his younger days. Halworthy had explored virgin planets, cataloged alien life forms,
and lived to tell about it. All of which added depth to his
lectures, or so it seemed to Dorn, who had looked up to the
older man as a surrogate father. Halworthy was gone now,
killed by a plague variant with a number instead of a name,
and his almost daily contacts with the slum people. How many
gardens produced more vegetables because of the old man?
How many children went to bed with full stomachs because
of his advice? Hundreds . . . maybe thousands.

That was a year ago now, a year in which two-thirds of the
alien microhabs had died, and local plants had moved in to
take their places. Plants that brushed Dorn's shoulders as he
made his way between them and threatened to obliterate all
that Halworthy had built. The hand-lettered signs were difficult
to read now, and the black irrigation tubing was hard to follow
as it snaked its way through the garden. There had been talk
of a new botanist at first, but it seemed as if no one wanted
the job, and Dorn couldn't blame them. Of the Confederacy's
more than 500 worlds, New Hope was one of the most backward.

Dorn followed a path that skirted the greenhouse and made
its way out onto a weed-encircled terrace. The city of Oro
shimmered in the afternoon sun and stretched for as far as
the eye could see. The slums, more than 300 square miles of
them, started beyond the electrified fence that circled the hill,
and spread out from there. Most of the buildings were one or
two stories high. A lack of steel reinforcing rods made it impossible to build anything taller. What little bit of iron ore
New Hope had was notoriously hard to mine, and the cost of
importing finished metal was prohibitively high.

So, with the exception of a small group of extremely

wealthy families, most citizens lived in grinding poverty—poverty that stemmed from a lack of natural resources, a highly stratified society, and systemic overpopulation.

Dorn knew those things as he looked out over the endless concrete hovels, the smoke that spiraled up toward a polluted sky, and the rivers of filth that flowed toward the sea. He saw the conditions but didn't *feel* them. And why should he? Especially since he'd been born on another planet and sent to New Hope for an education, or as a way to get rid of him, he wasn't sure which. New Hope was little more than a prison, so far as he was concerned, having nothing to do with him or his future.

The teenager looked around, verified that he was alone, and lit a stim stick. The smoke bit into his lungs, chemicals found their way into his bloodstream, and he felt better. The voice was unexpected and caused him to jump. "Mr. Voss? Are you there, Mr. Voss?"

The title "Mr." combined with the high, piping voice was a dead giveaway. A first- or second-year student had been sent to find him. Dorn considered extinguishing the stim stick and decided against it. An underclassman wouldn't dare report him, and the news that he'd been smoking would enhance his already seedy reputation, a reputation that kept both students and faculty at bay.

The "rat," as the younger boys were known, was about ten years old. He burst out of the undergrowth as if shot from a cannon. His hair was wet from the pool, his swimsuit was at least one size too large, and blood oozed from scratches on his arms and legs. His name was Wiley or some such, and he looked scared. "Mr. Voss! Come quick! The uppers grabbed Mr. Mundulo, and they're killing him!"

Dorn was seventeen years old and towered over the little boy. He took a drag from his stim stick and released the smoke the same way his favorite holo hero always did. He didn't like the way the younger students were treated but saw no reason to get involved. "Mr. Mundulo gets the crap beat out of him every day, so what's the big deal?"

"The blood," the little boy said earnestly. "It's all over the place and they keep hitting him."

Dorn sighed, tried to convince himself to let the matter drop, and failed. He could have asked, "Why me?" but he already knew the answer. Wiley and his fellow rodents couldn't go to the faculty, not with a hundred years' worth of tradition staring them in the face, so, since Dorn had been nice to them, well, not *nice*, exactly, but not mean either, they hoped he'd intervene.

The senior added the stim stick to the collection of butts already scattered around the terrace and gestured toward the bushes. "Lead the way, rat, and you'd better be right."

The little boy dashed away, and Dorn followed at a more dignified pace. What if the little shit was exaggerating the way rats tended to do? Appearances were important, and he had an image to protect. His peers wouldn't appreciate meddling and could make his life miserable if they chose to.

It took the better part of five minutes for Dorn to climb the stairs and make his way into the swim pavilion. He heard the beating before he saw it. The voice was loud and echoed off interior walls. "Hey, rat, take it like a man . . . What, you think I'm stupid? Faking won't work."

Dorn smelled chlorine and noted the water-slicked tiles as he passed through a gauntlet of frightened faces. The room had locker-lined walls and a bench that ran down the middle. Mist thickened the air. The rats came in all colors, shapes, and sizes. They stood in front of their lockers and shivered when the outside air hit them.

Dorn took them in with a single glance, along with the pitiful, nearly unrecognizable creature who occupied the center of the room. Mundulo had been tied to a pillar, beaten senseless, and beaten again. His eyes were swollen shut, his lips were pulped, and contusions covered his torso. Dorn saw blood bubble as air passed between the boy's lips and gave thanks that he was alive. A pool of vomit mixed with urine surrounded the rat's feet and added to the room's already funky smell.

The boy's tormentors, a group of uppers that the rats referred to as the Four Horsemen of the Apocalypse, turned toward Dorn. Confident smirks confirmed what Dorn had surmised. The coach was away and wouldn't return soon. Their leader, a sallow-faced youth named Cramer, waved a bloodstained hand. "Well, this is a surprise, the Voss-man himself. What's up, Dorn? Come to join the fun?"

Dorn shook his head. "No, a few laps, that's all. Are you finished here? I'd like to change."

Cramer looked skeptical. "You? Work out? Since when? No, I think it was something else that brought you here, something that looks and smells like a rat." The upperclassman's hand shot out and grabbed Wiley's hair. The little boy twisted free and started to run. An upper named Havlick grabbed the youth and held him off the floor.

Dorn frowned. "That's enough. Put him down."

"So," Cramer said softly, "the rumors *are* true. The Voss-man *is* a rat lover. Well, come on, rat lover, show the rodents how you love them."

Havlick looked doubtful. "I don't know, Cramer . . ."

"You don't know what?" Cramer demanded sarcastically. "Who your father was? Get real, Havlick . . . You don't believe that crap, do you? Have you ever seen Voss fight? No? Well, neither have I. Voss invented that martial arts crap to scare idiots like you."

Havlick licked thick, meaty lips and shrugged. "Sure, Cramer, whatever you say."

Dorn looked at the others, saw the hunger in their eyes, and knew there was no escape. None of the Horsemen had been present during the single fight that marked his first year at the academy. He remembered the long hours spent with his sister and the sound of her voice. "No, your other left, dummy . . . Start face forward, feet apart, arms hanging at your sides. Now, move your right foot back and out at a forty-five-degree angle. Okay . . . not bad for a geek. All right, bend your knees a little, rotate your hips to the right, and try to look scary. No, I said 'scary,' not 'stupid.' Good. Now, bend your left arm, keep your elbow low, and raise your fist. See? That protects your face and chest. In the meantime, you need to pull your right hand back to your hip, and hold your palm up. Perfect, or as perfect as a little turd like you is likely to get.''

The stance came naturally, as did the three commandments that went with it: Strike the target, snap back, and hit hard. The Horsemen came all at once, the way bullies tend to do, hoping to overwhelm Dorn with brute force. Dorn hit Cramer with the heel of his right hand. The boy fell and skidded. Havlick tripped on the body. The rats cheered as he went down.

The third upper, a weight lifter known as Malo, blocked a throat chop, threw a right, and connected with Dorn's chin. Dorn staggered, reset his stance, and threw a spin kick. Something crunched and Malo fell. He started to cry.

Cramer was back, as was Havlick, cautious now—but determined to hurt him. Dorn felt angry. Angry about what the uppers had done, angry about the way his parents dumped him on a piece-of-shit planet, and angry that he couldn't do anything about it.

He lashed out, felt his fists connect with flesh, and gloried in the contact. He took blows, channeled the pain into his anger, and fought even harder. It became a dance, a whirling, ducking, kicking, twisting dervish in which each move seemed to have been choreographed in advance and he knew exactly what to do. Blood spurted from Cramer's nose, vomit erupted from Havlick's mouth, and Malo rolled on the floor. But wait . . . where was—?

No sooner had he formulated the question than the fourth Horseman, a zit-faced troublemaker generally known as Pestilence, or the Pest, slipped a belt over Dorn's head, and pulled the ends in opposite directions.

Dorn's next move was completely unexpected, and he could almost hear his sister laughing as he threw a reverse elbow strike. It connected, and the Pest coughed, but hung on. Dorn pulled at the belt, struggled to breathe, and stomped on his opponent's foot. It made no difference. His vision blurred, the light started to fade, and darkness beckoned.

That was when George Albert Wiley III screwed up his courage, took six running steps, and launched himself into the air. The Pest staggered under the boy's weight and screamed as small fingers found his eyes.

Dorn nearly fell as the upperclassman let go of the belt. He gasped for air, saw Cramer start to rise, and kicked him in the head. He turned, left fist up, right fist back. The attack never came. The Pest was down and nearly invisible under ten squirming rats, each one of whom was determined to deliver five blows for every one received during the past year. Their arms moved with the regularity of pistons, and the Pest begged for mercy, but the rats weren't about to give him any. But, suddenly, a whistle blew.

At the sound, the rats jumped back, saw what they'd accomplished, and regarded each other with horror. What had they done? Fear replaced momentary jubilation. Payback is a bitch, and the uppers would exact a terrible revenge. Headmaster Tull entered, followed by Coach Mahowski. They were big men and radiated authority. Dorn relaxed his stance, tried to look casual, and found it hard to do. Not with a rat roped to the pillar, blood all over the place, and four of his classmates laid out on the floor.

Coach Mahowski hurried to Mundulo, cut the little boy down, and carried him away. Tull had piercing green eyes, and they swept the room like lasers. "Every single one of you will be sorry this happened. The first form is restricted to their dorm. Those upperclassman who need medical attention will get it and report to their rooms. Mr. Voss, you know where the detention room is . . . Go there."

Headmaster Tull kept Dorn waiting for two hours. Plenty of time to think, sweat, and wonder. But finally, after what seemed like an eternity, Dorn was ushered into a sparsely furnished office. Holo stats of dead headmasters stared from paneled walls, and the school's motto, "Learn that you might serve," had been carved into a ceiling beam. Hazy sunlight filtered down through a skylight and pooled on the surface of Tull's desk. It was bare except for an antique clock, a pen set, and a single pile of hardcopy. The printout looked like a school record, and it didn't take a genius to figure out who it belonged to.

Dorn had been standing there for a full five minutes before Tull entered. The headmaster gestured toward some guest chairs. Dorn waited till Tull was seated before accepting the invitation. A shaft of sunlight caressed the administrator's shoulders and gave the impression that he was on good terms with the local gods. He sorted through some hardcopy, found what he was looking for, and cleared his throat. "You've had quite an afternoon, Mr. Voss. You scored a C on your history exam, skipped fourth period, and fought a rather one-sided duel in the swimming pavilion. The dispensary hasn't been this busy in a long, long time."

Dorn couldn't think of anything to say. So he didn't speak. Tull nodded as if agreeing with his decision. "Yours is a difficult case, Mr. Voss . . . made more so by the rather complex circumstances. While I can never endorse physical violence as a solution for problems, especially when faculty are available to deal with such situations, I'm not so old, nor so out of touch that I've lost track of the social pressures fostered by an institution such as ours, or the fact that your actions stemmed from the most honorable of intentions." Tull paused. Dorn shifted in his seat. "In fact, the sad truth of the matter is that Mr. Cramer and his friends were overdue for a lesson in humility, and received their just deserts. Mr. Wiley and the other members of the first form had high praise for your courage and resolve, although I'm not sure that I believe you were in the botanical garden for the purposes of meditation, or that you suggested faculty mediation prior to beating the crap out of Mr. Cramer. However, all's well that ends well, assuming that you will refrain from such episodes in the future."

Dorn swallowed to clear his throat. "How's Mr. Mundulo?"

"Not very well," Tull answered darkly, "but he'll recover, and his assailants will be expelled from the school. And that brings us to you."

Dorn was puzzled. It seemed as if Tull had accepted the necessity of what he'd done, so what remained? Tull looked at the hardcopy as if checking to make sure that the text hadn't changed somehow. "Tell me, Mr. Voss, when was the last time you heard from your parents?"

Dorn felt a sudden queasiness in the pit of his stomach. "My parents? Gee, I don't know, six, maybe seven months ago?"

Tull nodded. "Is that unusual?"

Dorn became defensive. "A little. They usually send a package of stuff every couple of months, but they're busy."

Tull stood and looked out the window. His hands were clasped behind his back. "Yes, Milford parents *are* busy people." There was silence for a moment before the headmaster turned. He looked concerned, almost kindly. "Look, Mr. Voss, I'm terribly sorry to trouble you with what may be a false alarm, but we haven't heard from your parents in a long time. Simply put, that means the last installment of your tuition wasn't paid, and no deposit was made to your personal expense account."

Dorn frowned and tried to square the words with reality as he knew it. "But that's impossible . . . I bought some school supplies yesterday."

"Yes," Tull replied sympathetically. "I took the liberty of loaning you some of my funds. After all, your father was a student here, as was his father, and it's the least I could do."

Momentarily speechless, Dorn was numb with shock. His parents were worth millions, maybe *billions,* since they owned their own company, a fleet of ships, and a wormhole. One of only four gaps in the space-time continuum through which most of the Confederacy's fast freight was forced to go. That meant his tuition and expenses were little more than pocket change. Unless something awful had happened, and his parents were what? Dead? The teenager remembered his anger at being dumped on New Hope and felt a sudden sense of guilt.

In spite of the fact that lots of sentients had tried, no means of faster than ship communication had been discovered yet. If Dorn wanted to find out what, in fact, had happened, he had only one choice. "I need to find my parents, sir. I'll pack and leave on the next ship."

Tull raised a hand in protest. "I understand how you feel, son, and I wish it were that easy, but there are laws that govern what minors can and can't do. It's impossible for you to lift without your parent's permission. Not to mention the fact that a deep-space ticket costs a great deal of money, more than I can afford to loan you. No, we'll wait. A number of ships are scheduled to land soon, and I wouldn't be surprised if we hear something during the next couple of weeks."

Dorn tried to take comfort from the headmaster's words but found it hard to do. "And if we don't hear? What then?"

Tull looked away, then back again. "Eventually, if I receive no answer to the urgent letters already sent, you'll be asked to leave the academy. But let's cross that bridge when we come to it. School is the most important thing right now . . . and you're pulling a C in history."

Dorn nodded, mumbled his thanks, and left the office. Little more than fifteen minutes had passed, and his whole life had changed.

2

Tragedy, like good fortune, is little more than an illusion.

La-Da
Traa philosopher
Standard year 2097

The Planet La-Tri

The Mountain of the Moons loomed black on blue as the sun set and three satellites rose in the east. The moons glowed yellow-white, and La-Ma touched forehead, chest, and abdomen, an action that symbolized the unity between mind, heart, and body.

The priestess allowed her eyes to drift down along barely seen ridges, vertical cliffs, and hills of black volcanic rock to the high ground where ancient walls protected the Temple of Tranquility and the 3,333 altars within. It had been a fortress once, a place of comparative safety into which the priesthood could retreat, defending both themselves and the triune concepts of peace, harmony, and love. But that was hundreds of years ago, before the great reconciliation, and the unification of the Traa race.

All these thoughts and more made their way through La-Ma's mind as she watched the grand processional wind its way down the mountainside and into the temple. Every celebrant carried a glow rod that lit the area around them but was no more than a pinprick against the night. However, when combined with all the rest, the glow rods made a river of light visible from orbit.

The processional was an important symbol, made all the more so by the fact that each of the more than 2,500,000 individuals below were part of a three-person triad that included a priest, a warrior, and a commercial being. La-Ma was looking at roughly one-third of the Traa race, in her opinion the most important part, since the Philosopher Sept had responsibility for science, education, healing, as well as the spiritual and moral health of the Traa people. This fact both amazed and frightened her due to the responsibility involved.

Unlike the amazingly fecund humans, or the equally fertile Du'zaath, the Traa had an extremely low birth rate. Two or three offspring per triad were typical, though there were enough larger families to keep the population stable. This was a situation that theoretically made the race vulnerable to attack and caused the Warrior and Commercial septs no end of worry. Which explained why they advocated commercial domination, or failing that, all-out war—a war that the Philosopher Sept opposed lest it destroy the Traa rather than protecting them. Not to mention the suffering it would bring to millions of sentient beings and the harm it would do to their various planets. No, such a course was unthinkable, which accounted for the fact that La-Ma and her peers had resolved to hold the gathering over the objections of their own scientists.

Yes, they understood the mountain was stirring for the first time in eight hundred years; yes, they knew an eruption could be catastrophic, but the alternative was just as risky. It would take months, perhaps as much as a year to select another location, overcome objections from the traditionalist faction, and stage another gathering. More than enough time for the other septs to complete their plans and put them in motion. There were other ways to communicate, of course, but the Traa made decisions by consensus, and preferred face-to-face speech where matters of substance were concerned.

La-Ma thought of her own lovers, the warrior Ka-Di, and the commercial being Sa-Lo, and felt affection mixed with consternation. How could they be so blind? To believe that force rather than love would secure the future of the race? But they were as true to their septs as she was to hers.

Gravel crunched on the path behind her, and La-Ma turned. Like all of his kind, La-To had a short snout, omnivorous dentition, and horizontal nostrils. He wore the white robe of a priest, which, when combined with the short brown fur that covered his body, was sufficient for a warm summer's evening. He lifted a hand in greeting. It had three fingers and one thumb. "Peace unto you, La-Ma . . . La-Si told me you'd be here."

La-Ma pressed her hand against La-To's. "Peace unto you, La-To. La-Si spoke truthfully." She gestured toward the processional below. "Look, our brothers and sisters are beautiful, are they not?"

La-To looked and was about to answer when another mild earthquake shook the ground beneath his feet. He held his breath against the possibility that a worse tremor would follow. Nothing happened. "Yes, but we must hurry. The seismologists are concerned. The quakes are coming more and more frequently now. A steam vent opened to the east, and the sulfur dioxide emissions have increased. La-Si recommends we open and close the meeting as quickly as possible."

The temblors frightened La-Ma more than she cared to admit. She was quick to agree. "Yes, and let's evacuate the moment the ceremonies are over."

La-To considered her suggestion. It wouldn't be easy to move 2,500,000 individuals, especially when many had their hearts set on sleeping in one of the altar rooms, or within sacred hollows on the mountain's slopes, but it had to be done. Especially since the scientists agreed that even a medium-sized eruption was likely to spew tons of rock and ash. Thousands might be injured or killed. He gestured his agreement. "An excellent idea . . . I'll work on transportation while you handle the meeting."

La-Ma agreed and followed La-To down toward the valley

below. The ground shook as something shifted deep beneath their feet. A quake rolled through the Valley of Tranquility. An altar fell.

Hours had passed while the processional wound its way through the 333 stations of devotion and into the central cavern, a cavern created when molten lava flowed down the mountain's flanks thousands of years before, spreading fingers of red into the valley below. However, in spite of the fact that the rock *looked* solid, bubbles existed deep inside. They remained undisturbed as subsequent flows chose other less difficult paths.

A time came when free-roaming outlaws drove a band of peace-loving Traa up off the plains. There the first defensive walls were built, shafts were dug, and a bubble was breached. Soon other caverns were discovered and linked via underground passageways.

Hundreds of years passed, years in which food, texts, and gunpowder were stored in the caves, new engineering principles were discovered, and powerful machines were invented, all of which enabled the creation of a vast amphitheater with seating for nearly three million Traa. It was into this vast space, equipped with an elaborate multimedia communications system, that La-Ma stared, her heart beating heavily in her chest, the sound of her introduction still reverberating off the walls. This was the first time she had stood on the rotating platform and faced the entire sept. The responsibility weighed heavily on her shoulders. Her message was critically important. What if she failed? The other septs would continue their aggressive actions, the alien races would respond in kind, and a war would be fought. Millions of Traa watched her expectantly. La-Ma opened her mouth. Nothing came out. She tried again.

"Thank you, La-Si. It's an honor to address this distinguished gathering. The scientists among you are aware that the Mountain of the Moons has awoken from its long slumber. With that in mind I will keep my comments short and ask that you cooperate when we evacuate the temple."

There it was, the word "evacuate," which conveyed more urgency than "leave." It was already under way. For as La-Ma spoke, certain relics, artworks, and records had already been removed from altars and were being airlifted to safety.

The audience stirred. Objections were shouted, and some of the more unstable attendees started to panic. The traditionalists, who saw the suggestion as an unseemly departure from past ritual, demanded permission to speak. La-Ma held up her hands. "Yes, there is change, and with change comes danger, but that is the nature of life."

The saying, attributed to one of the sept's founders, had a calming effect, and La-Ma launched into her carefully prepared text. "Listen, my friends, for I bring news of a danger greater than the magma below, or the eruption it might cause.

"While other sentients developed civilizations in which people work together, but pursue personal goals, we evolved from three-person hunting triads. We act as a group. A group having familial *and* reproductive responsibilities. The two-male, single-female configuration ensures that the female has support and protection throughout her yearlong gestation period, and increases the likelihood that the child will survive, even if one of the parents is killed. This was a frequent occurrence hundreds of years ago.

"The two-female, single-male model confers benefits as well. Cubs born into this situation are almost guaranteed to receive sufficient nurturance, and, in the days prior to public education, often received more instruction than their peers."

"What is the point?" a voice yelled from the audience. "We know the history of the Traa race as well as you do!"

Such interruptions were common—and signaled intellectual engagement. La-Ma gestured her thanks. "The point is that the very things that helped our ancestors to survive threaten us today. Time passed, and the individual roles within the triads became more specialized, until the professions of priest, warrior, and business being emerged as separate activities. Each has its own skills, conventions, and traditions. In order to survive, and eventually to prosper, priests joined other priests in the pursuit of knowledge, warriors established alliances, and commercial beings entered into partnerships, and in some cases, cartels.

"A thousand years of anarchy ensued as religions were born and suppressed, city-states rose and fell, and armies conquered each other. Then came the Great Reconciliation during which the three great septs were formed, each a balance against the excesses of the others, each composed of individuals having similar attitudes and interests.

"And the system worked very well indeed until a few hundred years ago when our warrior-explorers made contact with the aliens. They discovered that the aliens number in the *billions* and that they could eradicate the Traa race if they chose to do so. That realization, and that possibility, has caused our loved ones deep concern."

A tremor shook the cavern, and tiny bits of rock showered down on the audience. They shifted uncomfortably and looked upward. La-Ma swallowed to ease her suddenly dry throat, and hurried to finish her speech. "We know the danger is *real,* that evil *exists,* and that some would take what we have. However, that possibility must be balanced against the findings of our social scientists, none of whom predicts war. The same cannot be said for our sister septs, however, since our monitors inform us that they *are* preparing for a campaign of military and commercial conquest, and that their actions could result in the very conflict they seek to avoid.

"That's why we must take a firm stand, not just as a sept, but as members of our individual triads. We must reason with those we love and convince them to abandon this insane drive for power. We can never control the other races, nor should we try to do so. Peaceful coexistence is the best strategy, and even more important, the *right* strategy. Please join me and the rest of the council in our efforts to counsel our brothers and sisters while disaster can still be averted."

The subsequent shouting signaled strong acceptance for La-Ma's point of view. She felt warm inside and exposed her neck in a sign of humility and submissiveness. La-Si, a somewhat chubby female of middle age, approached the platform and looked at La-Ma. "Thank you! Our sept owes you a debt of understanding."

She turned toward the audience. "I know many of you would like to question our speaker, but I request that you hold your comments until tomorrow, when she will make herself available for group interaction. In the meantime, the evacuation will begin at the rear of the auditorium, and proceed last row first. Transportation coordinators will guide you to maglev trains. Please remain with your row and help those who need assistance. May the truth enlighten and protect you."

The ensuing evacuation went surprisingly well. Those in the front rows chatted with each other while those toward the back followed coordinators through the exits. Pleased that everything was going so smoothly, La-Ma was turning toward La-Si when the earthquakes began. They came so quickly and close together that seismographs located hundreds of miles away recorded them as one continuous tremor. And as the earth shook, the mountain began to spew superheated gas along with a column of ash. It eventually rose thousands of feet into the air before the wind pushed it toward the east.

But La-Ma knew none of that as the floor pitched and rolled under her feet and she struggled to keep her balance. Some of the audience screamed and rushed for the exits, where the ushers turned them back. They were few when compared with the tens of thousands who remained where they were and closed their eyes in prayer.

A deep, resonant hum filled the chamber but was drowned out by an ominous rumble and a muffled explosion. Rock started to fall, and La-Ma barely had time to think cf her beloved Ka-Di and Sa-Lo before a section of roof collapsed and crushed the life from her body.

Meanwhile, up on the surface, the first train to leave the temple shuddered as its single rail strained against its mountings, and rocked from side to side. The operator knew what had happened and hit the manual override button. Even a mile could make a difference. The maglev leapt forward, and might have made it too, if the Mountain of the Moons hadn't picked that exact moment to explode. It took less than five minutes to bury the temple, trains, and landing fields under tons of rock and ash. Afterwards, rivers of hot lava flowed down off the mountain to seal the mass grave.

One-third of the Traa race was dead. It took weeks, and in some cases months, for the news to make its way to all of the Traa-held planets, and the entire race was convulsed with grief. But life goes on, or so the surviving septs told themselves, and there was work to do. Aliens were plotting against them and must be stopped.

3

God gives nothing to those who keep their arms crossed.

Bambara (West African) proverb
Date unknown

The Planet New Hope

Dorn Voss was expelled from the Milford Academy for Young Men exactly one month after meeting with Headmaster Tull. Each day felt like a week. One by one the hours crept by until the two o'clock mail call finally came. Some of the boys shouted with excitement as they tore into long-awaited packages, while those who received something nearly every single day yawned, and the less fortunate shrugged and wandered away. It was a painful process made even more so by the fact that Dorn had more than some stasis-packed cookies on the line. He was worried about his parents, and his concern deepened with each passing day. Nothing came, however, so Dorn stopped attending and made plans for the day when he'd be released.

The headmaster's office was as it had been during his previous visit except that rain pattered against the skylight, rain that would not only fill the city's cisterns but flood the slums as well. Tull was worried, and it showed. "Have a seat, son. The paperwork is ready."

In spite of the fact that the school boasted the latest in computer technology, a necessity if it was to attract students, the rest of the planet used old, frequently outmoded equipment. It was for that reason that Dorn's transcript, personal data, and release forms were issued on hardcopy as well as microdisk. The teenager signed his name in all the right places, pretended to hear Tull's well-intentioned advice, and wished the whole thing were over. The headmaster forced a smile. "It's no secret that whatever 'hope' the original survey team had for this planet was only partially realized. So, in spite of the fact that we have some serviceable hotels, there are many less reputable establishments as well. I took the liberty of reserving a room for you at the Starman's Rest. It's clean and reasonably priced. Here, take this," the headmaster said, handing Dorn some cash. "It'll tide you over."

The teenager knew the money belonged to Tull and felt even worse about the 250 credits he had liberated from his fellow students over the past few weeks. "Thank you, sir. My parents and I will repay the money as soon as we can."

The Confederacy was huge, which meant that all sorts of things could happen to people, even wealthy ones, so there was little chance that Tull would get his money back and they both knew it. The headmaster smiled, said, "Of course you will," and got to his feet. Dorn did likewise.

"So," the older man said, holding out an enormous hand, "while I have no authority over you once you leave the compound, I strongly suggest that you conserve what money you have, obtain any employment that may be available, and stay in touch with my secretary. Word will arrive from your parents any day now—and we must know where you are."

Dorn wanted to believe but couldn't. He managed a smile, shook the headmaster's hand, and left the office. He ignored the rain and made one last visit to the garden. Mud squished beneath his shoes, and branches rubbed his shoulders as the young man made his way out onto the terrace. The city was invisible behind a veil of mist and rain.

Dorn stepped into the dilapidated hothouse, leaned on the doorjamb, and listened to the rain drum against the plexiglas.

He knew he shouldn't cry, knew it wouldn't do any good. But he cried anyway. He watched the plants dance and sway to the rhythm of the rain and lit a stim stick.

The hotel was at least five miles away, a somewhat unpleasant march under the best of circumstances, and completely out of the question for someone burdened with two heavy bags. Besides, Dorn had never wanted for anything, not before today anyway, and the idea of walking to save money never even occurred to him.

A wave was sufficient to summon the least damaged of the three cabs waiting at the gate. The bags went into the trunk, and Dorn entered the worn but air-conditioned interior. Plastic, covered with official notices, separated the driver from the passenger compartment. It was difficult to see the cabbie, but the teenager had the impression of a small man with black hair and a nose stud.

Dorn looked out the back window as the hover car rose off the ground, swiveled to the left, and headed toward the flatland below. Rivulets of water divided the academy into mismatched chunks that were swallowed by the mist. He wondered if he would see it again. He hoped he would.

The rain slackened as the vehicle reached the bottom of the hill and vanished a few minutes later. A broad, four-lane boulevard had been established back in the early days of the planet's settlement, before the development grant ran out. By then it had become clear that two lanes would be sufficient. The road was awash in rainwater mixed with human waste. Children from the slums waved from an armada of crudely constructed ships. Dorn waved in return, knew his mother would disapprove, and did it again.

The children vanished behind a curve. An army of ragtag day workers appeared on the left. Two or three hundred of them lined the top of a levee, struggling to make repairs that one or two pieces of heavy equipment could have finished in an hour. But they were happy to work.

The taxi paused to allow a heavily laden wagon to pass, took a series of turns, and flared to a stop. Sunlight forced its way down through the clouds and speared the hotel. It was a modest structure by most standards but stood high above those around it, a sure sign that steel had been used to reinforce the concrete walls.

Dorn opened the door and felt warm, humid air flood around him. He wrinkled his nose at the smell and looked out at ankle-deep water. The hotel's entryway was more than two steps away and he was preparing to wade when a half-naked street urchin plopped a homemade stool in front of the door. She had black hair, big eyes, and a slightly protruding stomach. A sure sign of malnutrition, a fact that Dorn would have missed had it not been for Halworthy and his lectures.

Dorn smiled at the child, gave her a one-credit coin, and stepped on the stool. The curb was an easy jump. He turned and watched the waif scamper away. The sun had emerged by then, and the city started to steam. The cabbie, a quick, energetic man with half-rotten teeth, smiled and placed the teenager's bags on the curb. "That will be ten credits, young sir."

Dorn paid the man, added a two-credit tip, and turned to find that a young boy had taken charge of his bags. The ten-year-old, for that's the age he appeared to be, wore a none too clean loincloth and bore a striking resemblance to the stool-girl. He left a trail of feces-contaminated water behind him as he half dragged, half carried the suitcases across the hotel's gray synthimarble floor.

The desk clerk was enraged by this violation of his private sanctum—and the theft of his gratuity. He uttered a long string of obscenities, circled the chest-high reception desk, and hit the child with a stick maintained for that very purpose. The boy, fearing the loss of a much-needed tip, put his head down and forged ahead. Dorn stepped between them, smiled indulgently as the stick hit his arm, and felt for a one-credit coin. He found one in his right-hand pants pocket and tossed it into the air. The youngster caught it, flashed a thankful grin, and skittered out the door.

The clerk apologized profusely, launched into a diatribe against the local street children, and asked Dorn for a thumbprint. The teenager rolled his thumb on the registration plate, allowed the clerk to collect his bags, and followed him up-stairs. The room was on the second floor and looked out on an alley. The clerk opened drawers, mumbled something about room service, and held out his hand. Dorn tendered another tip, waited for the door to close, and scanned his surroundings. The furnishings were worn but clean. Not what he was used to . . . but acceptable under the circumstances.

It took less than fifteen minutes to unpack his clothes, in-vestigate the entertainment console, and flop on the bed. The springs squeaked, and a moldy spot decorated the ceiling. Viewed correctly it looked like a woman with her tongue stuck out. Though concerned about the situation he was in, the teen-ager had looked forward to being out on his own. But he felt none of the joy he had expected. Not with the continuing un-certainty about his parents. Where were they? What were they doing? Why had they deserted him?

Dorn was well on the way to feeling sorry for himself, but he pushed the emotion away. "If you want something done . . . then go out and do it." That's what his sister said, and that's what he'd do. His first objective was to obtain sufficient funds to buy passage on a halfway decent ship, and the second was to reach Mechnos, the planet on which his parents and their company were headquartered.

That being the case, there were two ways in which to secure what he needed. He could work for the money, a long, tedious process, or win the sum at cards, an easier and more practical approach. Dorn had been ranked as the best or second best electrocard player at the Academy, depending on whether you counted Ms. Fromsby or not. Besides teaching math, and un-derstanding the odds involved, she had a nearly photographic memory. Still, the Fromsbys of the world were rare, which meant that Dorn stood a fairly good chance. Or so he hoped.

So, where to start? The sort of game he envisioned would be a private affair, known only to a small group of well-heeled players. Dorn imagined walking up to the reception desk and asking for the location of the nearest high-stakes card game. Headmaster Tull had selected the rooming house for a reason. The clerk would rat on him for half a credit or less. No, he needed an alternative source of information, and the best way to obtain that was to scout around the neighborhood.

It took Dorn less than ten minutes to don his boots, insert the nose filters that most off-worlders kept handy, and make his way downstairs. He nodded to the desk clerk, left through the side door, and stepped into four inches of coffee-colored water.

The teenager paused to make sure his boots wouldn't leak, decided everything was okay, and eyed his surroundings. The side street steamed as the sun pulled moisture up into the sky. A shadow flitted by and a ship rumbled overhead. It was huge, and Dorn shaded his eyes as the vessel dropped towards the harbor. It had the stripped-down look of a free trader—which was perfect. The spacecraft dropped below the horizon, and Dorn resisted the temptation to chase it. Money first, transportation second.

The young man felt a hand touch his elbow. He turned. The boy had approached as quietly as a ghost. He was the same one who had carried his bags. "We meet again, sahib. It would seem the gods have plans for us."

"Or that *you* have plans for us," Dorn countered cynically.

"Not so," the boy answered easily, "for it is written that we are but instruments of the gods, acting parts for their amusement. Would you like a guide? I know the city like the palm of my hand."

Dorn looked down into a grubby little face and considered the lad's offer. Would the urchin lead him honestly? Or into an alley where relatives could rob him? The boy seemed to read his mind. "You have nothing to fear, sahib, for I am an honest guide, honor bound to see you home."

There was absolutely no reason to believe the boy even knew the meaning of "honor," or would feel bound by it if he did, but the words were expressed with such sincerity that Dorn nodded. "Good . . . you'd better be. What's your name?"

"Rali, sahib. It means 'sainted one' in my mother's native dialect."

"All right, Rali," Dorn said evenly, "I'm looking for a

certain kind of establishment. A place where men and women go during the evening.''

''Ah,'' Rali said with a knowing wink, ''I know the perfect place. All the boys and girls are virgins. They wear makeup, perfume, and fancy clothes. My sister plans to work there when she grows up.''

Dorn remembered the little girl with the footstool and shuddered. ''No, that's not the kind of place I mean. I'm looking for a place where they play cards.''

''Of course!'' Rali said brightly. ''I will take you there. Be warned, however, the sahib is young, and they might turn him away.''

''That's *my* problem,'' Dorn said confidently. ''You take me to the right sort of place and I'll take care of the rest.''

''As you command, sahib,'' Rali answered cheerfully. ''Shall I summon a cab? The sahib can travel in style.''

Dorn considered his dwindling cash supply and the need to learn his way around. ''No, I wish to walk.''

''It shall be as you say,'' Rali said obediently. ''Follow me and watch your step. There are holes beneath the water and you must be careful.''

The journey began with a series of right- and left-hand turns. Dorn tried to memorize the route but couldn't keep track. A stratagem on Rali's part? Or the natural consequence of the route chosen? There was no way to know. They passed dozens upon dozens of closet-sized stores. Specialization was the order of the day. There were shops that offered baked goods, meats, clothing, jewelry, cutlery, spices, tools, and yes, even electronics, although the selection was limited, and guards hovered nearby.

Vendors addressed the teenager in a variety of tongues, music filtered from partially shuttered apartments, voices haggled over prices, and a rich amalgam of odors found their way past Dorn's nose filters. The effect was rather pleasant, so much so that the youth decided to remove the plugs, and reveled in the smell of roasting meat, exotic incense, and fresh baked bread.

Most of the slum dwellers had little or no refrigeration in their homes. Shopping was a daily routine. The rain had kept many of them indoors, but they were out in force now, shopping bags slung over their arms, heading for their favorite stalls.

In spite of the fact that Dorn shared their brown skin and black hair, his clothes, carriage, and manner set him apart. Some of the natives hurried to get out of the young man's way, even jumping into the street to avoid him, while others made a point of nudging his shoulders, forcing him to the side of the sidewalk, or splashing rainwater on his legs. Since Dorn had accompanied Mr. Halworthy into the slums on two different occasions, the harassment came as no surprise . . . but the sense of vulnerability did. He had never felt so helpless, and it bothered him.

Still, the teenager didn't want to give the locals any satisfaction, so he ignored their insults and adopted an air of serene superiority. It might have made them even *more* angry except for the fact that Rali chose that particular moment to turn a corner.

The shops grew shabbier, dwindled in number, and gave access to an endless labyrinth of one- and two-story concrete hovels. Wives shouted at husbands, children screamed insults at each other, and chickens squawked. The street sloped downward and took a steady flow of rainwater along with it. A man pushed a heavily laden bicycle against the current and scowled when Dorn said hello. Light gleamed off water and Dorn saw the Krishna twist below. He knew the river originated to the north, wound its way through some of the planet's most fertile farmland, divided itself into three main channels, split yet again, and emptied into the sea. The city of Oro had been built on the delta at the river's mouth.

Rali took a right-hand turn and followed a narrow path down toward the cluster of buildings that marked the city's central business district. Dorn followed, careful of his footing and nervous about the ragtag collection of dogs that rooted in a nearby trash heap.

They reached an arterial minutes later, waited while a heavily laden hover truck roared past, and waded out through the still swirling water. Safely across, they followed the street for a while and turned into a parking lot. It was empty except for the homeless people camped along the back edge. Their clothes, still wet from the rain, were draped on a chain link fence, and flapped like multicolored flags. Vacant eyes watched the youth as he crossed the lot and passed beneath the dilapidated sign. It read ''Cantina Roja'' and was festooned with strings of lights. They might have been festive at night but looked junky during the day. Rali paused and gestured toward a gangplank. It sagged as if tired from its labors. ''There she is, sahib. You must proceed alone. I'll wait here.''

Dorn eyed the vessel at the other end of the gangway. It had been a river barge once, and like most of its kind, had been constructed from hand-planed hardwood. Pilings held it up, and had for some time, judging from their ragged condition.

The tide was low, leaving vast mud flats to await the ocean's return. They were dry now except for channels where ribbons of water continued to flow, stronger than normal because of the rainstorm, but too shallow for boats. Dorn watched the water surge through the ribs of a long-abandoned boat, spin around an old rubber tire, and splash a concrete block. The ground cars, oil barrels, and other metallic debris common to most planets were nowhere to be seen. They had been salvaged long ago or, more likely still, never discarded in the first place.

A great deal of the city's sewage had found its way down onto the mud flat, and the stench was appalling. Dorn fumbled for his nose filters, found them, and slipped them into place. He nodded to Rali. ''I'll return in a minute.''

The gangplank sagged wearily but held. The wood was slick, and cross cleats provided traction. The teenager looked over the side. Fish, eyes bulging, wiggled through the mud, encountered crablike things, and flopped end over end to escape. Most succeeded.

The cantina was clad in red paint, hence the name. The deck was weathered and splattered with white bird droppings. A large door barred the young man's way. Dorn pushed, and it gave under his hand. The interior was dim and relatively cool.

He walked past an empty reception desk and out into an open area. It contained fifteen to twenty pedestal-style tables. Chairs had been stacked on them, and a woman mopped the floor. She didn't look up.

A female voice came from the shadowed area on the far side of the room. "Yes? Can I help you?"

Dorn cleared his throat and tried to make his own voice sound deeper. "Yes, you can. A friend of mine suggested I drop by."

"You're from off-planet?"

"That's correct."

He heard footsteps and watched as a woman entered the light. Her face was beautiful, or had been years before. She still had a figure, though . . . a fact not lost on a seventeen-year-old male. The woman noticed and smiled. "What's your name?"

Dorn decided on the truth. The decision paid off. "Voss . . . Dorn Voss."

The woman raised a well-plucked eyebrow. "Really? Of the same family that owns Voss Lines?"

Dorn nodded modestly. "I'm their son."

The woman extended her hand. A serpent had wrapped itself around her forearm. It had gold skin and ruby red fangs. They were only inches away as her hand entered his. "Welcome to the Cantina Roja. My name's Carmen. I own the place."

"Pleased to meet you," Dorn replied politely, forcing his eyes up and away from her breasts. "When does the cantina open? I enjoy the occasional game of cards."

Miss Carmen noted the expensive clothes, the chroncomp on the boy's wrist, and arrived at the logical conclusion. The young man was a playboy, the son of shipowning parents, who fancied himself a player but lost vast quantities of money wherever he landed. Money *she* could use. A ship had arrived earlier, and he'd been on it. Her tongue slid across her lips. "We open at nine. Where are you staying? I'll send my car."

Dorn felt his spirits rise. This was more like it! "The Starman's Rest."

Miss Carmen nodded. ''Excellent. My car will arrive at eight forty-five. I can't promise—but there's a chance that my regulars will allow you to play.''

Dorn thanked the woman, left the cantina, and started the long walk back. A nap might be in order once he arrived. A long, profitable night lay ahead.

4

There is no greater evil than that practiced by parents on their offspring.

Author unknown
Dromo Book of Admonitions
Date unknown

The Planet Mechnos

Carnaby Orr, sole proprietor of Orr Enterprises, industrialist par excellence, and recipient of honors too numerous to mention, held the yellow ducky over the tub and allowed it to fall. Water splashed, and his son laughed delightedly. "Do it again, Daddy! Do it again!"

Orr smiled indulgently and did it again. Jason giggled happily, grabbed the duck, and pushed it under the soapsuds. The toy toured the bottom of the tub, then popped to the surface. The industrialist watched for a moment, then got to his feet. Jason laughed and splashed water over the duck. "Come on, son . . . it's time to get dressed. The doctors are waiting."

"I don't want any doctors," the little boy said petulantly. "I feel fine."

"Of course you do," Orr replied patiently, "but everyone needs to have a checkup from time to time. Come now, out of the tub, and grab a towel."

It took twenty-five minutes to towel Jason dry, put his

clothes on, and head downstairs. The staircase curved around a null-gravity well. A three-dimensional model of the Confederacy floated at its center. Stars were represented by balls of light. Planets boasted the correct number of satellites, cloud cover appropriate to the time of year, and precisely calculated orbits.

As chance would have it, 90% of the habitable planets were distributed along a barbell-shaped pattern. That being the case most of the Confederacy's population was located toward the ends. Transportation, plus a limited number of intense gravitational fields known as wormholes, made it possible for opposite ends of the barbell to trade with each other. Wormholes, also called "warps," enabled ships to take what amounted to a short cut from one end of the Confederacy to the other, or, in the case of warps known as "enders," to destinations from which no one had ever returned. Red lights identified each planet where Orr Enterprises had holdings of 50 million credits or more. There were hundreds of them.

"Carnaby, is that you?" The voice belonged to Orr's wife and had a sweet, vacant quality.

"Yes, dear," Orr replied patiently, "it's us. Jason had his bath and we're headed for the clinic. It's time for his six-month checkup."

Melanie Orr met husband and son at the foot of the staircase. She was beautiful but not especially conscious of it. She wore a white top with short sleeves and matching shorts. Her legs were long and tanned. Jason ran into her arms. "Can we ride the dasas this afternoon? Can we please?"

The sleek six-legged animals known as dasas were native to Mechnos and occupied the ecological niche filled by horses on Earth. Melanie smiled serenely. "Of course, dear. Right after your music lesson. Run along now . . . Mommy has a headache."

Jason was more than a little familiar with his mommy's headaches, and the multiplicity of pills, capsules, and shots that she used to fight them. He skipped toward the entry hall. Orr kissed his wife on the cheek, nodded to her bodyguard, and strode toward the front door. The schedule called for a beautiful day on Mechnos, and why not? Orr Enterprises had manufactured the components for the weather management system. It was programmed to produce rain between the hours of 2:00 and 5:00 A.M. Malfunctions were rare.

Three identical limos were waiting under the portico in front of the mansion. Logic dictated that Orr and son would be placed in the middle car where the other vehicles could shield them, which explained why the industrialist's security chief, Ari Gozen, directed her clients to the last car, and took the shotgun position. She was thirty-something, had a long lean body, and a face to match. She waited for the privacy screen to fall and wasn't surprised when it did. Orr spoke first. "So? What's happening?"

Ari knew what he meant and activated her implant. Information flowed into her mind. "We have the Traa under biological as well as robotic surveillance ... and they are monitoring *our* movements via airborne spy-eye and an Orr Enterprises security agent."

Orr nodded grimly. Double agents were an ongoing threat. No one trusted anyone else. Not with billions on the line. "Good. Tell the driver to take us to the clinic, and when the meeting is over, send the double to Reon IV. When the traitor arrives ... fire him."

The bodyguard nodded as the partition whirred upward. Reon IV was a frontier world located along the axis that connected one end of the Confederacy with the other. Once dirtside, cut off from his employers, the agent would be lucky to survive, much less return. It was a rather generous parting of the ways, since many of Orr's peers would have insisted on a more debilitating sendoff.

Ari checked her link, got a green on the route, and gave the necessary orders. The motorcade whispered along the carefully maintained drive. Topiaries passed to either side. Their foliage was lushly green. Jason bounced up and down. "Can I play with the console? Huh, Dad? Can I?"

Orr started to refuse, remembered what the doctors would do, and nodded instead. Video blossomed and stuttered from one channel to the next as his son played with the remote.

Jason didn't know it, but he was about to become collateral for a business deal worth billions of credits and, depending on how things went, control of the Confederacy itself.

The ship, the only vessel not seized by the Voss Line's creditors, rumbled in on commercial approach vector one-zero-niner, dropped into channel number six, and hit the water with a thump. Spray flew as the Class II freighter dropped water brakes, dumped forward momentum, and coasted toward a well-appointed data dock. Had the spaceship been larger, a tug would have sallied forth to bring her in. The vessel was relatively small, however, and continued under her own power. Due to the fact that the pier had been designed to handle data ships, rather than free traders, it was clean and tidy. Like all ships of her classification, the freighter required little more than a bank of fiber-optic cable ports to load and unload cargo, cargo composed of knowledge, plans, designs, entertainment, and other forms of digitized data. A camera focused on the "Orr Enterprises" sign and sent the image to the bridge.

Howard Voss sat toward the rear of the control room behind the three-person bridge crew. He spotted the sign on a forward vid screen and growled at his wife. "Look! The bastard took our sign down!"

Mary Voss, who was even more angry than her husband, gave a short jerky nod, and sat tight-lipped while the offending sign grew steadily larger. Red fingernails rattled against plastic until the first officer chose another camera shot. Mistakes had been made, and Mary took full responsibility. Howard, bless his loyal heart, was blameless. She was the one who had approved the terraforming project only to discover that the engineers had minimized the technical problems while the managers exaggerated revenue. All of which had bled Voss Lines dry and left its owners teetering on the edge of bankruptcy.

All was not lost, however. Not yet, anyway. The largest gem in a once glittering crown would save them yet. The wormhole known as the Mescalero Gap was theirs by right of discovery. The warp, and the advantage it conveyed to Voss Line ships, was the key to the future, which explained why Mary Voss refused to sell it. Not when a loan secured by the wormhole's value would do the trick, and Voss Lines could and would be rebuilt. Mary smiled grimly. Rebuild, hell; they'd create something better, and wipe the sneers off their creditors' faces!

The freighter bumped the dock as tractor beams locked the ship in place. Howard Voss released his harness and stood. He was a big man with a big man's strength and forceful persona. He had bright blue eyes hidden beneath bushy brows. "We have an hour before our meeting with Nat. Better get a move on."

Mary nodded, removed her harness, and followed her husband. It was too bad about Natalie's rebellious ways, but what could one expect? Natalie was her mother's daughter, and that meant independent. Perhaps Dorn would make the more reliable heir, not that Mary had any intention of relinquishing control in the near future, or later on for that matter. A limo stood waiting. They entered and were whisked away. It was sunny, and the day had definite possibilities.

Ka-Di felt the fur rise along the back of his neck as he followed Sa-Lo into the medical clinic. The act of walking into an enemy cave-home-fortress made him nervous. Alien odors assailed his nostrils, and a naturally produced stimulant entered his bloodstream.

Above and beyond the physical reactions to an alien environment, Ka-Di felt the persistent emptiness caused by La-Ma's death, and wondered what sort of counsel she would provide. The warrior didn't know why, or what alternatives might exist, but something told him she would disapprove. That made Ka-Di uncomfortable because La-Ma had been more than the mother of the triad's cub. She'd been his doorway to another world, a place where life came after death, and words made magic.

Now Ka-Di saw nothing but darkness. If the race had been outnumbered before, the loss of the Philosopher Sept made a bad situation worse, and left the survivors with no choice. Survival through domination. The strategy made sense to the remaining Traa and should have been comforting. It wasn't.

The warrior wore a knee-length cloak. It was projectile-resistant, and side slits provided access to twin hand weapons belted around his waist. They were ceramic and nearly undetectable. The knowledge made him feel better. A lot of aliens would die if they chose to attack.

The commercial being known as Sa-Lo saw the reception desk, made a quick calculation involving materials, labor, and durability, factored in cultural norms such as "face," and concluded that too much money had been spent. This was knowledge to be filed and used later. An alien rose to greet them, a female. She had flat, undistinguished features, what looked like a pair of chest tumors, and white furless flesh. Disgusting.

"Citizen Sa-Lo? Citizen Ka-Di? The chairman is expecting you. Please follow me."

Like all members of the Commercial Sept, Sa-Lo spoke flawless standard. "Thank you."

There was no sign of anything even remotely medical as the alien led them down a richly paneled hallway. Sa-Lo assumed it was an administrative area and that other parts of the building were devoted to patient care. The hallway ended and doors parted as they approached. Sa-Lo followed their guide into a long rectangular room. Light entered through high arched windows. Paintings, portraits mostly, warmed the walls. A rosewood conference table divided the space in two. Sa-Lo hated human chairs and hoped he wouldn't have to sit in one. A triad of humans waited toward the far end of room. Intentional? Or an accident? Time would tell.

A tall energetic flat-face who had lost all but a fringe of head fur came forward. Sa-Lo had studied human facial expressions and thought this one conveyed a mixture of forced joviality and a trace of fear. He liked that and knew victory could be had. "Citizen Sa-Lo . . . it's a pleasure to meet you."

Sa-Lo accepted the outstretched paw, released it as quickly as possible, and turned to the warrior. "May I introduce my associate? Citizen Ka-Di?"

"Welcome to Mechnos," Carnaby Orr said, shaking the Traa's hand. "How was your trip?"

"The human inquires as to the quality of our journey," Sa-Lo said in Traa.

"Tell him it would have been better if humans weren't so homely," Ka-Di replied, his eyes on the humans at the far end of the table. One of them, a skinny-looking female, reacted subtly. She knew Traa, or was receiving a translation. She matched the description he had been given of Orr's chief of security. Interesting. He would watch her.

Sa-Lo treated his companion to the Traa equivalent of a frown, and took liberties with his answer. "Citizen Ka-Di indicates that while our voyage was pleasant, a truly successful journey has a profitable ending."

Orr laughed appreciatively. "Excellent! Please inform Citizen Ka-Di that he's a being after my own heart. Business . . . that's what makes the world go round. And the Confederacy too. Shall we begin?"

"Nothing would please me more," Sa-Lo said sincerely.

"Good," Orr said agreeably. "I happen to admire Traa craftsmanship, and had the opportunity to purchase some investment-grade furniture. I hope you'll try one of the chairs."

The third flat-face, a male who introduced himself as the Orr Enterprises CFO, pulled a chair away from the table and gestured invitingly. The seat was made from narwood and slanted back to front as dictated by Traa anatomy. The T-shaped back was embellished with a hand-carved hunting scene.

Sa-Lo cursed himself for a fool. The aliens were more intelligent than he had given them credit for. Either the humans knew how much he disliked their furniture or they'd gone out of their way to make him comfortable. Either possibility suggested a Traalike attention to detail.

Both groups took their seats and turned toward Orr. The seat at the head of the table was regarded as a power position within both cultures. Orr had avoided it rather than seem presumptuous. "Here's the situation as I see it. Voss Lines is a family-owned company, and, thanks to a poorly chosen terraforming project, has negative cash flow. As a matter of fact, the only thing between the family and financial oblivion is a wormhole called the Mescalero Gap. I'm meeting with the principals this afternoon. By combining resources, we could buy them out. Our ships would transit toll-free. Lower costs would make both partners more competitive. So competitive that we could claim sixty percent of the long haul data business.''

There was a moment of silence while everyone considered the meaning of Orr's words. Beyond a requirement for navigational beacons, and overhead associated with billing, wormholes were free. The Traa were well acquainted with this fact since, unbeknownst to Orr, they already controlled two warps via secret agreements like the one under discussion. This strategy had allowed them to control half the commercially viable singularities without mobilizing other races against them. Sa-Lo cleared his throat. "There's truth in what you say. But what if the Voss family spurns our offer? What then?"

The silence stretched long and thin as Orr chose his words. "The Voss family travels frequently. Something horrible could happen. The heirs might prove more accommodating."

There was no mistaking the human's meaning, and while Sa-Lo approved of the strategy, something niggled at the back of his mind. He felt as though La-Ma was standing next to his shoulder saying something he couldn't quite hear. What would she want him to do? Ignore an incredible opportunity? Why? The flat-faces wanted an answer. He gave them one. "Yes, I see your point. Space travel *is* dangerous, and accidents *do* happen."

Discovery Bay was a large horseshoe-shaped body of water that opened to the west, and was subject to southerly winds that the weather management system hadn't been able to eliminate.

So, on days when the huge data freighters lay snug and safe beneath the headland that protected North Bay, the smaller and more numerous free traders pitched and rolled as wave after wave marched toward the south, swept past the partially completed breakwater, and broke against their glistening flanks.

But Natalie Voss was used to the motion and jumped from

hull to hull as she marched toward shore. Unlike the quiet, almost meditative feel that surrounded the data docks, Freeport bustled with activity. Sparks flew as repairs were made, voices shouted between ships, children hawked food from fragile boats, exoskeletons minced along the edge of the wharf, and birds screeched as a cook dumped table scraps over the side.

Natalie loved the sounds, the sights, and yes, even the smells that were part and parcel of Freeport. Taken together, they made up for the physical sensations that were absent while ships traveled through the vastness of space. Fact of the matter was that the young woman *liked* to load and unload cargo, which was good, because that's what the skipper insisted that she do.

Natalie jumped onto the last ship in line, crossed her deck, and stepped onto a gangplank. It was made of steel and rang with her footsteps. She arrived at the top, looked back, and saw someone wave from the *Sunbird*'s cooling tower. She waved in return, waited for an autoloader to rumble by, and wove her way toward the gate. A guard motioned her through. The path was clearly marked with bars, nightclubs, and flophouses. It took ten minutes to locate a dilapidated autocab, pry the door open, and climb inside. The onboard computer listened to her request, checked her universal account balance, and lurched into motion.

Natalie wrinkled her nose. The vehicle's interior smelled sour, like the inside of a tavern, and she ordered the window to open. It slid halfway down and jammed. The vehicle jerked into motion, pulled a U-turn, and followed Bayshore drive toward the city.

Million-credit homes jutted out from the cliffs, reminding Natalie of her childhood. Her parents owned one of those houses, though they didn't spend much time in it. Not with a shipping line to run, business deals to close, and planets to terraform. No, she and her brother had seen damned little of Howard and Mary, which was probably just as well, since neither one had any parenting skills.

The highway curved and traffic increased as the cab entered the city of Fortuna. High-rise buildings shot toward the sky, spidery skywalks tied them together, and aircars cruised vertical streets. It was typical of her parents to meet here, among the trappings of wealth, rather than in Freeport where Voss Lines had been founded. What nerve they'd had then, referring to a clapped-out freighter as their "flagship," and calling themselves "a line."

And later, when a drive failed during a deep-space voyage, and it looked as if it would take two years to limp back home, Howard and Mary had gambled on what might have been an ender rather than a commercially viable wormhole. That took courage. Real courage that paid off when the twosome emerged at the other end of the Confederation and registered their discovery.

Yes, Natalie's parents were special people, all right, which was why she spent as little time with them as possible. The cab pulled up in front of an expensive restaurant. The young woman grimaced, wished she had changed her clothes, and made her way up the steps. The doorman frowned but opened it anyway. Maybe lunch would be good. Maybe her parents had changed. Maybe hell would freeze over.

Jason looked small and vulnerable on the operating room table. Instruments gleamed as preparations were made. Orr swallowed the lump that had formed in his throat as the doctors and nurses laid sterile drapes back and forth across his son's tiny form. Monitors glowed and machines hummed as the anesthesiologist injected a sedative into the child's IV.

Jason's eyelids fluttered, he said something about dasas, and then he fell instantly asleep. The anesthesiologist looked at the surgeon, and she looked at Orr. The mask hid everything but her eyes, and they conveyed what? Horror at what they were about to do? If so, Orr understood how the doctor felt, because he felt a distinct queasiness in the pit of his stomach. He nodded. "Get on with it." The words emerged as a croak.

The initial part of the surgery was simple. An incision was made in the child's abdomen. Bleeders were located and cauterized. The first scalpel was discarded and a second incision was made. It went deeper this time, down through yellow baby fat to the peritoneum, where the surgeon paused again. A laser flashed, and the air grew thick with the smell of burned flesh. A pair of retractors scampered down a sterile ramp, positioned themselves to either side of the opening, and deployed their stainless steel arms. The hole expanded, and Orr felt dizzy.

He could have avoided the operation, could have waited outside, but had forced himself to watch. Doing so was his penance, his punishment for an act he knew to be wrong, but was determined to carry out anyway. Still, the knowledge that no harm would come to Jason, and that the son would inherit what his father built, salved Orr's conscience. The dizziness receded.

Orr opened his eyes and saw that the surgeon had cut down through the peritoneum and into the abdominal cavity. There was a pause as blood was sponged away, bleeders were cauterized, and the roboretractors repositioned themselves. The surgeon looked at the anesthesiologist, received a nod, and rinsed her gloves in a basin of sterile water. "Okay, people, let's get a move on. Is the organism ready?"

The industrialist looked across the operating table and into a Traa's tawny yellow eyes. Which one was it, anyway? The aliens were swathed in OR greens like everyone else, and the specially designed face masks made it difficult to tell them apart. The creature nodded as if to confirm the moment of contact. His voice was muffled behind the mask. "The organism is ready."

A nurse placed the specially prepared symbiote in a kidney basin. It was small, no larger than a prune, and similar in appearance. It pulsed with internal life, and the sight made Orr queasy. He fought the sensation with his knowledge of what would happen. Once in place, the alien organism would tap into Jason's blood supply and extract nourishment from it. In return for such sustenance, the symbiote would inject naturally produced antibiotics into the child's circulatory system, making both organisms resistant to disease. The only problem was that if left too long, the creature would grow its way out of the boy's abdomen and seek a larger body with which to partner, a process that would kill Orr's son.

So, to prevent that course of events, and guarantee his son's continued good health, the organism would be removed in three years. The symbiote could and probably would resist such interference, so chemicals would be used to subdue it.

Orr Enterprises scientists were already hard at work searching for the proper combination of compounds just in case a disagreement arose, though The Traa knew what the chemicals were, and were supposed to divulge that information in three years' time. It was their way of holding Jason hostage to his father's word, which was a rather important point from their perspective, since they were putting up more than half the credits required to buy the Mescalero Gap. They certainly didn't want their controlling interest to be known—not until the Confederacy was safely under their control, that is.

It was not what Orr wanted for his son, or what *any* father would have wanted, but it was necessary. Because if the industrialist had learned anything during his life, it was that nothing remains constant, and that success must be won over and over again. For, like the organism in question, Orr Enterprises had a single choice. It could find additional resources, and hope to grow larger, or remain as it was, and eventually die. The first alternative sounded a heck of a lot better than the second. The businessman smiled behind his mask. A microbot slithered down into the bottom of the incision, pulled the margins into alignment, and bonded them together.

Lunch went poorly, a fact that shouldn't have surprised Natalie but did. In spite of the fact that she should have known better, the young woman had hoped that her parents had changed, had matured somehow, and were genuinely interested in her. Nothing could have been farther from the truth. In fact, the dishes had barely been cleared from the table when the conversation switched from a perfunctory interest in her career to a terraforming project gone wrong, and what that meant to the company.

Not just *their* company, as her mother pointed out, but *her* company as well, since she and Dorn had been given equal shares in Voss Lines at birth, and would inherit someday. Not that Natalie especially wanted to.

In any case, it soon became apparent that the *real* purpose of the lunch was to advise Natalie of their intention to negotiate a loan and secure her thumbprint on the necessary screens, an approval Dorn didn't have to give since his eighteenth birthday was still months away.

So, with lunch out of the way, and conversation on the decline, the three departed for Orr Towers, a pair of high-rise buildings that dominated Fortuna's skyline and proclaimed their owner's power. The visitors were received with the pomp and ceremony that befitted both their past and present status, for even with their shipping line on the ropes, Howard and Mary Voss still owned a wormhole, and were theoretically wealthy.

As a high-speed, executive-only elevator whisked them toward the top of a tower, Natalie found reason to regret the way she was dressed for the second time that day—especially compared to her mother's custom-tailored business suit, tasteful gold jewelry, and perfect nails. She sighed. It was just one more way in which she failed to measure up.

The elevator stopped and the doors swished open. Carnaby Orr had been warned that they were on the way and came to greet them. He shook hands, exchanged pleasantries, and ushered them into a fashionably furnished office. It looked out on Discovery Bay. Natalie watched a free trader make its final approach, skim over the whitecaps, and belly flop in. Spray flew upward, and she wished she were there. Someone said her name and she took a seat instead.

Both parties knew what they wanted and were eager to begin. Mary seized the initiative. "You know why we came . . . your holding company and its subsidiaries have been buying Voss Lines piecemeal for the last six months or so."

Orr shrugged. "Properties came on the market and we liked them. It was business . . . nothing personal."

Mary Voss couldn't think of anything *more* personal, and knew Orr felt the same way, but understood his point. The industrialist hadn't done anything to destroy Voss Lines . . .

she'd managed that all by herself. "Of course. We never thought otherwise. Which brings us to the present. Howard and I have a business proposition for you . . . one that should be mutually beneficial."

Orr knew what was coming, and didn't have any intention of agreeing to it, but forced a smile anyway. "I love mutually beneficial business propositions. Fire away."

Natalie watched as her mother pitched the idea, explained how the loan would benefit Orr Enterprises, and minimized the extent to which she and her husband needed it. There were adders too, including language that would provide Orr's ships with a discount on tolls, and priority ratings that would shave days off shipping intervals. It was a masterful presentation, and might have worked, had Orr been interested. He waited for Mary to finish, nodded pleasantly, and said, "An excellent proposal, and tempting too, except that I have something different in mind."

Orr's counterpresentation was short and to the point. He, along with certain unidentified partners, was prepared to buy the Mescalero Gap outright, and for a rather generous sum, provided that the Voss family would agree to a large down payment, with substantial bubble payments each year for twenty years.

The figures were enormous, and Natalie felt her jaw drop as her mother not only refused, but took offense as well. Mary stood and looked at Orr through narrowed eyes. "The wormhole is worth *twice* what you offered, and you know it! Not that it makes a damned bit of difference. The gap is not now, nor will it ever be, for sale, especially to you. Good day, sir."

The atmosphere in the elevator was thick with anger as the threesome made their way down and into the street. Natalie had intended to ask after Dorn, to check on his progress at school, but she was dismissed with a kiss. Her parents couldn't wait to enter the private place where she'd never been allowed, where they could discuss the meeting and plan their next move.

Disappointed, and more than a little lonely, Natalie took a cab to Freeport. Once there she strapped herself into a loader.

The exoskeleton stood twelve feet high. It had been orange once, but the abrasive effects of time, salt, and constant use had leached the pigment out of the bright paint, and left islands of unadorned steel. But the machine made for an excellent vantage point and provided Natalie with an unencumbered view of the harbor.

She used the machine's optics to find her parents' freighter and watch it break free of the land. Clearances were given, drives were engaged, and repellors were fired. Water boiled and steam enveloped the ship as the hull broke free of the surface. Five or six seconds passed before the ship appeared over its self-generated shroud and rose toward the sky.

The spacecraft was approximately a thousand feet in the air when the first explosion shook its hull. The second came seconds later and was followed by a third. A miniature sun appeared, overloaded Natalie's optics, and vanished. Thunder rolled and broke 246 of Orr's specially treated windows, damaged thousands more within the city of Fortuna, and was heard fifty miles away.

The metal was still falling, still splashing into the water, when Natalie realized that her parents were dead, that she was alone, and that things would never be the same again.

5

Only by great risks can great results be achieved.

Xerxes
A comment made prior
*   to the invasion of Greece*
*   (which failed)*
Standard year 480 B.C.

The Planet New Hope

Dorn was ready a full hour before the agreed-upon pickup time, but made the driver wait for an extra fifteen minutes. It was something he'd learned from his mother, who said it made her seem more important, in spite of the fact that she *was* important, and had been for a long time.

Satisfied that the limo had been waiting for a sufficient length of time, and that the driver was impatient to leave, the young man checked the mirror and was pleased with what he saw. Dorn had dark hair, brown eyes, and a jaw that was firm like his father's. A pleasant, some said good-looking, face.

The suit had been in the last care package received from his parents. It was tight through the shoulders but consistent with the image he hoped to project. He wore a white shirt secured with a gold Voss Lines pin, a waist-length jacket, and a lot of gold braid. Black trousers and shiny half-boots completed the outfit.

Dorn checked to make sure that his bankroll was zipped

into an inside pocket, felt the fifty-credit note in his right boot, and surveyed the room. It was home now, which meant everything had its place, just like school.

The door made a reassuring click as it closed. The teenager tested the knob, assured himself that the lock was engaged, and made for the stairs. Dorn descended to the lobby, waved to the desk clerk, and stepped through the main entrance. The air was warm and humid. *Too* humid for the clothes he wore. Dorn half expected to find Rali crouched by the stairs but saw no sign of the boy.

The limo was an older model, but so well maintained that it looked new, and hummed like a much younger machine. The driver, a villainous-looking brute with long arms and an underthrust jaw, opened the door. Dorn nodded politely and slipped inside. The door closed, and he was enveloped by a cloud of perfume. The voice came from the shadows at the far end of the seat. It had a husky quality. "Hello, Dorn . . . my name's Candy."

A lighter flared as Candy lit a stim stick and offered the cylinder to Dorn. She was pretty, *very* pretty, and a few years older than he. "Smoke?"

Dorn felt very grown-up as he accepted the cigarette and took a drag. "It's a pleasure to meet you, Candy . . . thanks for the stim stick."

"No," Candy replied as she moved closer, "the pleasure is mine." Slender fingers caressed Dorn's thigh and slid up toward his groin. The teenager blushed as an erection pushed its way up to meet her touch. "Oh, my," Candy said softly, "look what we have here."

What happened next took Dorn by surprise. One moment he was sitting there, minding his own business, and the next thing he knew his fly was open, and Candy had taken him into her hot, wet mouth. The fragrance of her hair, combined with the delicious sensation, produced an almost instantaneous result. The pleasure was intense but brief.

Dorn was mortified, didn't know what to say or do, and wondered if the driver knew. He was relieved when his companion sat up and straightened her hair. She smiled. If she thought poorly of him, there was no sign of it on her face. "You needed that."

The teenager nodded gratefully, fed the cigarette to an ashtray, and dealt with his zipper. It was hard to be subtle. The limo had been in motion for a while now, and he had no idea where he was. Candy opened a bar. She offered him a glass. "Drink?"

Dorn accepted. He didn't like alcohol, but knew his character would, and took a sip. The liquor was sweet and glided down his throat. He waited for a moment, felt fine, and drank the rest.

"Another?"

Dorn nodded, allowed Candy to refill his glass, and was careful to sip rather than drink it. Better safe than sorry, not to mention the fact that refreshments could cost money, and he needed the credits he had. Which raised an important question. What about Candy? Were her services free? Or was he supposed to pay? His character would know, but he didn't.

The limo made a left-hand turn, entered the cantina's parking lot, and slid to a stop. A streetlight threw shadows across Candy's face. She looked older now and a little bit tired. Dorn finished his drink and cleared his throat. "Do I . . . ?"

Candy understood perfectly and shook her head. "No, but a tip would be nice."

Dorn fumbled for his roll, peeled a ten off the top, and handed it over. Candy seemed pleased, kissed his cheek in a sisterly fashion, and made the currency disappear. "Good luck, sweetie . . . I hope you break the bank."

Dorn thanked her, stepped out onto the pavement, and tipped the limo driver. The world swayed, then righted itself as the vehicle pulled away. The youth staggered, took his bearings from the cantina's brightly lit sign, and lurched in that direction. The air was cooler now and cleared his head. The sound of music reached up to the bank. He followed it onto the barge. Light streamed through the door and pooled on the deck.

The doorman called Dorn "sir," and smiled engagingly. A

man in evening clothes appeared, inquired as to his name, and snapped his fingers. A pretty young woman seized Dorn's arm and led him across the room. He used the trip to examine his surroundings. The room, which had been empty during his initial visit, was nearly full. There were locals out for a good time, spacers in from the black, and an assortment of other individuals who wore expressions of silent desperation and looked as though their entire futures rode on the next toss of their dice—a situation Dorn could empathize with.

There were null gravity roulette wheels, 3-D holo tables, virtual reality scenarios, and a variety of more traditional offerings, including Dorn's choice, a poker-derived electrocard game called Rockets and Stars.

The hostess led Dorn to a circular table and paused. It was occupied by a rather prosperous-looking middle-aged man, a woman dressed in a blue shipsuit with the name *Galaxy Queen* stitched over the left breast pocket, and an XT who, judging from the trade jewelry draped around his neck, owed his allegiance to an Alhanthian merchant clan. The alien had a pronounced supraorbital ridge, barely visible red eyes, and vertical nostril slits. He, she, or it looked around the table, gestured toward some upturned cards, and croaked, "Read 'em and defecate."

"That's read 'em and weep," the middle-aged man said indulgently, "although you may decide to follow your own advice when you see my cards."

"Cut the posturing and let's get on with it," the woman said curtly. "You gonna raise or not?"

The XT threw its cards on the table and leaned back. "Not."

"That's what I thought," the spacer replied contemptuously. "How 'bout you, Pops? You got the balls?"

"All my organs are intact, thank you," the man said urbanely. "But I choose to fold."

"Of course you do," the ship's officer said, raking the chips in, " 'cause you're a ground-pounding wimp."

The woman who had accompanied Dorn to the table cleared her throat. "Excuse me, gentlebeings, but I have the fourth player you requested. Citizen Voss, allow me to introduce Citizen Van Kirk, First Officer Harlan, and Citizen Pennuli. Five hundred credits are required to enter the game, the house takes five percent of each pot, and there are no limits. The dealer is using standard decks plus two supernovas. Questions? No? I'll buy your chips and bring them to the table."

Dorn felt the other player's eyes on him, wondered if they recognized the name, and hoped they didn't. He fumbled the bankroll out of its hiding place, wished he'd thought to do so earlier, and selected the correct number of bills. The hostess accepted the money, nodded pleasantly, and walked away. Van Kirk smiled and gestured toward a chair. "Take a load off, son. Welcome to the game."

Dorn nodded, took his seat, and tried to look impassive as the woman reappeared, placed three stacks of chips in front of him, and signaled a waiter. The drink was complimentary and warmed his throat. The dealer, a house-owned android, and one of the few that Dorn had seen on New Hope, was mounted at the center of the table. It could rotate 360 degrees and came equipped with a head, torso, and four arms. Each arm bore a finely articulated hand. Two shuffled a deck of cards while the others prepared to deal. The robot had a dour, nearly funereal expression, as if gambling were a serious business, which it undoubtedly was. A layer of dust frosted the upper surfaces of its black tuxedo.

"So," Pennuli croaked, "what the hell are we waiting for? Deal."

The machine bowed at the waist and servos whirred as it turned and dealt at the same time. Cards sailed out, skidded over green felt, and accumulated in front of the players. Dorn waited until his entire hand had been dealt before picking it up. The XT did likewise, while Van Kirk and Harlan examined each card as it arrived. Dorn fought the desire to arrange the rectangles in order of value.

Although the cards were as thin as their cardboard predecessors, they came equipped with high-definition video screens. Since each card had thirteen potential values, one for each card in a suit, a hand consisted of whatever symbol happened to be on-screen, plus the next image in queue. That meant each player could retain what they'd been dealt, trigger a new image, or fold. Dorn had two rockets, a planet, a star, and an asteroid. Not bad, but not good, not yet anyway. While he was not as experienced as those around him, the teenager had an excellent memory, and knew that the odds against making two pair were only 5 to 1, and that the odds against three of a kind were a quite reasonable 8 to 1, based on a three-card draw. The supernovas changed the odds, however—and the math made him squint.

Dorn glanced around the table, saw that the others were examining their cards, and made the obvious decision. A pair was better than nothing, so he'd keep the rockets and try for three, or even four of a kind.

The first round of betting took place before the players—those who wanted to—morphed their cards. Dorn felt his heart beat a little faster as he pushed the equivalent of twenty-five credits towards the center of the table. Then, holding his breath against what he might see, the teenager made the necessary decisions. The asteroid had the lowest value, so he pressed the card's lower right hand corner, and watched it morph to a comet. Damn! The planet came next. The teenager held his breath, triggered the card, and watched the image change. Planet to planet. Damn! The star, then . . . it had to be the star. Dorn tried again and felt a tremendous sense of excitement as the sun transformed itself into a rocket. He had triplets . . . and a chance of winning.

"So," Pennuli said, as he pushed a small stack of chips out onto the table, "twenty credits says homo saps are losers."

"Dream on," Harlan said tightly. "I'll see your twenty and raise you five."

"I'll pass," Van Kirk said easily. "How 'bout you, son? Are you in or out?"

Another drink had appeared next to Dorn's elbow, and the youngster took a sip. "I'm in."

The XT had a pair, Harlan had two pair, and Dorn took the pot. It, along with the alcohol that had found its way into his bloodstream, boosted his confidence. Time passed. Everybody took pots, but Dorn was most consistent. His chips doubled. He remembered Tull's advice. Assuming he had located a job, and saved every credit he made, it would have taken months to accumulate the chips in front of him. Dorn laughed, upped the ante, and finished the latest drink.

Cards hit the table, voices were raised in protest, and the teenager won again. The room felt warm and the chips wavered as he raked them in. Servos whirred as the droid dealt, and for reasons the teenager couldn't fathom, he felt lucky. And sure enough, after the others collected their cards, and were checking them over, he discovered he had three planets, a rocket, and an asteroid. The rocket morphed to a comet and the asteroid dissolved to a planet. Now he had clones . . . or four of a kind. The second highest hand there was.

The others must have held fairly good cards, though, because the pot grew and grew until half of Dorn's newfound wealth sat at the center of the table, and sweat soaked through his clothes. That's when disaster struck. The XT produced a pair, and Harlan had triplets, but Van Kirk blew them away. The older man had a star system consisting of a rocket, asteroid, planet, star, and comet. It was the equivalent of a straight flush—and beat the youngster's four of a kind.

Dorn felt fear gnaw his belly as Van Kirk pulled the chips toward his chest and built orderly stacks. The teenager considered dropping out of the game, but couldn't bring himself to do it. No, the older man had what amounted to *his* money, and he would win it back.

Hours passed, and while there were no further disasters on the scale of the first one, Dorn suffered a long series of minor losses, was forced to buy more chips, and wound up broke except for the fifty hidden in his boot.

But his luck had to change, or so it seemed to Dorn, so he stayed and waited for a break. It came at two in the morning. Dorn was looking at another so-so hand when the dealer droid slipped him a supernova, quickly followed by another, which was nothing less than remarkable, since the deck contained only two of them. Both cards were wild, meaning they could assume any value he gave them. Due to the fact that Dorn had three asteroids, he could claim the equivalent of a full house, the third highest hand possible.

Dorn struggled to hide his elation, bet, and bet again. The others, confident that they could beat the boy, went along. The pot grew larger and larger. Finally, certain of victory, and eager to capitalize on his hand, the teenager pushed the last of his chips toward the center of the table, pulled the fifty out of his boot, and tossed the gold Voss Lines pin on top of the pile. The stacks crumbled—giving way to a red, white, and blue chip avalanche.

There was a moment of silence while the others studied their hands. "I'm probably crazy," Harlan said slowly, "but I want to see what the boy's got. Or doesn't have. I'll see the last bet and call."

More chips were pushed toward the center of the table as cards went face up. Their eyes went to Dorn. He smiled, laid his hand out for all to see, and reached for the pot. He had just started to pull it in when Van Kirk grabbed his arm. "Wait a minute, son. A straight beats three of a kind, so what the hell are you doing?"

Dorn was still formulating a reply, still celebrating his win, while his eyes went to the cards. What he saw sent ice water through his veins. The asteroids remained as they were, but the supernovas were gone, replaced by a rocket and a planet. But that was impossible! That was . . .

Dorn came to his feet and looked around the table. Blood pounded in his ears, faces wavered, and his hands shook. "All right . . . which one of you did it? Empty your pockets. Someone used a remote on my cards."

No one moved, and Miss Carmen materialized on the far side of the table. She wore a red evening gown and the arm serpent he'd seen earlier. Two men, both larger than Dorn, stood to either shoulder. She looked cold and disapproving. "Good evening. Do we have a problem of some sort?"

"Yes we do!" Dorn said emphatically. "I had three asteroids, plus two supernovas. Then, just as I went to collect the pot, the novas disappeared."

Miss Carmen raised a carefully drawn eyebrow. "Really?

What are you suggesting? That you were cheated?''

"That's exactly what I'm suggesting," Dorn said grimly. "Search these beings . . . one of them used an illegal device to alter my cards."

Harlan wore a smirk, Van Kirk shook his head sadly, and Pennuli glared from deeply set sockets. It was as if they'd seen the whole drama before and knew how it would go.

The proprietress frowned delicately. "That's a serious allegation, Citizen Voss, and one that I take seriously, especially in light of the fact that it reflects on my customers and the cantina itself. First, allow me to say that *no one*, absolutely *no one*, gives orders to me, especially the drunken sons of bankrupt space trash. That's correct, *Citizen* Voss, I checked on your has-been family, and you are broke.

"In addition, it might interest you to know that the Cantina Roja is equipped with some rather sophisticated detection systems, so sophisticated that devices like the one you describe are discovered instantly, and confiscated moments later. You lost fair and square. Rudy and Sal will see you to the door. Don't come back."

Dorn tried to move, tried to respond, but discovered that the alcohol had slowed his reflexes. The bouncers moved with practiced ease, lifted the youngster off the floor, and elbow-carried him toward the kitchen. Hot, steamy air parted in front of his face as people in white turned to stare. A door opened, and he saw lights on the far side of the river. He barely had time to shout "No!" before being lifted into the air and thrown over the railing.

Time seemed to slow. Dorn remembered his previous visit, the river, and the exposed mud flats. Was the tide out or in? Would he land in mud or in the water? And what about pilings?

The fall ended. Shockingly cold water enveloped him and filled his boots. The boots, plus the water that soaked the teenager's clothes, weighted him down. Precious moments passed while the current pulled Dorn along. Curiously enough it was his old nemesis, Coach Mahowski, who intervened to save him. The voice, clipped and gruff, sounded in his head.

"This is a swimming pool, Mr. Voss, the purpose of which is not to provide you with entertainment, or provide the skills necessary to impress members of the opposite sex, but to help you survive in the element from which your ancestors crawled millions of years ago. The first rule to remember is that similar to most forms of excrement, underclassmen float, and that being the case, are equipped to survive in the water. What they lack, during the earlier years anyway, is brains—those amazing organs of thought, which, if employed properly, enable young men them to think their way out of most emergencies, or better yet, prevent them from happening in the first place."

Well, it was way too late to prevent the situation that Dorn found himself in, but it wasn't too late to think, and that meant losing some weight.

It was pitch black beneath the surface of the river, the current spun Dorn in circles, and his lungs were about to burst. It took a true act of will to bend over, pull his boots off, rip the buttons from his water logged jacket, and work his way out of it. The results were nearly instantaneous.

The clothing fell away and Dorn rose, propelled by Mahowski's flutter kick and the strength of his arms. They broke the surface first followed by his head and shoulders. Dorn spit foul-tasting water out of his mouth, inhaled great draughts of air, and kicked to keep his head up. He fought to get his bearings while an eddy spun him around. A long line of lights wobbled downstream, but before he could speculate on what they were, the river, working in concert with the outgoing tide, pulled the teenager over a series of rock ledges and into the blackness below.

The water stung as it made its way into countless cuts and scratches. His shoulder hurt where a rock had banged into it. Dorn ignored the pain, headed for the eastern shore, but didn't make much headway. He went ten feet downstream for each foot of lateral progress. The lights grew brighter and were overhead when the youngster hit the fishing net.

Later he would learn that silvers, a species of ocean-dwelling eel, liked to ride the incoming tide upriver to feed on the tiny organisms that flourished where fresh water mixed with salt—until the flow reversed itself, and the silvers were carried downstream. It was a cycle the locals took full advantage of by stretching nets across the river and harvesting as many of the eels as they could. But that knowledge would come later. This was now . . . and Dorn was in trouble.

Eels thumped into the boy's back, then pinned him against the net. Most of the silvers were one or two feet long and packed a wallop. He wondered what they ate and hoped it wasn't flesh. Dorn grabbed double handfuls of the net, looked upward, and saw a rickety bridge. The scrap lumber groaned under the force of the water and vibrated like a tuning fork. The teenager pushed his toes through the open mesh and tried to climb. He heard voices and shouted at the top of his lungs. "Help! I'm down here! Pull me up!"

There was a good deal of excited yelling followed by the appearance of a primitive fish-oil lantern and a pair of unshaven faces. One of them boasted a nose that had been flattened and reflattened in a long series of barroom brawls. "Well, look what we got here Packie, an extra big eel. I told you the sacrifice would work."

Packie, a man with high cheekbones and a gaunt face, remained unconvinced. "Sez you. Killin' a dog don't make no difference. It was dumb luck, that's all. The priests drink your money and laugh while you work. Come on, let's haul him out."

Strong, sinewy arms reached down to grab Dorn's wrists, pulled, and lifted him free of the eel-packed waters. The bridge was two planks wide, and it sagged under the combined weight of three people. The teenager looked down into water that churned with silvery life. He was about to thank the men when they grabbed his wrists. The cord went on with amazing speed. Dorn turned, tried to run, but was clubbed to his knees. He felt dizzy and allowed his forehead to rest against the water-slicked wood.

The first man shook his head disapprovingly and slapped the billy club against his left palm. It had dispatched a lot of eels and could easily break a skull. The lantern hung from a pole and cast long, hard shadows. "And where the hell do you think you're going, eel-boy? We caught you fair and square. Put the ropes on, Packie, the silvers are waitin', and we got work to do.''

It took the better part of two hours for the fishermen to harvest their catch, remove the net, and load everything, Dorn included, onto a makeshift cart. The wheels were made of wood rimmed with steel. For a penny apiece, plus another when the work was done, an army of street urchins grabbed the vehicle's hand-hewn tongue and pulled the conveyance through the early morning streets.

The fishermen, tired from their night's labors, lounged above Dorn's head and shared the contents of a stoneware jug. He, along with hundreds of dead eels, were thrown from one side of the wagon to the other as the exuberant children pulled their burden through narrow, twisting passageways. Where were they going? And more important, why? Those questions were at the forefront of the young man's mind. At one time or another he had offered the fishermen money he didn't have, and threatened them with Headmaster Tull's wrath, all to no avail. All he could do was wait and hope for the best.

Slums, the likes of which Dorn hadn't seen since his outings with Mr. Halworthy, passed to either side. The smell of sewage was so powerful it overwhelmed the odor produced by the eels and caused the teenager to gag. The thought of what he must have swallowed, and the bacteria that had access to his body, made Dorn thankful for the countless inoculations the school had given him.

The cart bounced into a turn, threw Dorn and the silvers sideways, and came to a grinding halt. By craning his neck and looking upward, the teenager saw a weatherbeaten sign. It read ''The Keno Labor Exchange'' and squeaked as the wind pushed against it.

What had been discomfort mixed with indignation quickly turned to fear. Though protected from most of the planet's less pleasant realities, and never allowed to venture out on their own, Dorn and his fellow students had heard of the so-called labor exchanges, places where sentients of every possible description signed their lives away in return for food and the bare necessities. It amounted to legally sanctioned slavery and had flourished for years.

Dorn struggled against his bonds, and was still struggling when his captors lifted him free of the cart, pushed their way through a crowd of goggle-eyed children, and carried him through a gate. The youth was suspended facedown. He saw mud squish out from under the men's homemade sandals, heard the babble of contentious voices, and the crack of what might have been a whip.

The next sound was the rasp of metal on metal, followed by a male voice. "Throw him in the holding cell and report to the office. Citizen Inwa will pay the finder's fee."

The fishermen took the voice literally, threw Dorn into a cell, and slammed the door behind him. Still tied, and unable to break his fall, the youngster hit hard and skidded across the muck-covered floor. He came to rest next to a man so emaciated he looked like a living skeleton. Sores covered his face, blood flecked his lips, and his eyes seemed dim. They blinked, blinked again, and closed. The words were so weak, so insubstantial, they seemed like ghosts. "Hello, son. Welcome to hell."

6

What the parents sow, their children shall reap.

Elwander the Wise
The Alhanthian Book of Truth
Circa 1600

The Planet Mechnos

The offices where Natalie had played as a child, and where her parents had hatched their multitudinous schemes, were silent now, emptied of people, machines, and furniture. The next tenant would arrive soon, causing the halls, offices, and conference rooms to hum with a different purpose.

The guard was a former Voss Lines employee who had found temporary employment with a security firm. She greeted Natalie with a hug and allowed her to roam the building. Just for old times' sake, so she could look around, and remember how things had been.

And remember Natalie did, bursting into unexpected tears when she entered the office her parents had shared, empty now except for cables that poked up out of the floor, and the remains of a once bushy plant.

Like any officer, Natalie was theoretically ready to handle anything from burnt toast to a runaway reactor. Nothing, however, had prepared Natalie for the death of her parents. She sat where the toy box had been and leaned on the wall. Tears trickled down her cheeks, and she used a sleeve to wipe them away. The only thing worse than watching her parents die was the feelings that had plagued her since. Sorrow, not for them, but for herself. Because they had abandoned her. How stupid. Especially in light of the fact that they had never been there to begin with.

It seemed as if they'd always been on the com, locked away in meetings, or traveling somewhere. Building toward what? A burst of bright light, followed by a sparsely attended memorial service and an empty office. She thought about Dorn, wondered how he was doing, and wished she could be with him.

How typical of her parents! To die at the same exact moment, so there was no room to squeeze between them, to know even one a tiny bit better. They'd been a unit for as long as she could remember, a single force that made its own rules and placed Voss Lines before everything else.

That's the way things were . . . and there was no use whining about it. No, she had responsibilities, not just to herself and what remained of her parent's empire, but to Dorn and *his* future. The kind of responsibilities she had left home to avoid.

However, like all officers, good ones anyway, Natalie understood the concept of duty. And duty dictated that she secure the one asset that remained, get as much for it as possible, and invest the money in a sensible manner. Then, and only then, could she return to the life she wanted for herself.

The problem was that you can't sell something you don't have, and Natalie needed the coordinates for the Mescalero Gap. An extremely valuable piece of information that her parents never divulged to anyone, even to the point of programming the adjunct memories themselves. For it was the AMs that, when connected to a ship's navcomp, provided the computer with the wormhole's coordinates, and erased the data one microsecond after use. More than a dozen would-be thieves had died testing their wits against the booby-trapped boxes.

Yes, there were other ways to locate gaps, but given that the wormholes were invisible to ordinary optics, such efforts depended on indirect evidence such as the influence they exerted on the matter that surrounded them, the radiation they produced, and the X rays they emitted. All of this might or might not lead the would-be traveler to the *correct* hole. And mistakes were fatal.

So, while a few foolhardy or desperate captains had no doubt used the gap for free and gotten away with it, most sentients preferred to fork over the fee and know that they would survive.

Natalie scrambled to her feet. There was little or no doubt that her parents had been carrying the coordinates on their bodies, but the data cube, or whatever device they used as a storage medium, had been destroyed along with them. But there were backup copies, she was sure of that, and her task was to find one. Because to sell the wormhole, and free herself from its grip, she needed a legal description of where it was. Not to mention the fact that she couldn't program the AMs—thereby cutting what remained of the shipping line off from its only source of income. Requests continued to come in, and she had no way to fill them. That's why Natalie had broken into the family mansion the night before, searched the now vacant house from roof to cellar, and searched it again. All to no avail.

Like most children, Natalie and her brother loved games, especially hide-and-seek, which the Voss Lines office staff had tolerated because of who they were. In the process of playing, and otherwise sticking their noses where they didn't belong, the children had discovered a variety of nooks and crannies. That included the drawer where their father kept some rather risque holo cubes, a drug stash that belonged to the firm's comptroller, and the crawl space where the maintenance woman took naps.

But of all the possible hiding places, the one Natalie considered most likely to contain what she was looking for was located behind the commode in her mother's private rest room. The first time the then-teenager noticed the stainless steel access plate, and used a nail file to remove the screws, the clean-out compartment had been deliciously empty. The perfect place to stash her diary or the stim sticks she was experimenting with. But, when Natalie removed the cover three days later, she discovered that someone, and her mother seemed the most likely candidate, had put the compartment to use.

A high-quality durasteel hand safe, complete with microcomputer and thumb lock, had been stored inside, and threatened to trigger a siren when she handled it. Fearful of what her mother might say or do if that happened, the girl returned the cube to its hiding place, replaced the cover, and decided never to touch it again. Not until now, that is . . . assuming it was there.

The carpet still bore the impressions left by furniture that had occupied the office for the last ten years. The matching desks that belonged to her parents, a variety of storage cabinets, and the display case that contained the nameplate from their first ship all had left their individual marks. Natalie crossed the invisible line that had separated her father's half of the room from her mother's and entered the private rest room. There was a counter, a commode, and a shower stall. The art, towel racks, and other fittings, many of them quite valuable, had been removed by creditors.

Natalie's ship-style high-tops squeaked as she crossed the tiles and knelt by the commode. It felt cold against her left arm. The stainless steel plate looked as it had years before. Or were there more scratch marks around the screws? As if someone had removed and replaced them numerous times.

The young woman's heart thumped against her chest as she pulled the multitool from its pouch, chose the correct driver, selected "reverse," and pressed the "on" button with her thumb. The motor whined as the screws spun out of their respective holes, clattered on the tiles, and rolled into grout-filled valleys. The access cover fell away from the wall and clanged on the floor.

The overhead light didn't work, and it was dark inside the hidey-hole. Natalie turned the multitool's handle to the right and was rewarded with a narrowly focused beam of light. She peered into the hole and missed the crawl cam that inched its way across the ceiling and stationed itself next to the burned-out light.

Unaware that she was under surveillance, and eager to retrieve the safe, Natalie reached into the cavity. The cube was cool to the touch and quick to complain. "Put me back! I belong to Mary Voss! Get your hands off me!"

"Yeah, yeah, yeah," Natalie said as she slipped the earplugs into place, "life is a bitch." In spite of the fact that she had anticipated the possibility, and come prepared to deal with it, the siren, combined with the noise generated by the carbide-tipped drill bit, was louder than she'd have liked. It was mercifully brief, however, as the tip tore through the safe's CPU, shorted the machine's circuits, and fried its brain.

Natalie was tempted to open the cube and peek inside, but knew the guard could arrive any moment. She dropped the safe into a handbag and was about to replace the access panel when the guard called. "Miss Voss? Where are you?"

"Right here," Natalie replied confidently, stepping out of her mother's bathroom. "I needed to freshen up."

The woman nodded understandingly and brushed a wisp of gray hair out of her face. "Yes, of course, dear. Your mother spent a lot of money on that powder room. It's a shame what happened to it. Did you hear a noise of some sort? A siren, perhaps?"

Natalie walked over to a window. It looked out on a busy downtown street. "Why, yes, I did. I was in the bathroom at the time, but there was a noise."

The security guard shrugged. "Ah, well, emergency vehicles come and go all the time. That would explain it."

"Yes," Natalie said agreeably, "it would. Well, thanks for letting me in. A lot of memories are stored here."

The guard nodded, allowed that what had happened to her parents was "terrible, just terrible," and saw her to the front door. She gave Natalie a hug, locked the door behind her, and watched the girl walk away. The guard sighed, returned to her desk, and poured herself a cup of coffee. It was a sad, sad day.

Ari watched the video fade to black and waited for the almost inevitable criticism. It wasn't long in coming. Carnaby Orr rose from his high-backed chair, walked to the recently repaired windows, and looked out over the bay. "So, let's see if I understand . . . Your staff swept those offices on two separate occasions, and missed the compartment behind the toilet?"

Ari wanted to point out that the offices were huge, that the spacer knew exactly where to look, but refused to take refuge in excuses. "That's correct, sir. We searched the place twice and missed the panel on both occasions."

Orr was disappointed. He'd hoped to grill Ari, to work her over for a while, thereby releasing some of the pent-up frustration he felt. Now she had denied him that, and dared him to fire her, which he'd never do. Not for a long time anyway, assuming that she performed in bed, and remained loyal— something he paid two subordinates to monitor.

"Ah, well," the industrialist said grudgingly, "these things happen. No harm done, I suppose, especially since we have a good idea of what the safe contained, and couldn't use them anyway. Not legally, that is."

"We do?" Ari asked coolly. "Based on what?"

"Common sense," Orr said smugly, turning his back to the window. "Natalie Voss is nobody's fool. She heard what I offered her parents and knows a good deal when she hears one. Especially since she has none of the overweening pride and ambition that made her parents so unpleasant. No, I think Natalie has the coordinates and will be eager to sell them."

Ari could think of other possibilities, plenty of them, but saw no reason to rain on Orr's rather optimistic parade. Especially in light of the access panel fiasco. She nodded. "So? What now?"

"We close the deal," Orr said comfortably. "My lawyers will meet with the young lady and extend the same offer that I made to her parents."

"And if she refuses?"

Orr smiled and cupped her chin. "Then it will be your job to change her mind."

Traffic was thick, much thicker than anything found on La-Tri, and Sa-Lo was driving. The Traa could have hired a driver or rented an autocar, but he was unwilling to surrender control. Horns honked and humans made rude gestures as Sa-Lo wove back and forth through traffic. The Voss female had an intimate knowledge of the city and seemed intent on making every right- and left-hand turn it was possible to make.

They had already followed the flat-faced female to the building where Voss Lines had been headquartered, to the Bureau of Trade where her parents' deaths were the subject of an ongoing investigation, and from there on a series of errands.

Ka-Di was nervous the way he'd *always* been nervous since La-Ma's death, the same sort of keyed-up fluttery feeling that preceded combat—only worse, since combat had a beginning, middle, and end, and this went on forever.

And, as if to make a bad situation worse, La-Ma had caused Ka-Di's condition, or rather her death had, and it was to her, or a person very much like her, that he wanted to turn for help. But none were left, not after the eruption that decimated the Philosopher Sept, which meant there was little or no hope for a cure. The knowledge, and the helplessness that accompanied it, felt like a mantle of lead.

Sa-Lo swung into oncoming traffic, accelerated, and slid back into his lane just as a green-and-white hover bus roared through the space he had so recently vacated. Horns blared, and the commercial being bared his fangs. "Mannerless scum."

Ka-Di watched his mate-brother from the corner of his eye. "You seem worried . . . is there something I can do?"

Sa-Lo responded with the Traa equivalent of a shrug. "Orr is wrong. He should wait until the investigation has been concluded before making an offer. This approach is too aggressive, too obvious, and might lead to trouble. It would behoove us to remember that while some of the authorities are stupid, some, like those recruited from your sept, are quite intelligent.''

Ka-Di had been comfortable with Orr's approach. After all, he was a warrior, and what was commerce if not symbolic warfare? The head-on attack is not only honorable, but frequently successful, and always worth consideration. Still, many are the ways of victory, and Sa-Lo could be right. Especially where Traa investigators were concerned. Though drawn from the Warrior Sept, they were required to sever all connections with it while they served the Confederacy. Not that they always did. The warrior chose his words with care. ''You may be correct, Sa-Lo, but this is the price we pay for working through others.''

Sa-Lo grunted an acknowledgment, slipped between a pair of trucks, and slammed on the brakes. The vehicle skidded to a halt. The female was in front of him. She executed two right-hand turns and entered her hotel. *Their* hotel, since the Traa were reluctant to rely on Orr's security apparatus and preferred to keep an eye on Natalie personally. The Traa followed the human down into an underground garage, parked their vehicle a discreet distance away, and waited while she entered the lift tubes. Natalie was in her room by the time Ka-Di and Sa-Lo arrived on the ninth floor, thumbed the lock panel on the adjoining suite, and let themselves in.

It took less than a minute to pop the lid on the surveillance case, power up, and check the female's activities. Five different crawl cams had been inserted into her quarters via the air-conditioning ducts, and two of them were close enough to provide clean audio when the doorbell rang. Ka-Di frowned and watched over Sa-Lo's shoulder as the flat-face answered the door.

Natalie thought she'd seen most everything. But the man in the hall was equipped with two heads. One rested where it should, centered between the shoulders of an expensively cut suit, while the other peered out from under his arm, and was first to speak. Head number two had a craggy brow, hooked nose, and thin, almost cruel lips. She knew it to be an Artificial

Intelligence, or AI, but thought of it as human. "Citizen Voss?"

Natalie positioned herself to slam the door in both faces. "Yes?"

"My name is Johnson and this is my associate, Frank Shank. Of the law firm Johnson, Shank, and Wong? Perhaps you've heard of us?"

Natalie shook her head. "No, I don't believe I have. But I don't spend much time on Mechnos. What can I do for you?"

Shank spoke for the first time. His face was too handsome, too perfect, to be real. "We represent Carnaby Orr. He sends his condolences regarding the death of your parents and wonders if we could be of assistance."

Natalie frowned. "Assistance? The law firm my parents used has responsibility for their estate."

"No," Johnson replied firmly. "Mr. Orr thought that you might be interested in a business proposal. May we come in?"

Natalie shrugged and opened the door. "Sure, make yourselves at home."

Shank thanked her, entered the room, and placed Johnson on the coffee table. The AI seemed comfortable there and looked around. A vid screen occupied the wall where a window might have been. The furniture was comfortable rather than stylish. The crawl cams radiated heat, and Johnson recognized them as belonging to the Traa. The machine smiled. "Nice room."

Natalie took a seat. "Thank you. So, tell me. What sort of business proposal does Mr. Orr have in mind?"

Shank removed an imaginary piece of lint from his sleeve. "You were present at the meeting between Mr. Orr and your parents?"

Natalie nodded. "Yes, I was there."

"Well," Johnson said, reclaiming control of the conversation, "while Mr. Orr would have preferred to have reached some sort of accommodation with Mr. and Mrs. Voss, or barring that, to have postponed this discussion until a later date, we advised him to move more aggressively. So, if a desire to pursue such discussions seems hasty, or lacking in taste, the offense is ours and ours alone.''

The handbag, and the safe that it contained, lay inches from Natalie's right hand. Seemliness, or the lack of it, was the farthest thing from her mind. Were the coordinates in the safe? If so, she had something to sell, and someone who wanted to buy. If not, she needed time. "No, my parents were business people, and understood the saying 'Time is money.' But there are other things to consider, such as fair market price, and the possibility that others may wish to vie with Mr. Orr for the rights to the Mescalero Gap.''

Johnson frowned ever so slightly and sent a scrambled radio signal toward a receiver located one floor below. "Yes, well, market conditions are an important aspect of any business arrangement. There is another saying, however: 'A bird in the hand is worth two in the bush.' Why wait if you can come to an equitable deal now?''

The words seemed to hang there, suspended in midair, as Natalie looked from the disembodied head up to the equally strange man who carried it around. This was what she wanted, wasn't it? Assuming she had the coordinates or could find them? A quick, efficient deal that would produce the maximum amount of money in the least amount of time. Then why did the lawyers look so evil? And why did the situation feel so wrong? The words seemed to form themselves.

"You make a valid point, Mr. Johnson, and one I will keep in mind. In the meantime, I beg your indulgence. I have a brother to consider. He'll be eighteen soon and should have his say.''

Ka-Di barely had time to look at Sa-Lo before Natalie's door opened, allowing three additional people to enter. A less experienced person might have assumed that Ari and her heavies had barged into the wrong room, or might have wasted time asking stupid questions, but Natalie had spent a lot of time on backwater planets and seized the initiative.

The officer came off the couch in one fluid motion. She grabbed Johnson by the ears and lifted him off the table. He weighed twice what a real head would have, and tried to bite her. She ignored the flashing white teeth and threw the machine at Ari. The security chief caught the head with a whoosh of expelled air and fell over backwards. She continued to fall as Natalie grabbed the handbag, twirled it around her head, and connected with the first assailant's face. He yelled, grabbed his nose, and danced a jig.

The other security person, a woman, grinned and gestured toward the handbag. "You've been lucky so far, honey . . . don't push it. Give me the purse and stay out of the hospital."

Natalie looked contrite and offered the bag. The woman latched onto the strap as Ari shouted, "No! Don't do it!" Natalie jerked the woman off balance and kneed her in the stomach. The double fist-strike, delivered to the woman's neck, finished her off. She collapsed in a heap.

Ari came to her feet. Natalie turned, entered the bedroom, and locked the door. The knob rattled as she stepped onto the balcony. Natalie slipped her head through the shoulder strap, climbed onto the railing, and teetered back and forth. It was a long way to the cement below. A body hit the door. Wood shattered and someone swore. Natalie threw herself forward. Wind rushed by her face.

7

No man can put a chain about the ankle of his fellow man without at last finding the other end fastened about his own neck.

Fredrick Douglass
American abolitionist
Circa 1850

The Planet New Hope

Moisture evaporated from the trenches that crisscrossed the holding pens as the yellow-orange sun climbed higher in the sky. The stench increased and the hours grew longer. Dorn's cellmate died about 3:00 in the afternoon but no one came for the body till well after dark. Dorn attempted to plead his case as they dragged the corpse through the door. "My name is Dorn Voss and I'm not supposed to be here. Could I speak with the person in charge, please?"

The men had agreed to collect dead bodies in return for extra food. One of them balanced the additional corpse on top of an already full cart while the other returned for the lantern. His feet slapped on wet concrete. He had unruly black hair, at least four days' worth of beard, and a gravelly voice. He held the light up, and a giant appeared on the wall behind him. "Take it from me, boy . . . none of us is *supposed* to be here . . . but this is where we are. Conserve your strength. Use it to survive. That's all anyone can do.'' The man exited the cell, the gate clanged closed, and the light wobbled away.

A bowl of steaming mush was shoved under the gate an hour later. It had a yeasty smell and contained lumps of what might have been meat. Dorn was so famished he didn't care what the mixture contained. He scooped the concoction into his mouth, chewed hungrily, and licked the bowl clean. The meal left him thirsty, but there wasn't any water beyond what had accumulated in the cell's lowest corner. He considered scooping some up but decided not to. Not with the bacteria that swarmed in it. Not yet, anyway.

The teenager wrapped his arms around his knees, ignored his thirst, and waited for morning to come. He wanted a stim stick and cursed his own weakness. Voices murmured in the next cell, a deep racking cough came from across the way, and a prayer drum could be heard in the distance. Dorn started the slide toward self-pity and was almost there when the corpse collector's words came back to him. ''Conserve your strength. Use it to survive. That's all anyone can do.''

The words amounted to little more than common sense but triggered an important understanding. Suddenly Dorn realized that *he* had responsibility for his life. Not his parents, not his teachers, not society in general. Yes, life had dealt him a bad hand, but only after a long series of good ones. It was *he* who had ignored Tull's advice and gambled his money away. Maybe someone would come to his rescue and maybe they wouldn't. His job was to survive, and that's what he would do. The key was to think about each move that he made and devise realistic plans for his release.

Rats chased each other up and down the far side of the cell for a while, but Dorn grew accustomed to their antics and drifted off to sleep. Nothingness felt good.

Dorn awoke to the sound of male voices and the clatter of chains. Light filtered through the bars and threw rectangles on the floor. His mouth tasted foul, and his shoulder ached from sleeping on the ground. A key rattled and hinges squealed. The guard was short and stocky. He smiled and slapped his leg with a half-coiled whip. "Morning, sweetums, time to rise and shine."

True to his new philosophy, Dorn wasted no time pleading his case before what amounted to a minor functionary and hurried to exit the cell. Mud squished between the teenager's toes as he stepped out into the sun. He blinked and stumbled as the man pushed from behind. "What's the matter, sweetums? You think I got all day? Get your ass to the other end of the line."

The line was reasonably straight. Dull-eyed men and women, some with children, stared at Dorn as he jogged past. Most were young to middle-aged, wore little more than rags, and appeared malnourished. Guards, all of whom had whips, smacked Dorn's head, shoulders, and arms as he passed. Not for any specific reason, but because they could, and that, plus a little more food, was all that distinguished them from the slaves they guarded.

The rearmost prisoners showed little interest in Dorn as he was pushed into position and shackled to a muck-covered drag chain—a valuable artifact on metal-starved New Hope. No sooner was the leg iron secured than a whip cracked and the line moved forward. Dorn led with his right foot, realized his mistake, and fell as the other foot was jerked out from under him. The teenager hit the ground, flinched under the whip, and scrambled to his feet. The line jerked forward, and he hopped to catch up.

It took an hour of starts and stops for the prisoners to snake their way through the holding pens and into a makeshift amphitheater. An assembly area had been established at the center of an old gravel pit and equipped with a makeshift platform. It boasted a red-and-white-striped awning, a simple wooden table, and a comfortable-looking chair. Concrete blocks fronted the platform. Due to the nearly random manner in which they were positioned, they looked like leftovers.

The guards took up positions around the perimeter. Their leader approached the head of the line, touched a wand to the first man's shackle, and kept on walking. The leg irons hit the mud one after another, and the prisoners drifted away. Two minutes had passed before the man arrived in front of Dorn. The teenager waited for the touch, heard the resulting click, and felt the bracelet let go. He massaged his ankle and saw that his skin was raw. A long walk would make it worse, and Dorn resolved to find some padding.

The prisoners stood in small groups, sat on the concrete blocks, or lined up for the chance to drink at one of two free-flowing spigots. The water gushed and made a puddle through which people were forced to wade. Dorn joined the right-hand queue on the theory that it would move faster but was quickly disappointed. Children slowed the process, and there were more of them on the right than the left. The slow, shuffling progress reminded the youth of school, when one of the more popular entrees appeared on the menu and everyone came.

The conversations were interesting, though. One man in particular seemed to have a pretty good grasp of what would happen next. He'd been through the process before, it seemed, and for reasons not entirely clear was going through it again. Whatever the case, the man claimed that a magistrate would soon appear, hearings would be held, and those judged vagrant according to the city's codes would be given over to the owners of the Keno Labor Exchange. They in turn would sell the condemned men, women, and children into what amounted to forced servitude. Not a pleasant prospect . . . but some information was better than none.

Forty-five minutes passed. Dorn was close now, so close he stood ankle-deep in mud, and could practically *feel* the cool liquid trickling down his throat. But what if the magistrate appeared? What if the guards ordered the prisoners to disperse? He'd lose his turn at the spigot, and the knowledge made him edgy. He started to see those in front of him as enemies, as people who, through their slow, dim-witted piggishness were out to steal that which was rightfully his. He fidgeted, resisted the urge to shove the person in front of him, and telepathically ordered everyone to hurry up.

A commotion was heard. Orders were shouted, guards stood straighter, and a processional appeared. It had a medieval feel, complete with an heraldic device and robes of black. The magistrate had arrived! Dorn was only three people away from the spigot now, his throat burning with thirst, his tongue swollen in his mouth. Water! He had to have water! The first person drank, stepped aside, and was followed by the second. An order, amplified through a bullhorn, boomed across the pit. "You! By the water spigots! Take your places at the platform!"

Dorn was about to drink, about to take his chances with whatever punishment might come his way, when a hand touched his arm. He turned, ready to snarl, and found himself face to face with a teenage girl. She had big brown eyes, a dirt-smeared face, and a six-month-old baby in her arms. The infant was clearly ill. The older child had a calm, matter-of-fact voice. "Please, mister . . . my brother has diarrhea. He'll die without water."

Dorn felt a terrible shame settle over him as he looked into that face, for the girl's lips were as cracked as his, but she asked nothing for herself. He forced the semblance of a smile. "Quickly, then . . . up to the spigot."

The look of gratitude the girl gave him reminded Dorn that no matter how desperate things got for him, there was always someone even worse off. A man attempted to push the girl aside, but Dorn blocked the way. The guards pushed into the crowd. Their whips cracked right and left. People screamed and hurried to escape. The girl appeared next to Dorn, shouted words he couldn't understand, and placed something in his hand. Then, still holding the baby, she was swept away.

Dorn turned toward the platform and followed the people in front of him. The youngster's hand felt wet. He examined the object, saw it was a scarf, and realized what she'd done. Working quickly, so as to conserve every precious drop, he crammed the fabric into his mouth and sucked as hard as he could. Nothing had ever tasted so good as the rusty, brackish water that trickled down his throat.

The moment the last vestige of moisture had been removed, Dorn pulled the scarf out of his mouth and tied it around his arm. A guard demanded their attention. "Court number six, of the Oro municipal court system, is now in session. Judge Janice Tal presiding.''

The hearings were conducted in alpha order, which meant that he had plenty of time to observe the way things worked. Moving slowly, so as to avoid negative attention, Dorn eased his way through the crowd. He joined the first row and craned his neck to see.

The magistrate wore her hair in a carefully constructed top-knot. She had thin, heavily plucked eyebrows, half-hooded eyes, and a slit-shaped mouth. The proceedings were more form than substance. A name was called; the person who answered to it was pulled, shoved, or dragged onto the platform where charges of vagrancy were read; a halting, often tearful defense was offered and gaveled to silence. The magistrate wore a boom mike, and her voice issued from a sphere that hung over the crowd. ''Guilty as charged. Sentenced to five years compensated labor. Next.''

Then the haggard man, woman, or child would be directed to the far side of the gravel pit, where the condemned waited, their chains laid next to them. More than three hours passed before the youth heard his name. ''Voss . . . Dorn . . . take the platform.''

Like most of his peers, Dorn had spent a lot of time analyzing Milford's faculty and playing to their weaknesses. Now, having spent the last few hours watching the magistrate, he had some theories. Judge Tal felt no sympathy for those who came before her, or if she did, hid it well. Sad stories and equally sad appearances had no effect on the sentences handed out. Only three people were found innocent, and every one of them had demonstrated the poise and bearing of the upper classes. So Dorn mounted the platform like a visiting dignitary. He kept his chin up, his back straight, and looked Tal right in the eye. ''Good afternoon, your honor . . . my name is Dorn Voss.''

Tal's eyelids hung at perpetual half-mast. They rose a quarter of an inch. ''Read the charges.''

The guard, who had already read the boilerplate hundreds of times, did so again. ''The defendant stands accused of vagrancy, a lack of visible support, and homelessness.''

The woman eyed Dorn in a speculative manner. "You heard the charges, Citizen Voss . . . how do you plead?"

Dorn stood even straighter. "Not guilty, your honor. I am a minor, my parents own a business, and I have rooms at the Starman's Rest. A call to the hotel or the Milford Academy will verify my story."

Tal tapped a stylus against her lips and looked thoughtful. "Yes, I'm sure it would, just as some com calls, intersystem record checks, and the expenditure of a modest amount of shoe leather would substantiate at least some of the other claims heard today. Unfortunately, niceties such as those cost money . . . more money than the good citizens of Oro have to spend. That's why we rely on identification cards and other evidence of solvency, such as credit chips or cash. Do you have any of these in your possession?"

A lump had formed in Dorn's throat and made it difficult to swallow. The half-lie came easily. "No, your honor, my residency card and money were lost when I fell in the river."

Tal shrugged. "That's what they all say . . . give or take a few details. Tell me Citizen Voss, or whatever your *real* name is, what college did your mother attend?"

Dorn felt his heart leap. Could it be? Did the Judge *know* his mother? If so, this might be the break he'd been hoping for. "The University of Mechnos, your honor."

Tal nodded approvingly. "Very good! Mary and I were classmates. Too bad about her death. The story made the news the day before yesterday. Including the fact that Mary graduated cum laude from the U of M. She even had a son about your age . . . though cleaner, I suspect." The magistrate turned toward the nearest guard. "Guilty as charged. Five years compensated labor. Take the imposter away."

The guard gestured toward the stairs. Dorn ignored him. "Dead? My mother's dead? How? When?"

But the magistrate ignored him, the guards grabbed his arms, and Dorn was half guided, half carried off the platform. The beating started the moment his feet touched the ground. The blows came hard and fast. The teenager tried to defend himself, fell under the assault of baton-style whip handles, and lay huddled on the ground.

The punishment might have been worse, and lasted even longer, had it not been for the prisoner who shouted obscenities and tried to attack the judge. A guard called for help, her comrades rushed to the rescue, and Dorn was left alone. He made sure that they were truly done with him, got to his feet, and stumbled toward the area where the others waited. He hurt all over, but nothing was broken.

Dorn chose a hunk of concrete and took a seat. A man moved in the boy's direction, saw the expression on his face, and thought better of it. Dorn turned his back on the other prisoners, thought about what the judge had said, and felt an overwhelming sense of grief. Sobs racked his body as tears ran down his cheeks. His mother was dead, and quite possibly his father as well. That would account for a number of things, including the lack of communication and the cessation of financial support.

Still, why hadn't he heard from the family lawyers by now? Or, failing that, from Natalie? Assuming she was aware of what had occurred. And even more important, why was he thinking of himself when he should be thinking about them?

Guilt, grief, and self-loathing combined to pull Dorn down. He thought about how foolish he'd been to gamble his money away, about the undeliverable letters that had arrived by now, and the likelihood that he'd never get to read them.

But something, the memory of his parents perhaps, or the knowledge that they never gave up, no matter what the odds, lifted him back up. Slowly, bit by bit, the sobs died away. Still, even as the teenager blinked the tears away and regained control of his breathing, he knew the empty feeling was there to stay.

A voice boomed across the gravel pit. "On your feet, scum. You have ten miles to walk before nightfall . . . so get those shackles on . . . and keep the line straight."

Dorn suspected that minute advantages could be realized depending on where one was located along the chain's length, but didn't know what they were, or how to harvest them. He remembered the chafing problem, removed the scarf from his arm, and tied it around his left ankle. The shackle was a tight fit, but there was no pain when the guard snapped it closed.

The prisoners were forced to wait for the better part of an hour as Judge Tal put her thumbprint on a four-inch stack of hardcopies, reviewed a transcript of the proceedings, and thumbed that as well. Then a man in a dirty gray turban appeared, transferred the correct number of credits to the Labor Exchange's account, and shouted orders to his guards.

Dorn felt hopeful when a rather plump doctor appeared and, accompanied by two assistants, walked the length of the line. He examined feet, listened through a stethoscope, and dispensed medications. Dorn realized the doctor was little more than a glorified maintenance technician, hired to minimize the wear and tear on recently purchased assets.

Still, Dorn welcomed the disinfectant that was sprayed on his many cuts and scratches, the antibiotics that were pumped into his arm, and the vitamins they insisted he swallow. Of even more value, to him at least, were the sturdy sandals issued to those who didn't have shoes. They were ugly as sin, but far better than bare feet. They would help during the march ahead.

The march, once it began, was almost pleasant at first. Dorn was rested and, thanks to the resiliency of youth, felt pretty good. At first the line went more slowly than he would have liked, but it picked up speed as it moved out onto the road, and a good steady rhythm was established. People, children mostly, swarmed out of the surrounding slums to witness the spectacle. Like the guards, most of the onlookers were only a residency permit and a few credits away from joining the procession themselves, and reveled in their brief moment of social superiority.

But there were others, kinder souls perhaps, who offered scraps of bread to some of the more pitiful prisoners, or bent their heads in prayer.

Dorn felt humiliated at first, and hated them with all his heart, until the first of many ground cars roared by and peppered the prisoners with debris. He tried to remember the outings he'd been on, and whether he'd seen a long line of prisoners marching beside the road, but nothing came to mind. Was that because he hadn't seen them? Or because such lowly creatures had no reality for well-fed schoolboys on their way to picnics? Dorn hoped for the first but feared the second.

They entered an area where the old road had been torn up and a new one was being laid. Hundreds of bare backs glistened in the sun as picks rose into the air, fell in a wave, and hit one after another. Though the workers were not linked at the ankles, it occurred to Dorn that they were slaves nonetheless. Economic slaves who had taken what they could get. Why else would they do such work? And if they suffered, what could he look forward to?

An hour passed, then two. The drag chain rattled as they walked. The slums grew thicker and crowded in on both sides as their balconies, makeshift arches, and badly eroded walls threatened to cave in on the street. Then, as twilight fell and the sun set behind them, the city dwindled away to be replaced by fields, lonely farmhouses, and the occasional dome-shaped temple. Candles flickered and prayer drums thumped.

The air quality improved as well, causing Dorn to take deep draughts of the stuff, reveling in the way it filled his lungs. The others seemed invigorated too, and the pace increased for a while, but fell off again. Unlike Dorn, who had been in top physical condition to begin with, the others suffered from a wide variety of maladies.

Physical problems cropped up with increasing regularity, and the line was forced to stop when a middle-aged man suffered a heart attack, and when a woman entered premature labor. Both individuals were unshackled, loaded into one of two hover trucks, and given treatment. The man died, as did the baby, but the woman pulled through. Dorn was glad for the break, realized what that meant, and felt lousy for it. It seemed as though there was no limit to his self-centeredness. The march continued.

Night fell, and every third person was provided with a battery-powered light and a headband to hold it in place. It seemed thoughtful at first, until Dorn realized the amount of damage a hover truck could do to the prisoners, and the money that would cost.

Still, no matter how cruel and calculating their new owner-employer might be, the prisoners had their own ways of helping out. Children, who were left unshackled for the most part, and were expected to keep pace with their parents, or whatever adult was willing to take an interest in them, were exhausted by now. They trudged with heads down, gradually fell behind, and ran to catch up again. Parents pleaded with them, guards hit them with whips, but it made no difference. The same thing happened over and over. Until something amazing happened.

One by one the children were absorbed into the line where they were hoisted onto backs or thrown over shoulders. Babies, carried by relatives up until that point, were passed up and down the column. Dorn wasn't exactly pleased when a five-year-old was loaded onto his back, but he knew it was the right thing to do and forced himself to cooperate.

The child switched mounts eventually, to be replaced by a six-month-old infant, who reminded him of the baby the girl had held in her arms. He carried the child for half an hour before a woman took over.

Finally, after what seemed like an eternity, the prisoners arrived at the point where two roads crossed each other, and they were ordered toward the south. A guard must have said something up toward the front, because the news rippled down the line like wind through a row of corn and raised everyone's spirits. ''The camp is on an island and we're almost there!''

Having spent the last few years in an institution, Dorn was skeptical of rumors, and was slightly surprised when this one proved correct. The smell of sea salt provided the first hint. It reminded him of Mechnos, a place so closely connected with his parents that the thought of it brought tears to his eyes.

He fought them back as the road ended and a wooden causeway began. It thundered with the impact of four hundred feet. The water, if any, was invisible beyond the light cast by their headlamps. Seabirds, disturbed by the noise, squawked and flapped away. The timbers beneath Dorn's sandals sloped upward with the curvature of the bridge, then downward again.

Lights appeared, and the line veered left and passed between evenly spaced tree trunks.

A graveyard, the markers made from tree limbs, piles of stones, and other debris, lay on the right, silent testimony to columns long gone.

It was three or four minutes before Dorn arrived at the turning point. He felt sand under his feet and fought the tendency to slide as he followed the others down an incline and into a bowl-shaped depression. It had clearly been used before and had the look of a regular stop.

A large fire had been built toward the center of the space, and guards had been posted along the perimeter. They appeared whenever the fire found an especially flammable piece of wood, then vanished when it was consumed. Dorn's stomach rumbled as he smelled the cereal-based mush, and he eyed a line of wooden water barrels.

Release came quickly, along with orders to stay in the immediate area and eat dinner. Dorn hurried to comply. He visited the water barrels first, followed by the chow line and a second trip to the water barrels.

Then, tired, but unwilling to accept sleep, the teenager set about the serious business of running away. The logic seemed irrefutable.

First, Dorn expected that his physical condition would deteriorate rather than improve.

Second, the school, and whatever help he would find there, was only twenty or so miles to the rear, but would be at least twice that distance away by nightfall the next day.

Third, it was safe to assume that the Sharma Metal Works, for that's where rumor said they were headed, would feature all sorts of fancy security measures designed to counter the sort of thing he had in mind.

Yes, no matter how one chose to look at it, conditions favored an immediate rather than a delayed escape attempt. The problem was, how?

Dorn yawned, spotted an open spot near the very edge of the security perimeter, and ambled that way. Once in place, with other prisoners to either side, he scooped a trough in the sand and lay on his side. He yawned for a second time, fought against the fatigue that threatened to pull him down, and forced himself to look around.

The fire had burned down by now, the area around it practically deserted because some off-duty guards had chased the prisoners away and claimed the fireside for themselves. Dorn turned away from their dark silhouettes, allowed his eyes to adjust to the dark, and quartered the campground. Hundreds of variously shaped mounds marked where his fellow prisoners had chosen to spend the night. Most were asleep by now, snoring, muttering, and in a few cases twitching, as if trapped within the most demanding of dreams. There were sobs, snatches of conversation, and the soft sound of the prayer drum that he'd heard before.

But nothing the youth heard or saw suggested a means of escape. The guards seemed alert, and, try as he might, no clever stratagem came to mind. Dorn had almost given up, and was drifting off to sleep, when luck made an unexpected appearance. Someone said, "Give me that!"

Someone else said, "Screw you!" and a fight broke out on the far side of the holding area. Every guard in that particular area, plus those seated around the campfire, headed for the scuffle. The rest, a motley assortment of drifters, stevedores, and beached spacers, stared toward the action, hollered advice, and wished something exciting would happen on their side of the camp. So they missed the shadowy figure that slipped between them, lost its footing in the dark, and tumbled head over heels onto the beach below.

Dorn scrambled to his feet, listened for the sounds of pursuit, but heard nothing more than the ruckus already underway. He ran down into the water. It was relatively warm and splashed his legs. He couldn't do anything about the footprints already made, but his trail would disappear in the surf, and leave his pursuers to wonder which way he'd gone. North? South? Out to sea? There would be no way to tell.

The water rushed past his calves, ran up the beach, and left a wavy line. The camp was located on an island, or so he'd been told, so it made very little difference which way he went, not in the long run anyway. Still, the road home led in a northwesterly direction, and that was the first place they'd look. With that in mind, Dorn turned to the right and headed south.

The waves broke against his left leg as he paralleled the beach. He watched for signs of pursuit and was prepared to drop when it appeared. The water would hide him and, with any luck at all, allow him to escape. The sand shifted under his sandals, found its way beneath the leather straps, and abraded his skin. That could become a problem if he let it go, since his feet would carry him home.

Still there was no pursuit, and Dorn started to relax a bit. He wasn't clear yet, not by a long shot, but he had five or six hours before the sun rose and the prisoners shackled themselves to the chain. That's when he'd be missed and the search would begin.

A wave broke against Dorn's waist, and he realized he had angled away from the beach. The teenager turned toward what he thought was the southwest and considered his options. He could make for the road, pass behind the camp, and sneak over the causeway. That was the most efficient approach, but the most obvious as well.

The other option was to find a place where he could cross the beach without leaving footprints, secure a hiding place, and wait for the searchers to depart. Time was money, or so Dorn assumed, which would limit the duration of the search. Once everyone left he'd emerge from his hidey-hole, double-time up the road, cross the bridge, and make his way to the academy where Tull would put everything right. Or so he hoped.

Satisfied that he'd selected the best of all possible plans, Dorn waded into the shallows and felt sand turn to rock. He tripped, nearly fell, and caught himself. The surf broke white where it surged along a two-foot-high ledge and ran up the beach. Dorn felt for a way up, found a series of stairlike ledges, and mounted what had been a lava flow.

He followed the outcropping shoreward, across the beach, and into the thick, junglelike undergrowth. The teenager pushed branches out of the way and forced a passage. Darkness consumed the stars, and Dorn felt his way forward. Leaves crackled under his sandals, animals scurried through the brush, and a seabird launched itself into the air.

Finally, when Dorn judged himself to be a hundred feet away from the beach, and almost certainly invisible, he sized a clearing with his hands, sat down, and listened for signs of pursuit. There were none. The teenager lay down, curled into the fetal position, and entered a dreamless sleep. That's where he was when the sun rose, branches snapped, and the whip fell across his back.

8

When God wills that an event will occur, he sets the causes that will lead to it.

Babikir Badri
Sudanese scholar
Circa 1900

The Planet Mechnos

The impact sent a jolt through Natalie's body. She grabbed for the wrought iron rail, missed, and grabbed again. The steel felt cool under her hands. It took every bit of her strength to pull herself up. A voice ordered her to stop. She ignored the impulse to look back over her shoulder, swung her legs over the rail, and stood on the balcony. The sliding glass door was locked. She swore, shook the handle, and tried again. Should she break the glass, and risk a cut? Or try another balcony? The second choice seemed best.

Natalie climbed over the rail and knelt on the narrow strip of duracrete. Then, having secured a grip on the lower part of the rail, she dangled over the edge.

In the meantime, the man named Shank, still carrying the head named Johnson, stood on what had been *her* balcony and hurled obscenities in her direction.

Natalie, determined to escape, forced herself to ignore them. Concrete pressed on the inner surface of her arm. It hurt. Natalie swung out, in, and out again. Then, as the outward motion completed itself, and the inward motion began, she let go. The balcony rushed upward, smacked the soles of her feet, and threw her off balance. She backpedaled into the railing, caught herself, and reversed the motion. Four steps carried her to the door. It was unlocked and slid out of the way.

Natalie entered as a naked man left the bathroom. He saw her, covered his genitals, and backed away. She waved cheerfully and left through the hallway door.

Natalie opened a fire door and ran down what seemed like interminable flights of stairs to the ground floor. She considered the rental car, assumed it was covered, and took a side exit instead. It opened onto a large courtyard. A walkway led her past the swimming pool and the cabanas, and into an alley. From there it was a short sprint to a side street and an autocab.

Most people would have called the authorities, but Natalie was a spacer, and like most spacers placed little trust in local police, even on Mechnos. So she headed for Freeport. Spacers, especially *free* spacers, take care of their own. The only problem was that it would be relatively easy for her pursuers to guess her destination and arrive there first, especially since the autocab was programmed to obey the legal limit, and ignored her orders to the contrary.

The cab crawled through traffic as its meter displayed an ever-ascending fare and the onboard computer obeyed each and every one of the city's multitudinous traffic laws. Natalie ground her teeth in frustration as she scanned the surrounding cars and prayed that the thugs were behind rather than in front of her.

Freeport, with its seedy demeanor, and even seedier residents, had begun to stir. Later, in three or four hours, things would start to hum. Still, a sprinkling of spacers, most dressed in their ship's colors, had already filtered up from the harbor and were wandering the streets.

Good. A call would bring five or six crew-beings to her side, most if not all of whom would be tougher than the dirtsiders at her hotel room.

Determined to walk the last few blocks and see what, if

anything, lay in wait for her, Natalie ordered the cab to stop. She ran her card through the scanner, wondered if Orr Enterprises had the means to monitor citywide credit card transactions, and decided it didn't matter. Such information would only confirm what common sense had probably already told them.

The autocab whirred away as Natalie walked the rest of the block, took a right at the Blue Moon tavern, and headed toward the harbor. The odor of briny water, deep-fried food, and recently released ozone filled her nostrils. She took a deep breath, nodded to an engineer she'd met somewhere, and smiled. This was home. For her, at least.

The street sloped down toward Discovery Bay, providing a good view of the harbor. At least fifty or sixty ships were bellied up to the docks. Most were loading or unloading cargo. And not symbolic cargo either, but the *real* thing, like variform cattle, critical machine parts, desperately needed antibiotics, weapons and ammunition, and much, much more.

All of which meant that the track-mounted cranes were hard at work, lifting cargo modules in and out of holds. Tractors, their beepers beeping, pulled lines of trailers along finger-shaped wharves while exoskeletons minced this way and that, their arms loaded with boxes.

Natalie paused at the bottom of the slope, searched the area for signs of pursuit, and heaved a sigh of relief when none was visible. She hurried across the maglev track, waved her pass in front of a bored-looking guard, and made for the terminal building. It crouched low as if seeking to avoid attention. The structure, and its single largest office, served as headquarters for Logenny MacAllister III, a notoriously crotchety man who carried the title of dock master, and served as Freeport's unofficial mayor, marshal, and magistrate.

She found MacAllister, as most people did, sitting in his office, monitoring his kingdom via sixty carefully placed vid cams, and smoking a pipe. A wreath of blue smoke encircled his head and drifted away from the incoming air. He was old, exactly how old no one knew for sure. He had a full head of white hair, and laser-bright eyes. He greeted Natalie the moment she entered. "So, lass . . . how were the hearings? Did they find a cause?"

Natalie shook her head and dropped into one of the dock master's mismatched guest chairs. They were arranged in a semicircle and fronted his beat-up desk. "Some say yes, some say no."

The dock master scowled, examined the bowl of his pipe, and emptied it into a much abused servo cover. "Talk, talk, talk, that's all they ever do. Here, have a cup of coffee."

Natalie couldn't remember seeing MacAllister without a cup of coffee, not in all the years she'd known him. He seemed to live on the stuff, and used it not only as a beverage, but also like some sort of universal balm, pouring great dollops of the brew on winches that refused to work, dogs that peed on the garden patch below his window, or anything else that annoyed him, including people. Natalie accepted the mug, took a sip, and looked through the steam. "I need help, Mac, and some advice."

The dock master shrugged and sat on the edge of his desk. "Of course. It's been a long time since pretty young ladies came knockin' for anything else. What can I do for you?"

It took Natalie the better part of fifteen minutes to tell her story, starting with the missing coordinates and ending with Orr's goons. Once she was finished, MacAllister nodded thoughtfully and said, "Well, lass, that's quite a story, and an interestin' one too, especially in light o' the hearin's and the lack o' cause. Starships don't explode very often, not in atmosphere anyway, and it makes ya wonder. Especially with the likes o' Mr. Orr pokin' around."

Natalie felt something heavy hit the bottom of her stomach. The idea had been there for a long time, lurking in the back of her mind. But it seemed too paranoid to be true. Until now. Maybe, just maybe, her parents had been murdered. A host of emotions fought for dominance. A sort of cold anger won. "So, what should I do?"

"Well," the dock master said thoughtfully, "first things first. Sounds like some real unpleasant people might be comin' ta visit . . . and I don't allow no riffraff on my docks."

So saying, the old man pulled a boom mike down in front of his mouth, gave some orders, and pushed it up again. ''That should cover it, lass . . . ain't no one takin' you where you don't want to go. Now, as for the coordinates you're lookin' for, how 'bout a peek inside that safe?''

Natalie felt a momentary pang of suspicion, decided that she had to trust somebody, and handed it over. The dock master nodded thoughtfully, motioned for her to follow, and led Natalie outside. Docks, not to mention the ships they serve, require endless maintenance, and the port authority's shops were second to none.

MacAllister led her to the machine shop. Metal screamed on metal, sparks fanned the air, and robots stalked through the gloom. The dock master handed the safe to one of the workers, yelled some instructions, and watched as they went to work. It took a minute to slice through the casing, three to let it cool, and part of a fifth for Natalie to peer inside. Nothing. The cube was empty!

Natalie struggled to hide her disappointment as she followed MacAllister out into the fading light. He shrugged. ''Sorry, lass . . . keep lookin'. You'll find 'em.''

Natalie smiled and gave MacAllister a hug. The dock master scowled and said he'd do the same for any other spacer, and knew he lied. Because there were plenty of spacers he wouldn't lift a finger for, and the truth was that he liked Natalie *in spite* of her parents, not because of them, especially in light of the fact that they had forgotten their roots and used the Gap to suppress free trade. That was transgression beyond all understanding. But their daughter, well, she represented what her parents *could have* been but never were.

They returned to the office together, and Natalie was just about to leave when the dock master touched his earplug and raised a hand. He listened for a moment, said something in reply, and pointed to one of the wall monitors. ''Look . . . your friends have arrived.''

Natalie bit her lower lip as she saw the woman and her goons get out of a limo and approach the security shack. The security guards, with automatic weapons slung across their chests, stepped out to meet them. Then, as if by chance, a pair of heavy-duty exoskeletons entered the area and assumed positions next to the gate. The display of strength must have worked, because the visitors reentered their vehicle and were gone moments later.

Natalie had allowed herself to hope that Orr and his minions would give up, would leave her alone, but the confrontation at the gate made it clear that they wouldn't. That, plus her failure to locate the coordinates, made her depressed.

She thanked MacAllister for his help, left the dock master's office, and walked toward the other end of the building. The guild hall occupied space leased from the port authority and served as an important gathering place, though not in the afternoon. Natalie followed another spacer through the beat-up green doors and into a large, rather undistinguished room.

The chairs were sturdy affairs, chosen more for strength and durability than for looks, and sat as they had the night before. Natalie could imagine the scene. A game, it didn't matter which one, playing on the wall screen, as bartenders dispensed endless quantities of beer, and spacers traded lies. But the party had been over for a long time, and with the exception of a med tech who lay unconscious across three carefully arranged chairs, the hall was empty.

Natalie's deck shoes squeaked as she made her way across the floor to the reception desk. It remained open around the clock and provided access to a variety of services. She waited her turn, rolled a thumb on the reader, and watched the clerk depart for her mail.

While he was gone she checked the desk term, confirmed that the *Sunbird* had lifted two days before, and wished her ex-shipmates a profitable run. She had hated to sacrifice her slot, not to mention the hard-won seniority that went with it, but hadn't been able to identify an alternative. The Voss Line might be dead, and badly in need of interment, and someone had to bury the poor thing.

That became even more apparent when the clerk returned with a box full of official-looking mail, dumped it on the counter, and hit her with a storage fee. He had a long, thin face, no chin to speak of, and a music implant. His head bobbed to an inaudible rhythm. "Here ya go . . . anything else?"

"Are the reading rooms open?"

The boy's head bobbed a little faster. "Five cees an hour . . . same as always. Take what ya want."

Natalie thanked the clerk, took her box, and headed for the reading rooms. Many spacers chose to live rent-free aboard their ships while in port, and used the little cubicles to handle their correspondence, or anything else that required privacy, including the sort of hanky-panky most COs forbade aboard ship.

Natalie checked to make sure the first cubicle was unoccupied, wrinkled her nose at the smell of disinfectant, and threw her bag on the well-worn couch. It was a simple matter to pull the plastic chair away from the beat-up desk and activate the computer. It was voice-capable and, like most of its kind, overly polite. "Hello . . . how may I help you?"

Natalie broke the seal on a data disk and dropped it into the appropriate slot. "Play the disk, please."

The computer played the disk, plus twenty-seven more, including nine interactive ads, a dissertation by the family lawyers, any number of hard luck stories from ex-employees, and a request for funds from the Milford Academy. She ran that one twice.

It seemed a man named Tull had attempted to contact her parents, failed, and hoped to hear from her. He went on to explain that while the school had kept Dorn on after his funds had expired, they wouldn't be able to do so for very much longer, and feared what might happen if he were out on his own.

Natalie frowned. Maybe she should head for New Hope, pull Dorn out of school, and bring him home. But to what purpose? There was nothing her brother could do, not until he finished school anyway, and that was a year away. No, the smart thing to do was leave Dorn where he was and find the missing coordinates. With that taken care of, she'd attend his graduation, pack his bags, and bring him home.

Natalie bit her lip, checked the balance in her savings account, and saw she had enough to cover the bill plus a tiny bit more. It took less than ten minutes to compose a reply, authorize the transfer of funds, and send the money on the first leg of a long journey.

The second message, the one in which she described to Dorn how their parents died, took the better part of an hour. Her words wouldn't help much, she knew that, but they had to be said. She sent that, plus her last hundred credits, and wished there was a speedier means of communication. Both letters would take weeks if not months to reach their destination.

With her brother's needs taken care of, for the moment anyway, Natalie continued to read her mail. There was a request for donations from an organization called the Free Traders Benefit fund, a political tract from the planet's governor, and a package protected by a governmental holo seal.

Natalie dropped this disk into the reader and watched two beings appear. The first was huge, and would have been reminiscent of an Earth-normal hippopotamus had it not been for the wicked horn that protruded from its forehead, and a beanie-shaped hat. She recognized the XT as a Dromo, a somewhat obscure race, known for their scholarly ways and inherent honesty. The other alien was small enough to ride on the first creature's neck. It had a pointed muzzle, leaf-shaped ears, and busy little hands. It was the larger creature that spoke. He, she, or it had a basso voice that rumbled like thunder.

"Greetings, Citizen Voss. Humans call me Rollo, and this is Torx. Please allow us to express our condolences regarding the deaths of your progenitors. The ceasing to be of one's birth beings is cause for grief in almost all of the Confederacy's many cultures."

Natalie raised an eyebrow, wondered if this was some sort of con, but allowed the message to continue.

The shot widened slightly and Natalie realized that the sentient named Rollo stood shoulder-deep in muddy water. He smiled, or seemed to, since a row of wicked-looking teeth appeared. "We work for the Department of Commerce and dispatched this communication to more than fifty different locations in hopes that a copy will find you.

"It is our belief that you have knowledge, or may come into knowledge, having a direct bearing on matters now under our investigation. Due to the fact that this investigation is of the utmost importance to the Confederacy and its citizens, we must request that you make your way to the planet known as The Place of Wandering Waters for immediate consultations. This request has the force of a legal summons, and there are penalties should you fail to comply. We apologize for the inconvenience and will provide remuneration for any and all reasonable expenses incurred while in transit. To check the authenticity of this communication, send a copy to the nearest branch of the Commerce Department. We wish you a safe journey."

Natalie bit her lip in consternation, read the message a second time, and sent a copy to the Commerce Department. The words "Official communication confirmed and registered," appeared on her screen a fraction of a second later. Suddenly Natalie realized what she'd done. By checking to make sure that the message was legitimate, she had unintentionally acknowledged receipt of it.

Damn! Damn! Damn! The last thing she needed was a governmental wild-goose chase. She hadn't done anything to merit the Commerce Department's attention, so the issue, whatever it was, had something to do with her parents and Voss Lines.

The spacer snapped orders at the computer, waited for one of the Voss Lines attorneys to appear, and sent a copy of the summons. It appeared alongside a shot of her face.

The attorney, a matronly type, listened to Natalie's story and nodded. "Interesting . . . I don't know what they want, but you'd better go. We have your power of attorney and will handle things here."

Natalie told her about the incident with Orr's lawyers, how the goons had barged into her room, and how she had managed to escape. The attorney listened, frowned, and raised a pencil-thin eyebrow. "Let me see if I understand . . . You grabbed Mr. Johnson by the ears and threw him at Mr. Shank?"

Natalie felt defensive and wasn't sure why. "Yes, but . . ."

"And they hadn't touched you?"

"No, but I . . ."

"No wonder they've been trying to reach me," the attorney interrupted crossly. "They'll file a personal injury suit, ask for a ridiculous amount of damages, and use the action to force negotiations."

Natalie was outraged. "You can't be serious! They invaded my room!"

"No," the older woman replied, "you let them in."

"But they attacked me!"

"No, not unless you misrepresented the facts earlier. The way I heard it, two women and a man entered the room, you threw Mr. Johnson at them, and attacked with a potentially lethal weapon. That's how they will tell the story. Skillfully presented, a jury will find in their favor. Unless they receive what they *really* want.

"All of which brings us to the following. Voss Lines Incorporated, which is to say you, owes something on the order of thirty-six million credits, give or take a few mil. The Gap is worth more than that, of course, a whole *lot* more, but only if we know exactly where it is. And, making a bad situation worse is the fact that we can't even rent the damned thing out. I suggest you find those coordinates."

Natalie wanted to snap back, wanted to say something like, "What the hell do you think I've been doing?" but knew the words would bounce off the attorney's surgically tightened skin. "So what are you telling me? That I have to respond to this summons? *Before* I look for the coordinates?"

"That's what I'm telling you," the lawyer said confidently. "A Confederate summons takes precedence over civil lawsuits. Or would you rather hang around and play legal patty cake with Johnson, Shank, and Wong?"

Natalie thought about that and knew the answer was no. "So what do I do now?"

The attorney was obviously impatient for the conversation to be over. "Find yourself a ride, honey . . . and take your swimsuit. I don't know where The Place of Wandering Waters is, but I'll bet it's damp."

9

While sentience takes many forms, love has but one.

Holmar Zylo-Nom
Dromo mystic
Standard year 1945

The Planet New Hope

Dorn rolled right, rolled left, and felt the whip bite his flesh. The guard had years of experience and landed the blows so they crisscrossed each other. The punishment lasted two or three minutes and the pain was nearly intolerable. Then, as suddenly as it had started, the beating was over. Hands grabbed Dorn's arms, pulled the teenager to his feet, and shoved him toward the beach. Branches slapped the boy's face and tore at what remained of his clothes. The guards, a man and a woman, were rather cheerful, as if the whole procedure was routine.

Dorn, who had assumed his escape was nothing short of remarkable, was taken aback. He looked from the man to the woman as they propelled him out of the jungle and onto the sand. Her head had been shaved and painted with intricate designs. "How did you find me?"

The woman chuckled and glanced at the man. "Shall we tell him?"

"Sure," the man chuckled. "Why not? The more that knows, the less runnin' we'll have to do."

"Good point," the woman said sagely. "We found you with this." The guard held a black box in her hand. It featured buttons and a small screen.

Dorn frowned. "You found me with that? What is it?"

"Nothing fancy," the man replied easily. "The mush you've been eatin' contains a small amount of radioactive material. The box tracks the emissions, plots them on a grid, and shows us where to look. The rest is easy."

"Pretty neat, huh?" the woman said brightly.

"Yeah," Dorn agreed sourly. "My compliments to the chef." The guards laughed as if genuinely amused.

Breakfast was over by the time the threesome made their way back to the encampment, and, in spite of the fact that Dorn *knew* the food contained potentially harmful chemicals, he would have given practically anything for a bowl of mush.

It wasn't to be, since the other prisoners had eaten and were ready to leave. They watched the teenager arrive with a mixture of sympathy and satisfaction.

As before, the first part of the day was relatively easy, and would have been enjoyable had the circumstances been different. The air was cool, birds chattered, and the road was flat.

The major problem was the trucks. They were invariably huge, had protective mesh over their intake ports, and highly individualized paint jobs that ran to red, orange, and blue. They carried steel reinforcing rods, sheet metal, and in one case, huge ingots of aluminum. Because the trucks and their cargoes were so valuable, the haulers mounted weapons blisters, each of which could fire a thousand rounds a minute, leaving all but the wealthiest hijackers to focus on lesser prey.

However, what amounted to little more than a bouncy ride for the truckers was a source of constant misery for the prisoners. They were peppered with gravel each time a truck passed, forced into the ditch when drivers hugged the edge of the road, and forced to eat dust long after a vehicle had passed.

The midmorning rest break was little more than a pause next to the road while people squatted over the ditch and children brought them water. Medics treated blisters for a while, quit the moment the whistle blew, and returned to their air-conditioned van.

As the sun rose in the sky and the air grew warmer, the prisoners crossed a long series of wooden bridges. Dorn realized they were following a chain of islands out into the southern ocean. Blue sky arched overhead, the chain rattled monotonously, and the jungle came and went as if unsure of its purchase. Water glittered through the green, teased Dorn with its cool promise, and vanished as the land pushed it away.

The sun eventually reached its zenith and hung like a fireball in the sky. Dorn began to sweat, children complained, and the line slowed. Whips cracked and the guards shouted. "Come on, people, pick up the pace, the next rest stop is only two miles away."

It might have been a lie, but the promise was sufficient to quicken the pace, and no more than an hour had passed before the foot-weary travelers were herded off the road and into a clearing. The camp was similar to the one they had occupied the night before and showed signs of constant use.

Once freed, most of the prisoners, Dorn included, headed for the water barrels. He drank as much of the brackish liquid as he could hold, used a double handful to wash his face, and joined one of the steadily growing chow lines.

The mush smelled wonderful, and much as the teenager wanted to go without, his body wouldn't allow it. The gruel, chemicals and all, disappeared quickly and left him hungry when it was gone. Others felt the same way, and scuffles broke out here and there. The whips cracked and order was restored.

Dorn had returned his bowl, and was headed for some shade, when a hand touched his arm. He turned to find the girl from the water line standing before him. She cupped a bowl of mush and held it up. "Here, it will protect your strength."

Dorn shook his head. "No, I had mine. You must have yours as well. If not for yourself, then for your brother."

The girl had brown eyes. They were large and brimmed with tears. Her voice was quiet and matter of fact. "My brother died last night. They buried him with the others outside the camp. Here . . . eat . . . I had kitchen duty. This was left over.''

Dorn accepted the food. He noticed her fingers were long and slender. They felt cool where they touched his skin. ''I'm sorry.''

The girl shrugged. ''So am I. But it was inevitable. If not last night, then tonight, or tomorrow. He was too young to work, medicine costs money, so the medics refused to treat him. Quick, you must eat, or the break will end.''

So Dorn ate, asked the girl questions between gobs of mush, and heard her story. Her name was Myra, and she, along with her brother, had been orphaned when the barge her parents had built capsized in the floods.

Myra, still holding her baby brother, had survived more by luck than skill and fought her way free of the current. She rested within a gently swirling eddy, placed the infant on a piece of driftwood, and paddled for shore. Dorn, who remembered his own experience in the river, was impressed by her bravery and presence of mind.

Once ashore Myra had searched for her parents, wandering the riverbank for two days before locating the wreckage of their boat, and her father's body. In spite of the fact that the rain-soaked soil was relatively soft, it took all of Myra's strength and the better part of a day to dig a shallow grave and drag the corpse out of the water.

Dorn imagined how frightened she must have been, and how determined, as the girl buried her father and did what she could for the baby boy. There was still no sign of her mother, she said, so it seemed safe to assume that she was dead.

Unable to salvage more than a few odds and ends from the wreckage, Myra made her way to the nearest road and followed it toward the city. Once there, she hoped to locate her mother's sister in hopes that her mother would be there, or, failing that, her aunt would take them in.

Such was not to be, however, since the bounty hunters caught them well short of the city and, when Myra was unable to prove her solvency, took both children into custody. From there it was a short, uncomfortable journey to the holding pens where she had first encountered Dorn.

Dorn, who like most of the boys from the academy had scant opportunity to meet girls, was drawn to her unaffected beauty, but more than that to the tranquility in her eyes, and the dignity of her actions. There were all sorts of things he wanted to say, but inexperience left him tongue-tied, and a guard preempted his words. "Hit the road, slimeballs. The last one in shackles gets a taste of the whip."

Pandemonium broke out. Dorn yelled, "I'll see you at dinner!" and caught her nod.

People ran back and forth. Men swore at each other, mothers called their children, and whips cracked as the guards herded the prisoners toward the road. For reasons not entirely clear, they had been ordered to maintain their positions in line. Dorn watched for the man in front of him, slipped into the slot behind, and wrapped the scarf around his ankle. Now that he knew Myra, the scrap of cloth had taken on more value and he didn't want to lose it. The shackle, which was oiled each night, closed with a click. Two or three minutes passed before the line jerked into motion. Dorn spent them peering ahead trying to spot Myra. He thought he succeeded but couldn't be sure.

The afternoon was long and hot with little more than occasional water breaks and glimpses of ocean to break the dusty monotony. That, plus the news about his parents, should have left Dorn tired and depressed. Why did he feel so energized, then? So excited? Verging on happy? He decided it was because of Myra. Which he felt didn't say much for his character, or his qualities as a son.

Here he was, a virtual slave, marching toward god only knew what kind of man-made hell, his parents recently dead, and he was all aflutter over a girl he barely knew. It was stupid, uncaring, and morally reprehensible. Unfortunately, however, Dorn discovered that knowing his thoughts were wrong, and changing them, were two different things. The sorry fact was that no amount of self-admonition was sufficient to change the way he felt. Dinner, and the opportunity to see

Myra again, had become his central goal in life. Nothing else mattered.

Dorn plodded on, thinking of little except Myra. The day wore on, and it was mid-afternoon, halfway between lunch and dinner, when a long black hover limo overtook the prisoners and started to pass. Empty trucks passed all the time, blowing their air horns and spraying the prisoners with gravel. But this was different. Partly because it was a car, and a rather expensive one at that, and partly because it eased by, as if the passengers cared about the prisoners, or wanted to look at them.

Dorn turned just in time to see that a middle-aged man with black hair and a slightly hooked nose occupied the front passenger seat, while a girl, perhaps Dorn's age or a little younger, sat just behind.

The man had no interest in the prisoners, to judge by his expression, but the girl did, and for the second time that day Dorn found himself staring into a pair of brown eyes, eyes that seemed to see and acknowledge him. Then she was gone, leaving the young man to wonder who she was, and why it mattered.

Time seemed to drag after that, but eventually passed, as did the heat of the day. Dorn had played horsey to a three-year-old for about two hours by the time the column veered off the road and entered a rest area. The prisoners knew the routine by now. Shackles were released, lines were formed, and food was served with minimum fuss.

Dorn spotted Myra almost immediately, resisted the temptation to rush over, and came to regret it as another youth sidled up and started a conversation. Dorn closed the distance as subtly as possible, entered the line behind them, and waited for Myra to look his way. His reward came a few moments later when she saw him, smiled, and turned her back on a clearly disappointed admirer. "Dorn! It's good to see you. Shall we eat together?"

It was like a dream come true, marred only by dirty looks from the would-be suitor, the always lumpy gruel, and the less than ideal circumstances. Dorn had never been part of a romantic dinner, but had seen plenty of them on vids, and knew the setting was way wrong.

Still, Myra was easy to talk to, and it wasn't long before Dorn heard himself blurting out nearly every secret he had, including his expulsion from school, the death of his parents, and his feelings of guilt. It turned out that Myra had similar feelings about her brother's death, and the commonality drew them together in a way that no amount of small talk ever could.

Finally, after what seemed like minutes but was actually hours, they looked around and realized that with very few exceptions, the rest of the prisoners were asleep. It seemed natural to lie side by side, and later, when a cloudburst drenched everyone to the skin, to wrap arms around each other so that bodies touched, and lips nearly met. It was then that Dorn felt himself harden, cursed his untrustworthy body, and recited math formulas in his head. The strategy worked. Myra fell asleep, and so, eventually, did he.

Morning dawned bright and clear. Dorn, who found his legs wonderfully tangled with Myra's, felt embarrassed, saw that she did too, and hurried to extricate himself. They headed for separate privies but met in the chow line.

Rumors, many of which were wrong, had been flying up and down the column every day. This morning's buzz, supposedly based on comments made by a guard, suggested that their final destination lay less than a half day away.

Dorn suspected the rumor was part of an elaborate trick, designed to make the prisoners more malleable, but Myra thought it might be true, and hoped that it was. And, despite his doubts, Dorn had to admit that the guards seemed more cheerful than usual, as if they had something to look forward to. Or maybe it was his imagination.

In any case, the breakfast chores were completed in record time and the column was underway shortly thereafter. Time passed quickly, and the terrain gradually changed. The wooden bridges that marked the more recent portion of their journey were all behind them, and ahead was a climb up through gently rolling hills.

Hand-fitted rock walls appeared to either side of the road, holed here and there by careless drivers. The vegetation, lush till now, grew steadily more sparse, until it virtually disappeared, leaving little more than wind-tortured shrubs to hold the nutrient-poor soil. The grade, and the consequent switchbacks, were both a help and a hindrance.

The good part was the fact that south-bound trucks were forced to slow down—their engines roaring as they climbed upward. The hindrance came as the result of the climb itself, which was hard for Dorn and represented a real trial for those less able.

Still, each footstep brought the summit a little bit closer, and with it, the promise of a downhill grade. Dorn looked up, hoped to see the top, and saw three wooden crosses. They were positioned like the letter X and bore the remains of three bird-pecked corpses. Mouths hung open as empty eye sockets stared into the sun. A breeze stirred their rags, raised dust from the ground, and touched Dorn's face. The odor of rotting flesh filled his nostrils and made him gag. Others had similar reactions and looked away. No one said anything. It could happen to them, any one of them. That was what they were supposed to think.

Finally, sluggishly, the column lurched over the hill's crest and wound down the other side. The view was both horrifying and magnificent. The hills dropped sharply in front of them and terminated on a flat, triangle-shaped point of land. Azure water sparkled for as far as the eye could see and foamed as it surged past partially scrapped spaceships, up the slightly rising beach, and onto dry sand. Some of the vessels were nearly intact, while others were so diminished they amounted to little more than piles of junk.

Dorn, who had grown up on and around spaceships, recognized the remains of Matsuzaki Data Liners, Sook Intersystem Freighters, Traa Drone Ships, Kilworthy Unihulls, Morgan High Haulers, and many, many more. It was an amazing and, for anyone who loved ships, depressing sight.

But as notable as the ships were, the human ants who worked on them were even *more* remarkable, especially in light of the fact that they were using hand tools to accomplish tasks that would normally fall to androids and cyborgs. Tiny sparks flew as plates were cut away, water splashed as beams hit the oncoming tide, and men rushed to recover the newly harvested wealth. It was difficult to see what happened in the surf, but the cranes were plain enough, as was the massive conveyor belt.

Now the trucks loaded with metal made sense, as did the efforts to find and import cheap labor. Labor that no doubt lived in the warren of huts, hovels, and shanties that stretched from the edge of the mud flats up and around the sturdy-looking one- and two-story buildings that crowded the delta's center. Here were the quarters in which they would live, close by the furnaces and mills necessary to melt, process, and finish the metal recovered from the beached ships.

Beyond it all, a pristine white mansion occupied the far-thermost tip of land, shimmered in the afternoon heat, and looked all the more palatial for the squalor that surrounded it.

Here then lay Dorn's young adulthood, assuming he survived long enough to have a future, given the conditions below.

The sight of what awaited them had a sobering effect on the prisoners, reducing them to silence by the time they reached the flats. The sign there was huge and bore the like-ness of a broken cogwheel. The name "Sharma Industries" had been spelled out in letters ten feet tall. Dorn figured it was for their benefit, since no one else was likely to see it.

The guards yelled insults at their peers as they herded prisoners through a checkpoint and were greeted in similar fashion. Dorn took note of the nine-foot-high durasteel fence, and the razor wire strung along the top, and knew escape was highly unlikely.

The line slowed, came to an occasional stop, and moved forward in a series of short jerks. One by one the prisoners passed under a strange-looking arch. A camera or something very similar hung over the prisoners' heads and winked as they passed below. Dorn heard cries of pain, the crack of whips, and felt his heart race. What did the thing do? And how did it work?

He soon found out. A guard ordered him forward, the device winked red, and the man in front of him clutched his face. A whip cracked, the line advanced, and the light flashed again. Dorn felt heat sear his forehead and stumbled. He caught himself, heard someone whimper, and looked over his shoulder. The woman behind was crying, and a bright blue bar code had appeared on her forehead. Dorn knew he now wore one as well. The workers had been branded.

Dorn was still feeling the pain when he heard a rumble. He'd been raised with similar sounds and scanned the sky. The ship was a twenty-five-year-old Kawabata Starlight Express. She had a reentry-scarred hull, registration numbers so faded they were nearly impossible to read, and a list to port. She approached from the west, and flew crabwise, as if subject to control problems. The freighter's repellors, the cyclonelike force fields that kept the vessel aloft during takeoffs and landings, were badly out of tune and screamed discordantly as they carved rooster tails through the shallows. Dorn heard six distinct sounds where there should have been one.

The teenager watched with increasing concern as the spaceship jerked, staggered, and resumed its inward drift. Either the pilot was incompetent or, and this seemed more likely, fighting a major malfunction. But the reason for the problem didn't matter much, not if the repellors hit land, not if they touched something structural . . .

Suddenly all the repellors stopped at once. The ship, which had been no more than a hundred feet off the ground to start with, dropped twenty-five feet, and Dorn's heart skipped a beat. Then, as if from an unwillingness to die, five out of six repellors came on-line, the ship caught herself, and continued her inward drift. Dorn shouted a warning, a siren began to wail, and five man-made tornadoes spiraled up the beach.

Workers were plucked off the ground, steel plates whirled like autumn leaves, and sand spiraled into the air. The prisoners tried to run, tried to get away, but the chain held them in place. It jerked this way and that as people ran in different directions.

A sudden wind tugged at their clothes as chunks of wood, fiberboard, and plastic sheeting flew into the sky, swirled like snowflakes, and fell toward the ground. In the meantime the deadly repellors cut parallel swathes through the shanties, killing countless people where they stood. Others, screaming in terror, were lifted into the air and released seconds later. Some fell on buildings, were impaled on poles, or, in the case of one lucky individual, landed on the sand.

Dorn yelled at the guards, ordered them to release the prisoners, but they were gone. The shadow arrived first, followed by a total eclipse of the sun, and heartrending screams as energy sliced through flesh. The teenager watched helplessly as an entire line of people, still connected by a twenty-foot length of chain, were pulled into the air. He thought of Myra, saw a woman ripped apart, and yelled her name.

10

You cannot travel on the path before you have become the path itself.

Buddha
Founder of Buddhism
Date unknown

The Planet Mechnos

The rain fell in sheets, drummed against space-black hulls, and formed puddles along the dock. The much vaunted weather management system that was supposed to prevent such occurrences had failed. Natalie delighted in the way the water splashed away from her boots. Puddles, and the opportunities they presented, had been the subject of many childish battles. Dorn had started them—well, most of them anyway—and laughed when she got wet. She missed his laugh and the companionship that went with it.

Lightning strobed, thunder rolled, and raindrops stung her cheeks. The ships were moored in orderly rows, with the exception of the xenophobic Grodd Drift Traders, that is, who clustered together.

The purpose of her journey was a job interview. It seemed a captain named Jord had an opening for a third officer, one step below her slot on the *Sunbird,* but beggars can't be choosers. Not with three or four applicants for every berth. Well, *most* berths, that is, Jord's being the exception, since he commanded what many spacers referred to as a "screamer"—a ship where all or nearly all of the crew were members of the same religion, and spent off hours preaching to each other.

The word "screamer" referred not only to the sermons themselves, but to what the more resistant nonbelievers wanted to do after a month or so, the rest either having been assimilated into whatever religion held sway or at least pretending to have been. Not a pleasant prospect, and one Natalie would have preferred to avoid, if it wasn't for the fact that the *Will of God* was bound for the planet known as The Place of Wandering Waters.

The ship, a Kilworthy Unihull, loomed large through the mist, and floated rock-steady within a web of tractor beams. She sat low in the water, as if already loaded, and there was no sign of activity around her.

Natalie checked to make absolutely sure that she had the right slip, approached the dock-mounted intercom, and touched the control bar. A face appeared on the screen. It belonged to a gray haired woman with the letter "S" branded on her forehead. "Yes?"

Natalie swallowed. "Natalie Voss . . . here to see Captain Jord."

The woman's head jerked up and down. "The captain is expecting you. Come aboard."

Natalie was about to say "Thank you" when the screen snapped to black. The aluminum gangplank bounced slightly and moved with the ship. A fragile-looking boat slid out from under the dock. It contained a water-drenched boy who propelled his craft with a single scull and an equally bedraggled girl who held a coffee mug aloft. "Ya wanta cuppa Joe, Captain? Just brewed and right for what ails ya."

Natalie shook her head, tossed a coin into the bottom of the boat, and stepped onto the Will of God's sea deck. The delta-shaped hull had manta raylike wings that doubled as outriggers plus fairings that directed air and water away from the heat exchangers, steering jets and other installations that marred the smooth uniformity of the vessel's skin.

The platform bore the word "personnel" in bright yellow letters. The spacer stepped aboard, touched a button, and waited as she was lowered into the lock. After Natalie stepped off, and the platform had been raised, the internal hatch opened and a tech appeared. He wore a plain blue overall and, like the woman on the intercom, had an "S" emblazoned on his forehead. His voice had the sugary-sweet quality of someone who's nice because they work at it. "Welcome to the *Will of God*, Third Officer Voss. My name is Peter. Please follow me."

Natalie frowned in response to the premature demotion, stepped over the raised coaming, and followed Peter into the ship's interior. Every ship has its own unique smell, and this one smelled of incense, spicy food, and just a hint of ozone. It looked a lot like the other Kilworthy Unihulls she'd seen, although cleaner than most, and host to a multiplicity of small altars. There seemed to be one dedicated to each department they passed. Or to a wide variety of individual gods, she wasn't sure which. There were differences, but all the shrines featured brightly colored figurines, and were decorated with candles and plastic flowers.

Everything else was fairly standard, steel gratings underfoot, pressure-molded side paneling that protected the wiring and fiber-optic pathways beyond, and the jumble of air ducts, storage compartments, sleeping cubicles, junction boxes, and other equipment that combines to create a fully functioning ship. Jord's cabin lay up one level, just steps from the control room.

Peter rapped three times, received a "Come," and gestured for Natalie to enter. The officer did so and stepped into a haze of smoke. It spiraled out of a brass incense burner, drifted overhead, and dived into a vent. Behind the smoke, Captain Jord sat on a mat facing the hatch. Outside of a white loincloth, he was completely unclothed. His eyes were closed and his legs were crossed in the lotus position. The smile appeared before the eyes opened. They were black and seemingly magnetic. "Greetings, Third Officer Voss . . . and welcome aboard. I am Captain Jord."

This was the second time she'd been demoted and Natalie

108 *William C. Dietz*

wondered what it meant. Had Jord misunderstood her previous rank? Or already given her a berth? There was no way to tell. She forced a smile. "Thank you. It's a pleasure to be here."

"Please," Jord said, indicating the mat near her feet, "have a seat. I apologize if you find it uncomfortable. Those who follow the path prefer simplicity over complexity, knowledge over comfort, and humility over pride."

Unsure of what response might be appropriate or expected, Natalie lowered herself to the mat, considered the lotus position, and decided against it. Not because of the religious significance . . . but because she wasn't sure she could pull it off. Jord snapped his fingers, and a wall screen came to life. Natalie saw the picture she'd sent along with her service record. Jord used the text to prompt his memory. "Twenty-seventh in your class at the Mechnos Trade Academy, complete with a pilot's ticket, additional qualifications as load master, plus an endorsement for ship-mounted class-three weapons control. Very impressive. Why seek a berth on a screamer?"

Natalie was taken aback by the directness of the question. She shrugged. "Slots are hard to come by . . . and you're headed for a place I want to go."

Jord had a receding hairline, the same "S" she had seen twice before, and prominent cheekbones. They gave his face a lean, vaguely sinister appearance. "You plan to leave the ship at our first port of call?"

"No," Natalie responded honestly, "not so far as I know. I was served with a Confederate summons. I'm supposed to report to a being called Rollo on The Place of Wandering Waters. Once there I expect to be questioned and released. That being the case, I will require passage back to Mechnos."

Jord nodded. "And what of our religious beliefs? Will they bother you?"

Natalie stirred uneasily. "I don't know. Not unless you force them on me."

Jord nodded. "I appreciate your honesty. You may be relieved to know that the crew includes other nonbelievers such as yourself. And no, we don't force our religion on others. Our cargo is loaded. We lift at oh-eight-hundred tomorrow morning. We pay standard rates. Please be aboard at least two hours prior to liftoff.''

Natalie thanked Jord, made her way to the lock, and stepped out into the downpour. It seemed the crew was strange but tolerable. Or so she hoped. A squall blew in from the bay and pelted her with horizontal rain. Natalie felt very lonely as she walked the length of the dock.

Orr's study was located in the west wing of his enormous home. Dark beams crisscrossed the white ceiling, wood paneling covered the walls, and well-chosen pieces of art hung, sat, or stood in all the right places. The fire in the fireplace burned year round. Orr's wife enjoyed the effect.

The industrialist's mind was as usual on building Orr Enterprises into the largest, most successful company in the Confederacy. Which was why he had agreed to speak with the Traa, in spite of his wife's rather unpredictable moods, a balky weather system, and a shitload of lawsuits, including farmers with flooded fields, rained-out athletic events, and at least one bride who wanted Orr Enterprises to pay for a ruined wedding ceremony. The list of know-nothing parasites was endless.

Orr checked to make sure that Ari and the rest of his retinue were out of pickup range, assured himself that they were, and gave the necessary command. A wall screen swirled to life and the Traa appeared. It was, Orr thought, the one called Sa-Lo. Though hardly an expert on alien facial expressions, Orr thought he detected open disapproval. Sa-Lo confirmed that impression. ''Time has passed, the female is scheduled to lift tomorrow, and your promises are as empty as a spendthrift's purse.''

''Don't hold back on my account,'' Orr said sarcastically. ''Say what you mean.''

The tonality was lost on Sa-Lo. ''You insisted on haste, your operatives frightened the girl, and the opportunity was lost.''

''So?'' Orr demanded. ''What would you suggest? Spacers look after their own. It would take an army to pull the girl out of Freeport. Besides, this isn't some rim-world backwater where you can do as you please.''

''We have taken the situation into our own paws,'' Sa-Lo said stoically, ''and will deal with the girl ourselves.''

Orr felt a sudden sense of alarm. Would the Traa cut him out? Was the deal slipping away? And what about his son? ''Wait just a minute. We have a deal . . . and what about Jason?''

''Our agreement stands,'' Sa-Lo replied, ''and your son is safe. And will be for as long as your interests are aligned with ours. We will contact you when the necessary documents have been signed.'' The video snapped to black.

The silence stretched long and thin. The first voice to break it belonged to a man. ''What cute little playmates you have . . . no wonder you want some help.''

Orr turned as the man stepped out of the shadows. He was tall, thin, and dressed in impeccable clothes. They were tight, with a touch of decadent lace. Thirty? Forty? Fifty? He could have been any of those. But the most striking thing about him was that his eyes never closed. Not even to blink. He looked like a statue, or a corpse come to life.

His name was Sanko, and like his father and grandfather before him, Sanko called himself a free trader, but made most of his money hijacking other captains' cargoes, running contraband goods, and anything else that would turn a fast credit. He had fallen under Orr's influence when he had jacked a load of highly addictive sleepy seeds, which, instead of belonging to a low-level drug cartel as he had believed, were actually the property of the Hildago Crime Syndicate, an organization sworn to slit his throat. Orr forced a smile. ''My furry friends are cute, aren't they? It would be a pity if something happened to them.''

Ari drifted into the light. She wore a frown and a much-handled sidearm. Data flowed through her implant. ''The call originated from a hotel in Freeport.''

''Which would tend to confirm your hypothesis,'' Sanko said thoughtfully. ''The aliens booked passage on the same ship the girl did . . . or hope to do so.''

"Exactly," Orr said grimly. "So do what needs to be done."

Sanko was a thief and a murderer, but he hated hypocrisy. He took pleasure in the exchange that followed. " 'Do what needs to be done'? What does that mean?"

Orr flushed. "What's the matter with you? Kill them . . . that's what it means. *All* of them. Is that what you wanted me to say?"

"Yes," Sanko said sweetly, "it is. And the *Will of God*. What of her?"

Orr shrugged. "She's yours . . . but not in-system. There would be an investigation, and we have enough badge pushers on Mechnos already. Take her at the other end of the trip. The law is thin out there . . . and news travels slowly."

"As you wish," the jacker said calculatingly, "but that means a long stern chase . . . and it takes money to run a ship like mine."

"Fifty thousand," Orr replied, "and not a credit more. Half now, and half when you return."

"A sum that will barely pay for my fuel," the jacker complained. "Seventy-five would be more like it."

Sanko felt something ram the base of his skull. His eyes flicked right, then left. The woman named Ari was nowhere to be seen. She was fast, damned fast, and the gun barrel hurt. Had it been anywhere else, on the street, or aboard his ship, his own bodyguards would have flayed her alive, but they'd been barred from the estate. Orr smiled. "Like I said, Sanko, fifty. Not a credit more."

The jacker nodded, felt the pressure disappear, and rubbed the sore spot. "All right—no need to get excited. Just business . . ."

"Good," Orr said. "Ari, see our friend to his car."

It took the bodyguard less than fifteen minutes to escort the jacker to his limo, see him off, and return. Her jacket was damp, and water dripped on the hardwood floor. Orr had just completed one com call and was about to make another when she entered the study. "Our friend is gone?"

" 'Friend' might be an overstatement, but he's gone,'' Ari replied.

"Excellent," Orr said cheerfully. "Sanko tends to overplay his hand at times, but he has his uses. Now, given the fact that little Miss Voss won't be coming back, we need to speak with her brother."

Ari frowned. "Why? I thought he was too young to put his thumb on documents."

"True," Orr replied easily, "but not for much longer. I checked, and guess what? Dorn Voss will be eighteen, thirty-six days from now. And if his sister had access to the coordinates, it seems safe to assume he does too."

"And if he doesn't?"

Orr shrugged. "Then we pay him a small sum, find the Gap the hard way, and open for business."

"So you want me to get him?"

"Bring the boy *or* his thumb," Orr said lightly, "whichever is more convenient."

Natalie went aboard the *Will of God* six hours prior to liftoff rather than the mandated two, and was familiar with the ship's systems by 0630. The rank still sounded strange to her ear. "Third Officer Voss to the bridge."

Natalie pushed a pedal, waited for the weapons pod to swivel left, grabbed an overhead rail, and swung out into the corridor. It took five minutes to reach the bridge, but she found it on the first try, and felt proud of herself. The first officer, a screamer named Russo, looked up from her computer screen. She displayed an S, a jeweled implant, and a practically non-existent chin. "Passengers are coming aboard. Meet them on the dock and bring them below."

The request could have been passed over the intercom, which would have saved Natalie the walk, but Russo had power and wanted to use it. Natalie had been around that kind of officer before and kept her face intentionally blank. "Yes, ma'am."

The passengers had arrived on the dock by the time Natalie got there. There were two of them, and they wore hooded cloaks that served to hide their faces as well as protect them from the rain. The officer thought they were humans at first, women perhaps, or adolescents, but soon learned differently. Each carried a small bag, and Natalie offered to help. "Greetings. I'm Third Officer Voss. May I take your luggage?"

The taller one replied. "Thank you, Third Officer Voss, but no, my companion and I prefer to carry our own belongings. Please proceed."

Though careful to avoid anything that would seem like a stare, Natalie was able to determine that the passengers were aliens and, if memory served her correctly, members of the Traa race. A highly competitive species known for their sharp but mostly honest dealings. And, while The Place of Wandering Waters seemed like a somewhat unusual destination for the aliens, the same commercial opportunities that attracted Jord might interest them as well.

The gangplank bounced as the three of them made their way down onto the same platform she had used earlier. It whirred as they were lowered into the lock. Russo was there to greet the Traa as the hatch cycled open and, judging from the heartiness of her welcome, regarded the Traa as VIPs. That they were was made even more clear when it turned out that the aliens had been assigned to the first officer's cabin, forcing her to bunk with Natalie.

Things went quickly after that, with a clearance to taxi, help from a busy little tug, and a final systems check. Natalie, whose launch station was aft in case of a bridge fire or similar emergency, pulled the harness across her body, checked to make sure her backup instrumentation registered the same readings that Jord's did, and nodded to the chief engineer. Both hung on as the *Will of God* shuddered, broke free of the water, and rose into the air.

Then, following one additional systems check, the ship roared out to sea and clawed through the atmosphere. It was slow going at first, but the drives roared, and the planet dwindled behind them. A short time later the *Will of God,* or the *Willie*, as the secular crew members called her, escaped the planet's gravity well, cleared planetary control, and directed herself toward a pinpoint of light.

One hour later, on an absolutely identical course, Tor Sanko, along with an unusually large crew, departed Mechnos on schedule. Their ship, a heavily armed Tully Trihull, had the ability to catch the *Will of God*, but made no attempt to do so. That, like the spoils to follow, would have to wait. The stars, eternally neutral in the affairs of man, wheeled through the void.

11

Friendship can flower in the most arid of fields.

Horbuth Neebarzer Dral Bod
Cycle Sayer to the Drodd
Standard year 2109

The Planet New Hope

The star ship's repellors functioned like man-made cyclones as they tore through the slums and sucked debris into the air. Dorn watched aghast as an entire line of people, still linked by the drag chain, were pulled off the ground. Arms waved and legs kicked, but to no avail. Dorn urged the others forward as Myra left the ground. "Quick! Grab them! It's their only chance!"

Much to Dorn's surprise, and perhaps theirs as well, the prisoners obeyed. Rushing forward, still hobbled by a section of chain, they grabbed the last of the would-be victims and held on. The dust was so thick that Dorn couldn't see. He wrapped his arms around someone's waist and hoped for the best as the vortex swung past. Then, just when it seemed the nightmare would never end, the sixth repellor came to life. The pilot seized the opportunity, took control of the ship, and veered toward the sea.

The trip back toward the water was as destructive as the

initial one had been, but took less time and killed fewer people. Dorn's attention was elsewhere. The body he held turned out to be Myra's, and she threw her arms around his neck. The kiss seemed natural and confirmed they were alive. Her lips were unbelievably soft, and Dorn had never experienced anything quite so good.

They were still in each other's arms when the guards crawled out of whatever holes they had disappeared into, blew their whistles, and herded the survivors toward a one-story building. Once there, and safely out of the way, the prisoners were placed under light guard and ordered to wait while the owner's medical staff did what they could for the wounded. The dead were carried to a makeshift crematorium, and work parties were recruited to clear the debris.

It was an uncomfortable afternoon, but the fact that Dorn and Myra were shackled right next to each other helped. There was plenty of time to talk, to touch the brands on each other's foreheads, and relive the last few days. There was time to wonder what would happen next, too . . . and the answer arrived all too soon.

The man in the dirty gray turban, the same one who had paid for the prisoners in Oro, appeared just before sunset. He scanned the prisoners, murmured something to one of the guards, and watched as his orders were implemented. The prisoners were ordered to stand and face outward. The teenagers did as they were told and waited to learn what fate held in store for them.

The man in the turban started at the far end of the line and moved their way. He spoke with some prisoners, but not to others. Selections were made, shackles were released, and what seemed like an oddball collection of men, women, and children were herded to one side. Some of the youngsters were removed from their parents and began to cry. A mother objected but a slap rendered her silent. Dorn started forward but the chain held him back. There was no rhyme or reason to the way the man made his decisions, none Dorn could discern anyway, and the process left him mystified.

Then, just as turban-man made his final selection and turned to leave, he spotted Myra. He looked, looked again, and ordered a guard to unlock her leg iron. The guard, an older man with badly yellowed teeth, did as he was told. Myra looked frightened, and Dorn grabbed the man's arm. "Please! What's going on? Where will you take her?"

"To the house," the guard said simply. "Now let go of my arm."

Dorn remembered the beautiful white mansion that sat on the tip of the peninsula. It didn't take a genius to figure out whom the house belonged to or that it would take a large staff to run the place. "How will they treat her? What will she do?" Dorn insisted, still maintaining contact.

"She'll receive better treatment than you will," the guard replied as he removed the shackle from Myra's ankle. "Four kitchen servants were killed when the ship drifted over the vegetable gardens. Your friend will replace one of them. Now back off."

Dorn did as instructed. He wanted to say something special to Myra, something she would remember, but there was no time. She was there one moment and gone the next as the prisoners were led away. She looked back, though, and her wave made him feel a bit better. At the same time, the expression on her face made him want to cry. Somehow, in a manner he couldn't explain, Myra had become an important part of his life. So much so that he would find her again no matter how difficult that might be or what the cost. Then she was gone, absorbed by the slums and the quickly gathering darkness.

What happened next was both disconcerting and unexpected. A guard, filthy from clearing rubble, worked her way down the line, released their leg shackles, and ordered a boy to collect the chain. Then, grabbing the end, she dragged it away.

Minutes passed and no one moved. They simply sat, squatted or stood there, backs to the building, awaiting their orders. Dorn realized that he, like those around him, was afraid to do anything. However, knowing it and acting on it were two different things. The prisoners watched as a constant stream of ragged-looking men, women, and children passed by. Many of them wore bandages, or leaned on each other for support. None wore chains.

Finally, after five minutes had elapsed, Dorn examined his surroundings, assured himself that no one was watching, and walked away. He waited for the inevitable whistles, for the shouts of outrage, but nothing happened. Thus emboldened, he walked faster and faster, until the building was left behind and the crowd closed around him. Dorn knew then that he was free, if anyone in a forced labor camp can be described as "free." Mr. Halworthy had always insisted that everything was relative.

It was dark now—but the serpentine footpaths were lit with smoky torches augmented with widely spaced halogen lights. Dorn spent his first half hour of comparative freedom wandering the muddy streets, absorbing the atmosphere, marveling at what his eyes saw, his nose smelled, and his ears heard.

The squalor he'd seen in the city was nothing compared to this. Yes, the open sewers were the same, but the people of Oro lived in houses, no matter how humble they might be. There were no such amenities here. Everything was made from scrap. Scraps of wood, plastic, and fiberboard, but never of metal, for metal had value, and belonged to the owners.

As Dorn followed the winding streets, and sought to avoid the deepest cesspools, he noticed subtleties that would have escaped him before. First, he noted the fact that the high ground was the most desirable since it was farthest from the sewers and subject to ocean breezes. That being the case, even the slightest rise was surmounted by the local equivalent of a mansion, the most elegant of which had been fashioned from standard twelve-by-six-foot plastic cargo modules.

Then, falling away to either side of the minimansions, and steadily decreasing in quality, came the makeshift huts, lean-tos, dugouts, and tents. Finally, along the very edge of the road, a line of pitiful figures crouched under scraps of plastic, and in one case, a much abused Voss Lines flag, just like the ones that had flown from his parents' ships as they taxied into

Fortuna's main harbor. It flapped dismally as if aware of its fate.

Dorn swallowed the lump that formed in his throat, wondered which of the family ships had expired on the mud flats, and continued on his way. As he wandered through the slums, he was struck by both the poverty and the energy with which the residents pushed it back. Everywhere he went voices offered clothing, haircuts, spices, alcohol, cookware, and sexual favors so exotic he'd never heard of them before, and wasn't sure he wanted to.

The food stands *were* tempting, however. He watched a little girl remove a strip of mystery meat from a tiny brazier, dip it into a pot of reddish-brown sauce, and offer it to a man covered with tattoos. He accepted the strip, handed the child a three-inch piece of insulation-stripped copper wire, and wandered away. Dorn felt his stomach growl, swallowed a mouthful of saliva, and drifted on.

Finally, as if unconsciously drawn to the center of the devastation, Dorn came to an area of almost unimaginable destruction. Smoke and dust, still visible in the light provided by the company-supplied floods, billowed up toward the sky. A rescue effort was underway as fifteen or twenty volunteers struggled to remove a pile of rubble. Their objective wasn't clear until Dorn heard a man shout, "I can hear them! We're getting closer!" and saw the others work with renewed energy. Suddenly, a siren sounded, and the would-be rescuers dropped their makeshift tools and hurried away. Dorn assumed they were headed for the buildings he'd seen earlier.

As the crowd departed, an alien emerged from the wreckage and waved his arms above his head. Dorn recognized the XT as a member of the Traa race and didn't need a degree in xenopsychology to tell that he, she, or it was upset. "Wait! Come back! We're so close! What if it was you? Come back, damn it!"

But the words were to no avail as the siren continued to wail and the humans hurried away. Dorn had drifted closer by then, and the alien saw him. He pointed a finger in the human's direction and sounded angry. "You! Yes, you! Why linger? Go with the others. Earn your meaningless pay.''

Dorn was confused. He shrugged. ''I don't know where they're going or why. I'll help if you show me what to do.''

The alien was closer now, and Dorn was struck by the humanlike fervor in his eyes, and the energy that crackled all around him. His bar code was old and faded. ''A newbie, huh? Well, so much the better. Come on, newbie, you and I will dig, and later we shall eat. It's the same deal the company would give you, except that our work will save lives, and theirs will cheapen it. Come then, grab that axe, and get to work.''

The axe head had been fashioned from a chunk of hull metal and mated with a hardwood handle. It was a tool so ancient, so common, that one could be had for two or three credits on most planets, and less if you bought them in bulk. But not on New Hope, where a meal cost a short length of copper wire, and guards were dispatched to recover a twenty-foot length of chain.

What if Dorn took the axe and ran? His legs were longer than the Traa's . . . and he felt sure he'd win the resulting race. But the alien had trusted him, and people were trapped in the wreckage, so Dorn pushed the idea away.

The Traa, who had a short snout, horizontal nostrils, and a sort of doglike aspect, led Dorn to a tangle of wooden beams, adjusted one of the homemade torches to maximize the somewhat dubious light, and called to the people trapped below. The reply was faint but encouraging. Dorn paused to analyze the situation, chose which beams to attack first, and went to work. The wood was dry, and chips flew with each blow. A beam cracked and fell in two. The human chopped while the alien hauled the pieces away.

It took two full hours of hard, unrelenting labor to reach the accident victims, all of whom turned out to be members of a single family. There was a man, his head coated with dust; a woman, an arm hanging limply at her side; and a child, crying from thirst and shaking with fear. They were dazed and suffered from cuts, scratches, and abrasions. According to the man, they had run from the ship, taken shelter in an abandoned dugout, and been buried as the spacecraft passed overhead.

Dorn was struck by the skill and gentleness with which the Traa placed a splint on the woman's arm, closed the worst of their cuts, and calmed the child. It was then, and only then, that the XT led the family to the main gate, spoke with a surprisingly respectful guard, and was assured that the family would be cared for. A few minutes later, after they'd left the guard station, the alien looked back. His words sounded strange. "Please forgive me, oh abiding force, for my actions made no great difference and have prolonged their suffering."

Dorn frowned. " 'Made no real difference'? How can you say that? They'd be dead if weren't for you."

"Yes," the Traa agreed sadly. "They will live through to-day . . . but what of tomorrow? And the day after that? True, each individual must do what he or she can to alleviate suffering, but what of the results? The medical treatment they receive will add a year to each of their contracts. And what of the evil upon which the entire system rests? That continues, and the responsibility is ours."

"How can that be?" Dorn asked in genuine amazement. "The guards have weapons and we don't. The responsibility is theirs."

"Ah, if only it were that simple," the alien responded. "All lives are part of a mutual weave, and the lack of resources, in this case weapons, does nothing to lessen our responsibility. But enough of that. Come, I promised a meal, and a meal you shall have."

It was a relatively short walk to the alien's home. Dorn was struck by the reverential manner in which passersby greeted his companion. He commented on the phenomena and received the same sort of response that Mr. Halworthy might have offered. "Yes," the Traa replied, "I give respect and others return it. And what, may I ask, is so mysterious about that?"

Dorn had no ready answer, but was reminded of his parents' world where respect stemmed from power, of the academy where the strongest boy ruled, and wondered how the alien's philosophy would work in such situations.

A winding path carried them past a variety of makeshift dwellings, up a hillside, and stopped in front of a well-maintained cargo module. The words "Hass Lines" could still be read on the front, and a piece of plastic covered the door. The alien swept it aside, lit a makeshift lamp, and offered the traditional welcome. "Be at peace here, for steel sleeps within leather, and all are septmen."

Dorn, who hadn't been welcomed anywhere in a very long time, thanked the Traa and stepped inside. Though relatively small, the interior was tidy, with shelving made from fiber-board, stools improvised from cable reels, planks on a pair of sawhorses, and a bedroll that lay across one end of the room. It was luxurious by local standards, and the human said so. "This is nice. Aren't you worried that someone will steal your possessions while you're away?"

The Traa, who was fussing with a tiny firebox made of hand-fired bricks, waved the question away. "My possessions come and go. Some steal while others give. Material objects are like clouds in an otherwise sunny day. The less one sees of them, the better."

Dorn wasn't so sure about that and drew on knowledge received during Miss Murphy's less than popular Contemporary Civilization class. "Some humans would agree with you . . . but not very many. And what of your own race? It was my impression that the Traa are reasonably materialistic."

The alien turned and looked at Dorn as if seeing him for the first time. "What you say is true. At least two-thirds of my race is as avaricious as yours. Sad, isn't it? Now, if you would be so kind as to feed small pieces of wood into the fire . . . I'll work on dinner."

They ate a short time later. The food was simple but good. Not because of *what* they were eating, which consisted of noodles and vegetables, but because of the way in which the dishes were prepared. Spices, combined with quick turns in a hot skillet, worked wonders. They ate in silence, Traa style, and it wasn't until Dorn had consumed three full servings that he put his plate aside and wiped his mouth on what remained of a sleeve. "That was good. Thank you. May I ask your name?"

The alien offered the Traa equivalent of a smile. Dorn was amazed by the number of teeth that appeared. "My name is La-So. And what of you, boy? How are you called?"

"Dorn," the teenager answered, "Dorn Voss."

If the name meant anything to La-So, he hid the fact well. "Pleased to meet you, Dorn. Help clean up and you can stay the night."

The surrounding slum was dark and more than a little foreboding. Dorn was quick to accept the offer. It took less than an hour to haul water from a public tap, do the dishes, extinguish the lanterns, and crawl into the makeshift bedroll. The floor was hard, but an Adams Line flag kept Dorn warm. It beat sleeping in the open. The alien chanted for a while, rolled over, and started to snore. Dorn was extremely tired, but thoughts of Myra kept him awake for a long time, and followed into his dreams.

12

Shit happens.

> *Human folk saying*
> *Circa 1998*

Aboard the *Will of God* and at The Place of Wandering Waters

While it was true that all of the computers, instruments, control boards, processors, wiring, and other equipment necessary to run the ship could have been crammed into a much smaller space, the *Willie*'s control room was spacious. This stemmed not from the generosity of the ship's owners, or whim on the part of the ship's architects, but from years of hard-won experience. Most species are happier and more efficient when given some elbow room.

So, in spite of the fact that Natalie had the con, and shared the bridge with two members of the crew, neither was closer than ten feet away. They sat within individual cones of light and monitored the constellations of green, amber, and red indicator lights that floated in front of them. Some blinked like stars seen through an atmosphere, while others glowed like beacons in the night.

The command chair was located at the center of the U-shaped control room with a position to either side. Information regarding the ship's course and external environment was available on a huge wraparound screen. Not that it made much difference, because there wasn't much to see or do, which was fine with Natalie. The peace and quiet suited her.

She had chosen the merchant marine to impress her self-absorbed parents, to get out from under their influence, and because she liked the feel of it. Beyond the travel, and the challenge involved, there was something almost religious about the chanting of checklists, the chapellike calm of the control room, and the interaction with the cosmos.

Come to think of it, the atmosphere might explain how ships became screamers, although she thought there were other reasons too, including a need for belonging, especially when loved ones were far away and voyages lasted so long. Peter's voice cut through her thoughts. "Excuse me, Third Officer Voss, but I have what may or may not be a ship at extreme range."

Natalie frowned. A contact? Way the hell out here? Though far from impossible, such encounters were rare and not without danger. "Thank you, Peter. Is there anything more? Hull configuration? Drive type?"

"No, ma'am. Not yet. She's too far away."

"Course? Speed?"

"Same as ours, ma'am."

Natalie pondered the tech's words. The contact was traveling in the same direction and at the same rate of speed. Coincidence? Or something more? The officer spoke, and a wire-thin boom mike captured her words. "Bridge to engineering."

The voice belonged to the chief engineer, a cyborg named O'Tool. He was stationed at the other end of the ship. He wore a headset and answered from wherever he was. The voice was crisp and efficient. "Engineering, aye."

"Give me a five-percent increase in speed. One-percent increments, please."

There was silence for a moment, and when O'Tool spoke,

his voice was doubtful. "Has the captain been notified? Fuel costs money, ya know."

"I'm aware of that," Natalie said coolly. "You heard my orders . . . carry them out."

There was a pause, followed by a reluctant, "Aye, aye, ma'am," and a nearly imperceptible increase in speed. Natalie waited until the full five percent had been applied, then spoke into her mike. "Communications."

Peter, who sat only ten feet away, turned in Natalie's direction. "Communications, aye."

"Monitor the contact. Inform me if it picks up speed."

The com tech turned to his board. "Aye, aye, ma'am."

Natalie leaned back in her chair. She had planned to wake Captain Jord, but couldn't. Third officers don't have much authority to begin with, and even less if they cave to someone like O'Tool. All she could do was wait and hope the contact increased speed. Anything else would prove the cyborg's point. The minutes ticked by.

Both combatants were naked save for the straps that held the woman's breasts in place and the pouch that secured the man's genitals. A makeshift ring had been established at the center of hold number three. The antagonists circled from left to right and growled at each other.

The man, a wiry weapons tech from Holdar III, pranced this way and that, head down, hands weaving patterns in the air. The woman, a thickly built load master with the words "Kiss this" tattooed on her right buttock, grinned, waved to a person in the crowd, and then, as the man looked in that direction, kicked him under the chin. His head snapped back, he staggered, and his supporters groaned. The woman pursed her lips as if offering a kiss, grinned, and circled left. Friends shouted words of encouragement to the man, placed bets with the ship's purser, and hurled insults at the load master.

Tor Sanko, who had sponsored the fight in order to entertain the crew, sighed and tried to care. The load master was going to kick the weapons tech's ass, anyone could see that, and the whole concept was boring. Sanko sipped from a bottle of

Mechnos spring water, sniffed the cologne sprayed on the back of his hand, and considered his surroundings.

The atmosphere was thick with smoke, the odor of un-washed bodies, and the smell of cooking, which, given the number of people crammed aboard the ship, never really abated. The conditions were enough to gag a ship's rat, much less a man of his sensibilities, but the additional bodies were necessary to take the *Will of God,* con her to the scrapyards on New Hope, and crew his own vessel as well. Especially if there were casualties, and there usually were.

Yes, the pirate decided, prize crews, and the problems as-sociated with them, were as old as piracy itself, which was very old indeed. His thoughts were interrupted by a voice in his ear. "Captain? Cowles here."

Sanko sniffed the cologne. "Shoot."

Cowles, a renegade policeman, convicted organ-legger, and any number of other things, all of which were bad, had the con. He was shorter than Sanko and smaller. The thronelike command chair was far too large for him, but he liked it. So much so that he hoped to possess it one day, an ambition he kept hidden from Sanko. The bridge crew, most of whom were watching the fight via a pair of security cameras, had their backs to him. He liked that too. "Our quarry increased speed . . . orders?"

Sanko reached into a pocket, found the squeeze bottle, and tilted his head back. If he didn't administer the drops, his eyes would become painfully dry. The liquid was cold and ran down his cheeks. It was the closest thing to tears he ever experienced. There were various options. He could match the other ship's speed and, if the screamers were aware of his presence, confirm their worst fears. Or, he could ease the other crew's concerns by maintaining his present speed, remember-ing he'd have to use more fuel to catch them later on, a factor that would lower his profit margin. The pirate lifted his head and dabbed at his eyes.

The weapons tech hit the load master in the gut. She gave a grunt, seized his shoulders, and brought her forehead down on his nose. The man clutched his face, staggered backwards, and fell into the crowd. Arms caught the tech and shoved him forward. If *he* lost, his supporters did too. Then the woman kicked him in the balls, watched her opponent collapse, and struck a pose. Muscles rippled beneath tawny skin. Her fans roared their approval. Cowles, who had grown impatient by now, cleared his throat. "Captain?"

"Yes," Sanko replied irritably. "I'm thinking. Try it some time."

Cowles, who thought *all* the time, spoke through clenched teeth. "Yes, sir. Sorry, sir."

"Yes, you are," Sanko answered serenely. "Very sorry indeed. But that's beside the point. The fact is that we should take them now, while they're scared, and a long way from planetfall. But Orr would throw a hissy fit, our crew is only half sober, and the screamers could get lucky. That's why I think it would be better to match their speed, keep the pressure on, and wait for a while. There's nothing like a little anticipation to wear the enemy down."

Cowles, who would have ignored Orr's preferences and to hell with the consequences, said "Aye, aye, sir," passed the word to engineering, and waited to see what would happen. The mouse had been warned. What would it do?

A V-shaped wave rolled toward the far end of the lake as nine large bodies propelled themselves toward the net. Rollo was the tenth. He nosed the ball forward, followed the team's center, and waited for the signal. It didn't take long. Torx, who had an excellent vantage point behind Rollo's neck, watched the defenders and sent a message with his knees.

An observer might have assumed that each nudge was identical . . . and would've been wrong. The duration of each contact varied slightly, as did the amount of pressure exerted, and the speed with which they were sent. Not only that, but specialized sections of a Dromo's epidermis served to facilitate communication. Rollo, his plate-sized feet touching bottom from time to time, surged forward, hooked the ball with his horn, and flipped it upward. Torx caught the ball, faked a forward pass, and dumped to Horlo, who rode a Dromo named Creed.

Creed, responding to Horlo's knee signals, went left, passed between two of the opposing team's guards, and pushed toward the net. Horlo eyed the distance to the goal, saw it was too far to throw, and dropped the ball in front of his still churning mount. Creed horn-hooked the globe into the air . . . and head-butted it toward the goal.

The goalies, a pair known for their miraculous saves, moved to intercept. The Treeth, using his mount's back as a springboard, leapt into the air, extended his paws, and swore as the ball passed between them. The visiting team came complete with its own pep squad. They were a rowdy group and bellowed their disappointment as the ball hit the net.

Rollo, being low in the water, had been unable to see the goal, and waited for Torx to pass the news. He did, and the Dromo roared his joy. The match, which had been broadcast all over the planet by means of tree-mounted vid cams, was an important step toward the regional playoffs.

The ensuing celebration, complete with a good deal of bragging, water churning, horn jousting, dra drinking, and weed feasting, went on for the better part of six standard intervals, and left Rollo unprepared for the summons.

It came as such messages usually did, not by means of the planet's perfectly good satellite system, but attached to the leg of a less than efficient courier bird, long forsworn by everyone but the council, and rightfully so, given the fact that the creatures took time out from their journeys to hunt, feed, and sleep, leaving the recipients of their questionable services only days, or in some cases hours, to make the long and somewhat arduous pilgrimage to the pool of contemplation, where the elders fed on prime bottom weed, wrangled over points of procedure, and occasionally made decisions. Or so it seemed to young and often impatient Dromos such as Rollo.

After having relieved the courier of its burden, and thumbing a print-sensitive receipt, Torx released the bird to the sky. The bird was low, and still beating toward the south, when the Treeth leaned forward and dangled the document before

Rollo's eyes. The larger creature read the message, fought to clear his dra-addled mind, and read it again. "Honorable blah, blah, blah, it is the council's pleasure to grant you an audience, and hereby orders you to appear pursuant to blah, blah, blah, at interval eight, day fifteen, of the second month . . . Torx! The elders granted our request for an audience! Come, we must leave immediately."

Torx, long accustomed to his companion's impatient ways, was quick to agree. He filed the document in a waterproof saddlebag and took his place on Rollo's neck. The other Treeth, disappointed to see Torx go, wished him a safe journey.

It was a short swim to the lagoon where both teams had left their motorized tugs. They were small machines, consisting of little more than a streamlined hull, rechargeable power cell, electric motor, sensor array, and onboard computer. The tugs served the same purpose ground cars did, pulling the Dromo over long distances and, thanks to a global positioning system, navigating the planet's complex waterways with ease.

Torx summoned Rollo's tug with a hand-held remote and guided his rotund friend into the harness without wetting his feet. Like all Treeth, Torx was descended from tree dwellers and regarded water as inherently dangerous. The tug surged forward, took up the slack, and pulled Rollo toward the south. A wave formed in front of the Dromo's chest, rippled along his flanks, and left a V-shaped wake. Torx, who had assumed a reclining position on his companion's mostly dry back, watched the scenery slide by. It was the only aspect of waterborne travel that he enjoyed.

Hours passed, the sun went down, and the sentients fell asleep. Hunters emerged from their daytime lairs, bodies slithered down through tall grass, and eyes peered into the darkness. The robotug sensed their presence, knew which ones to avoid, and ignored the rest. The motor hummed, the destination beckoned, and the tug bored through the night.

The *Willie*'s mess had been designed to accommodate the crew in three shifts, which accounted for why it was so crowded. All the ship's officers were there, with the single exception of Russo, who had the con. Also present, and none too happy about it, were Ka-Di and Sa-Lo, who had been invited by the captain himself. The assemblage stirred as Jord, fully dressed for a change, entered the compartment. His eyes, black as space itself, flicked around the room.

"Everyone's here . . . good. We have a ship on our tail, and, judging by the fact that it alters speed every time we do, it could be a pirate."

Jord surveyed the compartment and tested each individual with the intensity of his stare. "So," he continued, "the question is *why*. Why would a pirate ship take an interest in the *Will of God*? Especially in light of the fact that our cargo consists of hybrid water-weed seedlings, low-grade replacement parts, scientific data modules, and medical supplies. Yes, the cargo is worth money, but not the kind that would attract attention, not unless we have something else on board, something or someone of much greater value."

Natalie was still processing what the captain had said, still trying to understand what he meant, when Jord looked her way. "A couple of possibilities come to mind. The first has to do with Third Officer Voss. Her family owns a shipping line, or did, and the pirates might have ransom on their minds." Jord turned to the Traa. "Then there's our passengers to consider. Perhaps the pirates want them."

The Traa stiffened but were otherwise motionless.

Natalie thought about Orr, the lawyers he'd sent after her, and the explosion that had taken her parents' lives. Would the industrialist destroy an entire ship? Just to take her life? Maybe . . . but what good would that do unless . . . Suddenly it came to her, the fact that Dorn would be eighteen soon, and old enough to affix his print to legal documents. With her out of the way, and the right amount of pressure on Dorn, the industrialist could acquire the gap for a song.

Jord's voice brought her back. "I think we need look no farther than our third officer's face to confirm my theory."

Natalie scanned the mess and, with the possible exception of the XTs, who wore what she interpreted as neutral expressions, saw nothing but dislike on the faces that surrounded her. She tried to explain. "Yes, the people on the other ship *could* be after me, but it's far from certain, and I had no idea . . ."

"Please," Jord said holding a hand palm outward, "save the self-justification for someone else. Your family's tendency to put their interests above all others is well known. I should have known better, should have waited for a more reliable officer, but succumbed to my own impatience and greed. I hereby apologize to the ship's company and, assuming that we manage to survive, will give blood to the altar of life."

Natalie *wanted* to respond, *wanted* to explain, but knew their minds were closed. There were other nonbelievers aboard, but none held officer rank or were at the meeting. Only the Traa had what might have been sympathetic expressions.

"So what's the plan?" O'Tool asked, light glinting off the right side of his face. "Do we run or fight?"

"We run and *prepare* to fight," Jord said grimly, "assuming they stay on our tail. I propose to reach The Place of Wandering Waters before our pursuers do and deliver our cargo. Once down, we can wait or fight our way out. The choice will be ours."

There was discussion after that, but most of it was pointless, and the captain's plan was approved. The crowd dispersed, O'Tool brought the drives to max, and the *Willie* hurtled through space.

The pool of contemplation was a lake-sized body of water, fed by no less than two separate rivers and open to numerous waterways, each of which was guarded by a pair of ancient stone towers. Rollo knew that there were other, more modern means of defense hidden all around, but couldn't see them as the tug pulled him through "fool's" gate, where the rebels of 1810 had made their final stand.

Lagoons passed to either side. Some were empty, or thick with weed, but most teemed with life. Torx saw hundreds of Treeth and Dromos laboring in front of waterborne holo screens as announcements blared, flags snapped in the breeze, and robotugs churned this way and that. It was quite colorful, and very much what government should look like, or so it seemed to Torx.

Tugs were not permitted within the pool of contemplation itself, so Rollo surrendered his machine to an attendant and proceeded under his own power. Once he was within the ancient gathering place, formally sanctified by the great King Halory, time seemed to slow. A long series of attendants, each more solemn than his or her predecessor, greeted visitors, checked their credentials, offered ritual advice, and passed them on. Finally, after an hour of such nonsense, the summons that had brought Rollo from hundreds of miles away was read with the same agonizing deliberation given to changes in the tax code. Then, just when it seemed as if some progress had been made, and the co-marshals would be ushered into the pool, they were ordered to wait. Government officials came and went so slowly that their movements left no wake. The calendar slipped, then slipped again, as emergencies arose and were dealt with. Finally, as the sun started to set and the moon rose over the eastern horizon, a Dromo surfaced at the center of the lagoon. Her Treeth, a bedraggled-looking creature, much abused by all appearances, shook itself, and water flew in every direction. "Citizen Rollo? Citizen Torx? This way, please."

The Dromo found it difficult to swim as slowly as his guide did, and felt a growing sense of excitement as he was led out to the area where a ring of floating lights signaled which part of the pool was in use that day, surrounding as it did the seventeen elders, not to mention their various aides, assistants, advisors, and hangers-on.

Finally, after passing through a series of identity checks, detector screenings, and a rather insulting pat-down, Rollo and Torx were admitted to the center of the ring, where presenters traditionally floated, their audience arrayed before them. The Master at Arms, a huge bull who had been around so long no one could remember when he hadn't been, announced their presence. His voice rolled like thunder and brought an elder to the surface. He looked annoyed and had a giant wad of weed in his mouth. "The council has the privilege of greeting

Commerce Marshal Rollo Drekno-Hypont III, and Co-Marshal Pilo Horlon-Torx.''

An elder, barely visible in the quickly gathering darkness, blew water out through his nostrils. It spattered in front of him. ''Thank you for coming. The council reviewed your summary and is ready to hear the entire presentation. Please proceed.''

Rollo, who had been working toward this moment for months, remembered his mother's admonition to be careful what you ask for, and took a deep breath. ''Thank you. It's an honor to be here. Our thesis is as follows: First, in the absence of faster-than-ship communication, transportation and interstellar communication amount to the same thing.

''Second, that the steady consolidation of shipping lines through bankruptcy, mergers, and secret partnerships threatens to leave transportation and communications in the hands of an ever dwindling number of individuals and races.

''Third, that the use of wormholes, or gaps as they are more popularly known, serves to exacerbate the situation, especially in light of the fact that at least one and maybe two of these discontinuities have fallen under Traa control.''

''Implying what?'' a voice growled from Rollo's right. ''That the Traa are attempting to undermine the Confederacy? Or that they are extraordinarily successful? Which, to the best of my knowledge, continues to be legal.''

Rollo chin-splashed his respect. Like all of his kind, the Dromo had excellent night vision that grew even better after the sun had set. That's why he was able to see the elder and the injury that earned him the nickname ''Half-horn.'' He chose his words with care. ''You are correct. Any analysis by members of one race that reaches potentially negative conclusions about the motives, actions, and outcomes of another should be regarded with the utmost skepticism. And the evidence supporting such claims should be of the highest caliber.''

''And you have such evidence?'' an octogenarian named Grodley inquired, his equally elderly Treeth asleep on his back.

"Yes," Rollo replied calmly. "I think we do."

"Then let's see it," a third voice called. "It's late, and I tire of governmental babble."

Rollo, who didn't appreciate having his carefully rehearsed presentation characterized as "governmental babble," swallowed his ire. "Yes, ma'am. Torx?"

Torx, who had provided the council's staff with the appropriate data cube earlier in the afternoon, touched a button on his hand-held remote. The entire north end of the lake was replaced by a volcano, and no sooner had the elders identified the object for what it was than the mountain exploded, hurled rock hundreds of feet into the air, and released clouds of superheated gas. The lava, which hissed realistically where it flowed into the lake, was reddish orange.

Rollo checked his audience to make sure that he had their complete and undivided attention, saw that he did, and continued the presentation. "The Mountain of the Moons is located in the northern hemisphere of the planet La-Tri.

"The eruption took place about three local months ago, and, due to the fact that approximately one-third of the Traa population was gathered below, killed more than eight hundred thousand members of that race."

"Which implies a rather small population," Half-horn said thoughtfully. "Especially when compared to the humans."

"Exactly," Rollo said, pleased that at least one elder understood the importance of what he'd said. "And, since the Dromo and the Treeth are even less numerous than the Traa, we are uniquely qualified to grasp the enormity of what occurred.

"Of equal and perhaps more importance, however, is *who* died during that eruption. Traa psychology is significantly different from our own, in that it stems from a highly stratified society in which each individual belongs to one of three highly specialized septs. Generally speaking, these groups could be said to consist of commercial beings, warriors, and priests."

"So?" Council Member Grodley inquired. "What's your point?"

"Simply this," Rollo answered patiently. "Nearly all of

those killed by the volcanic eruption were members of the religious sept, and, because they represented a sort of racial conscience, the overall society is out of balance. That being the case, the commercial and warrior septs are doing what comes naturally, which is to control everything they can.''

There was silence as the elders took it in. Council Member Dor-Zander, his eyes glowing with reflected moonlight, was first to speak. "Let me see if I understand . . . You're saying that the Traa evolved a group, rather than an individualized, conscience, and lacking that, are mentally unbalanced. So much so that they are a threat to us, the Confederacy, and themselves. I find that rather hard to believe.''

"Really?" Rollo asked, peering through the dark. "Judging from appearances, I'd say that your Treeth companion is a good deal younger than you are. What happened to her predecessor? And how did you feel at the time?"

The bond between Dromo and Treeth was so ancient that neither race could be sure of its origins. But there was absolutely no doubt that they had coevolved, with the Dromo providing the protection needed on a hostile planet, while the Treeth contributed their hands and their subsequent ability to make and use tools, along with the capacity to go where Dromos couldn't—an absolute necessity where activities such as mining were concerned.

Later, as communication became more important to their joint destinies, the fact that the Dromos evolved spoken language, while the Treeth relied on various forms of nonverbal expression, had served to further bind the races together. All of which was known to the elders, as was the fact that the relationship between a Dromo and his or her Treeth, normally established during the first five years of life, was of much more importance than bonds with family, friends, or an eventual mate. Which was why Rollo had asked the question and Dor-Zander had been slow to respond. "Fabra died in an accident and I felt as if half of me went with her. I stand corrected. Comment withdrawn."

"So," Half-horn said slowly, "let's assume that you're correct regarding Traa psychology. What sort of data has been gathered to support your thesis?''

"An excellent question," Rollo answered respectfully. "Torx?"

The Treeth touched a button, and the first of twenty-five documents appeared over the lake. It took the better part of a standard interval to review all the data that Rollo and Torx had collected. Traa holdings had increased enormously during the last quarter, and, based on a combination of public records, reports of secret transactions, and a certain amount of educated guesswork, there was little doubt that the aliens were up to no good.

However, suspicions are one thing, and facts are another, as an elder named Horla Dormire-Proxley made clear. "You offer an impressive case, Marshal, very impressive indeed, but where's the proof? Most of the activities you documented are entirely legal, and the rest of your evidence is highly speculative."

Rollo knew she was correct, and was searching for the right reply, when Torx tapped one into his shoulder. He passed it along. "Yes, it *is* highly speculative, which is why we haven't charged anyone with a crime."

"Which brings us to the next logical question," Half-horn added. "Given the fact that you represent the Confederacy itself, and have its resources at your disposal, why call upon us?"

Rollo and Torx found themselves in a delicate position. They were planetary citizens, and as such had every right to appear before the council and ask for support, but as law enforcement officers, sworn to put the interests of the Confederacy above all else, they were expected to steer clear of politics. Which was a nearly impossible task, given the fact that the Confederacy was by its very nature a highly political organization. The Dromo chose his words with care.

"In order to implement their plans, and seize control of the Confederacy's economic infrastructure, the Traa seek control of a wormhole called the Mescalero Gap. The owners died under questionable circumstances, and their daughter, a human named Natalie Voss, will arrive here soon. Once that occurs, and the female comes under our protection, we will proceed with our investigation.

"At that point, or as soon as their agents learn of our activities, the Traa diplomatic corps will swing into action and do everything they can to block our efforts. They support a powerful lobby backed by a network of secret alliances, partnerships, and agreements. High-level officials will be persuaded to put pressure on our superiors at the Commerce Department, and, after a certain amount of squirming, they will attempt to limit our investigation."

"And you want our diplomats to counter such efforts and build support for your activities," Half-horn said thoughtfully.

"Yes, sir."

"Have you any idea of how difficult that will be?" the old bull demanded. "We'll be accused of everything from racism to public nudity. All of our initiatives will come under fire."

"Yes, sir."

"All right," Half-horn said wearily. "You heard him. All in favor of taking on a really difficult, thankless, and execrable job, say 'Aye.'"

Rollo heard a basso chorus of "Ayes," and not a single nay.

"So, it's agreed," Half-horn said. "We'll do what we can. Now leave us. The council has another two intervals' worth of work to do."

Rollo chin-splashed, made for an exit, and thought about what they'd accomplished. The first battle had been won. The second would be a lot more difficult.

13

The wise (adult female) adapts herself to circumstances much as water assumes the shape of the vessel which contains it.

Inscription on an earthenware jug discovered in the Forerunner ruins of Itchar IV Radiocarbon dated to 20,000 B.C. Standard

The Planet New Hope

Bright sunlight, which streamed in through a gap in the makeshift curtains, combined with the smell of food to bring Dorn up from a dimly remembered dream. He lay there for a moment and gloried in the comfort of his makeshift bed. Then, forcing himself to confront the chill morning air, he rolled out and scrambled to his feet. It didn't take long to slip into his trousers, brush his teeth, and wash his face.

La-So crouched in front of the brick stove. He nodded toward the nearly empty wood box. "Follow the main footpath north. When you reach the wood lot, ask for Sandro. Tell him La-So sent you. Breakfast will be ready when you return."

The words were gruff, as if the XT wanted to put him off, and Dorn wondered if he should just leave. But the odor of food, combined with a ravenous appetite, convinced him to follow the alien's instructions.

He opened the door, stepped outside, and found a trail leading down the side of the hill. The sun slanted in from the east and glazed the peninsula with golden light.

The shanties stood in ranks as if leaning on each other for support. Beyond them, where the slum stopped and the beach began, Dorn saw all manner of salvage large and small. There were hull plates, which, in spite of the fact that they had traveled millions of light-years through space, were stacked like so much cordwood. Orderly rows of reels, each fat with salvaged cable, occupied one section of beach, while bins filled to overflowing with smaller pieces of metal lined the security fence.

There were tools too, though surprisingly few, including a couple of yellow cranes, a barge that might or might not float when the tide came in, and a dozen or so exoskeletons, frozen in whatever positions their operators had left them.

Of even more interest to Dorn were the dimly seen shapes that lay beyond the curtain of mist that separated the salvage yards from the mud flats, because it was there, halfway to the point where brown met blue, that the half-consumed carcasses of once-mighty ships could be seen, wings clipped, hulls breached, ribs pointing toward the sky.

It was a sad yet compelling sight, and Dorn found himself torn between feelings of regret and curiosity. As a boy he had begged his parents for permission to explore old ships, ducking into musty compartments, fingering dead controls. But that was when he'd been younger—and firewood had been something that droids dealt with.

Dorn stopped long enough to make use of a partially screened privy. Insects whined around his head. He gagged on the smell and left as quickly as he could.

The main path was heavily used, and Dorn made the mistake of stepping in front of some children. They pushed on by, made fun of his appearance, and laughed as they pursued each other up the incline. Dorn, unsure of the best way to carry the wood box, followed along behind. Mud squished under his sandals, woodsmoke drifted across the pathway, and vendors hawked their wares. They lined the broader parts of the trail and vied for his business. "Fresh night fish! Fried just for you! Get 'em while they're hot!"

"Hey, mister! You want a bath? Lord knows you could use one . . . Just five inches of wire, a number-three fastener, or an L-bracket."

"Nice box young sir . . . how 'bout a trade?"

So it went until Dorn topped a slight rise and spotted the wood lot. It was surrounded by a four-foot-high adobe wall and guarded by half-starved dogs. The nearest one growled, lunged to the end of a badly frayed lead, and snapped its teeth.

Dorn kept an eye on the dogs, located the main entrance, and entered the compound. The wood had been sorted, piled, and priced by type. There was driftwood, nearly white from exposure to the sun; planks, or what had been planks, stripped off long-dead pallets; and branches, each shaped by the wind. Thanks to Mr. Halworthy's tutelage, Dorn recognized the latter as pieces of ironwood, an especially dense shrub that flourished on open hillsides. It burned like coal.

Dorn heard the *ka-thunk* of an axe hitting wood, wandered toward the sound, and was confronted by a woman in a red bandana, blue blouse, and homemade pantaloons. A pile of kindling lay heaped at her feet. Her eyes were blue. An explosion of wrinkles radiated away from them. "Yes? What can I do for you?"

"Is Sandro here?"

The woman bellowed, "Sandro! Someone to see you!" and returned to her work.

Kindling flew, and Dorn stepped out of the way. The voice came from behind and made him jump. "Yeah? What do you want? I don't give no handouts, if that's what you're after."

Dorn turned. Sandro was a small, wizened man. He looked as if every bit of moisture had been leached out of him, leaving nothing but leather. He regarded Dorn with the suspicion of someone who has seen everything . . . and none of it good. Dorn swallowed. "La-So sent me."

Sandro's features softened. "Oh, he did, did he? How is old snout-face, anyway?"

A little taken aback, unsure of how to respond, Dorn stuttered. "He's fine, that is, I *think* he's fine, though it's kind of hard to tell."

Sandro nodded as if he knew what Dorn meant. "Yeah, well, he can be a surly critter, especially when he gets to thinking 'bout his kin, which is nearly all the time. You know the story?"

Dorn shook his head.

"Well, there ain't much to tell," the man said gruffly. "Here . . . put the box down." He approached a pile of iron-wood, chose carefully, sectioned the pieces, and passed them to Dorn. "The Traa marry in threes, you know, kinda kinky if you ask me, but that's how they do it. Anyway, La-So and a couple of females came dirtside on a business trip. Here, take some roots . . . they burn longest. Now where was I? Oh yeah, La-So. You know them plagues? The ones that sweep through the slums every year or so?"

Dorn remembered Mr. Halworthy, and how he had died. "Yes, I do."

Sandro nodded. "Well, strange as it seems, the bug that killed La-So's wives didn't bother us humans. Oh, it gave some a headache all right, and a nasty case of the trots, but that's all. Anyway, the poor old slob went on the Traa equivalent of a thirty-day drunk, and woke up in the holding pens. You know the rest."

Dorn *did* know the rest, and lifted the box off the ground. It was heavier than it looked. "So how long has he been here?"

Sandro squinted into the sun. "Two years? Three? Time don't mean much around here. Not to me, anyway . . . though some think of nothing else."

Dorn nodded and looked at the wood. "I don't have metal of my own . . . and La-So didn't give me any."

Sandro waved the issue away. "That's 'cause snout-face knows I wouldn't take it. I owe him more than I can ever repay. You tell him that Sandro sends his best."

Dorn thanked the man, wondered what La-So had done to earn such undying gratitude, and made his way to the path. The box was heavy. Carrying it was easier when he hoisted it onto a shoulder. The downhill part of the journey wasn't bad, but the subsequent uphill stretch was more difficult, and he arrived out of breath. La-So's dwelling was just as he'd left it.

The teenager heard a humming sound and peered inside. A plate heaped with food sat on the makeshift table, and beyond that, face into a corner, sat La-So.

The Traa was humming a chant of some sort.

He put the wood by the stove, retrieved the plate of food, and carried it out front. The stoop made a good place to sit. The fact that the food was hot suggested that the alien had seen the human coming and wished to avoid him.

Dorn spooned mush into his mouth and wondered what the problem was. Did the alien's seemingly antisocial mood stem from sorrow, as Sandro suggested? Or did it flow from something else, like a different set of norms? Or an offense on Dorn's part? There was no way to know.

Dorn ate his meal, washed his dish, and stared at La-So's back. The chanting continued; Dorn shrugged and stepped outside. A siren sounded, people hurried toward the beach, and Dorn, having nothing else to do, joined the procession.

Men, women, and children materialized from all manner of huts, shanties, and tents, turned toward the sea, and followed paths toward the beach. Dorn, who'd been struck by the almost irrepressible good humor demonstrated by the camp's residents up till now, was now struck by the almost eerie silence that fell over them.

He considered returning, but remembered the alien's hard, unyielding back, and knew there was nothing to return to. He thought about Myra, wondered what she was doing, and hoped she was okay.

The paths converged one by one, leading to what amounted to an assembly area. Dorn saw the eight-foot-tall razor wire-topped fence that separated the lowermost slums from the salvage yards, the beach, and ultimately the ships themselves. Equally noticeable were the evenly spaced guard towers, the lights that would illuminate everything at night, and the signs that read: "All salvage belongs to Sharma Industries. Theft will be punished to the full extent of the law.''

Such precautions made perfect sense, given the fact that each time the workers passed through the heavily guarded gates they entered the local equivalent of a bank vault. So, if the workers weren't allowed to keep anything, and were denied access to the salvage when off duty, where did the pieces of wire, nuts, bolts, and other bits of metallic currency come from? Smuggled, perhaps? And if so, how? Knowing the answers to such questions, and taking advantage of that knowledge, would help Dorn survive. He would have to find out.

People milled for a moment, and then, as if governed by a single mind, divided themselves into three distinct groups. Two were composed almost entirely of men, with only a sprinkling of women, while the third consisted of women, children, and the elderly. Unexpectedly isolated, and feeling vulnerable, Dorn joined a group of males.

The siren, which had continued to wail, stopped suddenly, and the speaker system popped. The voice originated from a guard tower. ''All right, people, you know the drill, wreckers first, haulers second, and sifters third.''

The titles had a functional quality, as if they represented specialties of some sort, and, given the fact that the others had come to the assembly area of their own free will, or seemed to anyway, Dorn figured the work was compensated in some way. Another item to investigate and understand.

Dorn was nearly left behind as the group he had associated himself with shuffled toward a checkpoint, merged into a single column, and passed between a pair of guards. By peering around the people in front of him, Dorn could see up ahead. He noticed that each person was required to hold his or her hands out, and while most of the workers were admitted, some were rejected. This caused the line to move forward in a series of jerks. No sooner had Dorn made that observation than it was *his* turn in the gate. The guards looked bored. They used a minimum of words. ''Stop.''

Dorn stopped.

''Hands.''

Dorn held out his hands. The guard looked, frowned, and

shook her head. "You ain't ready for wrecking, newbie ... try hauling for a while."

Dorn turned, trudged to the end of the line, and fell in with the haulers. One of them, a middle-aged man with scar tissue where temple jacks had been removed from his head, nodded. Dorn offered a tentative smile. "I give up ... What does a wrecker do? And what's wrong with my hands?"

"Wreckers cut the ships into pieces, haulers drag the pieces to shore, and sifters sift through the mud and sand looking for the little stuff, which might be small but it all adds up in the long run."

"So? Where do hands come into it?"

The man shrugged. "It takes experience to be a wrecker. That's why they receive more pay. If you want to call what we get 'pay.' But it's hard on your hands, real hard, which is why most wreckers wind up with a lot of cuts, burns, and amputations."

It was sobering news, and Dorn was silent as the haulers formed a line and were funneled through the arch-shaped checkpoint. The light flashed and his forehead warmed. The reason was obvious. By scanning each worker's bar code, and running the information through a computer, the company could track how many days each person worked and ensure that they left at the end of each shift. Dorn added that fact to his hoard of knowledge.

The wreckers needed time to collect their tools, wade through the surf, and start work. So the haulers were put to work a hundred yards down the beach where the last shift had left a pile of durasteel plates.

There was nothing complicated about the work. Half the haulers were issued six-foot lengths of rope and told to find partners. Most had anticipated the moment and were paired off. Dorn, who had a piece of rope but no partner, felt a hand touch his arm. "You looking for some help, son? I'm available."

Dorn turned to find himself face to face with a black woman. She was at least ten or fifteen years his senior and built like a wedge. Years of hard physical work had widened her shoulders, thickened her arms, and narrowed her waist. She wore a sleeveless blouse, shorts, and sandals. Skin gathered over her nose when she frowned. "What? You think you're stronger than I am?"

Dorn gulped and shook his head. "No, ma'am."

The woman nodded gravely. "Good. Then I won't have to kick your skinny butt. Here, hand me the other end of that sling."

Dorn did as he was told. The woman took her end of the rope, led him over to the scrap metal, and accosted a pair of sun-darkened twins. They were thin but wiry. "Hey, you looking for partners? 'Cause the newbie and I match up pretty good."

The twins eyed them, nodded in unison, and headed for one of the plates. Dorn noted the ease with which the twins slid their rope under the steel slab and did his best to emulate their quick, sure movements.

Once both slings were in place a twin said, "One, two, three," and they lifted as one. The plate rose into the air and rode a half foot above the sand as they hauled it up the beach. It was heavy, and the sand made walking difficult.

The going became somewhat easier as they topped the incline and followed another team into the pickup zone. Once there, it was a simple matter to drop the plate, pull the slings out from under, and back away.

A cable dropped out of the sky, and Dorn watched as a pair of preteen boys dashed in, hooked a harness to the slab, and scurried out of the way. The crane jockey, perched a hundred feet in the air, squinted through the smoke created by her stim stick, released the clutch, and jerked a lever.

The five-hundred-pound slab of metal swayed into the air, drifted sideways, and thumped onto a conveyor belt. Dust rose into the air, rollers squealed, and the steel shuddered as the belt carried it upward. Dorn wondered what it would be like to try to sleep in the hovels that crept up within a foot of the belt.

The twins led the way down the slope, and Dorn fell in step

with his partner. She was open and direct. "My name's Jana . . . what's yours?"

"Dorn . . . glad to meet you, Jana. How long have you been here?"

"Seven long, miserable years. Which means that I know a thing or two about how to survive. Want to learn?"

Dorn nodded eagerly. "Sure! You bet!"

"It'll cost you."

Everything had its price. He should've known. Dorn felt his enthusiasm drain away. "Sorry, I don't have anything to pay you with."

"Oh, yes you do," the woman insisted. "Everybody does. I want to be paid in the same currency you'll receive . . . knowledge."

Dorn wondered if she was joking. Her face was serious. "What sort of knowledge? What little knowledge I have won't be of much use here."

"Knowledge is always valuable," the woman countered, "since merely having it provides pleasure. As for what you know, and what I *want* to know, let me be the judge of that. Time will pass and the payment will suggest itself."

Dorn wasn't so sure, but if Jana thought he had something to offer, why argue? The lessons began immediately. "Now," his partner said as they reached the bottom of the slope, "it's time to change sides. The work will seem easier, and balanced exercise will build both sides of your body. Watch what you eat, think about the work, and build yourself up."

Dorn did as he was told, wondered if the twins had done likewise, but couldn't remember which was which. The second trip was a copy of the first, as were the third, fourth, and fifth.

Finally, after Dorn had lost track of the number of times they had trudged up the beach, and the sun had grown a good deal warmer, the siren burped, and they surrounded the water barrels brought for their convenience. Salt tablets were available from a dispenser. Jana took two, washed them down with a generous amount of water, and suggested that Dorn do likewise.

With their thirst slaked, there was barely enough time for a ten-minute nap in the shadow cast by one of the guard towers before the siren wailed, guards yelled, the haulers got to their feet, and work resumed.

The existing supply of plates had been exhausted by now, which meant that it was time to march out through the incoming tide, take up positions around the slowly dwindling ships, and ferry the new metal in.

The water felt good at first, pushing against the front of Dorn's legs, foaming past the corner posts that marked where the sifters plied their monotonous trade, and sliding onto the beach. But that was before it grew knee-deep, a data liner loomed high above, and a huge slab of durasteel splashed into the sea not ten feet away.

Dorn learned then how treacherous the unseen sand could be, how it gathered along the inside surface of his sandal straps, and how it rubbed against his unprotected skin. And it was in the shallows, while struggling to slip a sling under a four-hundred-pound chunk of steel, that he had his first encounter with a shift boss.

He had knelt down, and was feeling for the steel plate's edge, when a larger than expected wave hit him in the face. He lost his balance, fell over backwards, and struggled to right himself. He wasn't aware of the exoskeleton until it appeared right next to him. The whip fell across his abdomen. It hurt like hell in spite of the fact that the water slowed the blow. The voice was amplified. "On your feet, stupid! What do you think this is? A private swimming pool? Your team should be halfway to the beach by now."

Dorn thought about fighting back, realized how hopeless it would be, but noted the man's heavily bearded face. The wreck master seemed to understand and nodded agreeably. "That's right, newbie . . . remember my face. I can't wear this rig twenty-six hours a day now, can I? That means you and I might run into each other on the beach, where it would be my pleasure to kick your worthless ass. The name is Castor. Nick Castor. Now stand or die."

The exoskeleton took a giant stride forward. The foot pod missed Dorn by less than an inch. Water splashed over him.

He turned into the waves, scrambled to his feet, and took his position. Jana tossed the rope; he grabbed it and staggered toward shore. The shift boss watched them go, spit into the surf, and turned away. Servos whined as he moved along the line.

"Nice work," the woman said through tightly clenched teeth. "Castor likes to pick on the same people over and over again. Looks like you're elected."

Dorn tried to think of something clever to say, failed, and decided to keep his mouth shut. The sun rose higher in the sky, the work grew harder, and the waves came in endless succession. Life was hard, and only the hard would survive. Dorn allowed a wave to break against his chest, pushed his way into the oncoming tide, and swore he'd be among them.

14

The wise and prudent man will draw a useful lesson even from poison itself.

Lokman
Ethiopian fabulist
Circa 100 B.C.

Aboard the *Will of God* in Deep Space

The dream was strange in at least two respects: Natalie *knew* she was asleep for one thing and her mother acted as narrator for another.

She watched the freighter taxi, pause, and vanish within its own cloud of steam. Then, as part of a miracle she had witnessed countless times before, the ship broke free of the water. Sunlight glinted off the hull as it turned slightly, and the drives growled. What made the whole thing so horrible was knowing what would happen next. *Knowing* and being powerless to stop it. Her mother's voice was calm and reflective. "I made many mistakes during my lifetime. The Braxton deal comes to mind, as does the terraforming project."

"What about me?" Natalie interjected, her voice echoing through time and space. "Was *I* a mistake?" Her mother couldn't or didn't want to hear, and Natalie watched the ship lift.

"Yes," Mary Voss continued, "I made many mistakes . . . not the least of which was ignoring your father more than I should have. Take this trip, for example. He was dead set against it and wanted to sweep the ship for explosives. I should have listened, I should have . . ."

The rest of her mother's words were lost as a miniature sun was born, lived for three seconds, and collapsed on itself. Thunder rolled, and windows shattered all around the bay.

Natalie awoke with a start, her heart pounding, sheets soaked with sweat. The compartment was dark, so dark that the clock and the indicators that surrounded it generated the only available light. Speed, course, and drive temps were all as they should be. Checking them, and knowing what they said, was a habit every deck officer had.

Natalie was preparing to get up and make her way to the head when the numbers vanished and reappeared. Something, or someone, had passed in front of them. "Russo? Is that you?"

A weight fell across Natalie's body, and a hand covered her mouth. She struggled, but to no avail. Her attacker had the advantage and knew how to use it. Her cheek encountered something soft, and the odor of cinnamon filled her nostrils. "Please, Citizen Voss, we mean you no harm."

"Then get the hell out of my cabin," Natalie replied, or tried to reply, since the hand kept her from speaking. She kicked and attempted to free herself. The pressure increased. The voice was concerned. "Your struggles are unnecessary. Relax and we will release you."

The voice and the accent were familiar. The Traa had entered her cabin. Why? What did they want? "We wish to speak with you," the voice said urgently, "privately. May I remove my paw?"

Natalie forced herself to relax and nodded. The paw disappeared, but the weight remained. Sa-Lo turned as the lights came on. Ka-Di, who lay across her torso, checked to make

sure she was okay, and pushed himself away. ''My apologies
. . . are you all right?''

''Fine, thank you,'' Natalie replied stiffly. She did a sit-up
and swung her legs over the edge of the bunk. The sweatshirt
extended halfway down her thighs. The officer knew the XTs
weren't interested in her anatomy, but she felt better knowing
she was clothed. ''So,'' she said, trying to sound as stern as
possible, ''what's going on?''

''We are business beings,'' Sa-Lo said simply, ''and you
own something we want.''

Natalie felt her heart beat just a little bit faster. So the Traa
had come aboard because of her. That being the case, there
was one thing they could possibly be interested in. ''You want
the Mescalero Gap.''

''Precisely,'' Sa-Lo said smoothly, ''and we're willing to
pay more than Citizen Orr offered. Providing that certain
agreements can be arrived at.''

Natalie's eyebrows shot up. ''You know about his offer?''

''Yes,'' the Traa replied simply, ''we do.''

Natalie knew there was more here than met the eye. The
same doubts that caused her to refuse Orr's proposal surfaced
once again. ''Well, I'm sorry. The Gap isn't for sale. Not for
the moment, anyway.''

Ka-Di, silent until now, fought the urge to grab the female
by the throat and force her agreement. Cooperation was best,
he knew that, and he managed to control himself. Words had
power, though . . . as did fear. ''Captain Jord was correct . . .
the pirates want you.''

Natalie felt a weight drop into the bottom of her stomach.
''*Me?* Why?''

''Because you refused Orr's offer,'' Sa-Lo said bluntly,
''The sooner you die, the sooner he can buy the Gap from
your brother.''

Natalie glanced from one alien to the other. Though not a
business person herself, she had inherited some of her mother's shrewdness, and she realized the Traa knew more than
they should have—unless they had links to the industrialist.

Which meant they couldn't be trusted. She tried another tack. "If *I* die, *you* die."

"True," Ka-Di replied easily. "Or it would be if we stayed aboard this ship. Come, and we will protect you."

"Yes," Sa-Lo put in. "Why not?"

Natalie wasn't sure why not, except that it had something to do with her parents' legacy, and her brother's trust. That, plus the fact that she was the *Willie*'s third officer, which meant that she had a sworn duty to the crew, the ship, and her cargo. The academy's instructors had gone to great lengths to pound that idea into her head, and, like most of the lessons they taught, it stuck.

Natalie braced herself, raised her right foot, and kicked Sa-Lo in the midriff. The alien made a satisfying whoosh and bent over.

Ka-Di saw the preparatory move, anticipated what the human would do next, and triggered the knife. It jumped into his paw and hummed as he touched the switch. The back-handed slash should have cut Natalie's throat but sliced through air instead. It seemed the female had martial arts training. A possibility that Ka-Di had failed to allow for.

Natalie came off the bunk, grabbed Sa-Lo, and used him as a shield. The force blade stopped, but just barely. Ka-Di growled and prepared to attack. But Sa-Lo made that unnecessary by triggering the sleep bomb. He carried five of them for use during their escape. A strange odor caught Natalie's attention, caused her nasal passages to constrict, and was gone before she could think about it. She hit the deck with a thump.

Ka-Di watched saw the human fall, gave thanks for nostril filters, and checked her pulse. It was slow but steady.

Sa-Lo, still short of breath, leaned on the bulkhead. "Humans are annoying."

Ka-Di signaled agreement. "Shall I cut her throat?"

Sa-Lo held up a paw. "No, the pirates will take care of it for us. Besides, you know how emotional the humans are. What if Jord gave chase? Our escape has priority."

The warrior signaled his understanding, restored the weapon to its sheath, and wondered what La-Ma would do. She'd spare the human, he felt sure of that, but what of the rest? How would she judge their plans to secure the wormhole with military force if necessary? Would she approve? There was no way to tell.

"Come," Sa-Lo said, "it's time to leave the ship."

Tor Sanko, comfortably ensconced in his wraparound command chair, placed a grape on his tongue, popped the tight green skin, and savored the juice that flooded his mouth. "Pilot . . . time to contact, please."

The pilot, a cyborg who was literally one with his ship, knew Sanko would be unhappy and kept his voice neutral. "Four hours . . . fifteen minutes."

Sanko glanced at the heads-up displays, tapped numbers into a keypad, and frowned. "The *Will of God* will enter the planet's atmosphere in four hours, *five minutes* according to my calculations."

The cyborg held his nonexistent breath. "Yes, sir."

Sanko's voice was dangerously calm. "Please explain. You indicated that we had more than enough time two hours ago."

The pilot wished he had legs, wished he could run, but knew he couldn't. "It would seem that the ship picked up speed, sir, not much, but enough to open a small gap."

"Then increase our speed, you fool," Sanko snapped, "or I'll cut your sensors."

The cyborg, whose only contact with the external world was through the ship's electronics, started to gibber. There was nothing he feared more than the deathlike darkness of sensory deprivation. "We're going full out, sir . . . ask engineering."

Sanko called the chief engineer, confirmed the pilot's data, and swore out loud. Assuming nothing happened to the other ship's drives, and she made planetfall as projected, the jacker would have a decision to make. He could follow the *Will of God* down and destroy her on the ground, or wait in orbit and attack when she lifted. The first was the more direct, and therefore more satisfying, possibility, but the second made better sense.

The Place of Wandering Waters carried a PTL rating of 16,

which suggested a primitive, largely undeveloped planet having some advanced technology. So, given the fact that backwater planets had an unsettling tendency to acquire missile launchers prior to microwave ovens, the locals could have all sorts of nasty little toys stashed in the trees. The thought made Sanko angry. *Very* angry. "The pilot needs a rest. Cut his feeds."

The second officer didn't like the cyborg. She caressed a row of buttons, gloried in the knowledge that the pilot could feel her touch, and smiled as she cut his sensors. The com link went last, so the crew could hear the cyborg scream, and reflect on what it meant.

Rollo was bored, irritable, and given to unexpected barrel rolls, all of which made him poor company, and a rather unstable platform on which to work, play, or snooze. That being the case, Torx did what any self-respecting Treeth would do under similar circumstances, and sought the company of other more reasonable beings.

Like his distant ancestors before him, Torx was well equipped for travel through the trees, and took pleasure in the long series of leaps that carried him from a platform near the pool of contemplation, deep into the sun-dappled woods. Despite the fact that his route carried him through the forest's upper canopy, the path had been used thousands of times before, and was clearly marked. Smaller branches had been broken off, while the stronger, more mature limbs had developed thick layers of protective bark and were worn from constant use.

There were breaks too, places where ancient giants had succumbed to the ravages of wind, water, and time. Torx could imagine roots breaking free from the wet, swampy soil, branches crackling as the disaster began, and a long, drawn-out groan as younger, still viable trees surrendered to the giant's weight and were carried to their deaths.

The result was a gap in the foliage, a place where the sun could coax new growth from the ground, and the forest could strengthen itself. When they encountered gaps such as those, the ancient Treeth had been forced to turn aside, or, if determined to proceed, face the carnivores on the ground, a situation that had led to the development of clubs, bows, and, after a sufficient amount of time had passed, firearms.

Those days were gone, of course, the gaps having been bridged by pulley-mounted T-handles on monofilament line. As if to emphasize that fact, an elder passed Torx traveling in the opposite direction. Her motor-driven pulley whirred loudly as it pulled her upward. Torx signed his respect and marveled at her dignity. To be dragged through the trees like a side of meat! So much for the benefits of old age.

The glen was huge, more than five hundred feet across, and ringed with trees. Most were old, dating to prehistorical times, but some were little more than hand-planted saplings, the giants of the future. Torx dropped through layer after layer of Treeth, all eating, playing, and gossiping, fingers flying as they signed back and forth.

The cradle tree, so called because of the way its branches had cradled his race, was thousands of years old, and so dominated the center of the clearing that nothing could grow in its shadow. It was said that the great Folar, companion to King Halory, had held court in the lower branches of the tree, arguing for the alliance that still bound the races together, and swilling endless tankards of dra.

Just being there made Torx feel good, and it wasn't long before he encountered beings that he knew. The first hour passed pleasantly enough, as he flirted with an administrator from the Department of Rivers, Lakes, and Dams, but the real payoff came as the result of chance.

Lorno, a rather tiresome Treeth who hailed from the northern swamps, and actually bragged of the fact, was busy complaining about his boss, a mid-level functionary in the Department of Defense, when he dropped what amounted to a juicy nugget. It seemed that a vessel named the *Will of God* had entered their system and requested emergency inbound clearance. A human called Tord . . . or was it Ford? . . . insisted that jackers were after them. Never mind the fact that the second vessel denied the charge and seemed peaceful enough. Could his audience imagine anything so absurd?

Torx could, and, having made some hurried excuses, raced to tell Rollo. Yes, the fact that *Will of God* had apparently been targeted by a pirate *could* be unrelated to their case, but Torx, like most law enforcement beings, had little faith in coincidence. No, there were other possibilities, all of them bad. The Treeth cursed his friend's unwillingness to wear a vibcom, picked his way up through the maze of crisscrossed branches, and felt the sun hit his face. He missed the initial jump, hoped no one had seen him, and grabbed a branch. The rest was easy.

Sa-Lo left the cabin, followed by Ka-Di. A quick glance confirmed that the corridor was empty. The Traa strolled toward the ship's stern. If discovered, they'd pretend to be lost. As with most vessels of her size, the *Willie* carried a number of auxiliary craft, including two shuttles that doubled as lifeboats, a pair of maintenance sleds, and four ten-person life pods, none of which had a propulsion system of its own. Which was why Ka-Di had chosen the shuttles as their escape vehicles of choice, and more specifically the starboard unit, since it was newer than its counterpart, and theoretically more reliable. He had checked the controls and discovered that they were well within his training parameters. Though long, and somewhat boring, the journey would be safe.

A hatch opened, a human emerged, and Sa-Lo felt a sudden stab of apprehension. They were a long way from the shuttle bays and clearly off limits. Light glinted off the man's face. His voice was gruff. "Sorry, but this section of the ship is restricted to crew. The lounge is this way."

Ka-Di nodded as if in agreement, allowed the human to pass, and slapped him on the back. The injector squirted liquid sedative through the engineer's clothes and the pores of his skin. A human would have folded, but O'Tool was a cyborg. He swayed and tried to communicate. "O'Tool to bridge . . . watch out for . . ."

Desperate now, and on the verge of a more permanent solution, Ka-Di tore the headset off. The engineer frowned, clawed at his back, and fell over backwards.

The Traa ran. Down the corridor, past the heat exchangers, and through an altar. A trio of plastic goddesses fell and rolled away. Voices yelled, and feet started to pound. The corridor curved away from the heavily shielded drives, along the ship's hull, and past the emergency control room.

Ka-Di started to lag. His breath came in gasps. Sa-Lo put an arm around his companion's waist, lifted him off the deck, and ran for the shuttle. It loomed ahead, its lock eternally open, ready for launch. Sa-Lo pushed Ka-Di through the hatch, hit the "launch" button, and pulled a hand weapon. He didn't *want* to shoot anyone, but was determined to escape. The hatch whirred, a computer droned instructions at them, and a face appeared. It was still there, shouting orders, when the hatch closed.

The *Willie* sealed herself against hard vacuum, a klaxon sounded, and the shuttle pushed itself off. Artificial gravity disappeared as the shuttle accelerated away from the larger and presumably dangerous freighter. The Traa lost contact with the deck. They flailed about, found handholds, and hoped for the best.

Captain Jord, who had been on the bridge during the entire episode, brought his fist down on the console with such force that a hand comp jumped and fell. "I want information . . . and I want it now!"

"I found Voss in her cabin, sir," a voice reported. "She's unconscious."

"O'Tool's coming around," another voice chimed in. "They hit him with a slap shot."

"It was the Traa," a third crew person volunteered. "I saw them board the shuttle."

"Shall I give chase?" Russo inquired eagerly. "We could nail them in fifteen minutes or so."

Jord rubbed his chin and scanned the readouts that hung in midair. The idea was tempting, damned tempting, but he had other things to think about as well. "The pirates? How are they doing?"

"Gaining . . . but slowly."

"Will we beat them into the atmosphere?"

"Yes, assuming both speeds remain constant."

Jord sighed. "Then let the pirates have them. There's no profit in a fight, especially if we lose. Keep me informed."

Having thrown their weight around, and successfully exaggerated their authority, Rollo and Torx gained entrance to the Defense Command's control grotto, an underground lake accessed by elevator. It was there, beneath the latticework of catwalks used by the Treeth staff, and hip-deep in the thermally warmed water, that Rollo, with Torx standing on his back, watched the drama unfold. Floating video screens, each shaped like a cube, told the story.

First, for reasons that weren't clear, a shuttle parted company with ship number one. That raised the possibility that the second, and allegedly hostile, vessel would snap it up, but no, they seemed uninterested. A rather boring period ensued during which the first ship, broadcasting all manner of emergency signals, headed for the atmosphere, while the second vessel, still protesting its innocence, followed.

Still, it wasn't too long before the *Will of God* entered the atmosphere and the situation became crystal clear. The second vessel, ominously silent at this juncture, ignored all orders from orbital control and followed the freighter down. Threats, which the locals were powerless to carry out, proved equally ineffective. The co-marshals, well aware that the woman who could be their most important witness was very much at risk, held their collective breath.

"They're heading for the surface," Cowles said disapprovingly.

"I have eyes," Sanko replied irritably, drumming his fingers on the console that adjoined his command chair. "Tell me something useful." Sanko was worried that the shuttle, long gone by now, carried the very people Orr wanted him to kill. Still, given the choice between chasing the shuttle, which might turn out to be a high-priced decoy, and pursuing the ship, which was worth a great deal of money, the answer seemed obvious. The shuttle thing was annoying, though—

and the jacker wished he could have snatched it up.

Cowles, who had grown increasingly weary of Sanko's arrogance, considered the energy weapon taped below the panel in front of him. He could remove the device, turn, and shoot Sanko through the head. But what of the crew? Would they back his play? Only if it was in their interest to do so. He wished they had the imagination to see how dangerous the situation was. Especially if Sanko followed the merchant ship down into the atmosphere. Neither vessel had been designed for combat under those conditions. And what of the locals? Would they stay neutral? Or side with the *Will of God*? There was no sign of military ships in the vicinity—but there very well might be surface-to-air missiles. The weapon beckoned, and the tension grew.

That part of the planet's surface not obscured by cloud cover was greenish blue. Sanko struggled with the decision. Should he follow the *Will of God* down? Or wait till she attempted to lift? The second was the more conservative choice, and therefore the safest. But what if a third ship arrived? The balance of power could shift in his opponent's favor and force him to run. Where to? Orr would find him, that was certain, and notify the Hidalgo Crime Syndicate. They'd do the rest. No, messy though it might be, it was best to take the ship now, or, failing that, destroy her in the atmosphere. The jacker leaned back, took some eye drops, and addressed the crew. "Secure the ship for battle. Arm all weapons systems. Take her down."

Natalie was strapped into the backup control slot. She'd been conscious for a couple of hours now, but had a headache, and wished the already subdued lighting was even dimmer. O'Tool, similarly recovered from the slap shot, reclined next to her. The encounter with the Traa had left Natalie angry and shaken.

Still, the crew interpreted the run-in as proof of her innocence, and that, plus the attack on O'Tool, had restored her credibility. So much so that Natalie had been asked to assume her previous duties, including the normally innocuous position of weapons officer, and the title that went with it. The pirates had followed the *Willie* down into the planet's atmosphere, and Jord was understandably worried. "Bridge to weapons control . . . how's it look, Guns?"

Natalie saw O'Tool out of the corner of her eye. Like the rest of the crew, he wore space armor in case they were holed. She couldn't tell where his body began and the pressure suit ended. He was watching and waiting to see if she'd make a mistake. Well, screw him. And the horse he rode in on. She scanned the board. The *Willie* mounted four missile launchers and an equal number of energy cannon. Light armament for a warship, but respectable for a merchant vessel. "All systems green, sir . . . standing by."

"Good," Jord replied, eyeing the information before him. "Okay, everybody, here's the plan. The pirate packs more throw weight than we do, that's a given, but isn't free to use it. Not without blowing the ship to dust. That being the case, I plan to turn and let 'em have it. Guns, you're the expert, what do you think?"

Natalie mustered some saliva and pushed it around her mouth. Having never fired a shot in anger, she felt anything but expert. The discussion of strategy would have been unthinkable on a cruiser but was typical of merchant vessels. The officer tried to sound confident. "Good strategy, sir. I suggest a diversion. Something to draw their missiles and give us a crack at them."

Jord had invited Natalie's input but hadn't expected to receive any. Damn the woman anyway! Time was passing, and she was about to waste some of it. "Yes? Go ahead."

The *Will of God* shuddered as she passed through a high-altitude jet stream. Natalie felt the seconds ticking away. The words poured out and nearly ran together. "Let's rig the life pods to run hot . . . and eject them as we turn. We wait, they fire, and blam! We take 'em." Every spacer knew it took at least five seconds to ready and fire a flight of ship-to-ship missiles, so Jord had no difficulty appreciating the value of Natalie's suggestion. He was surprised and struggled not to show it. "Excellent! We'll fire the cannon too. O'Tool, you heard number three. Rig the pods."

The cyborg winced at the extravagant use of valuable equipment and reached for one of his many keyboards. It swung into place and rippled with light. "Yes, sir. I need ten minutes."

"You have five," Jord said, watching the distance between the two ships narrow. "Make them count."

Cowles was afraid. He knew that for sure. What he *didn't* know was which option scared him the most: killing Sanko and dealing with the consequences of his treachery, or *not* killing Sanko and dealing with the consequences of that.

It should be a no-brainer. Wait in orbit, pot the *Will of God* as she lifted, and reel her in. Just like fishing with dear old good-for-nothing Dad. Except that Sanko chose to chase the merchant vessel and place his own ship at risk.

Cowles touched the weapon with his knee and turned so that Sanko appeared in his peripheral vision. It seemed as if the jacker was staring at him, eyes open wide, lips straight and narrow. Could the captain see his first officer thoughts? Ice water leached into Cowles's veins, trickled through his body, and froze his extremities.

Jord watched real honest-to-god video of the planet's surface as the freighter dropped through thick clouds and leveled out above an endless maze of lakes, ponds, pools, rivers, streams, and channels. It was a place of wandering waters indeed, and not where he hoped to end his life. His gods ruled Earth and extended their influence to New Delhi after that. Did the deities live everywhere? Or were they linked to the soil from which they had sprung? And how far did their influence extend? Far enough to find his soul? Most said yes. Were they correct? He pushed the question away. The ship slowed, reached equilibrium, and hovered in place. The combat clock continued to run. He waited for a row of zeros to appear and uttered a prayer. Echoes were heard in every part of the ship.

•   •   •

Sanko followed his quarry down through the clouds, grinned wolfishly, and watched the distance narrow. There were no signs of opposition. This was going to be easier than he'd thought. They'd catch up, force her down, and waste the crew. Orr would be pleased, he'd pocket half a mil, and the syndicate could kiss his ass. All he needed was a quiet planet, not *too* isolated, but away from . . . Cowles interrupted. "The merchant ship has slowed, sir."

Sanko nodded agreeably. "She's probably going to surrender. But keep an eye on her."

Cowles acknowledged the order, saw the *Will of God* turn, and knew Sanko was wrong.

In her capacity as gunnery officer, Natalie had temporary command of the ship. She moved the joystick to the right, swore at the cumbersome way that the vessel responded, and waited for the moment when she'd be bow-on to her pursuer. It seemed to take forever. Each passing moment exposed more and more of the *Willie*'s hull, until midpoint was passed, and their profile grew steadily smaller.

Sanko, confident that his vessel could take anything the freighter had to dish out, and eager to get the whole thing over with, spent the intervening time shedding all the speed he could. The strategy worked too, except that by the time the ships made visual contact the Willie was three-quarters of the way through her turn, and presented a much smaller target. However, due to the fact that Sanko wanted to capture the trader, not destroy her, the question was more academic than practical.

Natalie, her eyes locked on the screen, watched the other ship approach, willed the bow to come around, and breathed a sigh of relief when it did. She looked at O'Tool, received his nod, and launched the life pods. Three seconds later their specially rigged life-support systems went critical and their heat signatures started to bloom.

The weapons tech could still feel the pain in his testicles, not to mention his forehead. There was nothing wrong with his eyesight or reaction time, however. He saw pods bloom, blew chaff, and warned the bridge. "I have missile launch . . . repeat, missile launch . . . four and tracking."

Sanko had received the news direct from the ship's onboard computer. His eyebrows shot toward his carefully groomed hair. The sheep had teeth. "Destroy incoming missiles."

Lights glowed on the technician's board. He played them like a piano, felt the ship shudder, and watched telemetry. All systems green . . . missiles running true.

Energy cannon began to fire. The tech watched their heat sinks with one eye and the monitors with the other. Then the impossible happened. Never mind the fact that no merchant ship he'd ever heard of carried more than four launchers, and never mind the fact that it took a minimum of five seconds to reload, the *Will of God* fired a second salvo. Since she was a helluva lot closer this time, her ordnance struck before he could warn anyone.

The ship staggered under the force of three separate explosions; a cacophony of shouts, alarms, and klaxons was heard; and the bow started to drop. Smoke drifted, and voices babbled in Sanko's ears. He hit the override. "Get the bow up, damn it! Bring her around!"

The second officer did her best, but she wasn't half as good as the cyborg, and the response was painfully slow. Sanko began to scream at her, and Cowles realized what scared him most. His energy weapon bored a hole through Sanko's brain. His eyes were wide open when he died.

Rollo and Torx, along with most of the planet's senior defense staff, watched the pirate ship crash via airborne remotes, and turned to each other in amazement. Nothing like this had ever happened before. Not on *their* planet, anyway. Ground forces, medical teams, and an ecological contamination unit were dispatched to the crash site. Rollo and Torx assumed overall command. The Dromo was ebullient as he churned toward the elevator. "Time to get a move on, old friend. Our guests have arrived, and it would be rude to keep them waiting."

15

Scatter what you have to the winds. What you need will appear.

Insula Balloric
Du'Zaath mystic
Standard year 1916

The Planet New Hope

The *Nebula Storm* had taken up moorage toward the center of Oro's bay, where her crew would be safe from the latest plague variant and the intermittent labor riots that troubled the city. The bright blue water taxi pitched up and down as it passed through another boat's wake. Ari braced herself against the motion and marveled at the fact that the launch was made of wood rather than composites. She turned and saw the *Storm* wallow as waves rolled in off the ocean. She was an old beast, her hull scarred by countless reentries, patched where meteorites had hit. Her shape reminded Ari of the manta rays that roamed the oceans of old Earth. The boatman took exception to an unwieldy raft and passed as close as he could. The raft master's wife waved a frying pan and swore like the sailor she was.

It was hard to know what to feel. Should she be happy that the long, boring journey was over? Annoyed because the return voyage would start in just seven days? Assuming she found Voss, that is . . . which shouldn't be hard. No, it would be a snap. Find the school and you find the boy. Take the brat aside, explain the situation, and pay his way home. Simple as that. Or, take his thumb and arrange for an accident.

The alternative, which involved waiting for the next ship to arrive, was nearly unthinkable. All her research had led to the same conclusion: New Hope was a godforsaken pus pit. Certainly not a place to spend much time in. Still, supposing she had to stay, a thick wad of credits would see her through.

It was shit work, Ari knew that, but the pay was good, and she never stopped hoping that the on-again, off-again relationship with Orr would deepen and evolve into a more permanent relationship. Not love, that was asking too much, but a partnership similar to the one Howard and Mary Voss enjoyed. It was too bad about the bomb . . . she had admired their courage.

The waterman put the helm over, shifted into reverse, and brought her fantasy to an end as the boat bumped the wooden dock. "East landing, ma'am. Just like you said. Watch your step."

Ari paid the man less than she would have if her daydream had been allowed to run full course, hung the bag from her left shoulder, and mounted the water-slicked plank. It gave lightly, but cleats prevented her from slipping.

The embarcadero curved in both directions and served as a platform for warehouses, boats, nets, cargo modules, cranes, and makeshift shacks. The moment Ari reached the top of the stairs, she was mobbed by street vendors, most of whom were children who seemed intent on pushing, shoving, and yelling their way into her good graces.

Ari spotted a skinny youngster who looked a lot like she had ten years before, pointed a finger, and used her most authoritative voice. "You! Yes, you! I need ground transportation . . . but I don't need a mob. Lose the crowd."

The children were masters of the hard sell and more than a little reluctant to abandon a rich prize. It took the better part of five minutes for the street girl to disperse the crowd.

Finally, with the off-worlder all to herself, the youngster

motioned, and Ari followed. Horns honked as they crossed the street. Vehicles, some made more from wood than metal, chugged back and forth. Dense slums climbed the lower slopes of a cone-shaped hill. A blanket of warm, fetid air wrapped Ari in a damp embrace. Signs offered everything from food to acupuncture. The street waif, who continued to defend her client from a nonstop assault by vendors, beggars, and con artists, led the bodyguard into a narrow passageway.

Crude adobe walls rose to either side, bulged inward, and hung overhead. Strips of sunlight lit the way, and the smell of urine filled the air. Most people would have found the situation threatening, but Ari, who had been raised on the lowest sub-deck of an island-sized krill harvester, wasn't impressed. She did keep an eye on her back trail, however, and kept her gun hand free.

The juxtaposition of the spaceship in the harbor and the poverty around her spoke volumes. New Hope seemed like a strange place to send an only son, but, judging from her time spent with Carnaby Orr, rich people were weird. How else could you account for the fact that Orr, who was unimaginably wealthy, still wanted more?

A planter crowded with dead vegetation offered a rest for her boot. The tie didn't need tying but she tied it anyway. Ari checked behind her, and wondered why anyone would stop to admire a wall of graffiti. The tail was of medium height, slightly overweight, and too well dressed. She figured him for a thug, a freelancer employed by the Traa, or a pro repping Orr's enemies. The second seemed most likely.

The bodyguard finished her skit, nodded to her guide, and climbed a flight of terracelike steps. Children built dams, channeled the dirty water into quickly flowing streams, and launched scraps of wood. Some raced alongside while others yelled encouragement. Ari took comfort from the knowledge that while an empty passageway could signal an ambush, this one bustled with activity.

The alley, if that's what it could properly be called, narrowed and crossed even darker corridors to either side. Seeing that, Ari hurried to close the gap with her guide, pushed the girl into a passageway, and staggered under the force of a reverse elbow strike.

The girl, certain that her client meant to kill her, pulled a dagger as she turned. It was made out of green glass. Similar weapons were available from street vendors everywhere. Though not especially durable, they were razor-sharp. Ari backed away, shook her head, and held a finger to her lips. Would the girl understand? Or insist on a dart? The bodyguard gestured toward the alleyway and the man who would soon appear. The teenager paused, watched warily, and kept the weapon ready.

Ari offered what she hoped was an agreeable smile, motioned for the girl to wait, and watched while a woman with an enormous load of firewood passed the entrance.

Worried that his subjects had given him slip, and eager to catch up, the tail hurried into the trap. He was only fifteen feet away when the bodyguard stepped into the light. Her body hid the handgun. The man stopped, and Ari crooked her finger.

The tail looked surprised, took three steps forward, and reached under his jacket. Ari frowned disapprovingly and shot him in the right knee. The airgun made very little noise. The man screamed, grabbed his knee, and fainted.

Such were the conditions on New Hope that people disappeared into their dwellings and passersby averted their eyes rather than inadvertently get involved in a mugging.

Ari dragged the man into the dark, took his weapon, and slapped his face. His eyes popped open and he looked frightened. His pockets produced little more than a small wad of currency, a backup magazine for his pistol, and a porno reader. Ari tossed the cube over her shoulder and slapped him again. "Who the hell are you? And who do you work for?"

The man, who had folded himself into the fetal position, wrapped his arms around his injured knee and groaned. "A doctor . . . I need a doctor."

"Yes, you do," Ari said sympathetically. "That hurts, doesn't it? Now answer my question. What's your name?"

The man winced, bit his lower lip, and confirmed what Ari

had suspected. "I'm a freelancer. The name is Pardo. Sam Pardo. Please, I need a doctor now."

"In a minute," Ari promised. "As soon as you answer my questions. Who sent you?"

The answer both amazed and frightened her. The man grimaced. "I'm on a retainer from the Department of Commerce. They told me to watch for someone from Orr Enterprises."

Ari grabbed a handful of his jacket. "Why? What are they after?"

"I don't know," the man said, tears running down his cheeks. "They didn't tell me. I was supposed to tail you and report. That's all."

Ari believed him and was afraid that whatever passed for the local police would arrive soon. She stood, took aim, and put a dart through the man's temple. The girl was already in the process of backing away when the bodyguard turned and raised her pistol. It should have been easy to pull the trigger, and rid herself of a witness, but something stopped her. Pity? No. Well, yes, of a sort. The girl reminded Ari of herself, of who she'd been before she'd fought her way free of the harvester and left her home world behind. Or had she? How was this any different from the butchery of bilge city? Or the other hellholes she'd survived?

Ari holstered the weapon and left the next move to the teenager. Gradually, like a wild animal nibbling on a morsel of handheld food, the girl inched forward. The dagger slid into its sheath, and her steps became a swagger. Ari grinned, nodded approvingly, and gestured toward the sun-splashed passageway. "Come on. It's time to go."

The girl waited for the off-worlder to proceed her, slipped the man's gun into the waistband of her trousers, and followed along behind. The weapon was worth a lot of money. She could sell it or, better yet, model herself on the woman in front of her. The girl smiled and imitated the way Ari walked. Neither saw the glint of reflected light from a distant rooftop, the woman who had tears running down her cheeks, or the badge on her vest.

•   •   •

Though prepared for the worst, Myra found life in the Sharma household to be relatively pleasant, especially when compared with the obvious alternatives. She'd been assigned to the huge whitewashed kitchen, a bustling place full of spotless pots, pans, and utensils, all of which had their own special hooks, and were worth a considerable amount of money, a fact that hadn't escaped chef Ubi Fimbre, who imposed a rigid code of discipline and took inventory twice a day. That in spite of the fact that he had arrived in chains, established an open-air eatery down in the slums, and been recruited by the Sharmas.

Still, it wasn't long before Myra discovered that Fimbre's bark was a lot worse than his bite, and adjusted to her new surroundings. Fimbre was a small man with dark hair, a pencil-thin mustache, and quick brown eyes. Myra was headed for the storeroom when they fastened on her. He held a tray and shoved it in her direction. "Here, take this to Mr. Sharma and be snappy about it. He likes his coffee hot."

Like the rest of the servants, Myra knew that Sharma was either the most or second most powerful person in the house, depending on whether one subscribed to the theory that Mrs. Sharma was little more than an extension of her husband's will, or the theory that she was a clever manipulator who made him dance like a puppet.

In any case, Mr. Sharma was important, as was the errand, since only the most trusted members of the staff were allowed to serve the family. Myra sought such a position not because of the status involved, or the privileges attendant thereto, but because of the information that could be gleaned. Information she could use to free Dorn and herself from what amounted to slavery. There had to be a way out, and Myra was determined to find it.

The china, which had been made on one of the southern islands, was white with hand-painted blue fish that chased each other all around the rims. It probably cost more than her father made in a year. It rattled slightly as she carried the service into the formal dining hall, and from there to the day room, which was large and sunny, with lots of white furniture and enormous windows that looked out on the water. Water that was dotted here and there by the remains of gigantic starships. She wondered if Dorn was out there, cutting steel by hand, or dodging the pieces that fell from above.

Some said that Mrs. Sharma had a sharp tongue, but Myra had seen none of that in her contacts with the woman, and liked her in spite of the fact that she shouldn't. She was forty or so and had just started to thicken around the middle, a fact made less obvious by the colorful saris she wore and the quickness with which she moved. She had black hair, braided into waist-long ropes, and pretty eyes. They twinkled as Myra approached. "The table will be fine, dear . . . thank you."

Mr. Sharma, an intense-looking man with a slightly hooked nose, hardly noticed. He accepted a cup of coffee from his wife without taking his eyes off his hand comp. The liquid must have been sufficiently hot, because he made no comment to the contrary.

Myra had backed away as she'd been taught to do and was about to turn when Seleen, the Sharmas's daughter, entered the room from the main hallway. She was fresh from a shower and was drying her hair with a towel. In spite of the fact that Seleen was Myra's age, she looked older, and reminded the servant girl of the vid stars she'd watched in the village theater. Their eyes met, and Seleen tossed the towel in her direction. "Here . . . take care of that, would you? And tell Fimbre I want some tea."

In spite of the fact that their village was poor, the residents had treated each other with respect, and Myra felt blood color her cheeks. Words fought to be spoken, but she held them back. Myra had a plan, or the beginnings of one, and sacrifices must be made. She caught the towel, dropped a curtsy, and left the room.

Seleen, who had seen the conflict on the other girl's face, smiled and flopped into a chair. Life was boring on the peninsula, and fun was where you found it.

Jana was right. The shift boss *did* like to pick on the same people over and over, and, judging from the last eight hours,

Dorn was indeed elected. No matter how hard he worked, or how much metal he moved, it wasn't good enough. How many times had he heard servos whine as the exoskeleton approached? How many times had the whip fallen across his shoulders? How many times had Castor laughed, then stalked away? Ten? Fifteen? Twenty? It had been a long, miserable day, and, if it hadn't been for the leather armor that Jana had sewn for him, and secured beneath what remained of his shirt, Dorn might have been permanently injured.

As it was, he just *wanted* to die as the siren blew and the haulers waded ashore. He was tired, sore, and frightened. Would this be one of the days when the guards searched them? Plucking little bits of wire and metal from their rags and laughing while they tucked them away? And why didn't they search *every* day?

Jana said it was because the company benefited from the black market economy, and she was right. By allowing workers to steal small quantities of metal, the Sharma family enabled them to provide their own food and shelter. Still, the penalties for getting caught were quite severe, up to and including crucifixion. Dorn felt his pulse quicken, felt the beam brush across his forehead, and stepped through the arch.

Would a voice call? Tell him to stop? Order him to disrobe? He counted the seconds off and breathed a sigh of relief at ten. The others turned, grinned happily, and went their separate ways, Jana to her shanty, the twins to their hut, and Dorn to whatever shelter he could find.

A number of weeks, he wasn't sure how many, had passed since Sa-Lo had kicked him out. And, in spite of the fact that Dorn had spent a good deal of time and energy searching for quarters, he hadn't found any. Nights, many of them cold and miserable, had been spent out in the open. Tonight, though, thanks to some slivers of metal that Jana and he had surreptitiously worked free from a hull plate, he could count on a vendor-supplied meal and some floor space in one of the cleaner flophouses.

By working every day, and refusing to go there for anything more than a toothbrush, toothpaste, and a bar of soap, Dorn had managed to rack up a few credits at the company store. But he was saving those to buy some hand tools with which he could start a part-time business or, god forbid, secure medical attention if he were injured. Plus he had Myra to think about, and her needs. He was still determined to make contact with her.

Dorn followed one of the now familiar trails up from the beach and was headed for his favorite food vendor when he heard a commotion to his right. Sparks flew up as a crowd gathered around a fire. Curious, and eager for free entertainment, Dorn worked his way in. The sun had started to set, and the fire's warmth felt good against his skin.

A coarse-looking man, with eyes that seemed a little too bright, dragged a box in front of the fire and stepped on top of it. Then, reaching out like a minister to his congregation, the man addressed his audience. "Step right up, ladies and gentlemen! The merchandise is waiting and the time is now. Are you tired of fetching water? Hauling firewood from the beach? Battling the mud that cakes your floor?"

"You bet your ass I am!" one woman shouted. "Come on over, I'll put you to work!"

The crowd laughed and the man laughed with them. "Thanks for the offer, kind lady, and if it weren't for my love-mate here, I'd take you up on that. Besides, seeing as how there ain't enough of me to go around, the rest of the crowd would be disappointed. No, I have a better answer, and one that don't eat as much as I do neither. Come on, darlin', bring them little cherubs out here, and give these folks a look-see."

Dorn felt something catch in his throat as a woman stepped out of a cargo module, tugged on a rope, and pulled five children after her. They were a sad-looking bunch, with pinched little faces, eyes that seemed too big, and rags for clothes. None was more than ten years old, and Dorn was shocked. How could anyone sell another human being? Then he remembered where he was, checked the faces around him, and saw curiosity, interest, and yes, a little bit of greed. His fellows, being little more than slaves themselves, saw nothing wrong with the proceedings.

"So," the man said importantly, "who wants to make the first bid? Ten? Do I hear ten ounces of metal for this fine young specimen? Look at him, a good body, good bones, and as willing as they come. You'll never fetch water again."

"Three!" someone said. "I bid three!" and the auction had started. Dorn eyed the boy, a pathetic-looking creature with an open sore on his left leg, and fingered the metal in his pocket. He could buy the boy, and free him from his slavery, but what then? He had no food, no shelter to offer, and might be doing the child a disservice.

It was a moot question, however, since the bidding soon outstripped his ability to pay, and the boy went to a hard-looking woman who wore her hair in a bun. The rest of the children followed, some taking longer than others, until the last was sold. The crowd eddied, and was about to disperse, when the man waved his arms in the air. "Hold, friends and neighbors, we have one last offering. A bargain, if you will, a small but tasty morsel, who, though under the weather at the moment, will be of considerable value when she recovers. Bring that bundle of joy out here, honeybun, and show the people what a bargain looks like."

Dorn turned and watched as the woman entered the cargo module and reappeared with something draped across her arms. It was a little girl, perhaps seven or eight, so ill that she appeared to be unconscious. Her head hung over the woman's arm and bobbed loosely as she walked.

The crowd groaned. A man said, "Why, she ain't worth diddly squat," and a woman shook her head in disgust. "Geez, you call that merchandise? Give me a break."

The auctioneer, concerned lest the crowd desert him, held up his hands. "Wait! She's a bargain, I tell you! Heaven waiting to happen. How 'bout it, gentlemen? You like 'em young? Well, here's your chance."

Dorn, sick at what he'd heard, took a step forward. A second man did likewise. His tongue flicked over chapped lips. His eyes had a hungry look. "I'll take her . . . give ya an inch o' wire."

Dorn felt the metal in his pocket and guessed that he had

three or four ounces. "Three ounces of metal . . . and that's my final offer."

The slave owner looked at the other bidder, saw the shake of his head, and beamed broadly. "Sold to the boy for three ounces of metal! And don't forget, folks, we buy as well as sell 'em, so if you need a little extra cash, don't hesitate to stop by. See you next week."

Dorn handed the metal over to the woman, who transferred the girl to his arms and turned away. The girl moaned, said something incoherent, and lapsed into unconsciousness. The crowd began to disperse. A man said something obscene. People laughed. Dorn blushed and hurried away.

It wasn't until five minutes later, when Dorn found himself wandering down a path with nowhere to go, that he realized what he'd done. He had no place to take the girl, no medical skills, and, after paying for her, no means to purchase food. What would he do?

It seemed as if his feet had known the answer all along, because Dorn was halfway to La-So's cargo module before he made a conscious decision to go there. The trail was pretty much as it had been weeks before, less muddy if anything, but more treacherous with the girl in his arms. Night had fallen, and the Traa's door was closed, but light gleamed through the window.

Given the fact that it was nearly impossible to free up a hand, Dorn kicked the door instead. It opened, the alien took one look at the girl, and motioned Dorn forward. "Put her over there. What happened?"

Dorn explained while the alien checked the girl's vital signs, made strange clucking sounds, and marshaled his meager medical supplies. The female had a fever, that was obvious. But why? There were various possibilities. He worked his way through each one of them.

"So," Dorn said, bringing his narrative to a close, "I came here."

"It's well that you did," the Traa said evenly, "because the company doctors are reluctant to invest time, energy, and pharmaceuticals in anyone not capable of hard physical work.

Fortunately, one of my ex-patients works as an orderly at the clinic and steals medications one capsule at a time. Assuming my diagnosis is correct, this child will be better in five or six days. What's her name?''

Dorn shrugged. ''Somebody said she wasn't worth diddly squat, but I never heard them call her by name.''

''Then Diddly it is,'' the Traa said, ''until we think of something more fitting.''

Dorn nodded, stood, and backed toward the door. ''Thanks, La-So. I'll pay you the moment they pay me.''

The alien looked at the girl and up to the boy. There was something new in his eyes. Respect? Admiration? Affection? Whatever it was made Dorn feel good. ''No, I am the one who owes you, for the privilege of serving another. Make a bed on the floor. It is better than sleeping on the ground.''

Dorn ate the Traa's cooking and slept on his floor. It was the best night's sleep he'd had in a long, long time.

16

You learn something the day you die. You learn how to die.

Katherine Anne Porter
American writer
Circa 1950

The Place of Wandering Waters
and the Planet Mechnos

The pirate ship went in hard and cut a broad swathe through two miles of thick forest before slamming to a stop. The hull, parts of which were red-hot, started a class three canopy fire. In spite of the fact that hardly a day passed without some rain falling in the huge temperate zones that occupied most of the planet's northern and southern hemispheres, the topmost foliage received a great deal of sun, and was very dry. So dry that lightning started hundreds of fires every year, which, though momentarily devastating, had the meritorious effect of clearing old growth and making room for new. Young, healthy trees had an amazing ability to survive such conflagrations and even benefited from them.

Still, Torx didn't like the smoke that boiled up to merge with the lead-gray sky and, like his kinsmen, harbored a deep and abiding fear of habitat-destroying flames. This was a phobia not shared by his water-dwelling friend, who seemed oblivious to the sparks, branches, and other bits of burning debris that plopped into the water around them, hissed like death spitters, and were soon extinguished. Which was fine for Rollo, safe within his fireproof environment, but didn't help the Treeth one bit.

Conditions grew worse as they led a procession of battle-ready teams along one of the many channels in toward the crash site. The ship had buried its nose in a low-lying hill. In spite of the fact that the better part of a day had passed, flames still fed on combustibles within it, and licked at the vessel's badly crumpled superstructure.

Rollo touched mud with his plate-shaped feet, lumbered out of the water, and felt Torx stir. The reason was obvious. Although most of the canopy in the area over their heads had been consumed, isolated patches continued to burn, showering them with debris. There hadn't been much of a ground fire, however, since sunlight rarely touched the forest floor, and plants were sparse. The marines, each Dromo draped with body armor, their Treeth armed with automatic weapons, emerged to either side. Gallons of water ran off their flanks and trailed behind.

Rollo wore a military-style com rig. It had a speaker capability, and his voice boomed through the forest. "This is Confederate Marshal Rollo Drekno-Hypont the third. Throw your weapons to the ground, place your hands on your heads, and approach the beach."

There was no reaction until something exploded inside the spaceship. Fire shot skyward, and a patch of white cloth appeared over a fallen tree trunk. A voice yelled, "Don't shoot!" and a handful of humans staggered toward the water. They were unarmed, or appeared to be, and looked the worse for wear.

One of the humans, a scrawny specimen with a badly burned arm, identified himself as First Officer Cowles. He seemed especially eager to describe how he and his fellow survivors had been held against their collective will, done what they could to foil the evil captain, and survived the crash.

Rollo gave orders for them to be held separately, so the interrogators could compare everything they said, and led a sweep for stray survivors. He didn't find any. Then the officer in charge of the ecological contamination unit took control, and Rollo waddled toward the water. The *Will of God* had landed safely and he wanted to reach her as soon as possible.

The bedroom was almost totally dark, with nothing more than the hallway light to provide illumination. Something sharp pricked the surface of Carnaby Orr's skin. He awoke with a start, tried to sit, and found a knife at his throat. He could feel the needle-sharp point and saw light wink off the blade. A knee pinned him in place while a face floated into view. The industrialist expected to see an assassin, a kidnapper, anyone but his wife. Anger and hatred had distorted her normally beautiful face. He activated a subcutaneous alarm and tried to bully his way out of the situation. "Melanie? What is this? Some sort of joke? Stop this nonsense immediately."

The knife went in a quarter inch and sliced sideways. The blade missed the carotid but cut through a dozen capillaries. Orr felt something warm trickle onto his chest. He was bleeding! She'd cut him! He struggled, and the steel went deeper. Melanie was cold and sarcastic. "What's the matter, lover? Have an aversion to cold steel? It didn't bother you earlier when the aliens cut our son open and put a parasite in his belly. No, that was just god damned fine with you! Well, listen, asshole, your doctors are going after that organism, and if our son dies on the table, so will you."

Orr's mind raced. His wife had found out the truth about Jason's operation. How didn't matter. The threat to her son's well-being had somehow awakened her from the half-drugged state that had characterized most of her adult life. The challenge was to ignore the inconsequential and focus on that which was important: How much did she know? And where were his security people? They should have intervened by now.

Melanie grinned. "What's the matter, lover? Wondering where your lackeys are? They're late, aren't they? Ooops. Did

I forget to tell you? I made some changes after your whore left. The staff works for me. Luther, Munalo, escort my husband to the car.''

The knife was withdrawn, but hands seized his arms. They jerked the industrialist out of bed. The lights came on, and Orr made eye contact with Luther. Ari had recruited the high-grav wrestler and used him as a shield in crowd situations. Orr had been nice to the bodyguard and hoped for some loyalty in return. It was nowhere to be seen.

They had hauled Orr half way to the door when Luther spoke. ''Ya shouldn't have done that, Mr. Orr. Puttin' somethin' in Jason like that. We gotta take it out.''

The situation was clear. His security people liked Jason, and his wife had taken advantage of that. The bitch. Still, that's what insurance policies are for, to mitigate the impact of unforeseen catastrophes. Orr had one, but how to activate it?

Grim silence prevailed as Orr was escorted down the stairs, past the null-gravity well, and into the main hall. His son was there, thumb in mouth, head resting on the nanny's shoulder. The businessman saw open hatred on the woman's face as she walked past. Jason turned, removed the thumb, and pointed at his father. ''You have blood on your jammies. Are you coming with us?''

Orr, who had been forced to pause while his wife descended the stairs, forced a smile. ''I'll be there in a moment, son . . . save me a seat.''

''You're lucky we don't drag you behind the car,'' Melanie Orr said coldly. ''Take him outside.''

''I need to visit the bathroom,'' Orr said plaintively. ''You wouldn't want me to embarrass myself would you?''

''I don't care what you do,'' Melanie said unsympathetically. ''Let's go.''

Orr swore silently as Luther and Munalo manhandled him out through the front door. Triggers had been installed throughout the mansion. One was tucked away in the kitchen, two were hidden in the living room, and another had been installed in the bathroom off the hallway. Once he left the house and entered the family limo, there would still be one opportunity left. But what if they put him in a van? Or some other vehicle? Fear rolled itself into a ball and rode in the pit of his stomach.

The night air was sweet and made all the more so by the Oloroso vines that climbed the east side of the house. The limo was there, doors open, waiting for them to enter. Orr concealed a sigh of relief and hurried to enter first. It was too late. The nanny, with Jason on her lap, sat facing the front. Before Orr could adjust, his wife decreed that he sit in the center backward-facing seat. Luther took one side and Munalo the other. Things could have been worse, however. The backup security system boasted three triggers, two of which were within reach—

Melanie was the last to enter the car. She sat opposite him. She looked angry, very angry, and in spite of the fact that Orr didn't like the situation he was in, the male part of him noticed how beautiful she was. Which was something he hadn't thought about in a long time. Orr remembered their courtship. He had evaluated his weaknesses, designed a plan to compensate for them, and launched his campaign. And it had worked! Melanie had married him in spite of attentions from more attractive men, and the fact that he'd been relatively poor in those days. How had he done it? With words, that's how. Words carefully and faithfully applied. It was worth a try. He mustered a smile. "So, honey, how was your day?"

He saw amusement flicker in her eyes and hurried to follow up. "There is no parasite. I wouldn't do that. The organism is a *symbiote*. It takes nourishment from Jason's blood and provides immunity in return."

He heard the nanny snort in disbelief and ignored her. "Think about it, Melanie; when was the last time that Jason became ill? You can't remember, can you? That's because it was months ago."

Orr saw his wife's eyes widen slightly as she realized that it was true. There was another, less positive dimension to the situation, however, and the knowledge restored her anger. "But what happens when it becomes too large for its host? And is forced to tunnel its way out?"

She was about to say more, about to tell Orr what slime he was, when the nanny frowned. Her meaning was clear. Jason was present and unaware of his condition. Melanie bit off the words and crossed her arms. Her anger spoke louder than words.

The driver cornered too fast, the passengers leaned away, and Orr extended an arm as if to brace himself. The button was hidden beneath a decorative medallion. Orr felt it give under his hand. Luther frowned and pushed the arm away. Orr apologized and leaned back in his chair.

Fifty miles away, in the loft of what had been a small factory, a buzzer sounded and a light started to flash. It was a large space with white walls, wood floors, and a minimal amount of furniture. Mozart's Allegro in B flat was playing in the background. The man who lived there paused in the middle of his nocturnal workout, raised an eyebrow, and ordered the domocomp to kill the music.

There was no question as to where the summons came from. The man had retired many years before and retained only one client: a wealthy individual who could afford a fail-safe security system and knew better than to use it without reason. Though not in need of additional funds, the man used the obligation the client represented to keep himself sharp. To do otherwise was to die mentally, emotionally, and yes, physically, for the man judged everything according to its usefulness, and was unwilling to live without purpose.

The man, who had used many names over the years, was currently known as Riley. He hurried to the partitioned area that served as his office, activated some rather expensive electronics, and watched a grid appear on the wall screen. The orange lines represented streets. Names glowed blue. His client, represented by a flashing red light, was headed toward the business district.

Riley slipped into a black shirt, pants, and boots, armed himself, and grabbed a black duster on his way out the door. The rest of what he needed, equipment for almost every possible contingency, waited in his car. The night air smelled clean, and he was needed. Life didn't get any better than that.

The *Will of God* lay at anchor toward the south end of a large lake. A floating dock complete with cranes and auto-loaders was positioned alongside. The process of unloading the freighter's cargo was about half finished when a launch arrived and Natalie was summoned.

She, like the rest of the crew, had been working double shifts for days now. Time was money—and Jord had a schedule to keep. It took two minutes and forty-three seconds for Natalie to reach the main deck. Sparks flew as O'Tool and his technicians replaced a badly burned hull plate. Natalie knew the cyborg didn't like her, and probably never would, but she had earned his respect, and that was sufficient. He saw her, nodded, and returned to work.

Jord paced back and forth along the flat area in front of the ship's prow. He made it a habit to dress well while in port, both in an effort to impress the locals and to set a standard for the crew. His crisp white uniform, complete with shoulder boards, crackled as he moved. The official summons, and the temporary loss of his third officer, was just the latest in a long string of annoyances, especially in light of the fact that he and his crew had already spent countless hours bobbing up and down with waterborne bureaucrats. All because the pirates, for reasons known only to them, had targeted *his* ship. It was more than his heart or wallet could bear. He scowled as Natalie arrived. "So, more time wasted."

Natalie, who was present against her will, nodded in agreement. "Yes, sir. I'm afraid so."

"More nonsense about the attack, I suppose."

"Maybe . . . although I was summoned *prior* to our departure. Something to do with Voss Lines and my parents."

"I should have known you were too good to be true," Jord said sourly. "So tell me, are you and our ex-passengers connected?"

Natalie considered the truth, followed by a lie, and settled on a compromise. "*They* certainly thought so, which explains the visit to my cabin, but I still don't understand what they wanted.''

Jord seemed to accept the explanation, because he nodded and gestured to the sturdy launch that bobbed alongside. "Well, the locals want their turn. Let me know if I can help."

Natalie promised that she would, made quick work of the ladder, and dropped into the boat. It was spotless. A Treeth, resplendent in the uniform of the Water Guards, welcomed the officer aboard and cast off. An inboard engine made short work of the trip.

Clouds had gathered by the time Natalie stepped out of the boat, and raindrops hit her skin. A second Treeth, this one clad in civilian attire, dropped out of a tree. He motioned for her to follow. It was dry under the canopy and somewhat gloomy. Birds, or the local equivalent thereof, fluttered between the trees. Leaves brushed her shoulders.

The port authority's administrative park was unlike anything Natalie had seen before. Computer stations, all of which were linked via wireless technology, and personed by members of the Treeth race, stood in leafy glades, next to babbling brooks, and, in one case, up among some tree branches. A significant number of Dromo were present as well, shoulder-deep in their various pools, working their voice-activated computers.

Natalie followed her guide across a wooden footbridge and into a generously proportioned enclosure. The surroundings consisted of dense vegetation. It reminded her of an Earth-normal hedge, and it wasn't until she sat next to it and spotted the long brown thorns that she realized how deceptive appearances could be. The pond was small by local standards and designed for the convenience of Dromos. A series of waves followed by a cheerful "Hello!" announced her hosts. Natalie recognized the Dromo and Treeth as the same individuals who had issued the summons. She stood. "Greetings. Marshals Rollo and Torx, I presume?"

"None other," Rollo assured her. "Please, take a seat, make yourself comfortable. Do you require anything? Nourishment, perhaps? Many humans enjoy Treeth cuisine."

Natalie shook her head. "Thank you, but no. I ate aboard ship."

"Well, let us know if you need anything," Rollo said solicitously. "There's nothing worse than an empty stomach, especially one as large as mine."

Torx, safely beyond Rollo's field of vision, mimed a Dromo consuming the entire forest. Natalie laughed. Rollo was pleased with the response. "Thank you for coming, especially so soon after the ceasing-to-be of your progenitors, but the matter at hand is of the utmost importance. So much so that the outcome could affect the entire Confederacy."

Though unable to think of a way in which she, or anything she knew, could have a noticeable impact on the Confederacy, Natalie nodded gravely and waited. There was a lull as the Treeth tapped his fingers against the Dromo's neck pad. The message seemed to meet with the larger being's approval, because he nodded and cleared his throat.

"In light of the fact that you've been a cooperative witness, Torx suggests a departure from standard procedure. Rather than ask questions, and piece your answers together, let's exchange information. Agreed?"

Natalie indicated acceptance, swatted at a rather persistent insect, and listened to the briefing. What she heard both amazed and alarmed her. A natural catastrophe had killed one-third of the Traa race and left the rest psychologically crippled. So much so that they were determined to seize control of the Confederacy. A whole lot of things suddenly made sense. The trade in tools, pharmaceuticals, software, parts, food, weapons, and a thousand other items was important, all right, but not when compared to data traffic, most of which passed through wormholes. Wormholes the Traa sought to control.

Natalie told the co-marshals about Carnaby Orr, his efforts to acquire the Mescalero Gap, and the way in which the Traa had accosted her aboard ship. Finally, after Natalie had finished her recitation, Rollo spoke. "Your ship will be ready to lift soon?"

"Yes."

The Dromo delivered an excellent imitation of a human smile. "Good, because we're going with you."

Arrangements had been made and the clinic was open when the limo arrived. Melanie had thought of everything, it seemed—a realization that surprised Orr, but shouldn't have, given the efficiency with which she managed his estate, three vacation retreats, and any number of critical social relationships. All while partially stoned.

Luther and Munalo hustled Orr into the clinic. Jason, who recognized the smell, started to cry. Orr had just turned toward his son, and was about to offer words of comfort, when a needle stung his arm. He tried to react but felt his knees buckle. Luther grabbed Orr under the armpits, and with help from Munalo loaded him on a gurney. Though too weak to move, the industrialist could see and hear. People in OR greens came and went. A voice said, "Prep him." Another voice said, "Yes, doctor," and the ceiling began to move, or that's the way it appeared from his position on the stretcher. He wondered where were they taking him. Then it hit. The surgeons planned to remove the organism from his son and transplant it to him!

The horror of it sent adrenaline into Orr's bloodstream and enabled him to raise the upper part of his body. The industrialist yelled incoherently and fumbled with the safety strap. That's when a voice said, "Take him down," and Orr felt a second needle penetrate muscle. The businessman struggled, felt tired, and gave up. Melanie appeared and peered into his face. "So, lover, how does it feel? To know they're going to cut your belly open? But wait, I nearly forgot! The symbiote will *help* you. No need to thank me, it's the least I could do."

The face vanished, then reappeared a moment later. "Oh, one more thing. You know the empire you built? The one you were willing to sacrifice our son to? Well, my lawyers say half belongs to me, so kiss it good-bye."

The face disappeared, and half of Orr's life vanished with it. He was still absorbing that, still dealing with it, when they lifted him onto the table. The prep felt cold.

• • •

As with most medical facilities, the clinic had drugs and a system designed to protect them. It was a good system, and Riley spent twenty minutes finding his way through it. He eventually entered through a side door. He produced a semi-automatic handgun, chambered the first of fifteen hollow-point rounds, and reholstered it.

Then, hoping he wouldn't have to kill anyone, Riley drew a space-certified dart thrower, checked to make sure it was loaded with nonlethal flechettes, and held it ready. His client might be in trouble . . . but so were the people who controlled him. They just didn't know it yet.

The surgeons, three in all, had opened Jason's abdomen and were cauterizing bleeders when Melanie entered the room. Nearly all of them had attempted to talk her out of it, but she wanted to see with her own eyes. She saw the incision, fought the dizziness, and moved closer. Electrodes buzzed, and the odor of burnt tissue filled the air.

Whatever the creature was, it had grown over the last few months and established connections with Jason's circulatory, respiratory, and digestive systems via slowly pulsating tubes. Melanie gagged and turned away. A nurse took her elbow. "Come with me, Mrs. Orr . . . there's a chair over here."

The doctors started to sweat. The symbiote liked the boy's body and didn't want to leave. Every time a tube was severed, the symbiote lowered the child's blood pressure or slowed his respirations. The message was clear: "Stop or I'll kill him." The surgical team countered with drugs, but were doomed to failure. Much as they hated to admit it, the Traa had played a significant role in the initial operation, and the aliens were badly missed.

Finally, in what amounted to an act of desperation, the lead surgeon left for the neighboring suite. Consistent with Melanie Orr's instructions, her husband had been prepped for surgery. The medical team opposed the plan, but had performed one unethical operation and couldn't refuse another. Not if they wanted to maintain their extravagant lifestyles, that is. That being the case, the surgeon saw one last chance to snatch victory from the jaws of defeat. Orders were given, the staff obeyed, and the self-propelled table was guided through the doors.

Riley had no difficulty slipping up on Luther and Munalo. With Orr under sedation and strapped to a table, they were taking a break. Had Ari been present, she would have made provisions for a security zone, a primary escape plan, a backup escape plan, and a shitload of firepower. Luther, who was nominally in charge, hadn't even considered the possibility of an external threat, so he was hardly prepared for it.

The big man was halfway through one of his favorite wrestling stories when Riley pushed a cart full of medical supplies down the hall, approached the place where they were standing, flipped a towel off the dart gun, aimed and fired. Munalo jerked as the flechette entered his unprotected thigh, looked surprised, and collapsed on the floor. Luther started into motion but stopped when the semiauto appeared in Riley's left hand. "That's better . . . now tell me what's going on in there. And make it good."

Luther talked. Riley listened, nodded sympathetically, and shot him in the leg. That made the big man angry. He charged, took a dart in the neck, and dropped like a rock. Riley checked Luther's pulse, placed snake cuffs on his extremities, and donned some OR greens.

The medical team went to work. The first task was to notify the alien organism that a new host was available. Nobody knew what to do, but the lead surgeon had a hunch. In addition to the tubes connected to Jason's blood supply, a multitude of delicate white filaments had invaded his nervous system. By freeing one of the longer connectors, and pushing the patients together, the doctors were able to drop the filament into the father's recently opened incision.

What happened next was both frightening and disgusting. The connector, because the doctors couldn't think of a better name to describe its function, acquired a life of its own. The filament touched, recoiled, and touched again. It seemed more interested the second time, excited even, as it snaked here and there, felt around, and dived out of sight. Then, as if pleased with the reports it had received, the organism shivered and started to vibrate. Tubes popped loose, connectors broke free, and the organism prepared to move. A doctor scooped the creature up, dropped the organism into Orr's abdominal cavity, and watched as it took up residence.

The doctors, all of whom wished they had never agreed to work for Orr Enterprises, heaved sighs of relief, redivided themselves into separate teams, ordered that their patients be removed to their respective tables, and started to close.

Melanie felt better, elated even, and was about to speak with the doctors, when an orderly pushed a supply cart into the room. He seemed to recognize her. "Mrs. Orr?"

"Yes?"

"I work for your husband. I function as a backup for his regular security team, and, judging from the idiots out in the hall, a sorely needed one. What's Mr. Orr's status? And please, no histrionics."

The man produced a weapon and Melanie felt her knees go weak. She should have known that a first-class bastard would have a first-class backup plan. "Kill me if you must, but leave the boy alone."

Most of the security man's face was hidden by his surgical mask, but she saw his eyebrows rise, and realized he was surprised. "There's no need for that sort of thing. My only interest is in extricating my client from the present circumstances. Revenge is his concern. Now, if you would be so kind as to instruct your medical staff to close Mr. Orr's incision, I will arrange for transportation to a real hospital. The doctors will fabricate some sort of reason. Understood?"

Melanie gulped. "Understood."

"Excellent," Riley replied wearily. "Because I'm retired . . . and it's past my bedtime."

17

Take care where your footprints appear . . . lest the innocent follow.

Author unknown
Temple inscription Reon IV
Circa 1000

The Planet New Hope

Ari's mother had liked to dispense motherly advice. This in spite of the fact that she saw motherhood as a part-time job. Mom had some things right, though, like when she said that no matter how horrible things were, they could always get worse.

Maybe that explained why Dorn Voss wasn't where he was supposed to be, and why Ari, who had passed herself off as the boy's sister, was confronted by a clearly distraught headmaster. His name was Tull, and he rose from behind the desk like an iceberg rising to the surface of the sea. He circled the massive chunk of hardwood and perched on a well-worn corner.

"I'm sorry, Miss Voss, but my hands were tied. I waited for a considerable length of time, and, having received no word, and no money for tuition, was forced to let the boy go. He disappeared within one local day of leaving the academy. We traced his movements to a local gambling establishment where he won a small amount of money and left. The kitchen staff thought they heard a scuffle, and that raises the possibility that someone followed the lad and knocked him over the head. The casino is perched over the river, which was in flood at the time. The police believe he drowned, and I see no reason to disagree with them. We recovered your brother's belongings and left them in his room. There's some money too . . . left after you paid his bills.''

"Thank you," Ari said with what she hoped was the right mix of sadness and resignation. "You've been very kind. It's all so terribly sad. First my parents, now this. There's no hope that my brother's alive?''

Tull looked at his feet. He wanted to say yes, wanted to be positive, but hated to lead her on. She seemed like such a nice young woman. "Anything's possible, Miss Voss . . . but it seems unlikely."

Ari nodded soberly and stood. "Well, thanks for your time. My assistant and I may pursue an investigation of our own, just to confirm your suspicions, and provide my family with a sense of closure. May we call on you as a reference? Off-worlders get the runaround sometimes."

"How true," Tull said understandingly. "Please let me know if I can help."

The next hour seemed to last forever as Ari was forced to inspect the room where the boy had slept, take possession of his clothes, and sign for the money his real sister had sent him. All of which was a drag, but not nearly as bad as dealing with the mealy-mouthed teachers, and the scrawny little boys who talked about Dorn as though he were a deity of some kind. Who was this kid, anyway? She felt jealous and knew her reaction was stupid.

The bodyguard eventually won free and returned to her car. The street girl was still there. That was not too surprising, since Ari had taken the key with her, but it was commendable nonetheless. The girl claimed her name was Kara, but Ari wasn't ready to bet on it. Her own name belonged to a vid star, after all—and it was the first thing she'd stolen.

The bodyguard started the car, engaged the fan, and felt it

lift off the ground. The paint was shot, the interior smelled, and only half the accessories worked, but it moved. The driveway switchbacked down the side of the hill. "So, Kara, anything happen while I was gone?"

The girl shrugged. "A bird took a shit on the hood, and a security guard hit on me. That about covers it."

Ari, who didn't like the fact that the government had taken an interest in her activities, gave the girl a look. "Security? What kind of security?"

Kara made a face. "The disgusting kind, with a big belly, and hair growing out of his nose."

Ari felt the tension melt away. The description fit half the academy's security staff, and none of them mattered.

"So," Kara asked, "what's next?" She was doing her best to sound casual, Ari could tell.

"I think we'll poke around a bit," the older woman said thoughtfully, "and see what we can find. Maybe the Dorn kid took a shot to the noggin and maybe he didn't. The lack of a body makes me wonder. People disappear every day. Some want to."

The car arrived at the bottom of the hill and turned into the slums. The girl looked out the window. "There are lots of ways to disappear . . . some worse than death," she said slowly.

Ari honked at an overloaded cart and pulled around it. "Ain't that the truth? Well, stick with me, kid. If the little bastard is around, we'll find him."

The sky was blue, the sea sparkled, and the carefully manicured lawn was emerald green. The yard crew had spent two days erecting the red-and-white-striped awning, placing the tables and chairs just so, and laying crushed seashells on the paths. These paths would carry a hundred and fifty guests from the landing pads to the feast Myra and the rest of the kitchen staff had worked on for the better part of three days now.

Chef Fimbre shouted orders, people ran every which way, and Myra hurried to finish setting the tables. Each guest was provided with a water glass, a wineglass, a gold-rimmed dinner plate, a butter dish, and, light winking off their highly polished surfaces, real honest-to-goodness stainless steel utensils, including two forks, two spoons, and a knife.

All of which would have been splendid enough. But Mr. Sharma had gone one step further by engraving each guest's name on his or her table setting, a gift worth hundreds of credits.

Myra, who, like the rest of her peers, had grown up using fingers, chopsticks, and wooden spoons, marveled at the splendor of it all. There wasn't much time to gawk, however, not with Fimbre cracking the whip, and it wasn't long before the gleaming white tables were ready, the centerpieces finished, and a small army of carefully groomed children put to work keeping insects away.

Myra and three others were ordered to the rear courtyard where thirty-six hand-picked waiters and waitresses awaited final training. Each had survived a rigorous screening process designed to eliminate anyone lacking social skills, some brains, or the ability to communicate.

There had been no shortage of volunteers, since each person chosen received a shower complete with soap, a white uniform that they would be allowed to keep, and their share of what would almost certainly be a prodigious amount of leftovers. Half the candidates had no experience, so training was of utmost importance, and who better than the kitchen staff to provide it? All of which meant that Myra and the others had a big job to do.

The recruits were instructed to address each person as ma'am or sir, unless they were members of another race, when "gentlebeing" was acceptable. Each course should be served from the left, except where the Drog'na were concerned, because their culture forbade any being other than a blood-sanctified kinsperson to stand on their sword-side. And there was more, a lot more, which was why *real* waiters had degrees in xenoanthropology.

It was a great deal to learn in a rather short period of time, but the family's security team didn't want members of the great unwashed horde inside the family compound any longer

than was absolutely necessary. There had been a full-scale riot
three years before, which helped explain the fear that perme-
ated the house, and the sidearm Mr. Sharma wore. Although
the enslavement of sentient beings conferred certain benefits
on the owner, it carried a price as well.

Myra hurried into the courtyard, saw that the trainees had
been assembled, and joined the kitchen staff. Chef Fimbre was
only halfway through the list of things the waiters couldn't do
when Myra arrived. She scanned their faces and nearly missed
the one she was searching for. Dorn was so clean, so well
combed, that he looked like a different person. It was the char-
acteristic way that he stood, combined with an ear-to-ear grin,
that set him apart. The fact that he looked like an idiot, smiling
as Fimbre outlined the seriousness of the occasion didn't
bother her in the least. He'd found the means to see her; that's
all Myra knew, or needed to know.

Her heart beat faster, blood colored her face, and her stomach felt strange. She felt a desperate need to speak with Dorn,
find out how he was doing, and tell him about her plans for
escape. Well, not plans exactly, but intentions.

Fimbre wound down. "So, when the ship appears on the
horizon, and the announcement is made, it's extremely important that you withdraw to either side of the pavilion. I assure you that Mr. Sharma will be most unhappy with anyone
who blocks the view. Questions? No? Then pay close attention
to your training. Those who do well will receive something
extra when the dishes have been cleared. That will be all."

As Fimbre marched off to reassume command of his
kitchen, the trainees were divided into groups of six, and assigned to formally set tables. Then, with five would-be waiters
playing the role of guests, the sixth was put through his or her
paces.

Myra, who contrived to instruct the group that included
Dorn, found it hard to concentrate, especially after the way he
looked at her, and the way she wanted to look at him.

Finally, as the training period came to a close, and the first
aircraft came in for a landing, they had a moment alone. Myra
led Dorn around a corner and into a vine-shaded nook where

Fimbre took his afternoon wine. There was a table and two chairs. The furniture was damp from a sprinkler but they sat anyway. Dorn took hold of her hands and marveled at how small they were. "How are you? Do you get enough to eat?"

Myra nodded. "I'm fine . . . more than enough . . . and you? Tell me everything."

Another aircraft roared over the house, and Dorn grinned. "*Everything* would take too long, so the basics will do. I haul salvage in from the ships and steal metal to get by. And you? What do you do?"

"I work in the kitchen," Myra said quickly, not wanting to waste time on the seemingly endless process of meal preparation, "but I serve meals too. That means I hear things. The family talks as if we aren't there."

Dorn's eyes lit up. "Really? Good work, Myra. Perhaps you'll hear something we can use."

Myra's heart leapt in response to the word "we," as if they were a unit, and would naturally stick together. She was about to agree, about to say that she wouldn't leave without him, when a coworker stuck his head around a corner. "Hurry up, Myra. Fimbre's looking for you, and you know how he gets."

They stood. Myra looked up at Dorn. "I'll meet you during the fireworks. Dinner will be over, and the darkness will protect us."

Her lips were so close, and so clearly desirable, that it felt natural to kiss them. They were soft at first, then firm as the kiss was returned, and Dorn was lost in a host of wonderful sensations. The clean, fresh smell of her hair, the feel of her back under the pressure of his hands, and the sweetness of her tongue.

The voice was frighteningly close. "Myra? Where are you?" The girl pushed Dorn toward the courtyard, whispered, "Play along," and answered the summons. "I'm over here. One of the waiters wandered away, and I tracked him down."

Fimbre stepped out of the doorway, eyed Dorn's retreating back, and shook his head. "An idiot or a thief. Not that it makes much difference. Now hurry out front . . . the guests are arriving and we need your help."

Myra marveled at the extent to which Fimbre had distanced himself from his own humble origins, curtsied, and did as she was told. The beaching was only hours away, and there was work to do.

The trail led them from the hotel where the Voss boy had left his luggage, to the street urchin named Rali, and to the casino where the youngster had disappeared. There they ran into Miss Carmen and a wall of words, a wall that collapsed when Ari shoved a gun in her mouth and threatened to blow her brains all over the sparkly ceiling. A pair of heavies appeared and would have done who knows what except for the fact that Kara produced the weapon she wasn't supposed to have and threatened to shoot them. They believed she'd do it, and stood frozen in place.

Miss Carmen became quite cooperative after that. The river led to the fishermen, and they led to the Keno Labor Exchange, a foul-smelling warren of cells and pens where the boy had been held. Ari entered with no signs of trepidation.

Kara, who had originally viewed the off-worlder as a run-of-the-mill spacer born to be milked, cheated, and forgotten, followed her in. She knew the older woman was far from trustworthy but admired her anyway.

Or was it the other way around? Maybe she admired Ari *because* she was dangerous. The girl didn't know, and figured it didn't matter, so long as her employer paid at the end of the day, and didn't try to jump in bed with her. Yeah, the situation was pretty good, except for the stink that emanated from the pens, which was worse than anything even Kara's jaded nostrils had experienced before.

It took an hour of earnest conversation and a fistful of Carnaby Orr's money to circumvent the rather corpulent individual known as the Pen Master, and gain access to a scroungy-looking office where a second bribe was sufficient to send a cadaverous computerist to lunch, all of which left them free to browse through the none too carefully maintained records.

They were stored in a computer older than the bodyguard

herself and accessed through a rather archaic keyboard. Ari
didn't know how to type and used the hunt-and-peck system
to find what she wanted. She was feeling light-headed, and
very, very warm, which made the search go even slower. She
was hungry, she supposed.

The screen blanked, stuttered for a moment, and locked up.
All of the D's and half the E's were missing. The V's had
survived, however, and the bodyguard felt a rising sense of
excitement as she located the appropriate file and scrolled
through the list. Bingo! There he was. No less than six Vosses
had passed through the Keno Labor Exchange, but only one
of them was named Dorn. The entry next to his name indicated
that the youth had been declared destitute and sold to Sharma
Industries.

Ari shook her head in amazement, transferred the entry to
her hand comp, and entered a phony first name in place of
Dorn's. The computer asked if she really wanted to do that,
blinked agreeably when she indicated that she did, and gave
birth to a person named Jorge Voss.

The objective was to muddy the trail, not for the police,
who had already given up, but for the man, woman, or alien
who would be assigned to investigate the freelancer's untimely
death. Kara, who had followed the whole thing the way a
student observes a master, couldn't help but comment. "Hey
. . . that was slick."

Ari smiled at the unexpected compliment, wondered why it
pleased her so much, and wiped her prints off the keyboard.
She'd been more than a little surprised when Kara had backed
her play at the casino. Surprised, and pleased, since loyalty
was a rare commodity. Still, the fact that Kara had swiped the
gun and carried it all over hell's half acre worried the bodyguard. What would she miss next? Something that would kill
her? It was a frightening thought. Like growing old.

The room seemed to spin as the bodyguard gestured toward
the door. "It seems the little turd survived. Let's pay him a
visit."

•   •   •

Nearly all the guests had arrived, and the lawn in front of the mansion was filled to overflowing with New Hope's wealthiest citizens. There were touches of color, especially among the women, in spite of the fact that the vast majority of those present wore white, or, in the case of the men, blue blazers with white trousers. Conversation was muted for the most part and punctuated by bursts of laughter. The salvage work, which continued half a mile away, was largely ignored.

Dorn, who had responsibility for a table down toward the water, was struck by the similarities between this event and countless dinners hosted by his parents. The conversation was nearly identical, consisting as it did of business, gossip, and the occasional off-color story.

Of course he'd been a member of the privileged class in those days, had accepted personal service as part of his birthright, and grown irritable when it failed to meet his mother's rather exacting standards. Mary Voss would have been mortified to see the depths to which her son had sunk. The thought brought a smile to his lips.

Dorn had refilled the wineglasses, and was headed toward the kitchen, when a voice turned his head. The girl was his age or close to it and was very, very pretty. Not only that, but he'd seen her once before, riding in the back seat of the family limo. "Oh, waiter! Yes, you. Mr. Lott needs more butter."

It wasn't Dorn's table, but he knew how the request would be handled in a fine restaurant and acted accordingly. "Yes, ma'am. Right away, ma'am."

It took but a moment to swing by one of the back tables, grab a bowl of iced butter, and return to the young woman's table. He delivered it to her rather than Mr. Lott. "Your butter, ma'am." She looked and Dorn smiled. "It's nice to see you again."

Seleen frowned. It hardly wrinkled her skin. "We've met?"

Dorn smiled. "In a manner of speaking. You were in the back of your father's limousine and I was marching along the side of the road."

The frown became more pronounced. "You are extremely impertinent."

Dorn delivered what he hoped was a courtly bow. "And you are beautiful. You'll have to excuse me now . . . Chef Fimbre will be most upset if the soup arrives cold."

Dorn left, but her eyes followed him, and he cursed himself for a fool. What was he playing at, anyway? The whole idea had been to see Myra, fill his eternally empty stomach, and earn an extra bit of metal.

He decided to avoid the girl like the plague, like *all* the plagues, and entered the kitchen. Fimbre ordered him to hurry; he nodded obediently, and carried his tray back toward the water. It was heavy, but not as heavy as steel hull plates, so the youth had no difficulty hoisting it to his shoulder. He put it down and was in the process of serving the soup course when someone shouted, "Look!" A rumble was heard.

Everyone looked for the source of the noise, and Dorn was no exception. He saw the ship at the same moment that he heard the blare of recorded trumpets. The fanfare was followed by Mr. Sharma's voice. It boomed over the speakers.

"Gentlebeings! This is the the moment you've been waiting for. Prepare yourselves for a rare spectacle, as an enormous spaceship races toward you at more than two hundred miles per hour, and runs aground before your very eyes. Here it comes!"

A collective gasp was heard and the sound grew louder.

The ship was a long way off but grew larger with every passing second. Dorn squinted into the sun and bit his lip. There was something familiar about the vessel. Very familiar indeed. Form follows function, so many vessels look alike, but this one had the slightly droopy nose, raised brow, and side bulges typical of long-haul data liners. Especially those manufactured by the Drood Yards high above Langley II. More than that, this particular ship was huge, and reminiscent of the flagships his parents had commissioned. They'd been named after his mother and sister and were the pride of the Voss Lines fleet.

Just as his suspicions started to jell, Sharma took the microphone. "That's correct my friends, hold onto your chairs, because one hundred thousand tons worth of metal is headed straight for you!

"This ship, formerly known as the *Mary Voss,* will be cut into pieces, sold to you, and reshaped into tools, buildings, bridges, and thousands of other useful things, bringing jobs and prosperity to our planet. Remember this moment, because you won't see anything like it again!"

Dorn stood stunned as the very heart of everything his parents had worked to build hurtled toward the beach. Someone yelled, "I can't see!" and hands pulled him away. Obedient, but unwilling to take his eyes off the liner, Dorn tripped, recovered, and watched from outside the pavilion.

The *Mary Voss* was coming fast, much faster than was necessary or prudent, and the youth was reminded of the runaway ship and the destruction it had wrought. Would the same thing happen again? He almost hoped so, even if it meant that Sharma and all of his guests would almost certainly die. The fact that he would go with them was regrettable but worth it.

The *Mary Voss* was big now, *very* big, and the air displaced by her massive hull had created a miniature tidal wave that rolled in front of her. The sound of her mighty engines was so deep, so powerful, that the ground shook and cups rattled.

The sun was gone, eclipsed by the huge machine that had been mined from alien soil, steered through gaps in the space-time continuum, and condemned to serve out her final moments as mealtime entertainment. A memory surfaced briefly and was swept away. It had something to do with the ship and his seldom seen father, but Dorn couldn't focus on it. Not with tears streaming down his cheeks. Not for the ship, but for his parents, who were surely dead, for nothing less than their deaths could explain the sight before him.

The vessel slowed, hit the water with a gigantic splash, and sent waves in every direction. They broke against the older wrecks, swept haulers off their feet, and rushed toward land. Then, like a sea monster exhaling its last breath, the liner groaned and slid to a halt.

As Dorn wiped the tears off his cheeks, he felt something

small and warm nestle in his hand, and knew Myra had joined him. "I'm sorry, Dorn, really sorry."

Dorn swallowed the lump that had formed in his throat. "Thanks, Myra, that helps."

Myra's reply was interrupted by one of the guests. "Excuse me . . . could we have some service over here?"

Myra withdrew her hand. "Fimbre will be furious if he sees us standing around. We'll meet during the fireworks, remember?"

Dorn nodded soberly, returned to the busing station, grabbed a tray, and collected the empty soup bowls. Sharma offered the first of what turned about to be an endless round of toasts. The ceremony kept the guests busy, and made Dorn's job that much easier.

The hours passed, courses came and went, and the sun dropped below the data liner's massive hull. Finally, as the dessert goblets were cleared away, and the after-dinner drinks were served, a steady stream of aircraft started to arrive. Then, as the most important guests were escorted to the pads, the less fortunate were treated to a carefully programmed fireworks display, complete with lasers and three-dimensional holographs. These included twenty-foot-high portraits of the Sharmas, plus each guest in attendance, all captured during the afternoon's festivities.

Dorn searched for Myra and found her in the shadow cast by the house itself. They came together with the sureness of lovers. Her body, soft yet firm, melted against his. Lips met and met again. Light strobed as a holo lit the sky, and the guests clapped. Neither saw Seleen leave the house and stop to watch them.

18

Greed makes man blind, foolish and . . . an easy prey for death.

Rumi
Persian Sufi poet
Circa 1250

The Place of Wandering Waters, the Planet Mechnos, and Aboard a Traa Survey Ship in Deep Space

The rain fell in sheets, splattered across the spaceship's deck, and cascaded down her flanks. Natalie, who was soaked to the skin, and had given up all hope of ever being dry again, looked up and flinched as the raindrops hit her face. She pointed toward the lead-gray sky and held her hand aloft. The launch rocked gently and was dwarfed by the spacegoing leviathan above.

Captain Jord stood silhouetted against the dark gray sky. He wore foul-weather gear, and it was impossible to see his face. He remained motionless, as if to extend his third officer's misery. The entire crew knew their commanding officer held Natalie responsible for what he regarded as a bad run. Never mind the fact that the government would reimburse the owners as though the *Will of God*'s holds had been fully loaded, never mind the fact that they would pocket the difference between what fuel costs *would* have been with a full load of cargo and the lesser amount actually used, and never mind the fact that Jord would receive a bonus. The *Will of God* had been built to haul freight, and that's what she was supposed to do. Unscheduled side trips, no matter how profitable, were aberrations. Finally, after what seemed like forever, he gave the necessary nod.

Natalie gave a sigh of relief, checked to make sure the area was clear, and dropped her hand. The crane operator, who thought the whole thing was extremely entertaining, pulled a lever. A motor whined, the cable went taut, and water jumped away. The specially fabricated harness creaked under the strain, and Rollo felt heavier as the lake fell away. A sudden gust of wind caused him to spin one half-turn to the left. He felt helpless and awkward.

Though normally proud of his physique, especially when mingling with members of his own species, the Dromo felt momentarily envious of the smaller and therefore more agile races. Why couldn't he be like Torx, who had no need of cranes and the like? Such was the price he paid to venture off-planet, however, a necessity that had presented itself all too frequently of late. Still, the other choice, which would involve the sacrifice of his work, was too painful to consider. No, he was fortunate that the government indulged him to the extent that it did. Not that they could exclude his race and expect them to adhere to the Confederacy's laws. Still, the body that graced the rivers and swamps was a trial sometimes, which left him frustrated.

The crane operator, who was good at what he did, brought Rollo aboard with one smooth motion. Torx had supervised the creation of what amounted to a well-appointed stall. It was ready when Rollo's feet hit the deck. He felt better as the Treeth tapped a greeting into his receptor pad and freed him from the cable.

Rollo's freedom was short-lived, however, since only thirty minutes had elapsed before two members of the crew returned to rope his harness to the deck, and secure the hold. The announcement and matter-of-fact countdown seemed overly melodramatic.

The activity, combined with stress, served to stimulate his appetite. A bale of pond-marinated weed had been placed in front of him. Rollo attacked it hungrily. Chewing had always had a meritorious effect on the law officer's cognitive functions, so, by the time the *Will of God* had powered free of the lake, the Dromo was lost in thought. So much so that he barely noticed the additional gees or heard the announcements that were meant to reassure him.

The problem, as he saw it, had two dimensions. The first and most obvious thing to do was to locate the perps and take them into custody, a matter that had been made easier to some extent by the fact that a high-speed, eyes-only data torp had dropped into orbit the evening before and been accessed by Torx. It seemed that the head of Orr's security force had landed on New Hope, murdered a government agent, and appeared at Dorn Voss's school. It was a troubling development, but one that simplified the situation, heartless though that might seem. By focusing on the murder, the co-marshals had an airtight reason for investigating matters that their superiors might prefer to ignore. Which explained why they had commandeered the *Will of God* and were presently headed for New Hope, a locale sure to attract the Traa, and, with a little bit of luck, Orr himself. The problem was to arrive on the scene quickly enough to save the Voss boy *and* the coordinates. Assuming the youngster knew where they were.

The second and more puzzling part of the case stemmed from the triune nature of Traa society, and the fact that it had suffered the cultural equivalent of a nervous breakdown. Assuming Torx and he were able to intercept Carnaby Orr and apprehend the Traa, what then? The rest of the race would still be out of whack, and the same sort of nonsense would happen again. It was a depressing thought, and depressing thoughts made Rollo hungry. The second bale tasted even better than the first.

•   •   •

Carnaby Orr's eyes opened. His mind, normally fuzzy following a full night's sleep, was crystal clear. He took one look at the tubes, cables, and monitors connected to his body and knew exactly where he was. He also knew why.

Someone, and he would eventually learn who, had told his wife about Jason. And Melanie, god bless her medicated little heart, had emerged from a drug-induced haze. Then, having suborned his staff, and saved her son from what she saw as a fate worse than death, the woman he had loved had gone one step farther by having the symbiote transferred to him.

The knowledge that it was there, snuggled in between his organs, had terrified him at first. Not any more, though. No, Melanie had done him a favor. He had undergone major surgery, conked out for a few hours, and felt like a million credits. No, make that a *billion* credits, since that would be little more than pocket change once his plans were implemented. All because the symbiote was taking care of him. How long would he live, anyway? A hundred years? Two hundred? Life was good. Or would be, the moment he left the hospital.

Orr sat up in bed, jerked the IV out of his left arm, ripped the contacts off his skin, and threw them aside. Buzzers buzzed, lights flashed, and people started to run. A nurse and an orderly arrived first. Both happened to be male. They saw Orr and assumed the worst. It had happened before. A patient awakes, doesn't know where he or she is, and becomes hysterical. They smiled reassuringly and moved forward.

Orr waited with the confidence of someone who knows what he can do, opened his arms in a gesture of welcome, then grabbed the backs of their heads and slammed them together. They crumpled to the floor. Orr loved power, and had accumulated quite a bit of it. But not like this. Never like this. Not *physical* power of the sort that allowed him to impose his will on people directly. It felt good, damned good, in spite of the fact that it flowed from chemicals produced by something alien living inside of him. But so what? Results are what count. Ask the bozos on the floor.

Having found no clothes of his own, Orr slipped into the hospital-issue robe and tied the belt around his waist. He left the room and was twenty feet down the hall when the next wave of medical personnel ran past. The industrialist smiled. The previous Orr would have stopped at the desk, apologized for what he'd done, and released himself from the hospital. His lawyers, armed with blank checks, would have handled the rest.

Not this Orr, though. He was different. Freed from his traitorous wife, his fortune reduced by half, he was psychologically reborn. He had placed his trust in others, and they had betrayed him. Well, not any more. What was the old adage? If you want the job done right, do it yourself? That made sense, a lot of sense, and he would put it into practice.

The fastest way to rebuild his sagging fortunes was to seize control of the Mescalero Gap and the revenues that would flow from it. Then, with his assets restored, he'd go after Melanie. Not physically, because that would be too easy, but financially. He'd make her watch as he took her possessions away, one at a time, till she was begging on the streets. And then, just when it seemed that things could get no worse, he'd use his influence to take her son. She was a drug addict, after all . . . and there were laws against that. The thought made him grin.

Voices shouted, another alarm was heard, and Orr stepped through a door marked "Exit." His yacht was moored in the harbor and would make short work of the trip to New Hope.

The *Search for Opportunity* was registered as a survey vessel, one of many in the Traa fleet, and mounted weaponry similar to that found on Confederate cruisers. This stratagem allowed the Traa to circumvent the Treaty of Stars, through which all races had agreed to decommission their warships in favor of a single peacekeeping force.

In the unlikely event that the ship's commander was questioned, she could honestly say that the ship was searching for a black hole, never mind the fact that it had been in use for years, and belonged to someone else.

Her name was Na-La, and although she was theoretically equal to Sa-Lo and Ka-Di in rank, her position as the ship's commanding officer gave her an edge. She used this advantage to make the operatives slouch lower in their chairs and avoid direct eye contact, the Traa equivalent of pack-style submissive posturing. The setting, which consisted of her day cabin, added weight to her position. The lighting was dim, consistent with the race's better than average night vision, and the bulkheads were ascetically bare.

"So," she said lazily, "let's see if I understand. After forming an alliance with the human named Orr, and using him to screen your actions, you ventured off on your own." Sa-Lo saw where the conversation was headed and, true to his training as a negotiator and deal-maker, remained silent. Ka-Di, always the warrior, launched a counterattack. His demeanor changed, as did his posture. He was on the attack now, fur standing up along his neck, teeth visible. "What are you saying? That we're incompetent? That we should have stayed on Mechnos after the Voss female left? Recycled air grows stale at times. A tour in the field might clear your head."

The words caused fur to bristle along Na-La's neck. "Perhaps *you've* been in the field too long. Actions without results are like seeds on poisoned soil. Energy wasted and opportunity lost."

Ka-Di growled, and was about to retaliate when Sa-Lo intervened. Ka-Di, though not intentionally trying to do so, had provided him with the opportunity to play peacemaker, a position that seemed innocuous but gave the incumbent power over both sides of the dispute. He postured openness.

"Come now, you two. There's little point in dwelling on that which failed. Success belongs to those who nose the correct trail . . . and this one leads to the Voss boy."

Na-La felt mollified and tried to seem open. "What about the female? Additional pressure could change her mind."

"Perhaps," Sa-Lo replied soothingly, "but no amount of persuasion could produce information she doesn't have."

"You're sure of that?" Na-La asked skeptically. "Sure she doesn't know?"

"Nothing is sure," Sa-Lo said gently, "but the odds are good. Everything we know about the female suggests that she intentionally rejected the family business in favor of her current career. Why seek to preserve something already refused? And why would the flat-face visit her parents' offices on Mechnos, if not to find the coordinates? Coordinates she'd sell if she had them.''

"Let's assume you're correct," Na-La said thoughtfully, "and the female doesn't have the coordinates. What leads you to believe that her sibling has them?''

"Nothing," Sa-Lo replied honestly. "But what if he does? How many ships are currently involved in trying to locate the Gap using conventional means?''

Na-La looked away. "Three.''

"And why haven't they been successful?''

Na-La's features took on an expression of profound sadness. "Our best physicists died when the mountain blew, and the rest refuse to help. They regard our project as ethically untenable.''

Sa-Lo and Ka-Di, both of whom knew how La-Ma would have viewed their activities, signaled their understanding. The naval officer continued. "That being the case, we are left with nothing but scientific texts and alien contract personnel to do the job. The fact that black holes are optically invisible makes for slow work. You can track the X rays they emit, you can look for Doppler shifts, but you can't see them directly. And, to further complicate things, there are *two* kinds of black holes, the kind that spin and provide a shortcut from one point in space to another, and the kind that don't and will crush you like a bug. All of which means that while we know roughly where the Gap should be, and have some preliminary evidence that it's there, we aren't sure that it's the right one. Not until we find a way to send drones through without the government or our own scientists catching on.''

"Fabulous," Ka-Di said disgustedly. "Just frigging fabulous.''

Sa-Lo, who disapproved of human colloquialisms, shot his partner a dirty look. "Thank you, Na-La. Forgive my marriage-brother. He spends too much time with aliens. The discussion has been most helpful, if only to reaffirm our existing strategy. Time was lost while you came to get us. That's why we must make all possible speed for New Hope. The flat-face youth may or may not be in possession of the coordinates. We have no choice but to find out.''

19

Courage has many faces . . .

General Zeen-Nymore Dronk
On the civilian defense of Lake Hypont
Standard year 1613

The Planet New Hope

The sun had risen in the east and threw long black shadows down across the hillside. Thin plumes of smoke, each fed by the minimum amount of wood necessary to cook one family's breakfast, twisted toward the sky. Dogs barked, a door slammed, and the stamping mill thumped its eternal dirge.

Dorn, clad only in a towel with the name DataCom Freight embroidered across the bottom edge, left the relative warmth of the cargo module and headed for the makeshift shower. It consisted of a wooden framework covered with plastic. Water was stored in a fiberglass tank salvaged from a lifeboat. The girl once referred to as "Diddly" now answered to the name Dee Dee. She was fully recovered. That meant she loved to play, and like most children her age, especially those who live in squalor, had a talent for getting dirty. *Very* dirty.

Which was why Dorn, who had grown tired of organizing baths, constructed the shower. And, having done so, took advantage of it himself. The water was damned cold in the morning, though—something Dee Dee took immense pleasure in, since it was her job to fill the tank, and then, when Dorn gave the command—or a tiny bit before, if she felt mischievous—to dump the cold liquid on his semiwilling body. Her voice had a high, piping quality, and came from the ladder located at the rear of the enclosure. "Ready?"

Dorn gritted his teeth and nodded. "Ready."

Dee Dee grinned sadistically, pulled a lanyard, and laughed as the water splashed onto Dorn's head and shoulders. She wasn't supposed to peek—but did anyway. Dorn, whom she had come to regard as part friend and part brother, danced under the cold water and uttered a series of war whoops.

The shower ended two minutes later as Dorn rinsed, pleaded with Dee Dee to stop the water, and toweled himself dry. Breakfast was ready, and he followed the smell. Once they were inside, La-So ladled one of his delicious concoctions onto mismatched ship plates, ordered Dee Dee to wash her hands, and reminded Dorn to lather up.

The lotion, if that's what the thick, gooey mess could properly be called, was a neighbor's creation, and it worked surprisingly well. Smeared liberally over the user's body, the gunk was proof against sunburn, heat rash, and, if the substance's inventor was to be believed, attack from foraging needlefish, which was a rather dubious claim but comforting nonetheless. Careful to minimize contact with the cargo module's furnishings, Dorn slid into his salt-stiff work clothes, herded Dee Dee toward the table, and sat down to breakfast. It was his favorite moment of the day. The prayer, led by La-So, affirmed that each would be granted an opportunity to learn, help others, and harmonize with the universe.

Dorn and Dee Dee chanted the prayer in Traa, while the previously moody La-So smiled approvingly and guided them through the appropriate hand gestures. The change in La-So's personality seemed both miraculous and inexplicable until Dorn learned the importance of triads. When Dee Dee joined the household, she completed the necessary three-person unit and restored balance to La-So's life.

The prayer ended, and Dee Dee waited for La-So's nod. He

gave it, and she started to eat. Not like an animal, as she had at the beginning, but with something approximating the manners Dorn had acquired from his sister, and been taught at the academy. Manners that had been intended to be of assistance as he made his way through the highways and byways of upper crust society. His present circumstances were somewhat different, and he smiled at the irony.

"So," La-So said sternly, ever ready to heap more food onto Dee Dee's already full plate, "what sort of mischief do you have planned for today?"

Dee Dee, who had dealt with the same question every morning for weeks now, and who regarded the alien as a sort of grandfather, tried to appear solemn. "Well, work comes first, so I'll do my chores, study the lessons Dorn prepared for me, and then, when you least expect it, I'll follow you around and get in your way. How does that sound?"

"Terrible, just terrible," the alien replied gruffly, "but I have no choice. It's penance for my many sins."

"Maybe," Dee Dee answered serenely, "or just bad luck. Like when Dorn's and my parents died. You never know."

"No, you don't," the Traa replied, "nor do you need to, since we must dwell in the ever present now. Eat some driftweed . . . it's good for you."

Dee Dee made a face, Dorn laughed, and the meal was soon over. When the table was cleared, and Dee Dee had started her chores, Dorn left for work.

He knew the trails by heart, which left his eyes free to roam. They went to the *Mary Voss* like magnets to metal. Approximately two weeks had passed since the beaching party and, thanks to other ships already aground, the data liner was relatively intact. Dorn still found it difficult to believe that she would be cut into pieces, fed to the mills, and rolled, stamped, and extruded. Into what? Screwdrivers? Soup ladles? Axe heads? It made no difference. No matter what they made from her flesh and bones, it wouldn't add up to a spaceship.

Suddenly the memory that had been eluding Dorn came flooding back. He was transported back in time, to one of the rare occasions when his father had taken him to the best of places, a spaceship. The liner was to be christened that day, and in response to the boy's whining, or on a personal whim, the senior Voss took his son on a tour. The ship smelled new, and to a child the odor of plastic and ozone seemed like a ticket to the places his parents talked about, distant planets that teemed with aliens. He remembered the engineering spaces, followed by vast multilayered memory banks, and long, empty corridors. Most of all, he remembered the U-shaped bridge, control boards, and wraparound view screens. And—the best—the captain's chair, a powered affair with rows of touch-sensitive controls built into both arms, and a swing-out com monitor.

Dorn had been allowed to sit in the chair for only the briefest of moments, and had just begun to explore its many wonders, when a hand pulled him away. The next place they saw held little interest for the boy but seemed important to his father. The captain's cabin was small but nicely finished. Howard Voss dropped to his knees, took a small hand in his, and pressed it against the smoothly finished metal. "Forget the captain's chair, son, the *real* power is here. Do you feel it boy? Vibrating under your hand? It'll be yours someday."

Dorn had felt nothing other than a certain coolness and the urgency in his father's voice. He nodded. "Yes, Daddy."

Howard Voss nodded. "Good. Now, look at the plate. See anything different about it?"

Dorn shook his head. "No, they all look the same."

"Darned right they do," his father replied, "but they aren't. Make a fist and thump three times. Quickly now."

The child did as instructed. Nothing happened in response to the first two thumps, but the third produced a surprising result. A mechanism whirred, and the panel opened. The recess was shallow and lined with foam padding. The ball bearing, for that's what it looked like, was nestled at the center of the space. It gleamed with reflected light. "There it is," Howard Voss said proudly, "the jewel of our empire. We keep a copy aboard every ship we own. The crews don't know about it, not even the captains. It's a way to safeguard our most important secret. But you must tell no one, not even your sister. Promise?''

Dorn had given his word and kept it too. And now he was glad, because he knew, or thought he knew, what the shiny metal ball contained: the coordinates for the Mescalero Gap. What was it his father had said? ''. . . Our most important secret''? What else would qualify? Yes, Natalie might have the coordinates, or know where to find them, but what if she didn't? What if his parents had died without passing the secret along? Would that explain why the money stopped?

His thoughts practically tripped over each other as they moved through his mind. The voice that interrupted them was gruff and accompanied by a shove. ''Hey, buster, what the hell's wrong with you? Move or get off the path.''

Dorn realized that he'd been standing there, staring at the ship for what? Five minutes? Ten? He mumbled an apology and followed the other workers down toward the beach. He felt different somehow. It was as if everything had changed. The memory was an elusive thing. It had surfaced at the party, or tried to, and been buried by emotion. Not any more. Now it was at the very center of his being. Burning like a star. He had to find the correct plate, open the secret compartment, and retrieve the sphere. Nothing else mattered.

A crowd had formed, and Jana was there. She smiled broadly and waited for him to join her. ''Hey, Dorn, I memorized those times tables . . . you wanna hear them?''

''Yeah,'' Dorn lied, ''but not right now. There's something I have to do . . . and I need your help.''

Jana frowned. ''I don't like the sound of this, Dorn . . . What's happening?''

''I need to go aboard the *Mary Voss,* and that means joining the wreckers. And I might need to stay all night, so if I don't show up, tell La-So I'm okay. Got it?''

Jana opened her mouth to object, but the siren overrode her words, and Dorn disappeared. The nearest members of the wrecking crew glanced at him as he joined their ranks. They had seen him around and weren't especially surprised. Most haulers tried for the next step eventually and he looked sturdy enough, especially after weeks of hauling.

Jana's coaching, plus lots of hard physical exercise, had packed muscle onto his previously slender frame. Now, with long, sun-bleached hair and a heavy tan, Dorn looked the part of a barbarian. All muscle and very little brain. But he had brains, and used them as the group shuffled toward the entry gate.

His hands, which had failed the first test, were more callused now, and the surreptitious addition of grease from the outer surface of his arms, and reddish-brown clay, gathered while adjusting one of his sandals, made them appear more rugged than they actually were.

The line jerked forward, the man directly in front of him stepped through the gate, and a guard looked Dorn over. "You a hauler, ain't you? The one that works with the black woman. She's somethun' else, that one is. Well, let's see them hands. Maybe you ready, and maybe you ain't."

Dorn held his hands out for inspection. The guard took hold of them, examined the backs, and flipped them over. "Not too bad . . . reckon you ready. Welcome to the wreckin' crew."

The scanner read the bar code imprinted on his forehead, sent the new classification to a computer, and logged him in.

Dorn thanked the guard and stepped out onto the sand. He hadn't gone more than fifty feet toward the tool bins when an amplified voice boomed across the beach. "Hey, boy! Yeah, you! Where ya going? You ain't no wrecker, not till we run out of men anyway."

Dorn didn't even need to look around to know who it was. The shift boss named Nick Castor had been after him since day one. Why would today be any different? He stopped and turned toward his tormentor.

Castor, clad as always in a rusty yellow exoskeleton, strode across the sand. Servos whined as the landward leg shortened itself to deal with the slope. Dorn steeled himself against the inevitable abuse. The exoskeleton towered over him. Castor, his features nearly hidden by a thick growth of beard, smiled sadistically. "Get your ass over to where the haulers is workin'. You ain't got no business workin' with *real* men and women.''

Castor was intimidating, and Dorn was sorely tempted to obey, but the compartment beckoned. Was the sphere really there? Tucked inside its bed of foam? He had to know. ''I'm here because the guards approved me.''

Castor nudged a chin switch. His voice, amplified till now, still sounded loud. ''Listen to me, you little shit, the guards work for the beach master, and if it wasn't for the fact that I need a favor from her every once in a while, I'd override their decision and send your ass back to where it came from. But that might piss her off, so I'm gonna let you play your little game, remembering that the wrecks belong to me. Which means that *you* belong to me. Unless you get killed, that is, when the fish take over. Now grab a wrecking bar and hit the water.''

Dorn did as instructed and followed the other wreckers into the surf. Demolition had begun three days previously, but because the workers ripped the interior fittings first, and worked their way out, the vessel looked intact.

Long accustomed to the impact of waves hitting the front of his legs, followed by the backward pull of the water as it went in the other direction, Dorn was free to examine the hull that loomed above him. It was black as space itself and bore scars caused by micrometeorites, an encounter with a concrete pier, and who knew what else. And there, just below the point where the metal curved up and in, he could see the heat-resistant white letters, badly faded by now, but still readable: *Mary Voss.*

It was an emotional moment, but not one that Dorn could afford to indulge in. The entire wrecking crew was waist-deep in water by now, chest-deep when the waves rushed by, and burdened with their steel tools. A cargo net hung against the ship's side, and Dorn watched a man and woman scramble upward. They climbed with one hand instead of two, reserving the second for whatever tool they'd been issued, the loss of which was worth ten years of forced labor.

The ascent involved a rhythmic grab, pull, release, grab,

pull, release pattern that continued till they reached the deck. They made it *look* easy, but Dorn knew it wasn't. The fact that the others were watching, waiting to see if he'd make it, confirmed his suspicions.

Dorn allowed the veterans to precede him, jumped for a cross rope, and grabbed with his right hand. It took a moment to find the right foothold, push his body upward, and position for the next grab. He went for it, missed, and fell backwards into the sea. Water roared around his head. The bar pulled him down, but he held on and eventually found his feet.

Just as he was ready to rise, a wall of outgoing water threw him forward. He floundered, reestablished his footing, and struggled to stand. A voice hollered words of encouragement, and he waved. Faces lined the deck and peered downward.

The net, unburdened since the others had gained the main deck, flapped in the breeze. Dorn, determined not to fall in front of so many witnesses, jumped again. He felt the cross rope hit the palm of his hand, pulled, found a foothold, and pushed. The second grab was timed correctly, and so was the next. He moved steadily upward. Finally, with the L-shaped wrecking bar triumphantly clutched in his left hand, he reached the main deck. The jokes, grins, and friendly insults all said the same thing. The others had been there and knew how it felt. The initiation was over.

The courtyard bustled with activity as lower-ranking members of the house staff carried supplies into the house. In addition to the high-quality foodstuffs ordered by chef Fimbre, there were luxuries including an airtight canister of Mr. Sharma's hand-rolled cigars, a three-pound box of Mrs. Sharma's chocolates, and cosmetics for Seleen. All of it had to be inspected and signed for.

Myra had initialed the final item when she felt someone approach from behind. The truck driver, who had been raised in a village not far from her own, pretended to inspect the list while actually peeking down her neckline. Myra, who wore a scooped-neck peasant blouse, allowed him to look. His breath was terrible. "So, sweet stuff, was everything there?"

"Yup," Myra answered lightly, "thanks to you."

The truck driver, who would have cheerfully stolen the entire load had there been any chance of getting away with it, nodded soberly. "A man ain't got nothin' if he ain't got his integrity. That's what Momma said, and she was right. So, honey, how 'bout it? You ready to shake this place or not?"

Myra took a quick look around, assured herself that no one was looking, and kissed his cheek. "You know I am, Jake, but not without my brother. I could hide in the back of the truck, but what about him? He works on the wrecks and has no way to enter the courtyard."

Jake wasn't too thrilled about the brother aspect of things, but had resigned himself to giving the poor sod a lift. Assuming he didn't get in the way, that is. He spat on a sun-warmed cobblestone. "I'll slow down in front of the mill, you open the door, and he jumps inside. Whaddya think?"

Myra shook her head as if amazed. "It's brilliant, Jake, just brilliant. When's your next run?"

"Four weeks from today," the driver answered eagerly. "You'll be ready?"

"I sure will," Myra whispered suggestively. "Will *you*?"

"You can count on it," Jake answered thickly, taking her hand and pressing it against his groin. "I'll be ready and waiting. Hell, I'm ready now!"

"And so you are," Myra said sweetly, removing her hand as quickly as she could.

"Is everything off the truck?" The voice belonged to Fimbre, and originated from the other side of the courtyard.

"Yes, it is!" Myra answered loudly. "Jake's about to leave!"

Fimbre waved and disappeared into the house. Jake eyed Myra's shapely little body, licked his lips, and shook his head. "It's gonna be a long four weeks . . . you take care."

"You too," Myra said sincerely. "Drive carefully."

Jake winked, aimed some spit toward the mansion, and entered his cab. Life was good, or would be in four weeks, brother or no brother. The turbine whined, air filled the chamber, and the truck wobbled off the ground. Myra waved, watched the rig pass through the security gate, and made her way to the kitchen. Fimbre, who was touching, sniffing, and tasting some of the just delivered off-world spices, heard her enter. "Seleen requested some lemonade . . . would you take it up?"

Myra wanted to say, "Tell the spoiled little so-and-so to get her own lemonade," but knew that Fimbre would force her to do it anyway. Even worse was the fact that the chef would observe her movements more carefully, making it that much more difficult to leave the compound, and tell Dorn about her plan. She smiled sweetly. "Sure . . . I'd be happy to."

Fimbre, who was well aware of Myra's feelings toward the Sharmas, looked up from his spice canisters. Sarcasm, like other manifestations of defiance, couldn't be tolerated. Not if he wanted to retain his position of privilege. The chef was pleased to see that the servant girl's features were empty of resentment as she prepared the tray and carried it up the stairs. He nodded knowingly. Some took longer than others, but the smart ones, people like himself, accepted their fate and made the best of it. The fact that Myra had made the necessary adjustment raised his estimate of her intelligence.

Myra, unaware of the chef's thoughts, knew as everyone did that Seleen preferred to sunbathe before the sun grew too hot. Her favorite place to do that was on the balcony that ran along the mansion's west side. Knowing that, Myra padded the length of the upstairs hall, nodded to one of the house-maids, and made her way out onto the breezeway that circled the house.

A black anodized railing, salvaged from the engineering spaces on a Morgan High Hauler, ran along the right-hand side, potted plants filled the niches between windows, and the sea glittered beyond. A breeze, the same one that ruffled the surface of the ocean, touched Myra's face and moved her hair.

Of all the hulks, the *Mary Voss* was closest. Myra could see wreckers moving around on her decks, carrying pieces of metal to the side and throwing them to the haulers below. She could imagine Dorn standing waist-deep in the water, squinting upward as the salvage started to fall, then fighting to get out of the way. What if he didn't make it? What if he was killed before she even got to know him? There would be none other like him, she felt sure of that, and prayed he would survive the next few weeks.

The sun was warm, but Myra shivered as she stepped out onto the balcony. Seleen was there, beautifully brown and glistening with oil. She wore a white two-piece swimsuit and looked breathtaking. Myra wondered how she would look in a similar suit but assumed she'd never find out. Seleen gestured toward a glass-topped side table. Her eyes were unreadable behind dark sunglasses. "Put it over there."

Myra did as she was bid, poured some lemonade into a prechilled glass, and turned to go. The voice was flat and unemotional. "How's your boyfriend?"

Myra felt an ice-cold hand grab her stomach. The turn was slow and deliberate. "Boyfriend? I have no idea what you mean."

Seleen took a sip from the condensation-covered glass. A bead of sweat from high on her temple paused, as if deciding what to do, and then ran down the side of her face. "Oh, but I think you do. A rather handsome young man who wouldn't give you the time of day under normal circumstances."

Myra's heart tried to beat its way out of her chest. Seleen knew! She couldn't know but she did!

"That's right," the girl said lazily. "I checked Daddy's records, made a few calls, and put the story together. His name is Dorn Voss, his parents were killed in some sort of explosion, and he owns a wormhole. Or will, if he lives long enough to claim it."

Myra, too shocked to pretend ignorance any longer, became angry. "You know this? And you allow it to continue?"

"Maybe," Seleen said indifferently, "and maybe not. His future depends on you."

"Me?" Myra asked in disbelief. "What do I have to do with it?"

"He likes you," Seleen said calmly, "and, even though his reduced circumstances would account for most of that, your somewhat grubby charms may have caught his eye as well. It's a problem—but not an insurmountable one.''

Myra was amazed. ''I can't believe it . . . You want him for yourself! That's what this is about, isn't it?''

Seleen dabbed at her forehead with a towel. ''Yes, I do. Unless something better comes along. And why not? How many wealthy young men do you think I meet on this god-forsaken planet? Not very damned many. And, all things being equal, neither do you. What were you going to do, anyway? Find a way to escape? Live happily ever after? Not while I'm around.''

''So,'' Myra asked shakily, ''what will you do? Tell your father?''

''Why?'' Seleen asked sarcastically. ''So Dorn could go free? And take you with him? I don't think so. No, I plan to leave our wealthy young friend right where he is. Unless you break off the relationship, that is . . . which would create a host of possibilities. Hmm, let's see now, how should the rescue go? I just stumbled over his name in the computer? And remembered the news story? No, too unlikely. Oh, well. I'll think of something. I always do.''

Myra made a choking sound and raced toward the other end of the balcony. Seleen watched the other girl go, pushed the sunglasses higher on her nose, and took a sip from her drink. The lemonade was cold and pleasantly tart.

If Dorn had learned anything over the last few months, it was that things are never as simple as they seem. Wrecking was an excellent example. Spaceships, especially those designed to survive multiple reentries, are built to last. So, while brute force may be sufficient to rip paneling off bulkheads, and pull ductwork down from the overhead, some installations require more finesse.

The huge radiation-sealed engines were a good example, as were the data banks, solar accumulators, and control boards, all of which could be reconditioned and sold to the shipyard in Oro. Dorn, who had no idea how to ready such equipment for removal, wasn't allowed to touch it. No, his activities were limited to the relatively brainless work of carrying materials freed by others up onto the main deck, where they were tossed over the side, usually without looking below.

Dorn, who had been dodging sheet metal only the day before, tried to convince the other wreckers to be more careful, to consider the safety of the haulers, but met with limited success. Yes, the wreckers knew fellow workers had been killed by falling materials, but it was as if they wanted the haulers to run the same risks they had. Dorn refused to follow suit, however, and looked before he tossed salvage over the side. Jana waved on occasion, and he waved back.

The day progressed slowly, and while Dorn had escaped the push and pull of the sea, the work was equally hard. The metal was heavy, and the task of carrying it up to the main deck consumed a great deal of energy. Still, he was in excellent shape and had little difficulty matching the others.

The problem was his inability to access the captain's cabin. Oh, he passed the compartment all right, not just once, but many times. The shift bosses seemed to haunt that particular area, however, and one occasion, Dorn saw Castor himself, ensconced in his yellow walker, clanking down the corridor. The fact that the wreck master wore the rig aboard ship was a testimonial to what? His ego? Insecurity? Cowardice? Dorn wasn't sure and didn't care. He lifted a four-by-eight sheet of fiber panel up next to his face and hurried by. The wreck master, his mind on other things, failed to notice.

So, as the day wore on, and it became increasingly obvious that he wasn't going to gain access to the cabin, Dorn made plans to stay the night. The most pressing need was for a light of some sort. A portable generator powered the work lights that were strung along the ship's corridors, but Dorn knew the crew would kill it when they left. There were other possibilities, however, thanks to the fact that the ship was in the early stages of salvage. Spacesuits stood like suits of armor along the main corridor, and bins, many filled to overflowing with emergency repair packs, first-aid kits, fire extinguishers, and yes, rechargeable flashlights, waited near the main lock.

Dorn waited till no one was around, grabbed a likely look-

ing hand light, and stashed the device in the partially disman-
tled galley. He hoped no one would find it there, but knew
they wouldn't be suspicious if they did. After all, who knew
where crew beings put things, or why? The wreckers came
across more interesting things nearly every day—including the
occasional stash of money, drugs, or jewelry.

Proud of how provident he'd been, Dorn was secretly
pleased when the bins were taken topside and a crane lowered
them onto a barge. Yes, he felt pretty good about himself.
Until a really horrible thought raised its ugly head. What if
the flashlight required charging? Dorn called himself every
name in the book—and prayed that he would survive his own
stupidity.

Time passed, the tension grew, and the shift eventually
ended. The siren was a muffled but still audible wail when
Dorn stepped into his carefully chosen hidey-hole, slid to the
deck, and wrapped his arms around his knees.

The lights went out. It took a while for the footsteps to die
away, and for the voices to disappear, but they finally did.
Dorn was tempted to abandon his hiding place, but forced
himself to wait. He didn't think he'd be missed, not immediately anyway, but there was no way to be sure. Minutes ticked
past as the temperature fell and the ship groaned, creaked, and
popped.

Then, just when Dorn thought he had adjusted to the darkness, and the sounds that never seemed to stop, metal clanged,
a man swore, and sandals clattered across loose gratings. The
voice belonged to an assistant shift boss.

"Wake the hell up and come out of there, boy! A nap's one
thing, but you don't want to stay out here. Hey, you think
Castor rides your ass now? Just wait till you come crawlin'
up the beach. He'll take whatever you stole first, beat the crap
out of you second, and beat the crap out of you third. It ain't
worth it, son. Come on, now, I'll tell him you were sick, and
he won't be half so rough."

Dorn, who had yet to come up with a strategy that would
soften the almost inevitable consequences of what he'd chosen
to do, was sorely tempted. Still, the vision of the data ball,

nestled within its bed of foam, rendered him mute. The punishment wouldn't be pleasant, he knew that, but it couldn't be helped.

"All right," the assistant shift boss said, his voice steadily dwindling. "Have it your way, son . . . but don't say I didn't warn you."

The darkness seemed especially dense after the assistant shift boss left. Dorn waited long enough to be reasonably sure he was really gone, eased out of the hiding place, and felt his way to the galley.

The hidey-hole wasn't hard to find, which was fortunate, since the darkness was absolute. His fingers touched the flashlight, accidentally pushed it away, and found it again. The device was cylindrical and cool to the touch. He found the switch. What if he pushed it forward and nothing happened? The whole thing would be for naught. Yeah, he might find his way on deck through pitch blackness, but he might not. It would be easy to lose one's way in the maze of corridors and wander all night. The thought made him sick.

Dorn licked his lips, swallowed some saliva, and pushed on the slider. A beam of bright yellow light leapt forward and wobbled across the bulkhead. He mumbled the Traa prayer of thanksgiving, padded the length of the corridor, and paused by the captain's cabin. His heart beat like a trip-hammer. Here it was, the chance he'd been waiting for, winner take all.

Dorn entered the compartment, proceeded to the opposite bulkhead, and knelt before the panel his father had shown him years before. Conscious that the security guards could arrive any moment now, and eager to end a day of suspense, he hammered on metal. *Bam! Bam! Bam!*

Nothing. He tried again. *Bam! Bam! Bam!* Nothing. Panic mixed with frustration. No, he musn't let emotion rule, he must think. What was wrong? What was missing? The whirring noise! He should have heard a whirring noise but hadn't! Why not? No power, that's why. The mechanism was wired to the ship's electrical system!

Dorn gritted his teeth in frustration, returned to his hiding place, and retrieved the wrecking bar. He returned to the cabin, located four hair-thin cracks, and went to work.

The tool made a horrendous noise as it clanged against the metal. Dorn gritted his teeth and tried again. Craters formed around a sturdy metal frame. A ragged hole appeared. He shoved the flat end of the tool inside, pulled on the shaft as hard as he could, and heard something creak.

The metal surrendered without warning and dumped him on the deck. He scrambled to his feet, grabbed the light, and aimed for the newly created hole. The cover, which had protected the recess for so many years, hung from a single hinge. And there, surrounded by foam and glinting with reflected light, sat the data ball. Dorn reached out, touched the highly polished surface, and pried it loose. The device popped free and landed in his hand. He had no more than wrapped his fingers around it when a voice called his name. "Voss? You down there, Voss? I sure hope so . . . 'cause I came all the way out here to kick your ass." The voice belonged to Wreck Master Nick Castor, and his pleasure was obvious.

Dorn got to his feet, slipped the data ball into the single pocket that didn't have a hole in it, and turned toward the hatch. Every light in the ship came on followed by Castor's maniacal laughter. It grew louder with each passing moment. "That's right, boy . . . I want you to *see* what your insides look like."

Dorn was frightened. One part of his mind took note of that fact, while the rest tackled the problem. The exoskeleton gave his opponent a huge advantage. Dorn could beat on the machine all day without putting a dent in it. What he needed was an antitank weapon or, barring that, an exoskeleton of his own. There weren't any aboard the ship . . . or were there? An idea popped into his head. Dorn took it and ran.

The wreck master enjoyed his stroll along the main corridor. Castor liked to inflict pain on others, but, due to budget strictures imposed by Mr. Sharma, had been forced to conserve the work force. Except for occasions like this one, when harsh measures were called for, lest open defiance trigger rebellion. So, even while such moments were rare, the delay made them that much more enjoyable, especially savored as he planned to do. First he would draw the process out by chasing the kid all over the ship, and then, just when it seemed that he could escape, snatch freedom away. Then, while the unfortunate young Mr. Voss screamed for mercy, Castor would rip the boy's arms off, wave them under his nose, and toss them away. The legs would follow—or would they? It might be amusing to watch him run this way and that, blood spurting from arteries, unable to use one of the ship's multitudinous first-aid kits.

Castor smiled at the thought, made his way past the galley and into the eating area. A quick look around revealed no sign of his quarry, so he stepped through and headed for the opposite corridor.

Dorn, who had pressed the access button on the first set of space armor that looked large enough to accommodate him, bit his lip as the suit powered up, and very nearly shouted when the heads-up display board went to green. Yes! Like his sister Natalie, who had gone on to become a full-fledged rocket jockey, Dorn had cut his teeth in space. His skills included the operation and maintenance of his own spacesuits.

He stood perfectly still as the exoskeleton lumbered by the rows of identical armor, waited until Castor's back was turned, and made his move. Like the wreck master's machine, Dorn's suit mirrored his movements and amplified his strength. His first instinct, which he knew to be wrong, was to wrap an arm around the other man's throat and choke him. A none too sophisticated strategy that might work on an unprotected victim, but would do little more than annoy his armored opponent.

Three strides took Dorn into striking range. A bundle of cables, all of which led to servo-operated joints, was in easy reach. Dorn grabbed two and yanked. They pulled free at the same moment that Castor detected his presence and launched a backhanded blow. The impact bounced Dorn's head off the inside of his helmet and triggered rows of indicator lights. The suit comp, which assumed that its client was operating in the vacuum of space, squirted sealer into a zigzag puncture. Castor boomed through Dorn's speakers. "So, the rat-boy fights back. Clever . . . but not clever enough."

The words might have had more impact except for the fact that the severed cables left the wreck master with only partial use of the exoskeleton's right leg. He lurched forward, arms outstretched.

Dorn backed away. He remembered how his sister had taunted him, had insisted on a workout in spite of his sprained ankle, and called him names while he limped around the room. He'd wondered about those sessions . . . Were they training, as she claimed? Or an excuse to kick his butt? Consistency suggested the former, while her manner hinted at the latter.

"You sprained your ankle? So what? You think that's going to slow 'em down? Hell, no, they're going to work on that ankle and hope to take you out. Which is what *you* should do if you ever get the chance."

Dorn stepped in, faked a head strike, pivoted on his left boot, and launched a kick toward the weakened leg. It made contact, and something gave. Castor swore and fell in Dorn's direction. Dorn backpedaled but didn't make it. Metal forearms hit his shoulders, followed by the full weight of Castor's steel body. The wreck master grinned, raised the head cage, and smashed Dorn's face plate.

Dorn, still falling backwards, clutched the other man's machine with his left hand, and delivered a blow with his right. It hit a metal crosspiece, and the wreck master laughed. "You might as well accept it, boy . . . I'll be walking the beach while you feed the fish!"

The suit protected him from most of the impact as Dorn hit the deck. But something, he wasn't sure what, passed through six layers of fabric and stabbed him in the side. The pain was intense. He struggled to concentrate.

Every single one of the suit's indicator lights had turned red, all except for the auxiliary tool drivers, both of which glowed emerald green. Dorn looked into the other man's eyes, produced a weary grin, and chinned a switch. "So long, asshole . . . try this on for size!"

The drill made a screeching sound as the eight-inch bit bored through a sheet of rusty yellow metal and entered the wreck master's side. He screamed, and thrashed from side to side as the red-hot metal entered his body, but Dorn held on. It was only when the light left the wreck master's eyes, and his body went limp, that Dorn lost consciousness.

When he came to, a damage alarm was beeping in his ear and Castor was staring at a point somewhere over his head. He positioned his hands under the exoskeleton's frame, pushed, and felt the suit amplify his effort. The machine rolled off him and clattered against the deck.

Now that it knew he was conscious, the space armor printed a message across his heads-up display, and spoke the words as well. "You sustained a serious penetrating wound to the lower left quadrant of your back. There has been no damage to internal organs insofar as this unit can tell, but you suffered significant blood loss, and require emergency care. You sustained . . ."

Dorn chinned the voice off, ordered his body to roll over, and felt something fall away from his back. It clanged against the floor. The wrecking bar! He'd fallen on his L-shaped wrecking bar, and the end-piece had punched a hole through the suit. It would've been funny if it wasn't so stupid.

Dorn stood, fought the dizziness that threatened to push him off his feet, deactivated the safety, and hit the release switch. The much-abused suit made a horrible grinding noise as it clamshelled open. Dorn half stepped, half stumbled out and fell to his knees. The pain was so intense it made him retch. Nothing came up. He couldn't see the wound and wasn't sure that he wanted to. He had to reach help.

Dorn pushed the deck away, made it to his feet, and simply stood there. The vertigo seemed to lessen after a minute or two. The trip to the main deck took forever. The bulkheads, the gratings, the lights seemed to crawl by.

Finally, after what seemed like an eternity of pain, he stumbled into the lift. It made the trip upward relatively painless, and the cool night air smelled wonderful. Weaving like a drunken spacer, Dorn made his way to the port side and sat on the deck. It took an enormous amount of effort to turn, lower himself to the point where his feet rested on a cross rope, and start the laborious trip downward.

Dorn had made it a third of the way down the netting when a wave of dizziness overcame him, the strength left his hands, and he fell backwards into the sea. He was aware of the impact, felt the pain as salt water entered his wound, and wondered if what they said about needlefish was true. Did they *really* know when something was dying? And home on it? He knew he should care, but couldn't muster the energy. Darkness beckoned, and Dorn followed as the sea carried him toward the shore.

20

Be careful what you ask for, you may just get it.

American folk saying
Circa 1996

The Planet New Hope

Ari awoke to the ancient odors of vomit and diarrhea. Lemon-scented disinfectant tried to cover them but never quite made it. The smell was bad enough, but the knowledge that she, invulnerable to all but the occasional head cold up till now, had fallen victim to a microbe was even worse. Plague Derivative NH7462-5, to be exact. Ari remembered becoming dizzy at the slave pens and seriously ill after that. She'd been admitted to the hospital sometime during the night. That had been what? A week ago? A month? She wasn't sure any more. It seemed as if the room, and the routines associated with it, had been her universe for a long, long time.

The view, on the infrequent occasions when she'd felt well enough to consider it, consisted of dingy ceiling tiles, 179 of them, since one had fallen, leaving blobs of adhesive to mark where it had been. The light fanned from wall fittings and pooled along the floor. And this was one of the finest rooms in the hospital, light years better than the humanity-packed wards that lay fifty feet beyond.

The otherwise still air swirled as the door opened and closed. Ari knew who it was. Thanks to the dirt-cheap labor available on New Hope, those fortunate enough to occupy a private room had benefit of a full-time attendant as well. Two, actually, since one handled the day shift, while the other stayed through the night. It was dark within the air shaft, so this was Rosa, a kind-hearted individual, who, through her very cheerfulness, set Ari's nerves on edge. The voice arrived first. "Buenas noches! How are we tonight? Better, much better. Rosa can see that."

Ari, who had long ago become immune to Rosa's rough-and-ready psychology, waited for the woman to come into view. She was plump, the way poor people can be plump, with black hair and matching eyes. She had perfect teeth, and they flashed when she smiled. "Dinner will arrive any moment now."

Ari, who had been feeling nothing but nausea at the mention of food, felt her stomach growl. She was hungry! An excellent sign indeed. She pushed herself into a sitting position. "That sounds good, Rosa. Here, lend me your arm."

Rosa nodded agreeably and offered a substantial arm. Ari took hold of it, wiggled her way to the edge of the bed, and allowed her feet to dangle over the side. It wasn't the first time she'd gotten up, but it was the first time she'd *felt* like getting up, and that made it special.

The smoothly finished concrete felt cold beneath her feet. She released Rosa's arm and tottered toward the bathroom. The door stood open and bore a half-length mirror. Ari shrugged, and the nightgown fell away. She was shocked by what she saw. Lean to begin with, her body looked skeletal now. Enormous eyes stared back from deep-set sockets. Her breasts had nearly disappeared, and her ribs, each one of which was clearly delineated, tapered to a waspish waist. That was as far as the mirror went, and as far as her eyes wanted to go.

The shower was good, and dinner was even better. Meat, vegetables, and rice. Ari ate two servings of each, belched, and demanded her clothes. Rosa, proud of her patient's recovery, yet uncertain of what the doctor might say, stalled for time. The stratagem worked, and the doctor appeared before Ari's patience expired.

He was young, as were most of Oro's physicians, since the plagues killed most of those willing to work with the poor. He was prematurely bald, had a hooked nose and tired eyes. They came alive at the sight of a patient who was up and around. His hands were warm, and the stethoscope was cold. "Two servings, you say? Wonderful! Just wonderful! I'm proud to say you're cured, Miss Gozen...a statement we make all too seldom in this hospital."

"So, I can leave?" Ari said hopefully.

The doctor shrugged. He hated to admit it, but the hospital was a dangerous place to be. Patients who survived one disease risked contracting another. His answer reflected that reality. "Yes, so long as you take your medications, eat properly, and get moderate exercise. It's important to rebuild your strength."

Ari assured the doctor that she would, thanked him for all he'd done, and requested her clothes. They were new and fit perfectly, a seemingly impossibility given the weight she'd lost. Ari took a turn in front of the mirror. She looked as good as a scarecrow could. "Rosa? Where did the clothes come from?"

Rosa was stripping the bed. Another patient would arrive soon. She spoke without turning. "Miss Kara had them made. From measurements I gave her."

Ari had assumed that the street waif had disappeared the moment the money stopped flowing. The fact that she had stood by her came as a shock. "Kara? She's been here?"

"From the day you arrived. I saw her when I came to work this evening."

"She never visited my room."

"The guards wouldn't allow it. Each patient is allowed one visitor, *if* they can pay for weekly checkups, and few can. That's how we keep disease from entering the hospital."

Ari nodded thoughtfully, packed her belongings, and gave Rosa what amounted to a month's wages. An equal amount was placed in an envelope for the daytime attendant. Then, on legs that felt like rubber, she made her way down onto the street.

The air was cold and clammy. Fires, fueled with scraps of wood, and medical waste burned here and there as relatives waited for their loved ones. Ari looked for Kara but found it difficult to see. A boy approached and held his hand out for money. "Could ya spare some metal, miss? Daddy's got the plague, and me mom and me is hungry."

Ari slapped a number three washer into the street urchin's hand. "I'm looking for a teenage girl. About this tall. She calls herself Kara and doesn't take shit from anybody. Have you seen her?"

The boy nodded earnestly, gestured for the bodyguard to follow, and headed into the murk. Ari's hand rested on her gun butt as she stepped over and around blanket-clad bodies. Eyes followed her, but no one moved. The kid led Ari down a side street and along a wall. And then, just outside an alcove behind some stairs, he pointed to a tightly rolled blanket. "There she is, that's her. Can I go now?"

Ari peered into the darkness, confirmed the girl's identity, and dropped a second disk into the boy's hand. His sandals clattered as he ran away. The decision should have been easy. She needed a guide and Kara filled the bill. So where was the problem? Wake the girl and go. It was that simple. Or should have been. But something, she wasn't sure what, kept her from touching Kara's shoulder. Did it have to do with the fact that she liked the girl? That for all Ari had been through, and for all the chances she'd taken, she was no better off than she had been? Not in the ways that counted, anyhow . . . since money was essentially meaningless. How would Kara end up if they stayed together? Doing what she did? For assholes like Orr?

Ari sighed, turned on her heel, and walked away. Kara, her fingers wrapped around a dead man's gun, continued to dream.

Dee Dee waited until a sufficient period of time had passed, and La-So's breathing had stabilized, before sliding out from under her covers. The black woman had sworn that Dorn knew what he was doing, and would reappear the next morning, but the girl wasn't so sure. Everyone knew the rules: Don't steal from the man, but if you do, don't expect to survive. That meant Dorn was in trouble, *deep* trouble, and was going to need help. *Her* help, since the adults didn't seem ready to provide any.

Quietly, gathering clothes as she went, the little girl slipped out of the cargo module, paused to fasten her sandals, and half walked, half ran downhill. A pair of boys, the very ones Dorn had cautioned her to avoid, waited by the fence. The towers seemed huge as seen against the stars. Searchlights winked as they rotated and swept adjoining quadrants of sand. "Here she is," a voice whispered. "Just like I told you."

"Yeah?" another replied. "So, big deal. Bet she doesn't go under the fence."

"You're on," the first voice said. "Let's see the color of your metal."

"Cut the crap," Dee Dee said, skidding to a halt. "Just open the tunnel and keep your mouths shut."

"Not before we get paid," the second voice insisted, his face a blur. "Show us what you got."

Dee Dee was going to be in deep trouble when La-So discovered her theft, but that didn't matter. Not while Dorn was in danger. She took a chunk of angle iron from her pocket and handed it over. "Now, show me the tunnel."

The boys, who had bragged about their tunnel for more than a week now, and had used it to glean a half-pound of aluminum from the shallows, motioned her to the ground. Dee Dee followed as they low-crawled to the fence. The first youth, who was named Ahmad, gave the briefing.

"Timers control the lights. To stay out of their way you gotta memorize which way they go and for how long. The guards are real lazy. They don't do half what they're supposed to. But the dogs are dangerous. Dig a hole if you see 'em coming, stick a straw in your mouth, and pull sand on top. Who knows? It might work. We been through three times and never had to try it."

"Too bad," Dee Dee replied dryly. "And how do I get a straw?"

"No prob," the boy answered cheerfully. "You can borrow mine. Here . . . mind you don't lose it now. And don't forget to sweep your tracks."

Dee Dee accepted a length of plastic tubing, shoved it into a pocket, and watched the second boy clear some trash. The tunnel lay below. "Thanks, Ahmad. You're okay for a pimple-faced, good-for-nothin' piece of camp trash."

"You too," the boy said with a grin. "You sure you gotta do this? I was lookin' forward to strappin' you on when you got old enough."

"In your dreams," Dee Dee replied tartly. "And when I do the wild thing, it'll be with someone who takes a shower once in a while. Now, remember what you promised?"

"Yeah, yeah," the second boy said irritably. "We'll be here come sunup . . . but not a minute longer."

"Good," Dee Dee replied, "'cause leave before then, and I'm gonna kick your butts."

The boys laughed. Dee Dee plunged into the tunnel and wormed her way toward the beach. The clay felt cold under her fingers and brushed against her back. The knowledge that the unsupported ceiling could collapse, and bury her forever, hurried her along. She bumped the other end, pushed a sheet of fiberboard out of the way, and stuck her head out. Night turned to day as the searchlight swept across her section of beach. Dee Dee pulled back, knew it was too late, and waited for the shouting to start.

Seconds passed. A minute. Nothing. Heart pounding, Dee Dee looked again. The way was clear. The previously dangerous tunnel felt like home now and she was reluctant to leave it. There was no other way, however, so she grabbed the sawed-off broom and backed onto the sand. It retained some of its daytime heat and crumbled around her toes. She didn't want to sweep but had no choice. If a guard happened along, the tracks would be a dead giveaway.

The lights, still on a distant part of the beach, turned and started the inexorable journey back. Dee Dee worked faster. The sand became increasingly firm and harder to sweep. Finally, as the tide lapped around her feet, and the lights hopscotched up the beach, she turned and ran. Water splashed away from her sandals, the smell of the sea filled her nostrils, and Dee Dee wished she knew how to swim. Dorn wanted to teach her, and would have too, had workers been allowed on the beach. Dorn . . . where was he? The question filled her thoughts as a wave rolled past her knees and she dived forward.

Light swept over the child's head as she held her breath. Sand gave under her fingers. Then, as quickly as it had come, the illumination was gone. Dee Dee surfaced like a whale, blew water out through her nostrils, and rolled as a wave hit. She turned to get her bearings. The camp lay to the east, and the *Mary Voss*, her work lights inexplicably burning, made a smear to the southwest. That's where Dorn had gone—so that's where she'd go as well.

The incoming tide made the water deeper. Unable to swim, and eager to move, Dee Dee returned to the shallows. About calf-deep in water, she moved parallel to the beach. The lights weren't a problem since she could submerge whenever she chose. The broom got in the way, but Dee Dee hung on. She'd need it on the trip back.

The little girl was about halfway to the *Mary Voss* when something strange happened. A man appeared on the ship's main deck, stood silhouetted against the work lights, and staggered to the rail. He sat, or fell, she wasn't sure which, and disappeared from view. Was it Dorn, returning from whatever errand he'd set for himself? Or one of the security guards patrolling the wreck? There was no way to be sure. She continued to move, her eyes firmly fixed on the *Mary Voss*.

As Dee Dee continued to stare into the darkness, she saw movement followed by a loud splash. Dorn! It had to be Dorn! A security guard wouldn't fall into the water, would he? Well, maybe, but it *felt* like Dorn—and that was good enough.

She attempted to run, but the water made it difficult. Her legs pumped and got nowhere fast. Still, the girl made *some* progress, and aimed for the point where Dorn was most likely to come ashore. He'd be angry with her, Dee Dee expected that, but knew he'd relent when he saw the tunnel. Wait a minute . . . what was that? A log? Like those that came ashore sometimes? Whatever it was seemed lifeless, rolling with each successive wave.

Dee Dee forced herself through the water, recognized Dorn, and grabbed what remained of his shirt. She saw blood, a slit where something had penetrated his back, and more blood. Of more immediate concern, however, was the fact that he was face down in the water. The girl rolled Dorn over, and gasped when she saw the damage done to his face. "Dorn! Wake up! Please wake up. You're too heavy to carry."

There was no response.

Dee Dee frowned, drew her hand back, and slapped Dorn across the face. His eyelids fluttered, then opened. Dorn coughed. "Wha? Where am I?"

"In deep shit," Dee Dee replied earnestly. "Come on, Dorn, you've got to help."

Dorn groaned, fought to establish some sort of footing, and felt a hand tug at his waistband. "This way, we've got to go this way, so we can hide when the light comes."

Everything seemed to sway, and the words had no particular meaning, but Dorn followed where the child led. Something told him she shouldn't be here, that he ought to be angry, but he couldn't remember why. Walking was difficult, very difficult, and he fell, over and over again. Each collapse, each disaster, felt like it would be the last. But Dee Dee wouldn't hear of it. Not for a moment. She never stopped pushing, cajoling, and prodding. Begging Dorn to rise, ordering Dorn to rise, praying for Dorn to rise.

And rise Dorn did, until the lights came, and Dee Dee pulled him down, forcing his face into the water, calling him names. The names made him so angry he pushed the bottom away. In fact, the light was still in the process of passing over their heads when he rose dripping from the water and lunged forward.

Dorn wanted to wrap his fingers around Dee Dee's neck. That would shut her up, oh yes it would, and he could hardly wait. She backpedaled and he staggered forward. He came close at times, extremely close, but not close enough. Dee Dee kept walking backwards and waving a broom in his face. The nightmare seemed to go on and on, and he had decided to call it quits when she pushed on his chest. "This is it! Stop! We're opposite the tunnel."

"Tunnel?" Dorn asked stupidly. "What tunnel?" He could have grabbed her at that point, could have cheerfully drowned her, but he didn't care any more. He tried to tell her something, forgot what it was, and collapsed in a heap.

Dee Dee swore, slapped Dorn's face, and got no reaction. Then, while she was still thinking about what to do next, the siren burped three times, two of the spotlights converged on the *Mary Voss,* and shouts were heard. Dee Dee stood, saw movement to the south, and ran toward the fence. "Ahmad! Dougie! Come through the tunnel! I need your help!"

There was no response at first. Had the boys broken their word and gone home? But then a head appeared, quickly followed by another. "Dee Dee? Are you crazy? They're after you!"

"No, they aren't," the girl responded urgently. "They're after someone else. See? The action's down there. Come on! I need your help!"

"For what?" Dougie asked suspiciously.

"The biggest piece of aluminum you ever saw," Dee Dee said enthusiastically. "Help me, and a third of it belongs to you."

"Half," Ahmad said pragmatically. "Let's go."

To the south of them, just opposite the *Mary Voss,* voices shouted and guards ran every which way as the boys followed Dee Dee down to the water. Dougie was first to note the obvious. "Shit! That ain't metal! You lied!"

"Yes," Dee Dee said calmly. "Grab his armpits and drag him to the tunnel. I'll sweep the tracks."

"Why the hell should I?" Dougie demanded defiantly. "Drag him yourself."

"Do it," Ahmad growled, "or I'll tell your brother what happened to his knife. You know, the one in your pocket."

Dougie glared, swore under his breath, and did as he was told. Dorn's heels left two parallel grooves in the sand. Dee

Dee backed up the hill, sweeping as she went. Ahmad entered the tunnel first, and was in the process of dragging Dorn through, when the dogs started to bark. Dee turned and saw an all-terrain vehicle bounce onto the beach. Guards walked to either side, and an exoskeleton brought up the rear. The fence blocked an escape to the east, and the water was too far away. Dougie took one look, shouted, "Dig!" and went to work. He was six inches down before Dee Dee started. The headlights, which had been tiny at first, grew with each passing second.

Carnaby Orr liked to pilot his own yacht, especially when it required some skill. Which was fine unless you happened to be his pilot and were forced to sit by as he dropped through the stratosphere like an ore barge on autopilot, then grinned and leveled out. "That was fun. No wonder you pilots like your work. Not bad for an amateur, huh?"

"An excellent entry, sir," Lawson lied, "just excellent. Shall I take her in?"

"Sure, why not?" Orr answered magnanimously. "You have the controls."

"I have the controls," Lawson agreed thankfully, and surreptitiously dumped speed.

Orr, his mind already on other things, released the harness and made his way toward his quarters. His wife had supervised their design and decor, which meant he didn't care for them. Maybe Ari would try her hand at some redecoration. The thought brought a chuckle as he sat behind his desk. "Voice communication—ship to surface."

The computer acknowledged the command in a husky voice, a voice Orr liked so much he had launched an effort to find the woman it belonged to only to discover that it was synthesized. Still, he liked the way it sounded, and would ensure that it survived. The computer, unaware and uninterested in its owner's thoughts, responded to its programming. "Please provide a number, name, or other identification sufficient for linkage."

"Ari Gozen, Orr Enterprises staff implant 341, connect now."

A thousand miles to the west, on a road south, Ari battled to keep her eyes open. She was tired, very tired, and should've been in bed. But weeks had passed, valuable weeks, during which she should have completed her assignment and headed home. But she had been sick instead. Not the sort of thing her employer was likely to forgive. The miserable bastard. So, why did she care for him anyway? And want him more than anything else? Perhaps it was a sickness equal to the one she'd survived.

The car, which liked to drift, veered to the right. Ari struggled to correct it. The mental "pop" as her implant came to life after months of silence scared the hell out of her. She swerved and almost ran off the road. The "voice" was equally unexpected. "Ari . . . Carnaby Orr here . . . how the hell are you?" Gravel flew as Ari flared to a stop. The skirts thumped as she cut power. She subvocalized. "Carnaby? Is that you?"

"Of course it's me," her employer replied matter-of-factly, throwing his booted feet up onto his desk. "I thought I'd drop in and see how things are going. If you have what I'm looking for, I'll give you a bonus so big you can buy a piece of the company. We could be partners."

Partners? The implication *seemed* obvious, or had she read something into his words "No, not yet anyway. Our subject disappeared, but I know where he is. Or *was*, anyway, assuming he survived."

"Excellent," Orr replied cheerfully. "How can I help?"

Reassured by her employer's high spirits, and cheered by the prospect of seeing him again, Ari considered his offer. Insects chased each other through her headlights and thumped against the windshield. "As a matter of fact, there *is* something you could do. There's a local company called Sharma Industries. Owned by a family of the same name. They run a salvage operation. I have reason to believe that the individual we're looking for is trapped in one of their camps."

Orr took his feet off the desk in surprise. "Slave labor? You're kidding!"

"It's a long story," Ari replied, "but suffice it to say that when his parents died, and the money stopped, our friend made some rather poor choices."

"Good!" Orr said happily. "Very good. As long as he has what I'm after. Tell me what to do."

"Contact the Sharmas," Ari said forcefully. "Buy the rights to the boy, meet me at their camp, and bring some muscle. I don't know what these people are like . . . better safe than sorry."

"How true," Orr said, remembering his wife, and the knife at his throat. "I'll take care of it. And, Ari . . ."

"Yes?"

"I'm looking forward to seeing you. *All* of you, if you catch my drift."

Ari thought about her emaciated body and wondered what he'd think of it. It occurred to her that a darkened room might be best. She allowed some very real excitement to color her voice. "Me too, Carnaby . . . as soon as this is over."

Orr smiled and broke the connection. He was more aroused than he could ever remember being—just from thinking of sex! A side benefit provided by the symbiote? What if he obtained a similar creature for Ari? They could live forever! And screw their brains out in the bargain. He laughed and went to work.

It was dark beneath the sand, and Dee Dee felt something akin to pinpricks as sand ants cut minute chunks out of her skin, grasped them in tiny mandibles, and headed for home. But the darkness was bearable, as was the pain. What *really* bothered her was the uncertainty. How close were the security guards? Would the dogs find her scent? And what about Dorn? What if he died? It would be like losing her parents all over again. She wanted to cry but couldn't without giving herself away.

The plastic tube had spent most of its existence in a coil and liked that shape. That being the case, the upper end of it curved downward and came within a quarter-inch of the surface. Tiny grains of sand were sucked through the tube and into Dee Dee's mouth each time she took a breath. It was annoying and potentially dangerous. She could adjust the tube, but what if the guards saw her? Still, what were the odds? Heavily in her favor, she assumed. Dee Dee flexed her fingers, and about was about to reach for the tube when the sand began to vibrate. Something heavy approached.

Sand was packed in and around Dee Dee's ears but allowed some sound to get through. She heard the deep throaty rumble of an engine, a sort of thumping sound that might have been exoskeleton pods hitting the sand, and a voice too distorted to understand.

Someone stepped onto the sand that covered her right ankle and sank till boot touched skin. There was more pressure than pain and her heart nearly beat its way out of her chest. She wanted to scream but bit her lip instead. Then, just when the girl thought she couldn't keep still any longer the pressure vanished and the guards moved on.

Dee Dee forced herself to count to a thousand, raised her head, and confirmed that the search party had passed them by. It was a hundred yards down the beach tossing a pile of trash. Staying low so as to reduce the chance that she'd be silhouetted against the lights, Dee Dee rolled out of the depression, spat sand out of her mouth, and probed for Dougie. He came up spluttering. "Frigging dogs . . . one of them peed on me!"

"It beats the hell out of what else could have happened," Dee Dee replied unsympathetically. "Now move your butt . . . the tunnel should be clear by now."

The tunnel *was* clear, and the youngsters wiggled through. Ahmad was waiting. "About time, you two . . . This guy is heavy. I barely pulled him through."

Dee Dee, fearful that Dorn was dead, checked his breathing. It was shallow and came less frequently than it should have. She turned to the boys. "Ahmad, find Jana. Tell her to come. We need her muscle. Dougie, wake La-So. Tell him what happened. Hurry."

Dougie paused for a moment, then shrugged his shoulders. "What the hell. But you owe me . . ."

The boy disappeared into the darkness before Dee Dee

could reply. With them gone, and help on the way, she threw an arm across Dorn's back and whispered into his ear. "Dorn? Can you hear me? Please don't die. I couldn't stand it. Not twice. I'll do my chores without being asked, learn *all* of La-So's prayers, and study real hard. I promise."

Dorn groaned, and spat water. "And I won't let you forget," he croaked. "Where the hell are we?"

"Down by the security fence," Dee Dee answered, her heart leaping with joy.

"Which side?"

"The land side."

"Thank god. You're amazing, Dee Dee. Reach into my pants pocket."

"Which side?"

"The right, I think."

The girl did as she was told, found a round metal ball, and pulled it out. "Is this what you want?"

Dorn looked and saw light gleam off the data ball's mirrorlike surface. His eyelids felt heavy and he allowed them to close. "Yeah, keep it for me, and don't let anyone know you have it. Promise?"

Dee Dee heard the sound of voices and recognized one as belonging to La-So. She had pockets, but lost things on a frequent basis. The voices grew louder. She popped the ball in her mouth and swallowed. "I promise."

Dorn allowed himself to relax. "Good. I knew I could count on you."

Dee Dee bit her lip and allowed the tears to stream down her face. "You can count on me, Dorn. Always, always, always."

Voices yelled, a siren whooped, and the hunt continued.

21

Beware of that which blossoms hide.

Col. Valtrath Bin-Iznar
A Manual for Forced Landings
Confederate Armed Forces
Standard year 2346

The Planet New Hope

The *Will of God* made a picture-perfect landing in Oro's bay. Due to the never-ending plagues, and the fact that the *Willie* had no cargo to discharge, the harbor master ordered the vessel to take up moorage at buoy three. It was shaped like a cone and, judging from the stains, was home to at least one bird, which flapped away as a tug nudged the ship into position. Chief Engineer O'Tool tagged the float with a tractor beam.

A tech lowered the *Willie*'s umbilical to the tug, watched critically while the smaller vessel hauled it to the buoy, and delivered a thumbs-up when the connection was made. It cost less to buy shore power than to run the ship's reactor, an economy Jord was determined to capture. Plus, there were maintenance procedures that required them to power down.

No sooner were those arrangements made than a veritable armada of water taxis, food scows, makeshift rafts, and other rickety craft headed out toward the ship, each loaded to the gunwales with sales beings, con artists, tax collectors, and other assorted riffraff. Captain Jord wasn't about to allow such unsavory individuals aboard his ship, and posted guards bow and stern.

None of this was apparent to Marshals Rollo Drekno-Hypont III and Pilo-Horlon-Torx. They had been hard at work ever since the ship entered New Hope's system and, thanks to their diligence, had amassed an interesting set of facts.

It seemed Dorn Voss had been expelled from school for nonpayment of tuition and had disappeared shortly thereafter. This was news that came as a shock to his sister, who blamed herself, and sank into a deep depression. Then the next message arrived, suggesting that the younger Voss was alive, and being held in a forced labor camp. This was information obtained by following Orr's agent rather than arresting her.

Natalie, just released from her watch station, was overjoyed yet worried nonetheless. She made her case while the crew members released Rollo from his safety harness. "So, given what we know, I suggest we notify the police, go to this horrible place, and set my brother free."

Rollo thanked the crew people and treated Natalie to what any member of his race would have recognized as an expression of pained bemusement. "Your anxiety and eagerness do you credit. Any being having parents capable of multiple birthings would be fortunate to possess a sibling such as yourself. However, much as Torx and I might like to take the actions that you suggest, we are unable to do so. Not immediately, in any case. The Confederacy was built on compromises . . . not the least of which concerned matters of jurisdiction. We believe your brother is a material witness to criminal activity. However, *believing* is one thing, and *proving* is another. We need proof to force the sort of tactics that you recommend."

"So, my brother rots while you do nothing?" Natalie demanded angrily. "Not while I'm around!"

"We beg to differ," Rollo replied reasonably. "I think you'll agree that Torx and I have been rather active up till now, and I can assure you that we have no intention of slacking off. In fact, if memory serves me correctly, it was we who summoned *you,* not the other way around. Next, it's our duty to notify you that the sort of unilateral action you mentioned will land you in jail. Questions?''

Torx, who had been a bystander up till now, nodded his agreement and tapped a message into Rollo's side.

Natalie scowled, started to say something really unpleasant, then thought better of it. "I'm sorry, Rollo. I know you and Torx are doing everything you can. I was out of line. The rules are frustrating, that's all. Is there anything I can do?''

"Yes," the Dromo replied soberly, "there is. I prefer to swim ashore. Members of my species look quite absurd riding about in boats. Please open the cargo hatch and step out of my path.''

Natalie remained where she was. "Can I go with you?''

"Do you know how to swim?''

"Yes.''

"Excellent. Torx abhors contact with the water and prefers to be lowered onto my back. You can take his place.''

Natalie tried to imagine what it would be like to climb aboard the alien's back and dive three stories into a badly polluted bay. She didn't care for the images that came to mind, but couldn't refuse. Not if she wanted to go along. She forced a smile. "I'd be honored.''

It required no particular courage to open the hatch and ride Rollo to the door. The next part was scary, however. Especially when the marshal backed up until his hindquarters touched the bulkhead, charged across the hold, and launched himself into the air. The ancient war cry, delivered on the way down, was an obvious afterthought.

Natalie saw a blur, felt air rush by her face, and gasped when they hit. The impact threw her into the water, and she started to sink, but fought her way to the surface. It required three attempts before she was able to reclaim her position on Rollo's back. Once aboard, she surveyed the damage.

The marshal's belly flop, the most impressive such maneuver ever witnessed in Oro's harbor, had generated considerable chaos. Dozens of people had been soaked by the spray, a vegetable scow had overturned, and waves still rolled toward shore. Rollo, who fancied himself as something of an athlete, looked back over his shoulder. "Quite exhilarating, eh? Come, let's collect Torx, and be on our way. There's work to do."

The Dromo turned, churned his way through a sea of still-bobbing vegetables, and approached the ship. It rose huge and black before them. Suddenly Natalie realized where she was and what she was doing—riding an alien law officer through the waters of a distant planet! It was the sort of adventure she'd imagined as a child, and though she knew she shouldn't be happy, not while her brother was missing, she was.

The message arrived while Myra was scrubbing the kitchen floor. It came via one of the servant children, her hands still grubby from cleaning vegetables. The words tumbled from her mouth. "Myra! I have a message for you! From the camp!"

Myra straightened, brushed a wisp of hair from her eyes, and took a quick look around. The kitchen was empty, or seemed to be, although experience had taught her that in a house filled with people, appearances could be and often were deceiving. "Softly, dear . . . the walls have ears."

The little girl nodded and glanced around as if searching for wall-mounted ears. "Sorry . . . I forgot."

"The message?" Myra said gently, her heart beating a little bit faster. It was from Dorn. It had to be from Dorn. "A girl brought it. Her name is Dee Dee. She says Dorn was hurt . . . but feels better now. He's in trouble and the guards are searching for him. He wants to see you. Dee Dee will lead the way."

Many thoughts chased each other through Myra's mind. She remembered Dorn telling her about Dee Dee, and the alien they lived with, so that part made sense. The fact that he was hurt was worrisome and gave rise to a variety of questions: How serious were his injuries? Who, if anyone, was caring for him? And what about their escape plan? Could he travel? And trouble . . . what sort of trouble? There were various possibilities, none of them good; but Myra would have bet what little bit of metal she had that the *Mary Voss* played some sort of role in the trouble. Excitement danced in the little girl's eyes. "Will you go? Well, will you?"

Myra was still on her knees. She took the child by both

arms. "Maybe, I don't know. Now listen, Nadi, don't breathe a word of this to anyone, not to anyone. Not even your mother. Understand?"

Nadi nodded solemnly. "Yes, Myra, I understand."

"Good," Myra said gently. "I stashed a cookie in the usual place. Take it and get back to work. Fimbre will make his rounds soon."

The little girl smiled, retrieved the cookie from behind a broken pot, and scurried out the door. Myra returned to scrubbing. The decision was easy. If Dorn wanted her, she would go. Even though it meant sacrificing a relatively privileged position and subjecting herself to danger. The only questions were how and when.

Honley was a seaport approximately two hundred miles south of Oro. Though the smaller and less populated of the two cities, it was more than adequate for Carnaby Orr's needs. He watched the last of the toughs board via the main hatch and head for the lounge. Perhaps one in fifty had even *seen* a spaceship before. Mouths hung open and heads turned as they surveyed the metal-rich surroundings. They were a scurvy lot, and the very thought of allowing them to ride in the yacht's salon would have driven his wife crazy—assuming she could be any crazier than she already was.

Anyway, who cared what the musclebound idiots did to the decor? So long as he took possession of the Mescalero Gap and the leverage that went with it. Orr's greatest fear was that he'd find Dorn Voss only to discover that the kid didn't have the faintest idea where the coordinates were. The industrialist strapped himself into his seat, ordered everyone else do likewise, and took the controls. Lawson, not looking forward to what would happen next, tried not to care.

Repellors roared, steam flared, and the ship staggered into the air. Once aloft, the industrialist turned the yacht on its own axis, aimed her bow toward the open sea, and took her out. His repellors tore a fishing boat in half and he didn't even notice. The camp was less than an hour away by air and Orr was expected for dinner, a rather boring prospect but necessary nevertheless. The ship accelerated, pushing the passengers back into their seats. They tried to look tough. Some succeeded.

Seleen had made a study of Myra and knew the servant girl was up to something the moment she appeared. The occasion was lunch. Myra was one of two servers, and she performed flawlessly. So well, in fact, that the very perfection of it drew Seleen's attention to the excitement in Myra's eyes and the energy around her. Something was up all right, and the something was Mr. Dorn Voss. Nothing else made sense.

Seleen had listened while her father described the wreck master's murder to her mother. His narrative included the fact that the primary suspect was a worker named Dorn Voss. Her father had a low opinion of Castor, that was clear. But he was still concerned. There had been riots in the past, horrible riots, and a murder, successfully carried out, could trigger them again.

Seleen nearly spoke then, nearly told her parents all she knew, but couldn't bring herself to do it. Yes, the information she provided would almost certainly get Dorn Voss out of trouble, or lessen it at least, but what then? He'd go free, the servant girl would win, and she would lose. A nearly unthinkable outcome.

No, there had to be a better way, a means by which she could bond with Dorn, and use the relationship to reach the next level of intimacy. He wanted her the same way all men wanted her, was good-looking in a rough-and-ready sort of way, and theoretically rich. What more could any girl desire? Especially if the relationship took her away from this house, this peninsula, this entire planet. Myra appeared to Seleen's left and proffered a pitcher of ice-cold tea. "A refill, miss?"

Seleen checked to make sure that her parents were engaged in one of their interminable private conversations and kept her voice intentionally low. "So, how's our friend? Well, I trust?"

The other girl's reaction told Seleen everything she needed to know. The fear-filled eyes, the half-bitten lip, and the suddenly shaking hands. Myra knew where Dorn was or knew how to find out. Seleen smiled and waved the pitcher away. "No, thank you. I have what I need."

Sharma's guards arrived at approximately three in the afternoon. They'd been through the area twice before and it seemed as if they'd never give up. One of them banged on the door with his truncheon. "Security! Open up!"

"Coming! I'm coming, damn it."

Dorn listened to the floorboards creak as Sandro made his way across the room above. The wood vendor and his wife were the third set of people to give him shelter. All had one thing in common: Their lives had been enriched by an alien named La-So. The door opened and Dorn blinked as light sliced down through the boards and made a path across his face. Dust motes drifted through the air, and the voices were muffled. "Torly, turn this place upside down. You, what's your name?"

"Vitrus Alexander Sandro."

Dorn flinched as boots thumped over his head and moved toward the rear of the shack. Mrs. Sandro said something unintelligible. Something crashed as Torly tipped it over. The first guard put a finger against the wood lot owner's chest and pushed. Sandro took a half-step backwards. "We're looking for a murderer. His name is Voss. Dorn Voss. He bought wood from you."

Dorn, his eye no more than an inch from the crack, saw Sandro shrug. "I sell wood to hundreds of people. I know some better than others."

"And Dorn Voss? Did you know him?"

"No more than the others. Who did he kill?"

"Wreck Master Castor."

"Too bad. Is there anything else I can do for you?"

Boots clomped toward the front of the house. Torly appeared, chewing on one of Mrs. Sandro's locally famous biscuits. "I didn't find nothin', Hank . . . I suppose they're clean."

"And see that you stay that way," the first guard said ominously, subjecting Sandro to another finger attack. "We'll be around."

The door closed, the light disappeared, and Sandro swore: "Pigs."

Dorn grinned and winced as he lay back on the makeshift bed. It was important to rest while he could. After Jana carried him up from the beach, La-So had pumped him full of blood volume expanders, closed the puncture wound, and stuffed a handful of antibiotics down his throat. He felt better now, a lot better, but didn't know what to do. He couldn't stay, not with the guards looking high and low, but he couldn't run. Not unless Myra's plan was ready. Her letters, each smuggled out via the children who ran errands for Chef Fimbre, were full of hope. Dorn imagined how the truck would slow as it passed through the slums, how he would jump aboard, and Myra would pull him in. It was easy to imagine her eyes, lips, and body. Sleep followed.

It wasn't every day that an enormous alien, with still another alien riding its back, and a human thrown in for good measure, swam in from a spaceship, bid a fisherman good day, and waddled up a heavily used boat ramp. Once Rollo gained the top of the embarcadero, it was necessary for him to push his way through the steadily growing crowd. Natalie, still damp from her immersion, sat behind a bone-dry Torx. She used halting touch-code to tap a message into his shoulder. "Where going we?"

The Treeth reached back, touched her calf, and responded in kind. She had long since learned that it was easier to read the code than send it. "One of our agents was murdered. His backup, a woman known as Rikki, saw what happened, but couldn't intervene. She was too far away. The perp, a professional bodyguard employed by Carnaby Orr, was allowed to remain at liberty. We will meet with Rikki and hear what she has learned."

"And my brother? Does she know about my brother?"

"Perhaps," the co-marshal signaled. "Time will tell."

Unable to pry additional information from Torx, Natalie examined her surroundings. Their entourage, composed mostly of children, dwindled steadily as they left the harbor behind. The once-white adobe buildings loomed to the left and right. Dwellings, each shoulder to shoulder with its neighbors, gave way to warehouses as Rollo followed Market Street along the hillside. How he knew where he was going was a mystery, but Torx had confidence in him, so Natalie allowed herself to relax.

Signs, many of which hung low enough to touch, passed just above her head. Most were carved and announced everything from boat builders to food wholesalers. People stared out of doorways and their heads swiveled as Rollo passed. They wondered what he was. Most assumed he was an exotic beast of burden, similar to the genetically engineered cattle grown by the first landers, the descendants of which still plowed the fields.

The spacer noticed that anything that could be manufactured from wood had been—giving the area an ambience unlike any place she'd been before. It would have been charming except for the rich amalgam of sewer, fish, and lord knew what else that hung in the air.

Finally, after countless twists and turns, the Dromo paused as if consulting a map tucked away in his memory, and headed for a large dilapidated warehouse. Insects circled in front of the partly opened door and buzzed Natalie's face as Rollo entered. It was dark inside, and she peered into the shadows. A voice echoed off distant walls. "Marshals Hypont and Torx?"

Rollo made a grunting sound that Natalie recognized as a laugh. "How many beings of my description wander in here, anyway? Yes, I am Marshal Hypont, Rollo to my friends, and Torx, who never walks when he can ride, is seated on my neck. The human is none other than Natalie Voss, sister to Dorn Voss, and a ship's officer. And you are?"

"I go by the name of Rikki," a woman said, stepping into the light. "My real name doesn't matter."

"Exactly," Rollo said agreeably. "Thank you for meeting with us. You brought the girl?"

"Yes," Rikki said matter-of-factly, "I did. Kara, step out here, please. The marshals want to see you."

Kara, her heart pounding ever so slightly, did as she was told. The act of doing so was the final installment of her revenge. By the time the night attendant told her that Ari had been discharged, two days had passed. Which meant that the bodyguard, like everyone else in Kara's short life, had knowingly deserted her. So, seething with anger, she had gone in search of someone like Rikki, a person with the power and the reason to find Ari, and having done so, to punish her. Because the man Ari had killed, the man whose weapon Kara had stashed away, had been Rikki's cousin. Yeah, payback *was* a bitch, but so what? The bodyguard had it coming. The light hit Kara's face and she waited for the questions. She'd heard them before.

The arrival of Carnaby Orr's yacht, and the commotion it caused, gave Myra the opportunity she'd been waiting for. The servant girl drifted toward the fence, waited until the unexpected landing had claimed the guards' attention, and slipped through the open gate. Then, with a basket hung over her arm, she hurried down the hill.

Had the girl chosen the right moment to look back over her shoulder, she would have seen a second figure slip out of the compound and follow in her footsteps. She didn't, however, and, in her hurry to put as much distance between herself and the mansion as possible, barely noticed her surroundings. A group of children spotted her, recognized the household uniform she wore, and swarmed around her. "How 'bout it, miss? You got metal?"

"My momma's got vegetables . . . you want some?"

"Hey lady, follow me, we got class-A number-one jewelry."

In fact, the street urchins were so loud, and so insistent, that Myra nearly missed the child she was looking for. Someone tugged on her skirt. "Myra . . . my name is Dee Dee."

It took a moment for the words to sink in, but once they did, Myra stopped. A sea of faces looked up at her. One of them belonged to a girl with sun-bleached hair, a slightly up-turned nose, and bright blue eyes. She matched the description Dorn had given her. "Dee Dee?"

The little girl grinned. "That's me! You're pretty, just like Dorn said you were."

Myra felt herself blush. "And so are you," she said truthfully. "How is he?"

"Better," the girl said, shooing the others away. "Much, much better. Boy, will he be surprised!"

"Surprised?" Myra asked. "About what?"

"About you, silly," Dee Dee replied, taking Myra's hand and pulling her down the road. "He doesn't know you're coming!"

Myra felt a sudden sense of alarm. "He doesn't? Then who sent the message?"

"I did," Dee Dee answered brightly. "I wanted to cheer him up."

And turn me into a fugitive, while destroying our escape plan, Myra thought bitterly. Still, there was no point in scolding the girl. She loved Dorn too . . . and was trying to help.

Dee Dee led Myra into the slums, and Seleen, careful of where she placed her 200-credit shoes, hurried after them. The sun settled in the west and the air began to cool. Seleen shivered, pulled her cape around her shoulders, and continued down the trail. Dilapidated huts dotted the slopes around her. Miserable things full of good-for-nothing people. Oh, how they would love to get their hands on her perfect body! Seleen shivered once more. There was danger in the air, and it felt good.

It was another in a long series of beautiful evenings. A slight breeze stirred the awning, the scent of zucherro vines filled the air, and the sun hung only inches above the western horizon. Mrs. Sharma had ordered dinner to be served on the veranda in front of the house. The meal, one of Fimbre's finest, included locally caught fish, vegetables straight from the garden, and a frothy concoction that tasted of lime. Though they were somewhat provincial by his standards, Orr found the Sharmas to be *his* kind of people, meaning they were shrewd, and knew how to slice a credit six ways from Sunday.

Take their ships, for example: By tracking the financial performance of various shipping lines, and keeping elaborate records on the age and condition of their fleets, Mr. Sharma could forecast the market. Orr was further impressed by the fact that his host could list the ships Orr Enterprises owned from memory, place an approximate value on each one of them, and, based on the kind of usage it had received, predict the month and year when each would hit the scrap market. Of course, savvy wasn't everything. Artificially low labor costs and a strong local market conveyed huge advantages. Orr took a drag from one of Sharma's cigars, raised his glass, and proposed a toast. "To shipping . . . new *and* old."

"To shipping," the Sharmas echoed in unison.

Mrs. Sharma lowered her glass. "I'm sorry you missed our daughter—she would have loved to meet you."

Mr. Sharma had wondered where his daughter was but was afraid to ask. Seleen had moods, most of which were unpleasant, and kept to her room a good deal of the time. He knew she felt confined and blamed him. Business seemed like a safer subject. "So, you have an interest in one of our workers . . . which one?"

Orr flicked ash off the end of his cigar. It exploded when it hit the deck. "Yes, a trivial matter really, but success is built on details."

Sharma, who didn't for a moment believe that someone of Orr's importance spent his time on trivial details, nodded agreeably. "Yes, how true. The life of a businessman is never easy."

"My point exactly," Orr said indulgently. "Take the Voss boy, for example. No sooner was he expelled from school than he went slumming and wound up in a labor exchange. And a good thing too . . . since the Sharmas treat their workers well, from what I hear."

Sharma frowned. Voss? The one who murdered Castor? Yes, probably. And there was something else too, something he couldn't quite put his finger on, something that should have been obvious. There could be danger here . . . or the possibility of profit. It was his experience that the two frequently went hand in hand. "Thank you. A happy worker is a productive worker, I always say. Voss, is it? Not *Dorn* Voss, by any chance?"

"Why, yes," Orr replied, sitting a little straighter. "Do you know the boy?"

"No, not personally," Sharma replied, "but I know *of* him. He murdered one of my employees. My security people are looking for him."

Orr felt a sudden stab of fear. To be so close to his goal and have the boy snatched out of his grasp would be intolerable. He wanted to jump out of his seat, grab the man by the throat, and shake him like a rat. He struggled for control. "Really? They won't hurt him, will they? It's imperative that I speak with him."

"What a strange coincidence," Mrs. Sharma said brightly. "We have a ship named the *Mary Voss* . . . and that's where Castor was killed."

Mr. Sharma blinked, realized his wife had supplied the missing piece, and marveled at his own stupidity. Dorn Voss . . . Mary Voss . . . he should have put the two names together. Still, all was not lost. If there was money to be made, he would find it. Sharma made a steeple with his fingers. "Yes, that is a strange coincidence, isn't it? Tell me, Carnaby, is the boy related to the shipping family of the same name?"

Orr saw the glint in the other man's eyes and knew it for what it was. Greed. He could stonewall and lose Sharma's support, or cut the other man in and get what he wanted. The decision was simple. The negotiations began.

Once Myra arrived, and Dorn was summoned from his hiding place, the Sandros gave them the use of their bedroom, which, though separated from the rest of the shack by little more than a Kent Line tablecloth, granted them a small amount of privacy.

What the wood lot owner and his wife made of the long silence that followed the initial exclamations of joy, or the whispering that followed, was anybody's guess, but one thing was for sure, Dorn Voss wore an enormous grin when he escorted the girl to the door an hour or so later. She slipped through the opening, and he watched as Dee Dee led her away.

Much as Dorn hated to part with Myra so soon, common sense dictated that two fugitives—for a fugitive was what Myra was about to become—were more than any one family could, or should be expected to, support, especially when it was so hard to feed themselves.

Euphoria battled with fear as Dorn turned away, thanked the Sandros for their kindness, and headed toward the back door. Fearing that the next search would be more thorough, Sandro had prepared an enclosure at the center of a wood pile. Though open to the sky, it was otherwise secure, and sure to be less claustrophobic than his previous hidey-hole. Dorn was little more than halfway across the room when a knock came at the door.

The sound was so unexpected, so threatening, that his heart nearly stopped. He looked at the Sandros, and they stared back. They all wondered the same thing: Had Myra been spotted? Were the security forces waiting outside? The back door would be covered if they had. Still, where was the truncheon and the demanding voice? Sandro, clearly thinking the same thoughts, peered through a crack. "It's a girl, all by herself as far as I can see."

"A customer, then," Mrs. Sandro said, "out for some last-minute fuel. Let her in."

Dorn pulled the curtain across the room, and was headed for the back, when the door creaked open and he heard her voice. "Hello, I'm sorry to bother you, but I'm looking for Dorn Voss. He's in trouble . . . and I can help."

In spite of the fact that he'd heard the voice only a few times, Dorn had no trouble recognizing it as belonging to Seleen Sharma, and felt his heart pound against his chest.

There had been plenty of time to fantasize, until the last day or so in any case, and when he was not dreaming of Myra, Seleen had filled the empty spaces. And why not? The hair, the face, the perfume, everything about her reminded him of the girls on Mechnos, the kind he assumed he'd marry some day. In fact, one of his fantasies dealt with recovering his inheritance and landing a ship in front of her parents' house. How surprised she'd be! And impressed by his transformation from slave to industrialist! Still, that was fantasy and this was the real thing. How had she found him? What did she want?

Sandro had cleared his throat, and was about to deny all knowledge of the boy's whereabouts, when Dorn opened the curtain. "Seleen? What are you doing here? And how did you find me?"

The girl brushed the hood away from her face. A wave of beautiful black hair fell over her shoulders. The Sandros recognized who she was, looked at each other in alarm, and stood frozen in place. The girl took three steps forward. Her eyes were huge. "I followed Myra . . . and waited till she left."

"But why?" Dorn said, wonderment in his voice. "Your father has enough people searching for me. Did he need you, too?"

"I didn't come for my father," Seleen said simply. "I came for me. For *you*. I know *who* you are."

Dorn felt a sudden stirring of hope. She knew who he was! Did that mean what he hoped it did? That Seleen would intervene with her father? Give him a chance to tell his side of the story? And make contact with Natalie? It was like a dream come true. "Really? How?"

"You were different from the others," Seleen said truthfully. "I was curious. I looked for your name in my father's records, found it, and ran a background check. The off-world stuff took a while, but the answers came back. I'm sorry about your parents."

One aspect of Dorn's mind was taken with the girl's magnetism and sincerity, but another part was wary, and wondered why she'd chosen to come alone, and more than that, allowed the search to continue, if she really wanted to help.

The former Dorn Voss, the one who had gambled his future away and wound up in a slave labor camp, would have fallen for it, would have jumped at whatever crumb Seleen had offered. But he'd grown since then, and learned some lessons about himself and others as well. One of which was that when someone or something looks too good to be true—it probably is. Still, there was the chance that the girl was what she seemed to be, so he kept an open mind.

"So, your parents know? I'd like a chance to talk to your father, to tell him why I went to the wreck, and what happened once I got there."

"No," Seleen said, her perfume floating around his head. "I thought I should check first, make sure you were who I thought you were, *then* tell my parents."

The story was fairly plausible, so Dorn went along. "All right, let's go . . . we'll have to avoid the guards, though . . . I don't think they'll wait to hear what I have to say. They're pretty quick to shoot."

"Of course," Seleen said matter-of-factly. "They have to be. How else can they keep order? Surely *you* understand. The workers know nothing beyond feeding their miserable faces. I imagine *your* family has the same kind of problems."

Dorn was struck momentarily dumb. His mouth worked, but nothing came out. Finally, he exploded. "Are you crazy? Or just plain stupid? These people are just like you and me. Some are nice and some aren't. They had *bad* luck . . . and you had *good* luck. If you call sitting in that mansion 'good.' I'd rather die in the surf than live like you do."

The words hit Seleen like so many slaps across the face. *Never,* not in her whole life, had anyone dared speak to her in such a manner. Her eyes blazed and her chin trembled. "Then enjoy the next couple of hours, Dorn Voss! Because the guards will find you! And when they do, I'll applaud when they haul what's left of you to the top of the hill and strap it to a cross!"

With that the girl turned, made her way to the door, and slammed it behind her. Mrs. Sandro was the first to react. "Stop her! She'll bring the guards down on us!"

Sandro jumped for the door, followed by Dorn. They hurried outside and ran toward the path. The dog was barking but the girl was gone. In minutes, an hour at most, the men with the guns and truncheons would arrive.

22

The fundamental principle is that no battle, combat, or skirmish is to be fought unless it will be won.

Che Guevara
Cuban revolutionary
Circa 1950

The Planet New Hope

Carnaby Orr liked Sharma's cigars. He was going to have a second one. And why not? The symbiote would mitigate the negative effects. He lit one, took a deep, satisfying drag, and surveyed the slums below. The mansion's defensive wall was four feet thick and offered an excellent vantage point. The paths were illuminated by torches. A breeze blew off the ocean. One of the torches sputtered and disappeared. Shadows moved, and a baby cried.

The industrialist heard footsteps and turned toward the sound. Ari looked lean and lanky, maybe *too* lean and lanky, but he liked her that way. His orgasm had been much more intense than usual. The result of his self-enforced celibacy? Chemicals the symbiote added to his bloodstream? Whatever it was felt good. He gave the bodyguard a hug. "You slept well?"

"*Extremely* well," Ari replied meaningfully. "Thanks to you."

Orr laughed delightedly. "Good. It doesn't seem fair, given what you've been through, but we have work to do. Once the wormhole belongs to us, there will be plenty of time to rest. The Voss boy is here, we know that for sure, and so are the coordinates. I can *feel* it. They were hidden on a Voss Lines ship, the kid either knew it or figured it out, and murdered a man to get them. His mother would be proud."

Ari looked out over the slums. The stamping mill was silent. It seemed as if the whole peninsula was holding its breath. Waiting. The hair rose on the back of her neck, and she took Orr's arm. "It's *too* quiet. I don't like it."

"Yeah, Sharma said the same thing," Orr replied casually. "He says they're lying in wait for us. So what? We've got his guards plus hired muscle. We'll go down, break a few heads, and take the place apart. It should be fun."

Orr? Breaking heads? Having fun? Ari looked to see if he was serious. Judging from his expression, it seemed that he was. First the hyperintense sex—now this. Her boss had changed. He seemed more powerful somehow. The bodyguard smiled. "Yeah—well, don't get carried away. I need you. For a good night's sleep if nothing else."

Orr knew she was playing to his ego and didn't mind a bit. He laughed and took her hand. It felt good to be alive. "Come on . . . opportunity waits."

The waiting room had never been intended for someone of Rollo's size and temperament. That, plus his propensity for pacing back and forth, made the receptionist nervous. The fact that Torx had fallen asleep on her couch and was snoring loudly didn't help. The truth was that the High Commissioner could have seen the co-marshals during the previous day or nearly anytime since. Could have, but chose not to, for reasons she could only guess at.

Maybe it had something to do with the message torps that had arrived during the last twelve hours, or the aliens who came and went through the back door. Whatever it was had driven her to take up smoking after years of abstinence.

The floor creaked as Rollo reached the far end of his ten-

pace journey, turned, and bumped her favorite plant. It toppled
and fell. The Dromo was nudging the half-empty pot with his
horn when the intercom buzzed. The receptionist touched a
button and checked the screen. "Yes?"

The Commissioner looked tired. "Send them in."

The receptionist killed the link and breathed a sigh of relief.
"Marshal Hypont?"

Rollo looked up from the plant. "Yes?"

"The Commissioner will see you now."

"It's about time," the Dromo grumbled. "Hey, Torx! Wake
up! We've got work to do."

If the sound of the plant crashing to the floor hadn't been
sufficient, the head nudge certainly was. The couch slid three
feet and bumped a wall. Torx yawned and stretched. His fingers fluttered. "What time is it?"

"Four hours later than the last time you asked."

"Ah," the Treeth replied, "that would explain why I feel
so rested. Nice couch—nearly as good as a tree. Did his high-
ness send for us?"

"That he did," Rollo said grimly, "and just in time. You
know how what happens when I get frustrated."

"Tsk, tsk," Torx signed. "None of that now. We can't
afford the damages. And we sure can't afford to lose our pensions."

"Screw our pensions," Rollo replied ominously. "There's
the door . . . you first."

The receptionist waited for the marshals to pass, righted her
plant, restored the soil to its pot, and went to grab a quick
smoke. Aliens. Who could understand them? She'd be glad
when they were gone.

The Commissioner was a middle-aged man with thinning
hair, slightly protuberant eyes, and an upturned nose. He'd
been on the fast track once, a sure bet for Secretary of Commerce, when this sponsor, a senator from Earth, had taken a
bribe. The scandal had ruined her career and capped his. The
posting to New Hope seemed ironic at first, the final insult
from a cruel, uncaring government.

Four years had passed since then, and the Commissioner

had concluded that there were worse things than a high-ranking position on a backwater planet. Like swimming in political sewage all day, kissing ass all night, and hating what he was. All it took was the right amount of maturity to see his post for what it truly was, a paradise where his superiors never chose to visit and no one cared what he did. Or didn't do. Not until now anyway, when a pair of unlikely badge jockeys, a wayward rich boy, and a shipload of influence-wielding aliens had conspired to compromise his little hide-away. He could tell there were big uglies hiding in the bushes, the kind of big uglies he didn't want any part of, the kind that would draw attention to his hidey-hole. All was not lost, however. The Commissioner had a plan, and, assuming all parties agreed to it, he would rid himself of the entire lot.

The door opened, and the Commissioner rose. The marshals were no surprise. The Commissioner had met members of both species before. In fact, anyone who had ever witnessed a Dromo consuming hors d'oeuvres at an embassy reception while his companion swung from a chandelier wasn't likely to forget the spectacle anytime soon. His number-three smile conveyed welcome and a touch of pained superiority. He bowed at the waist.

"Marshal Torx . . . Marshal Hypont . . . I apologize for the wait. However, it seems that any number of government officials are interested in your case—and have opinions on how it should be handled. More on that in a moment. Please allow me to introduce gentlebeings Ka-Di and Sa-Lo. They represent the Traa government and hope to be of some assistance."

The aliens had been seated, albeit somewhat uncomfortably, on a pair of straight-backed wooden chairs. They stood at the mention of their names, nodded, and bore no discernible expressions. Rollo and Torx recognized the Traa as the same ones who had approached Natalie and absconded with one of Jord's shuttles, but gave no sign of their knowledge.

Rollo knew a bureaucratic ambush when he saw one. *Assistance*, bullshit; the Traa wanted the coordinates, and saw the investigation as a quick way to get them. The very ploy that Torx and he had predicted. So how to play it? Hard, as in there are penalties for interfering with a murder investigation? Or easy, as in we'd just love to have your assistance—please tell us more?

Torx had an opinion and tapped it out. "Let's hear what they have to say . . . we might learn something. If they tell too many lies, or attempt to lean on us, we can arrest them for stealing the shuttle."

The advice made sense, so Rollo forced a somewhat toothy smile. "Citizen Ka-Di, Citizen Sa-Lo, it's a pleasure to meet you. Particularly if you have information that would aid our investigation."

The Traa, who had absolutely no intention of aiding anyone with anything, tried to look sincere. It was Sa-Lo who answered. "The pleasure is ours."

The Commissioner, happy that things were going so well, started to offer seats, and realized his mistake. The Dromo would crush anything he sat on, assuming such a thing was possible, and the Treeth had appropriated a chair. That left him with nothing meaningful to say. Still, like millions of bureaucrats before him, the Commissioner said it anyway. "Well, now that everyone's acquainted, we might as well get down to business. Marshal Hypont, perhaps you'd be so kind as to characterize your investigation."

Rollo decided to play dumb, something Torx claimed he was good at, and frowned when the official lit a stim stick. Rather than lay out what they knew about Traa society, and their efforts to capture the Mescalero Gap, he focused on the murder investigation instead. It took less than ten minutes to review the murder, the trail that pointed toward a forced labor camp, and the need to search it, both for Ari Gozen, who was their main suspect, and the Voss boy, who, assuming he was alive, might be in danger. The only impediment was the requirement for a warrant—which the High Commissioner could and should issue. Having said that, and having choked on the Commissioner's cigarette smoke, the Dromo turned the tables.

"So, gentlebeings, in light of the murder investigation presently underway, Marshal Torx and I would like to hear whatever information you have to offer, as well as a detailed description of the assistance you hope to render. Oh, and one more thing . . . Commensurate with Section 27, page 318, paragraph 4 of the rules, regulations and procedures covering intersystem criminal investigations, law enforcement personnel are required to record all relevant conversations, discussions, interviews, and interrogations. Please proceed. Taping now.'' Torx produced a small recorder and smiled disarmingly.

The Traa looked at each other in alarm. The last thing they wanted to do was speak for the record. The entire point of the exercise was to blunt the inquiry, or, failing that, to co-opt the investigation and redirect the process. However, due to the fact that the co-marshals weren't the out-planet hicks the Traa had hoped for, the first objective seemed increasingly unrealistic. Sa-Lo tackled the second.

Everyone knew, or thought they knew, about Sharma's mercenaries and why they were present. The wreck master abused the Voss boy, the kid punched his ticket, and the owner wanted revenge. More than that, he wanted to make an example of Voss, something most workers could live with, except for one thing: Past manhunts, like the one directed at Dorn Voss, had been indiscriminate, and had affected the entire community. Plus, La-So liked the kid, and claimed he was innocent. So they were willing to fight. Never mind that La-So abhorred violence and begged them not to.

Some of the workers had been soldiers and took charge of the semiorganized defense effort. The strategy originated with Lawrence Kane, a onetime sergeant major. Like the others who been around for a while, he knew what would happen. The security forces would exit the compound through the main gate and follow the road into the slums. Then they would split into groups and follow side paths out into the community. During the premeditated rampage that followed, men would be beaten, women raped, homes looted, and neighborhoods burned to the ground. With one quick stroke the security forces would make the workers more dependent on the company *and* destroy whatever socioeconomic infrastructure had established itself since the previous cleansing. An infrastructure that, like a noxious weed, was certain to sprout culture, norms, and worst of all, leaders, none of which was acceptable.

Like any good strategy, the one Kane came up with was simple. By sealing the side paths and forcing the security forces down a funnel, he would push them into a trap. People understood the plan and liked it. Word spread, and work began. Teams of haulers dragged raw materials to the edge of the road, where wreckers wove junk into eight-foot-tall barricades, which they would defend using long wooden spears, each crafted by a sifter and tipped with contraband metal.

Dorn, who felt personally responsible for the crisis, offered to turn himself in. Kane, along with other community leaders, refused. The ex-sergeant major was not especially large but radiated strength and authority. He wore a carefully groomed handlebar mustache and hair so short Dorn couldn't tell what color it was. He had green eyes, and they glittered when he spoke. "That took guts, son, and if we thought it would save lives, they'd be strappin' you to a cross right now. Only trouble is that it wouldn't make much difference. Sharma ain't about to back down, not with the muscle he hired, and that Orr guy egging him on. The best thing you can do is lend a hand. Nobody blames you for what happened. Pull your weight—that's all anyone can ask."

Dorn pulled his weight and then some as he teamed with old companions to haul materials up from the beach. It was hard work, damned hard work, and equal to working the surf. He didn't mind, though, and neither did the others, because they were determined to strike back.

The foursome loaded their slings with an odd assortment of lumber and hauled it up the hill. A gang of children ran by, water trailing from the buckets they carried, heading toward a fire station. La-So had enlisted Myra as a medic and, along with other volunteers, was building a makeshift hospital. Dorn wondered how Myra was doing, prayed she'd be okay, and released the sling. The boards crashed to the ground. The barricades were impressive and growing by the hour. He wondered how much time remained and hurried down the hill.

•   •   •

Torches flickered and bottles passed back and forth as Orr's toughs and Sharma's security forces mingled in the compound. Exoskeletons had been brought up from the beach. Servos whined and shadows flickered as the machines stalked from place to place. Past experience had proved them invaluable for ripping the roofs off shanties.

Sharma entered the courtyard through the kitchen. He was furious with his daughter. First because she'd left the family compound without permission, and second because she'd known who the Voss boy was and kept it to herself. All of which had led to the potentially disastrous situation before him.

The slums were like a well-maintained compost heap, in that they required turning from time to time. Not *too* frequently, however, since excessive churn led to high costs and low productivity. Not that Orr cared. No, the industrialist had decimated Sharma's cigar supply and hijacked his security forces all without so much as a by-your-leave. Now he planned to grab the Voss boy *and* his wormhole. Owning a wormhole! Imagine! It could have been his, *would* have been his, if Seleen had any brains.

Sharma sighed, checked to make sure his sidearm was loaded, and left the porch. He didn't relish a foray into the slums, but Orr was going, and that left him no choice. Not if he wanted to retain his people's respect and limit the amount of destruction they caused. But everything wasn't lost. No, Orr might be a tough negotiator, but so was Sharma, and the industrialist had affixed his thumbprint to an exclusive salvage contract. Not a wormhole, perhaps, but millions over the next ten years, and all for the family. Except for Seleen, that is, who would spend the next four years with a rather strict religious sect, making prayer rugs for the poor. The thought made the salvage operator feel better and put a spring into his step.

Orr was about to address the troops when he saw Sharma move into the courtyard. Ari shouted for their attention and got it. "Hey! Listen up! Mr. Orr has something to say."

Orr, conscious of the fact that Sharma resented his presence, pointed toward the salvage operator. "Let's hear it for Mr. Sharma!"

A cheer went up and died away. It was a nice gesture, and Sharma was pleased. Orr placed hands on hips. He looked as if he'd conquered the wall rather than climbed on top of it. "All right, people, you know who we're looking for. His name is Voss, Dorn Voss, and he's wanted for murder. Justice must be done. However, before this young man pays for his crime, I want to speak with him. I'll pay one thousand credits to the man or woman who drags him in. Providing he's alive, that is."

Ari stepped forward. Her eyes were bright and her voice was hard. "Did you hear that? One thousand credits! Let's hear it for Mr. Orr!"

A cheer went up. Ari noticed that it was at least ten times louder than the one Sharma had received. Orr waved his cigar in acknowledgment. "The talking's over—go get 'em!"

The cheer was spontaneous this time, and they surged toward the gate. It opened on well-oiled hinges. Ari noticed that in spite of her efforts to integrate all of them into a single force, Sharma's security people had instinctively clumped together, as had the mainland toughs. This troubled the bodyguard and didn't bode well for a coordinated effort. Still, the task before them wouldn't call for much cooperation, Ari assumed. Both groups crowded through the gate and started down the hill. Spirits were high, and there was no attempt at discipline.

A group of household servants had gathered to watch. Most favored the slum dwellers. Fimbre stood to one side and frowned. He found the whole thing distasteful. Yes, discipline was an absolute requirement for a stable society, but this was uncalled for. A role for each, and each in their role. That's what he believed in. Anything else led to anarchy. He thought about sending the servants inside, decided the show would expire on its own, and retired to his room. A glass of sherry and one of Mrs. Sharma's books—now that was the way to pass an evening.

• • •

Dee Dee, Ahmad, and Dougie were hidden amongst the junk that bordered the slums. The area immediately behind them had been evacuated on the theory that the toughs would strike there first. Dee Dee had recovered the data ball and wore it in a pouch that hung from her neck. She twisted the thing this way and that while they waited. Ahmad saw movement and pointed toward the gate. "Look, Dee! Here they come!"

Dougie saw the exoskeletons marching out front, heard dogs barking with excitement, and wanted to pee. This in spite of the fact that he'd gone only fifteen minutes before. "Come on, you two . . . we gotta tell Kane."

"Not yet," Dee Dee countered grimly. "Kane said to count 'em, so we gotta count 'em."

"What if there's more than ten? I can't count more than that."

"So, count the skeletons," Ahmad said patiently. "We'll handle the people."

Dougie swore, fought his bladder, and counted exoskeletons. They, like the people behind them, were silhouetted against the mansion's security lighting. "Three . . . four . . . five. There's five! I see five!"

"Good," Dee Dee replied. "I counted sixty-three goons. Ahmad? How 'bout you?"

"Sixty-one," the boy answered. "But it's hard to tell with people moving around."

"We'll split the difference," Dee Dee said pragmatically. "Sixty-two it is. Let's tell Kane." The children backed away, faded into the shadows, and scampered toward the center of the slums. Dougie ran fastest of all.

The barricades were as good as they were going to get. They were wide where the slums began and narrowed until they closed on what Kane referred to as "the killing zone."—a cul de sac surrounded by head-high walls.

Dorn, who still felt guilty about his role in precipitating the crisis, had volunteered for what Kane referred to as "the bait patrol," a mixed force of workers who would engage the goons and draw them into the killing zone. It was dangerous duty, the worst possible, which explained why Dorn sought it out. Having done so, it seemed natural to accept a steel wrecking bar and march next to Jana. She and Sandro had been named as noncoms and led teams of twelve people each. Dorn noticed the axe the woodcutter carried and shivered. If someone was wounded with it, there would be little chance of survival. There was a hollow feeling in his stomach.

Orr had fought hundreds of intellectual duels in which the victor fired words and the loser hemorrhaged money. However, with the exception of some boyhood fistfights, and one barroom brawl in college, he'd never been part of an honest-to-god battle. The prospect was quite invigorating, and made even more so by the knowledge that unlike those around him, he'd survive anything short of a bullet through the head. Yes, Orr thought as Ari took her place in front of him, the prudent man has at least one insurance policy, and two if he can afford it.

Though ostensibly civilian craft, Traa landers were equipped like assault boats, including high-performance propulsion units. They raced just above the whitecaps and traveled at four hundred miles per hour. Torx was impressed but careful not to show it. The decision to accept a ride from the Traa had been part pragmatism, part politics. The Traa, who had previously blocked their attempts to obtain a search warrant, proved remarkably cooperative when invited to come along. The invitation to use their in-atmosphere flight craft followed. That, plus the fact that Captain Jord had refused to loan the marshals his remaining shuttle, led to an agreement in which both parties would arrive simultaneously and monitor each other's activities, an arrangement that was sure to come apart if Jord learned the Traa were involved.

The lander rocked from side to side as a gust of wind hit from the south. Rollo, who'd been roped to the cargo area's deck, braced himself, and put a curse on bipedal ship designers. Natalie Voss freed herself from a Traa-style jump seat and crossed the deck. She grabbed a strap, jerked the slack out of it, and secured the loose end. "There, that should do it."

The marshal looked back over his shoulder. "Thank you. I was built to swim . . . not fly."

Natalie patted his back. "Still, you get around when you need to."

The Dromo smiled. "We do what we have to. Don't worry so much. Your brother is fine."

Natalie forced a smile. "You think so?"

The Dromo delivered a human-style nod. "Absolutely."

Natalie smiled. A real one this time. "You're probably right. Dorn's fine and I'm worried for nothing."

Having been alerted by Dee Dee, Ahmad, and Dougie, Kane ordered the bait patrol to make contact. Like thousands of soldiers before him, Dorn felt a rock hit the bottom of his stomach and heard blood pound in his ears. Everything was clear and sharp—the smell of his own sweat, the feel of gravel beneath his sandals, and the glow up ahead.

The street curved, and it wasn't long before they saw the exoskeletons, torches, and a mass of undifferentiated bodies. The blob looked like a monster with thirty arms, thirty legs, and too many heads. It roared and rushed to meet them.

"All right," Jana shouted over the noise. "Remember the plan. We engage, then retreat. Are you ready?" The team roared their defiance, and Dorn yelled with the rest.

Jana lifted her wrecking bar over her head. "Charge!" The battle was joined.

"You ready?" Dee Dee asked tersely. "We gotta be quick."

Dougie looked out onto the street. The bait patrol was running uphill and the goons were running down. In seconds, a minute at most, the whole lot of them would collide in front of him. Then he and his friends would dash out, hook a rope onto an exoskeleton, and pull it over. It was a stupid, nearly suicidal plan. He checked Dee Dee and Ahmad. They appeared eager and ready to go. What was wrong with them, anyway? Couldn't they see how stupid it was? Or did the problem lie inside him? Dougie swallowed the lump in his throat. His voice was thick and raspy. "Yeah, I'm ready. Let's get it over with."

The combatants came together. There were grunts of expelled air, a variety of oaths, and the clank of steel on steel. Some of the goons had firearms, but weren't supposed to use them. Not when each death lowered Sharma's profits by two or three hundred credits. A wrecking bar stabbed at the salvage operator's groin. He parried and back away. The key was to *look* aggressive but survive.

Orr uttered a shout of pure joy and waded into the battle. Besides the weapon holstered on his hip, he carried a four-foot nightstick wrapped with metal. It rang on pipe. The wrecker holding the pipe was strong, very strong, and pushed the industrialist back. Orr's fear turned to rage as the symbiote added chemicals to his blood. He pushed the other man off balance and struck with the club. It fell on an unprotected shoulder. Bone cracked; the man fell to his knees and begged for mercy. Orr laughed, raised the club, and crushed the man's skull. He died instantly. It was a new kind of power, and Orr drank it in.

Dorn discovered that the strength gained as a hauler and the martial arts techniques learned from his sister made an effective combination. A man moved forward, raised his baton, and prepared to strike. Dorn shifted his weight, aimed for the man's knee, and launched a side kick. The blow connected, cartilage gave, and the man went down.

The goon was still falling, still screaming, when something hit Dorn from behind. It knocked him facedown, drove the air out of his lungs, and opened his wound. He rolled right and fought for air as a rust-covered pod landed next to his head.

An exoskeleton! The thought had no more than crossed Dorn's mind when the rest of the machine towered above him. He watched the pod rise, center itself over his chest, and start to fall. He rolled clear, and was scrambling to his feet when a group of children appeared.

One yelled, "Hey, shitface," while another hooked a rope to one of the exoskeleton's legs, and the third pulled. Nothing happened until the other two tailed on. A pod came off the ground, the machine swayed, and toppled over. Dorn recognized Dee Dee and shouted her name. He might have followed, might have caught her, if Jana hadn't yelled over the noise.

"Fall back! It's time to fall back!" Sandro echoed the order, took a blow to the head, and fell. The battle passed him by. It took a while to disengage, to retreat as a unit, but the workers managed to do so. Orr, seeing the enemy waver, charged forward. The mercenaries followed.

Ari broke a man's arm, put a needle through his temple, and frowned. Fall back? Why? The workers had held their own. It didn't make sense. Not to be outdone by the mercenaries, Sharma's security forces followed their lead. They ran full out, yelling their heads off, oblivious to their surroundings. Their employer, clearly wishing he were somewhere else, followed along behind. That was when Ari noticed the barricades, the way the street narrowed, and knew what lay ahead. The bodyguard started to jog, to call Orr's name, but knew it was too late. A wall of flesh and steel appeared, parted to let the fugitives through, and closed behind them. Orr attacked like a madman. The rest followed.

Torx watched pinpricks of light grow larger until they took on meaning. Huge starships, hulls eternally grounded, flashed under the fuselage. A mansion, lights blazing, stood on a promontory. Hundreds upon hundreds of torches outlined streets and paths. A blob of light appeared, and Torx strained to see. The pilot said something in Traa, Ka-Di barked a reply, and the aircraft banked to the right.

Rollo struggled to stay upright and spoke into a Dromo-sized headset. "Torx? What's going on?"

The Treeth tapped an answer into his belt pad. Each contact created a corresponding vibration against the Dromo's skin. "A battle of some sort," the Treeth answered calmly. "Right at the center of town."

"Order them to put us down," Rollo said firmly, "and I mean now."

"Your wish is my command, oh lawful one," the Treeth replied. It took some gesturing to communicate with the pilot, but he got the idea eventually, and switched the landing lights on. They carved paths through the night.

Orr bellowed his triumph as the workers wavered, broke, and fell back. Ari was there, shouting something into his ear, but he refused to hear. Not while faces filled with fear, flesh gave beneath the force of his weapons, and blood roared in his ears. The industrialist waved his bloodstained truncheon and urged the troops onward. Ari followed for a ways, stopped, and let the mob go. The street was only fifteen feet wide, and the end was near. She was standing there, watching the insanity, when Sandro, who had come to his senses, and stumbled down the street, cut her down.

Dorn turned on his pursuers. He was angry now . . . too angry to run. Five or six lassos settled over the remaining exoskeleton and pulled it over. A cheer went up, and the troops looked confused. Dorn waved a fist at them. "Come on, you bastards! Fight!"

A hand grabbed Dorn's belt and jerked him backwards. He swore, stumbled, and fell. The barricade opened. There were five surviving members of the bait patrol. Four staggered to safety, and Dorn, alone except for the goons, remained where he was. The attackers turned in his direction and were about to finish him off, when the sifters slid their spears through holes provided for that purpose and skewered those within reach. Orr's mercenaries, and Sharma's men panicked, ran toward the mansion, and were blocked by a company of angry wreckers.

Sharma, along with a number of his security people drew handguns, and were about to use them, when beams of white light pinned them in place. The Traa ship rumbled ominously as it circled above. The repellors hummed and debris flew into the air and whirled through the lights. A voice came from above. "Remain where you are . . . do not move. Confederate marshals are on the ground . . . do as they say."

Rollo, happy to be off the damnable ship, pushed his way through the workers. Torx, armed with a submachine gun, rode his neck. The muzzle commanded the crowd. Natalie followed behind. The Dromo spoke into his headset. "Make way, make way, Confederate marshals coming through." Mouths dropped open and faces registered surprise as the law enforcement officers pushed toward the center of the trap.

Natalie, eager to see, moved to the left. She recognized Dorn the moment she saw him. He was bigger now, much bigger, and covered with blood. The bar code looked like a sun-faded tattoo. He stood alone, until a man she recognized as Carnaby Orr stepped into view. He took two steps forward and raised his pistol. Time seemed to slow. "Dorn Voss?" he asked.

Natalie's blood ran cold as she heard her brother answer, "Yes, I'm Dorn Voss."

Orr looked curious. "Did you find them? The coordinates?"

Dorn felt strangely calm as he stared down the pistol barrel. Would he see anything as the bullet emerged? His voice came from a thousand miles away. "Yes, I found the coordinates."

Orr nodded as if satisfied. "I was right, then. Well, say good-bye to your friends, son, because you and I . . ."

Later it would seem strange that the person who took Carnaby Orr's life had never heard of him before. His name was Jorge Petras, and he had survived the camp for twelve long years. Though not especially smart, he was resourceful and extremely resilient. Petras lived while others died. Still, the years took their toll, and finally, after what seemed like an eternity of suffering, he could take no more. He had to strike back. Orr made an obvious target.

The spear was a homemade affair, taken from a woman who had fallen. The point, fashioned from a piece of hull metal, gleamed with reflected light. The yell came from deep within, from ancient ancestors long dead, and shattered the silence. Petras charged. He sensed bodies moving to intercept him, heard someone shout, and saw Orr turn. The pistol winked red.

Petras felt the bullet tear his body, staggered, and kept his feet. The spear was heavy now . . . it took all his strength to hold it up. Petras knew he would die and looked forward to it. He took two additional bullets before the spear entered Orr's belly. Freedom felt good.

Orr was surprised when the spear point went in. Surprised that a scarecrow could take so many bullets and live, surprised that anything like this could happen to him, and surprised that it hurt so much. Where was Ari? Damn the bitch anyway. He grabbed the shaft, tried to pull it out, and felt the ground slam against his back. He was conscious, which seemed like an advantage. But it wasn't.

The industrialist felt something stir deep inside his belly. He wasn't sure what it was at first. Then he knew. The symbiote! It had assessed the damage and written him off. Orr screamed as the organism enlarged the hole in his belly, ripped connectors free from his nervous system, and worked its way to the surface.

Dorn stared in open-mouthed amazement as loops of intestine slithered out of Orr's abdomen and onto the ground. Something, he wasn't sure what, separated itself from the mess and humped its way toward one of the wounded. It was halfway there when a huge, plate-sized foot landed on it. The symbiote made a popping noise and ceased to exist. Orr died a moment later.

"The party's over," Rollo announced calmly. "Surrender your weapons."

Sharma ordered his men to obey, and a wide assortment of clubs, spears, and wrecking bars clattered to the ground as Natalie approached her brother. "Dorn? It's Nat."

Dorn grinned. "Hi, Nat. You sure as hell took your time."

Natalie laughed and gave him a hug. His body was covered with blood. She wondered how much was his. "Dorn . . . Mom and Dad . . ."

Dorn hugged his sister and realized she was shorter than he was. "Yeah, I know. We have lots of catching up to do."

"Dorn? Are you all right?" The voice came from behind. Dorn turned to see Myra hurrying toward him. She held Dee Dee by the hand, and La-So brought up the rear. Truth was, his wound hurt again but he ignored it. "I'm fine, just fine. Myra, Dee Dee, and La-So, this is my sister Natalie."

Myra looked self-conscious, Dee Dee peppered Natalie with questions, and La-So turned his attention to one of the wounded. The lights reappeared, chased each other around the ground for a moment, and centered on Dorn. The assault craft hovered to one side. Rollo recognized the voice as belonging to the commercial being known as Sa-Lo. "Surrender the co-ordinates or die. The choice is yours."

Dorn blinked in surprise. What the hell was going on? Everyone seemed to know about the coordinates. He pushed the others away. "Then kill me! You can't have them!"

La-So got to his feet and wiped the blood off his paws. The voice, a Traa voice, sounded familiar, very familiar, and he shaded his eyes against glare. His voice was loud and carried well. "Sa-Lo? Is that you? Stop this nonsense immediately. You should be ashamed of yourself."

Silence reigned. A light found La-So and bathed him in brilliance. Then, unable to trust what his eyes were seeing and his ears were hearing, Ka-Di emerged from the shadows. He approached, stopped, and exposed the back of his neck. "Greetings, Uncle La-So. Many years have passed."

"They have treated you well," La-So said ritually. "Have you followed the one true path?"

"Yes . . . no . . . I'm not sure," Ka-Di replied soberly. "The Mountain of the Moons exploded. Most of the Philosopher Sept was killed. La-Ma was there and we miss her counsel."

Sadness filled La-So's eyes. "I am sorry, Ka-Di. Come, let us leave these beings in peace. You will tell me all that transpired and we will make things right."

The warrior nodded obediently and followed where La-So led. The ship, still hovering above, did likewise. Natalie watched them go, then turned to her brother. "So, Dorn, where *are* the coordinates?"

Dee Dee giggled and held the data ball up to the light. It gleamed, and somewhere in the deep blackness of space, a wormhole waited.